Softly Falling

CARLA KELLY

SWEETWATER
BOOKS
An Imprint of Cedar Fort, Inc.
Springville, Utah

ISBN 13: 978-1-4621-1395-8

Published by Sweetwater Books, an imprint of Cedar Fort, Inc.
2373 W. 700 S., Springville, UT, 84663
Distributed by Cedar Fort, Inc., www.cedarfort.com

LIBRARY OF CONGRESS CATALOGING-IN-PUBLICATION DATA

Kelly, Carla, author.
  Softly falling / Carla Kelly.
      pages cm
  Leaving her uncle and his English estate, Lily Branson, 24, travels to Wyoming to live with her father on his ranch. Since Lily has no dowry, her uncle thinks she might fare better in the United States. But when Lily reaches Wyoming, she finds that her father has gambled away the ranch and is working as an accountant for another rancher. Now she must find a way to survive before the harsh winter comes.
  ISBN 978-1-4621-1395-8 (perfect)
  1. Women pioneers--Wyoming--19th century--Fiction. 2. Man-woman relationships--Fiction. 3. Frontier and pioneer life--Wyoming--19th century--Fiction. 4. West (U.S.)--Social life and customs--19th century--Fiction. I. Title.
  PS3561.E3928S66 2014
  813'.54--dc23
                          2014034870

Cover design by Kristen Reeves
Cover design © 2014 by Lyle Mortimer
Edited and typeset by Melissa J. Caldwell

Printed in the United States of America

10 9 8 7 6 5 4 3 2 1

To Marilyn and Gordon Bown
and Kemari Rawlings with love.

When you have exhausted all the possibilities, remember this: you haven't.

—THOMAS EDISON

PROLOGUE

ᘒ

*B*ecause Lily Carteret had a generous soul, she understood why her uncle couldn't look her in the eyes when he gave her the ultimatum—long overdue, in her opinion.

"Lily, my fiancée is wondering who you are, and I am disinclined to tell her."

His fiancée. Oh heavens, his fiancée was gat-toothed with thinning hair, but her father was a baronet, and the Carterets were a pretentious bunch. A prosperous ship-building company wasn't enough. Uncle Niles Carteret, widowed himself, craved even the shadow of a title to cross his path, and Lady Sophronia Wadsworth seemed the answer to his prayer.

"To avoid any disclosure, you are sending me where?" Lily asked. She kept her voice level and well modulated, as she had learned at Miss Tilton's School in Bristol, a city not known for social airs, but good enough for Lily Carteret.

"Wyoming Territory, to your father's ranch."

Uncle Niles spoke as though Wyoming had a bad odor. Or perhaps "father's ranch" was the bad odor, or maybe just "father." Lily couldn't really tell, but she had her suspicions.

Wyoming, was it? She had finally been banished too. Sitting there in the Blue Room, reserved for any unpleas-antness at the manor, Lily glanced out the window at the

1

rain and merely wondered if it rained so much in this Wyoming. If not, then hallelujah.

"When do I leave?"

"Lady Wadsworth will be here Thursday next for a visit. Monday would be best. I've made arrangements."

Uncle Niles rose, and Lily did too, head high, for she had been the soul of grace even before her incarceration at Miss Tilton's School. Her hand was on the knob when her uncle cleared his throat.

"In his last letter—two years ago, in '84, if I recall— your father mentioned how well the cattle business was going. I'll send one hundred pounds with you, for him to invest on my behalf. He said anyone can make a fortune on what they call the 'open range.'" He lowered his voice like a conspirator. "I think Wyoming has turned him toward responsibility."

I doubt it supremely, she thought. "Do you still send his remittance checks?"

"Every quarter, as directed by Papa's will. I am an honorable man," he assured her. "Send me a report, eh?"

She nodded. India had failed Clarence Carteret, or vice versa; Australia, ditto. And now he owned a ranch in Wyoming Territory? Doubtful.

When she just stood there, privately amazed that her uncle was still so gullible, he cleared his throat, her signal to give a slight curtsy and leave.

Lily vetoed the curtsy, her first tiny blow for liberty. She was being released too, and it didn't feel half bad.

CHAPTER 1

The fact that he couldn't read was Jack Sinclair's little secret. He'd learned to sign his name for the paymaster during the War of Northern Aggression, but as the war lengthened and Confederate funds shortened, he hadn't overused his sole bit of education. Maybe someday he'd have time to learn, but so far, no luck.

Maybe everyone already knew he couldn't read and just didn't want to embarrass him. That seemed unlikely, because he didn't live in a society interested in sparing a person's feelings. Still, that might be the case, if he could believe a comment from Vivian, a faro dealer he knew at the Back Forty, Wisner's sole saloon.

"Jack, you're just a nice man," she had told him. Maybe she meant it. Maybe people didn't want to hurt the feelings of a nice man. A fellow could hope, anyway.

He pocketed Madeleine's scribbled note to pick up flour and sugar at Wisner's only general store and hoped that the clerk could read what looked like chicken scratches. Jack had stopped to tweak little Chantal's pigtail. She looked up from the dough she was rolling and turned tender eyes on him.

"I'll see if the clerk has some old penny candy gathering dust," he whispered to her. She was just six, but she could stand on an upended milk pail and roll dough.

Mrs. Buxton's note had been much neater. Jack came to her room, Stetson in hand, because she didn't hold with anyone wearing a lid indoors. He had learned long ago just to go upstairs to her bedroom and knock, because she hadn't the energy to walk very far, and downstairs constituted very far. Sickly, stern, and pitiful rolled into one disturbing invalid, she gave him her usual once-over.

"Mr. Sinclair, get a haircut."

"I was going to ask Preacher to cut it toni—"

"A haircut in town. Can't cost more than fifteen cents, with a nickel gratuity."

Jack was too shy to explain that nearly two bits wasted in town meant two bits he couldn't spend on grain for Bismarck, placidly adding muscle and bone in his own private pasture.

"Yes'm," he said and held out his hand for the list.

She handed it to him. "Make sure it's Pond's Healing Cream and no imitation."

"Yes'm." He felt the warmth rising from his neck at the thought of leaning across the counter, giving the clerk his leveling stare, and demanding Pond's Healing Cream. A real man could hardly do that, but try to explain that to the boss's wife.

Jack started for the door, but Mrs. Buxton wasn't through. "Mr. Sinclair, tell the post office clerk distinctly that there is a package for me and he needs to look a little harder."

He almost grinned but stopped in time. Trust a boss's wife to demand packages to materialize, even if they weren't there. He regarded her with some sympathy but not a lot; he didn't think there was anything wrong with her except disappointed hopes and too much Wyoming.

"Ma'am, I'll demand your package and give the clerk a good shake if it isn't there. Won't shoot him, though. That'd be rude."

Why he bothered to tease, he didn't know. Mrs. Buxton had no sense of humor.

She gave him a fishy look. "One more thing. Mr. Carteret wants you to stop in his office."

Jack held in his sigh until he was on the stairs. Would it have killed the Buxtons' clerk to come to *him*? Jack had been ranch foreman long before Clarence Carteret became a clerk. Thirty a month and a two-room house, and Clarence felt superior to everyone. Maybe it was the English accent. What an irritant the man was. Any day now, the boss would figure it out and fire the skinny weasel.

Still, Jack's mother had raised him right, or right enough. He went down the stairs quietly, because Mrs. Buxton always whined about a headache. He stood outside the closed door at the bottom of the stairs. Jack stalled long enough to man himself for a visit to the clerk.

He glanced through the lace curtains to the outside wondering if someday he would have a house like this with lace curtains, his reward for learning the hard business of ranching in Wyoming. After twenty years, discounting the years where he shivered, starved, and learned his trade in a place foreign from Georgia, Jack could run a ranch. Compared to the consortium's Bar Two Dot (usually shortened to Bar Dot), his few acres nearby were paltry indeed. So he knocked on the door with a grimness about his mouth that he couldn't totally blame on the man at the desk.

"What do you need, Clarence?" he asked with no preamble.

"That's Mr. Carteret to you," Clarence said.

Jack knew better than to argue, and he knew "Clarence" was good enough for a remittance man, who couldn't get by without that quarterly check from England, and a man barely sober on a good day.

"What do you need?" Jack repeated, without benefit of first or last name this time. Maybe he just felt like twitting all that pretension sitting behind a desk.

"My daughter, Miss Lily Carteret, will be on the afternoon train. Pick her up."

Gadfreys! The man wasn't going to come along? Although he didn't relish riding any distance with Carteret, it was only four miles to Wisner.

"I'm taking the four-seater buckboard, so you're welcome to come along. Your daughter?"

"My daughter," the clerk replied. "I don't need to meet her."

Suddenly Jack understood. The worm wasn't brave enough to tell this Miss Lily Carteret he'd gambled away a paltry two-thousand acre spread. Obviously the little twerp had never learned to own up to a misdemeanor.

He tried again. "How long's it been? She'll probably want you to meet her."

Carteret turned his attention back to the ledger before him. "Nine years," he muttered.

"Suit yourself," Jack said with a shrug, grateful that his own father, a hard enough man, was never so callous. "In case the platform is loaded with young ladies, how about a brief description?"

"You'll recognize her," Carteret said, obviously reluctant to continue the conversation. "She was tall for her age at fifteen. Looks like her mother." His voice grew almost wistful. "Her mother was from Barbados."

That was it? Did Mr. Remittance Man think Jack Sinclair was going to walk up to every woman on the platform and ask if her mother was from Barbados? "More information would be nice. Maybe even helpful," he suggested.

Carteret gave him a long look. Jack thought he saw a little embarrassment in it, but he could have been wrong.

"Sinclair, do you know what *café au lait* is?"

"No, I don't."

"Didn't think you would."

Jack ordered himself to count to ten. By twenty, he felt better. He gave Carteret his patented stare-down-his-long-nose look that generally worked with new hands and salesmen. Amazing, but Clarence couldn't meet his glance. Jack hadn't used the stare in a long while, but it still worked, apparently.

"What about cambric tea?"

With a shock, Jack understood. "I'm to look for someone not pasty white," he said, feeling suddenly sorry for Miss Lily Carteret, who deserved a better father, no matter what her hue.

Clarence Carteret surprised him. "She looks like her mother," he said again, and with greater dignity. "Quite a lovely woman. You'll find her."

⁓

In the past decade, Jack had made the short drive to Wisner more times than he could count, but as this hot and dry summer turned the corner into September, he was starting to dread the trip. The sky had been bright blue since April with no hint of rain. Brittle grass and parched ground outlined with cracks widened in the soil.

Too many cattle nosed in the dry brush and lowed by shrinking ponds. The commission agents had offered so little for this year's four-year-olds that most of the ranchers chose to winter over their herds and hope for better prices in '87. Jack shook his head as he threaded Sunny Boy through a regular convention of steers complaining about their lot in life.

He glanced west toward his own few acres. On the rare chance that the Cheyenne Northern was actually on time, he'd better ride for Wisner, get ranch business done first, collect Carteret's mulatto daughter, and stop by the Two Jay on the way back to the Bar Dot.

Wisner wasn't much, not an up-and-coming town like Wheatland, which had a merchants' club and three banks. One bank, a post office, a Methodist church, one general store, one undertaker, a hotel, a greasy spoon, a lawyer, a saloon, and a sporting house made up Wisner. What more did a Wyoming town need? A doctor might have been nice.

Mrs. Buxton's package was waiting for hm. The clerk handed it over with a frown. "Shake it."

Jack shook it and rolled his eyes. "Let's hope Mrs. Buxton ordered a parcel of broken glass from Monkey Ward."

The clerk turned back to targeting pigeonholes with letters. Jack watched a moment, wondering what it would be like to receive a letter and be able to read it.

The chair in the impromptu barbershop constituting a corner of the general store was more comfortable than he remembered. Since the Cheyenne Northern was late as usual, he felt rich to the tune of another fifteen cents and included a shave with his haircut. Glory, but it felt good just to sit there with a hot towel on his face. If only there was someone to knead the knots out of his neck, which had tightened into bullets after a summer with no rain.

A visit to Vivian's faro table would have been nice, but he had to save money. No telling how much hay and grain he'd have to buy for Bismarck and his harem this winter. He wasn't any great shakes at faro, but Vivian was nice to talk to.

His face in the mirror was always a shock. His little scrap of a shaving mirror at home only showed a bit of personal real estate; here was his whole head. At least his hair wasn't thinning, even if that strawberry blond color seemed childish for a man going on thirty-five. He had enough weather wrinkles to avoid the nickname of Babyface. Or at least no one called him that to his face, since he was the foreman and had certain powers of hire and fire.

Observing him, the barber was not helpful. "You could maybe grow a handlebar to cover that scar. Get it in the war?"

"Sure did." He smiled at the barber. From his speech

he was a Yankee, and he still held that shaving razor. No sense in mentioning that *his* army was Lee's. "I earned it. How much?"

Transaction completed, Jack handed over his notes in the general store portion of the building and added Mrs. Buxton's admonition about Pond's Healing Cream. Good thing he never had acquired a wife or he might have had to pick up something that would make him blush. He doubted foremen blushed, and he didn't intend to be the first.

As it was, the clerk handed over the jar with a flourish and added it to the pile. Madeleine's chicken scratch seemed legible to the fellow, which relieved Jack.

"How's Madeleine doing, anyway?" the man asked as he wrapped Jack's purchases in brown paper and twine. "Must be a little tough without old Jean Baptiste to bring in wages."

"It is." He sighed, wondering how much to disclose of the cook's anguish at her husband's death. "Three little kids . . ."

Jack was no fan of small talk, but the brief exchange reminded him of the penny candy he had promised Chantal, rolling dough so diligently, and a bag of peppermint drops for Manuel, minding his ranch and Bismarck. Jack found what he wanted and kept it separate from ranch purchases, adding in a dime's worth of lemon drops for himself. That and the shave constituted his splurges for the summer.

He put the parcels in the buckboard, which already held the windmill parts he had picked up earlier. A brief visit to Stockmen's Savings and Loan assured him that he could treat himself to lunch at the greasy spoon, grandiosely named the Great Wall of China. It was run by a Chinaman who wielded a great cleaver to send poultry to a better place.

But there was the Cheyenne Northern, less late than

usual. Maybe Miss Carteret wouldn't be too refined for the Great Wall of China.

One middle-aged lady got off the train and looked around. Her anxious expression changed to relief when a middle-aged gentlemen stepped up, Stetson in hand. Jack watched them out of the corner of his eye. When all they did was shake hands and leave considerable distance between them, he figured her for a mail-order bride. Give'um a year and there'd be a baby. Someone had to populate this sparse territory, since he wasn't doing any heavy lifting in that regard.

The train next coughed up what looked like a preacher and a salesman. He watched, and there she was.

How in the world did she do it? Every person who got off the Cheyenne Northern was windblown and blowsy. There wasn't a hair out of place on Lily Carteret's head, from what he could see of her dark hair under the small hat, tipped forward so stylishly. He knew she had been traveling from New York City, long enough for her clothing to be wrinkled and travel stained. But she looked as though she had just stepped out of a fancy store, as neat as wax.

"*Jee*-rusalem Crickets," he murmured. "I have died and gone to heaven."

CHAPTER 2

❦

*I*t couldn't be anyone but Miss Lily Carteret. Clarence Carteret was absolutely right about the cambric tea color of her skin, but that wasn't the first thing Jack noticed. In fact, it was way down his manly list.

Like the other lady, she stood on the top step, looking around, but with a striking difference. She seemed to be assessing her surroundings instead, weighing Wyoming Territory in the balance. He couldn't tell from her expression how the scale tipped.

As he stared at her, he decided it was her eyes that held his attention, even before her shape, which was bounteous without being ostentatious. Her eyes were deep brown. He saw no fear or doubt in them, only interest, as though she was trying to figure out what life planned for her here.

It was impossible to ignore her beauty. Her skin was indeed cambric tea, or that pretentious French phrase Clarence Carteret had tossed about. A bold man could stare at her for some time, wondering if she was English, French, Spanish, or African. Since he knew something about her, he knew she was all of that, and she wore it well.

She helped herself down, since the conductor had turned away. Jack didn't have to gird his loins for this. He knew that meeting Lily Carteret was going to be a pleasure. There had been so little genuine pleasure in his life that he almost didn't recognize the emotion.

Grateful he had visited the barbershop, Jack took off

his Stetson and stepped forward. "Miss Lily Carteret?" he asked, also grateful that his voice did not squeak. He was well beyond that particular felony, thank the Almighty.

"That would be I," she said, and he nearly swooned—if men swooned—with the loveliness of her English accent.

He had become familiar with proper English because the Bar Dot was a British consortium, pompously titled the Cheyenne Land and Cattle Company. The various owners had visited the ranch through the years, and he liked to listen to them. None of those men sounded as well-bred as Lily Carteret.

"I'm Jack Sinclair, foreman on the Bar Dot," he said, using the ranch's nickname. "Your father asked that I escort you to the ranch."

"And his first name is . . . ," she began. Jack silently applauded her circumspection. This was not a woman to be easily gulled by some flat looking at her luggage for her name and taking advantage.

"Clarence Carteret," he answered.

"Bravo," she said and held out her hand.

If she was disappointed that her father was not here to greet her, she didn't let on. It seemed to Jack as if she did not expect him, anyway.

"He, uh, said he was busy, and, uh . . ." *Stop, you idiot*, Jack ordered himself. *Just stop talking.* "It's a busy time of year, ma'am."

She smiled at him and looked over his shoulder, which made him turn around too, like an oaf. "My luggage."

Her voice was so lovely. Someone watching him would think he had never seen a pretty lady before. He must have, but he couldn't remember when.

He picked up the suitcases. "If you'll just follow me."

"Why should I do that?" she asked, sounding completely reasonable. "Papa never mentioned a foreman. Yes, you know his name, but after only an overnight sojourn in Cheyenne, I've decided everyone knows everyone in this territory. Do set down my luggage until we sort this out."

He couldn't help smiling. "You're right there, ma'am. It's that small a territory." He set down Miss Carteret's suitcases. Obviously she needed a little more explanation to budge herself off the platform. "You don't have foremen in England?"

She shook her head, showing no apprehension, but also showing no inclination to move until he proved up. "Do you tend the cattle?"

He thought of all his duties, most of which involved monumental cursing and brute force against stubborn animals. *Tending* sounded so kind, almost benevolent. Miss Carteret was in for a rare experience, if he ever convinced her to come with him to the Bar Dot. "I . . . I suppose I do. The Bar Dot is a huge spread."

"Papa told me his ranch was two thousand acres, so that must be huge. He also called it simply the Carteret, not Bar Dot."

Now what? Did he have to explain what had happened before this person would take another step? "It's like this, ma'am," he began, after a lengthy pause.

She put up her hand, her eyes kind, the starch out of her, somehow. "There's no ranch, eh?"

Jee-rusalem Crickets, why in the world did Clarence Carteret have to be a fool *and* a coward who couldn't even do his own dirty work? "There is and there isn't."

She drew herself up taller, and he suddenly saw that this conversation was diminishing her and that she felt the need for height. He had done that a time or two in his life, when opposition loomed. Nothing loomed now except the disaster that was Clarence Carteret, and she somehow knew.

"Papa doesn't own it anymore, does he?" she asked, her voice soft.

Jack shook his head, impressed with her courage, as

though she had known all along that this was going to happen. The women he knew out West weren't the type to shrink and faint at bad news when their own lives were hard enough, but Lily Carteret was a lady. He thought he heard a small sigh, but that was all.

"Tell me, if you know: How did he lose this ranch that I will never see?"

"He lost it in a card game."

Her head went back a little, but that was all. "I'm not surprised," she said. "Would I have liked the ranch?"

Even a deaf man would have heard the wistfulness in her voice. She was doing her dead level best not to show her disappointment.

"Yeah, you would have liked it. Begging your pardon, ma'am, but two thousand acres is small potatoes out here. Still, there's a wonderful little spring on the place, which I don't think Clarence knew about. He, uh, didn't spend much time there. Maybe he never saw the spring."

"Was there a house?"

"More of a shack. Two rooms, but he put up wallpaper, if you can believe that."

"I can," she said, getting into the spirit of the thing. "Papa has his standards." Her shoulders sank a bit, as if she knew there was no pretense or courage to maintain, not with news like this. "You seem to know the place pretty well."

Go ahead and tell her, he thought. *She'll find out soon enough.* "Yes'm, I do. I'm the fella who won the ranch in that card game."

Jack couldn't help wincing, certain she would come apart now. She looked away, as though the magpie hawking and spitting on the saloon roof fascinated her more than speech. When she turned back, she was even smiling, and it looked genuine. You could have barreled Jack over with a broomstraw.

"Sounds to me as though you love the place, Mr. Sinclair. How long have you owned it?"

"It was the result of a January card game."

"Were spirits involved?"

"Most certainly." No point in telling her that the only drinking man was her father. She probably already knew. After Clarence Carteret, eyes red, won three hundred dollars and declared himself lucky, no force in the world could have kept him from slapping the deed on the table. Jack had seen gamblers like that before, but he was usually watching the game, not sitting at the table.

He didn't know what else to say. "It's a grand little ranch," he said, blundering on. "All fenced and with that spring."

"Does your wife like it too?"

"No wife, ma'am. I have an old Mexican, name of Manuel, living there and taking care of Bismarck."

"Bismarck?"

He saw the defeat in her eyes, and he didn't know what to do. He could tell her about Bismarck, but maybe he should just get her to the Bar Dot so her slimy father could explain. Jack only made seventy-five dollars a month. No one paid him to mend a suddenly broken heart, which he knew he was looking at, even if the casual passerby couldn't tell. You had to stand close to Lily Carteret to see the pain in her eyes.

His stomach rumbled. "I can tell you about Bismarck, but . . . but how about some chop suey at the Great Wall of China?"

"Chop suey?"

"You'll like it."

She seemed to perk up. Maybe she was hungry too, or maybe she was again the adventurous person he had noticed when she stepped off the train. "Nothing would suit me more than a spot of luncheon, Mr. Sinclair."

He chuckled to himself over that, wondering how loud his cowhands would hoot if he suggested a spot of luncheon during the cow gather.

She made no objection this time when he picked up one of her suitcases, and she surprised him by picking up the other one.

"I can do that, ma'am," he assured her,

"I can too, Mr. Sinclair," she said. "Quite possibly I'll be doing more of that in future, considering circumstances. What is chop suey?"

CHAPTER 3

❧

~~T~~here was one thing Lily could say for the Great Wall of China café: She didn't have to fight her way to the counter for a sandwich. No one rushed in, shouldering her aside as they had when the Union Pacific screeched to a twenty-minute stop, all the way across this interminable country. Not until Grand Island, Nebraska, was she brave enough to use her elbows to good effect and actually reach the counter in time for grisly beef and coffee with an oily sheen on it. (Tea was unheard of, and only brought tired smiles.)

The Great Wall was dim, if not cool. At the moment, she preferred dim to cool, because how long could a lady keep up the pretense that nothing had rattled her with Mr. Sinclair's wry announcement? She would study him and keep her mind off her increasingly precarious future in this Wyoming Territory.

But first there was the Chinaman, wiping his hands on an apron that should have been washed weeks ago.

He bowed to Lily, then turned to Mr. Sinclair. "Boss, where you find pretty lady?"

"On the train, Wing Li," Mr. Sinclair replied, without even a blush. "No ladies in Wisner."

That seemed to be as far as Mr. Sinclair wanted to delve into the matter. "You got any chop suey?" he asked, motioning away the menu.

"Always for you, chop suey," the cook replied. "If you

have twenty minutes, I kill a chicken. Whoosh! You have chicken and dumplings."

Mr. Sinclair glanced at Lily. She tried hard not to laugh, because she was imagining such a conversation in Carteret Manor. She thought of all the boring meals she had endured with Uncle Niles, who only wanted to get back to his ledgers and avoid his niece. She decided this was better, if more rustic.

"And you, pretty missy?"

"I'd like the chop suey, Mr. Wing," Pretty Missy said. "Or is it Mr. Li?"

Mr. Wing or Mr. Li giggled.

"What's in it?"

"I've never asked," the foreman said in a low voice. "What *is* in it, Mr. Li?"

Mr. Li shrugged. "Some of this. Some of that." He frowned, perhaps considering better food on another continent. "Comes with soy sauce."

"Which hides a multitude of evils," Mr. Sinclair whispered. "Hasn't killed me yet, Miss Carteret. Price is right, too—fifteen cents."

"That's the deciding factor," Lily said, thinking of her thin purse. "Chop suey for me too."

"I'll buy," Mr. Sinclair said when the Chinaman retreated behind a beaded curtain and started shouting orders to whoever worked there.

"You needn't," she said quickly, not wanting to be obliged to the man who won her father's ranch in a card game.

"I asked you if you wanted lunch, so it's my business," he told her with a certain dogged air that suggested he wasn't used to argument.

"But . . ."

"No discussion," he said with real finality this time.

"Tea, missy?" Mr. Li asked, back from the kitchen.

"Oh, my word, yes," Lily said. She couldn't even

remember her last cup of tea. Apparently no one in the United States drank it except Chinamen.

Wing Li retired behind the beaded curtain again. Lily prepared herself for conversation, but Mr. Sinclair got up and walked to the counter, to a row of thick china coffee cups. She felt a smile coming on as he looked over the mugs carefully, perhaps after one with no chips and sort of clean. She hadn't expected such nicety, and it charmed her.

While he took his time, Lily watched him. He was tall and had that hip-sprung walk she had noticed on other men from mid-Nebraska on. She had never seen better posture, not even among the men who comprised her uncle's hunt club back in Gloucestershire. They just rode on occasion; this man rode for a living.

He had left his hat on a peg by the door. From the look of his hair, and the white line on his tanned neck, she knew he had recently sat in a barber's chair. His hair was blond, his eyes brown like her own. She looked down at her ungloved hands; his skin was even darker than hers. She knew that his would change with the seasons, while hers would remain the same.

Straight back, straight nose. He might have been a handsome man, except for a scar that ran from his left nostril down to the corner of his mouth, giving his lips, nicely chiseled, a lopsided look.

She hadn't meant to stare. Maybe he was sensitive to observation. He stopped his inventory of the china mugs and looked at her. "I earned it at Sayler's Creek," he said with no embarrassment. "I call it Sinclair luck. I fought through two years and got wounded in the last battle before Appomattox. I was fifteen."

Sounds like Carteret luck, Lily thought.

He didn't seem to mind talking about either defeat or his wound. "Someone dragged me to a Yankee aid station. They still had chloroform, so it could have been worse."

He couldn't help going a little grim about the mouth. "Can't say I was sorry to miss Appomattox."

He saw her puzzled expression. "The War of Yankee Aggression, ma'am," he explained. "Maybe you called it the War between the States." He gave her a wry look. "You know, we could have used some help from England. Just sayin'." He returned his attention to the mugs.

He had the same starved look as other cowmen Lily had noticed. She decided that western men were well enough, but there was no denying a certain gauntness of face, the look of hardworking men who never quite got enough to eat. She found herself hoping that Wing Li's portions of chop suey were prodigious.

He found a cup to his liking, reached over the counter to a coffee pot, and filled the cup. Another reach brought a tin of canned milk, followed by several scoops of sugar.

She hadn't meant to stare—so impolite—but she must have, because he grinned at her, which made his face look less gaunt. He did have good teeth. "The hands tell me I don't drink manly coffee, but I don't like it black. Do you?"

"I don't like it any way," she said frankly.

He chuckled. "In that case we'd better stop at the mercantile and get you some tea," he told her, then glanced around as the beaded curtain rattled. "Slap my knee, Mr. Li, you've outdone yourself."

Slop mah nay, Lily thought, wondering what on earth he meant. He did have a lengthy way of speaking that she hadn't heard before. Would it be impolite to ask the man where he came from? And what did he mean by "hands"? *I thought we spoke the same language.*

Mr. Li slid a plate of something questionable in front of her and stepped back, perhaps expecting some sort of admiration.

"Lovely," she said, trusting that to be adequate.

It must have been more than adequate, because Mr. Sinclair looked away and smiled at the wall. "There you go, boss," the Chinaman said as he slid a plate in front of him. "You get more rice, even though she tall too."

Mr. Sinclair nodded. When Mr. Li retreated to the kitchen, his shoulders started to shake. "He's a piece of work, Miss Carteret."

Lily observed the steaming mound in front of her, trying to identify something familiar. "Seriously, what *is* it?"

Mr. Sinclair started eating through what fifteen cents bought at the Great Wall of China. "I told you, never ask," he replied. He pushed a brown bottle toward her. "Soy sauce?"

Uncertain, she sprinkled it on the chop suey. Maybe if it all turned brown, she wouldn't wonder about its origins.

"He's probably never seen a tall woman before," Jack said, taking the soy sauce from her when she finished, and dousing his meal. "Don't know why he wouldn't think you'd be hungry too."

"I've never been convicted of being dainty," Lily said, discarding once and for all anything she knew about polite conversation.

Mr. Sinclair winked at her, then turned his whole-hearted attention to the chop suey. He ate with some relish, so she picked up her fork and tried. Not bad; not good, either.

"What do you think?" he asked, after a few minutes.

"I'm pleasantly surprised," she told him and then nodded to Mr. Li when he brought a tea cup, no saucer, and a pot. She poured fragrant green tea into the cup and felt a care or two slide from her shoulders. Papa had told her once that the English could solve any problem with tea. In his case, it wasn't true. Still, it was tea and not to be trifled with.

She knew she had not a single thing in common with the man seated opposite her except species and planet, but here she was, and here she would remain until she thought of something else. Lily took another bite and considered Mr. Sinclair's one comment spoken with affection.

"Why Bismarck?"

He chewed, swallowed, and put down his fork. "A grandiose name for a bull, I'll admit, but I expect great things from Bismarck."

Lily felt laughter welling inside her, not that bulls were objects of humor, but that this conversation was going to be unlike any she had ever been party to anywhere. Her uncle would drop dead from mortification, but she gloriously did not care.

"Sir, what makes him so special?" she asked, pushing aside her chop suey.

His eyes were merry, as if he knew precisely what she was thinking. "Do you seriously want to know?"

"I believe I do."

"You won't have heard of his kind before, but he is a Herferd."

He had a poor accent, but she knew precisely what he was saying, and she understood. "It's Hereford, sir, and I have heard of his kind. A red cow with a white face?"

"You got it, ma'am. How'd you know?"

"I'm from Gloucestershire, which is hard by Herefordshire. I have seen these cows."

She moved her plate of chop suey farther away, noting how his eyes followed it. *Uncle, here comes another social gaffe of enormous proportions*, she thought with some glee. "Mr. Sinclair, you are welcome to finish my chop suey."

"Not to your taste?"

"Not really."

She glanced toward the beaded curtains as they rustled, and there stood Mr. Wing Li, his brow furrowed, his lower lip drooping, his eyes on her rejected plate. "Oh dear, he doesn't take kindly to my lack of appetite," she whispered to the foreman. "Is it a personal thing?"

"I don't pretend to know, ma'am," he whispered back, his eyes on her plate too. "He scares me and he has that cleaver."

Lily laughed. Without a word, she pushed the plate toward him. Without a word, he forked the chop suey onto his plate and kept eating. "Hairiford, Hairiford," he said around bites. "Sounds better than Herferd. Miss Carteret, after I won your father's ranch, I spent my whole life savings on a bull. He resides in majestic splendor on two thousand acres of fenced land with his harem of two cows." He put down his fork. "I am the laughingstock of the entire territory, but I have a plan."

His enthusiasm was undeniable. Lily sipped her tea, wondering about a man who ate chop suey, won a ranch in a card game, and gambled everything on an English hunk of beef. She had never met anyone like him.

"I've never had a plan," she said, setting down her cup. "I envy you."

Mr. Sinclair merely shrugged. "No need. Get a plan of your own, Miss Carteret." His look was kindly then, as far as Lily understood kindness. "I'm speaking out of turn, but any daughter of Clarence Carteret should get a plan."

"Pretty soon?"

"Almost immediately."

CHAPTER 4

*M*r. Li insisted that Lily take a handful of almond cookies. "He make you give him your dinner?" he asked in a voice loud enough for Mr. Sinclair to hear as he twirled the cleaver, with its congealed blood and chicken feathers.

"No, Mr. Wing. I have been on the train for four days and my stomach is . . . is . . ."—Lily patted her middle—". . . unsettled."

Mr. Li brightened. He held up one finger as though to keep her there and rattled back through the bead curtain.

"What have I done?" Lily whispered to the foreman.

"I don't know," he said doubtfully. "But whatever he brings out, you should probably drink."

Lily closed her eyes when she heard the beads rattle again. She opened her eyes when he set down a porcelain cup, its content the same color as the soy sauce.

"Bottoms up, Miss Carteret," the foreman said with a grin. "Better you than me."

She gave him a speaking glance and picked up the cup. "My stomach doesn't hurt that bad," she said to Mr. Li.

"Drink it, missy," he said, still twirling that cleaver.

She felt her stomach give a great heave as the brew landed inside and probably crawled away to some dark corner. She set the cup down and waited to die.

Nothing. "I am cured," she told him. Why not gild the lily a bit? "Mr. Wing, you are a wonder."

The Chinaman beamed at her and nudged Mr.

Sinclair's shoulder. "You bring her around anytime, Jack. She better than the bad girls at Lucy's."

I will sink into the ground, Lily thought. She glanced at Jack, whose face had gone as red as a man lost three or four days in the Sahara.

"Um, well, yes," Jack managed, then stood up. He plunked some money on the table and nodded to Lily without looking at her. "We'd best be on our way."

He was halfway across the café when she joined him, taking his proffered arm. She could tell he was suffering in the worst way, and she liked him. *Uh, best to put him at ease*, she told herself, falling into the vernacular.

"Mr. Sinclair, I have decided not to be embarrassed by anything I see or hear in your territory," she told him in her most serene voice as he hurried along the boardwalk.

"I don't go to Lucy's." He turned even more red. Probably without being aware of it, he glanced up the street toward a building painted a color not found in elevated social spheres, where two women hung out the window, calling to passersby.

Time to put the poor fellow at peace. She stopped. "Let us come to a right understanding, Mr. Sinclair. What you do or do not do in your spare time is your business."

"Seriously, I don't. I do play cards now and then."

Lily found a larger concern as wind started to tug at her skirts. She released her hold on Mr. Sinclair's arm and fought to keep her steel-taped bustle sedately behind her where it belonged. Another gust at the corner flared out her skirts, giving anyone who might be looking more than a glimpse at her legs. Her mortification grew as a man in a long linen duster whistled and tipped his hat to her. "Jack, you dog," he called. "You're the envy of nations!"

"Mercy," she murmured, taking her turn with embarrassment, suddenly grateful that the ranch was several miles away and she wouldn't have to set foot in Wisner again until she left it.

"Just a Wyoming zephyr, ma'am," Mr. Sinclair said, kind enough to keep a straight face at her predicament.

"I'd hate to be here when the wind actually blows," she joked, wishing the wagon were closer.

Once across the street and back on the wooden sidewalk, the buildings blunted the force of the wind. Lily took his proffered arm again and found herself nudged toward a store.

"Forgot something," he said. "I'll just a moment."

The store was cool and dark and a blessed relief from the wind. Interested, Lily looked around to see bolts of cloth on shelves and kegs of food. She followed him to the long counter, peering into the kegs and seeing raisins, flour, and cornmeal. There were several boxes with pungent dried fish. In the distance, hoes and shovels had taken up residence next to horse collars and crockery.

"Imagine, all this in one store," she said.

"You don't have general stores in England?" he asked.

"No, indeed. We go from shop to shop," Lily said. "I believe I like this better."

At the counter, while she waited for Mr. Sinclair, Lily admired German dolls with bisque heads and tiny feet in the glass-fronted case. Wooden trains and knives were jumbled next to dominos and packs of cards. Overhead were strips of gluey material with flies stuck to them, trapped in mid flight. As repugnant as that was, Lily couldn't help but admire the enterprise of someone manufacturing and selling fly strips. The United States and her territories were going to be an unceasing interest, she decided.

"Here."

Mr. Sinclair held out a small paper bag to her. She took it, surprised at its weight.

"It's a nickel's worth of lead shot," he explained. "What you do is sew a handful of these into each of the hems of your skirts."

His kindness touched her. "I'll never be a spectacle in Wisner again."

She looked inside the little bag with lead shot, and it suddenly became something much bigger. Somehow, accepting the bag from a man that was essentially a stranger had cracked open her book of life for the first time. What had gone before—the shame of being a remittance man's daughter, a woman of color, a poor relation— was only prologue. She couldn't have put her finger on it, but accepting that bag meant she was going to live large now. Whether for good or ill remained to be seen.

"A little lead in each hem?" she asked, grateful for his small gift.

"Just drop in one lead ball and sew a little vertical seam on either side of it. Six inches later, repeat the process."

"Where'd you learn this, Mr. Sinclair?"

"I could lie, but why? A faro dealer at the Back Forty told me that's how she kept her skirts from flying in the wind."

Lily nodded, appreciative of his honesty. He had no airs to put on and probably nothing to prove. "She is a wise woman."

"Indeed she is. Vivian tells me she's saving money to open a millinery shop in her hometown. Everyone needs a plan."

⁐

They drove in silence, but it wasn't an embarrassed silence, not even after his plain speaking. Jack thought he ought to say something, but he noticed that Lily was looking around, noticing everything. She pointed at a brown and white deer-looking creature.

"Antelope. You'll see them with the cattle a lot. Don't know why, really. Maybe they're sociable."

He drove slowly, then looked back at Wisner, a middling sort of place with a background of low hills. It was the kind of town that needed a few more churches and then a school, and maybe ladies would come and there would be families. He hadn't thought of the matter, but here was Lily Carteret sitting beside him, observing. Maybe that was why he saw Wisner through different eyes.

"It's nothing like your home, is it?"

She shook her head. "I haven't really had a home, Mr. Sinclair. As you were plain speaking, so shall I be."

He waited, wondering what she would say, but half knowing, because he knew her father.

"I've lived at the mercy of begrudging relatives all my life," she said, looking straight ahead now. "They fed me, clothed me quite well, and educated me because they had to. To their credit, I have never gone without anything I needed, not once. Uncle Niles owns a shipbuilding yard in Bristol. He's a wealthy man and aiming for a match with a lady who is plain and prim, but the daughter of a baronet." She paused and looked at him, hoping he understood what she didn't say.

"And . . . and maybe you don't fit into the world he wants?"

"I don't. He decided to send me on my way to his younger brother, a remittance man. That way, two of us are out of sight and out of mind." She raised her hands in her lap and then lowered them. "I don't know what will become of me here, but I intend to count somewhere."

Jack thought of his own life and felt an amazing kinship with the pretty lady who was neither fish nor fowl, and who had absolutely nothing in common with him. "I came out here after the war. There was nothing left for me in Georgia. I starved and I probably should have died, but I learned about cattle."

"You understand me then," she said.

He didn't mind her subsequent silence. He was content to breathe the pleasant lavender of her hair or clothing. He tried to imagine the landscape through her eyes: the edge of the plains as it met low hills and the mountains beyond; the dry air and the wind-chased dust devils; the enormity of the sky. Everything was tawny now in late summer, more parched and thirsty than usual, even in this dry land.

Cattle roamed everywhere, crossing the dirt track that passed for a road, idling around shrinking water holes, on the search for grass. Beyond them were the drift fences—slatted affairs paralleling the road but not attached to each other—that he knew she would question.

"Those fences can't hold anything in," she commented finally.

"They're drift fences. Look around you. You won't see any bob wire, or maybe you have wooden fences at home."

"Some, and stone fences. Even hedgerows." She turned to look at him then, and he saw all the intelligence in her lively eyes. "But these don't keep anything in. How could they?"

"It's open range, Miss Carteret. Each ranching district has drift fences, which are supposed to keep the cattle from wandering too far." He gestured to the wideness around them. "You're looking at cattle from several ranches. They just mingle together until the cows gather. The boys from different ranches separate them according to brand. Usually the four-year-olds go to market."

She must have heard his uncertainty. Jack reckoned she was a hard woman to fool.

"But . . . but they didn't go this year? Is that what you're . . ." She chuckled. ". . . you're *not* saying?"

"They're too puny, what with no rain and no grass. The buyers from Chicago made lowball offers and most of the ranchers decided to hold them over for another year."

"You sound skeptical," she told him, and again he was impressed with her awareness.

"I am. Who is to say this will be an easy winter, with enough snow and rain in the spring?" He spoke to his horses and pulled back to slow the wagon, just watching the cattle, something he did all the time, because they worried him.

"You'd have sold anyway, wouldn't you?"

He couldn't hold back his admiration, and the sudden realization that he had a most unlikely ally. "Bravo, Miss Carteret!"

"Oh, now," she said with a low laugh. "You're teasing me."

"No, I'm not! I wouldn't. I'd have sold the whole lot, even at a loss." Might as well unlimber his whole gripe on her. "That's what I told Mr. Buxton, but he ignored me. Said the consortium knew best. What was I but the foreman who works the cattle?"

She peered at his face in a way he found endearing. "*You're* the one who knows. Who is Mr. Buxton?"

"He's my boss, but he never rides the range. He works for a whole bunch of Englishmen who have sunk amazing fortunes into cattle. They call themselves the Cheyenne Land and Cattle Company." He started the horses in motion again. "I'm the one who knows, but who listens to a man making seventy-five dollars a month?" He couldn't help his sarcasm. "They're piling in thousands of dollars and *that* makes them experts."

He could have said more, but Jack was curious to know just how bright she was. She looked at the vastness of the plains, full of cattle, and then up at the sky without a cloud in sight.

"What's going to happen, Mr. Sinclair?" she asked. "What do you know?"

"I'll show you when we get to the river."

CHAPTER 5

*H*ang onto the seat," he told her. "Or grab my belt. It's steep here. Don't be shy."

She gripped the wagon bench as they started down toward the Sublette River, hardly more than a creek now. She pressed her feet against the wagon boards as the pitch grew and then grasped his belt, trying not to slide. He enjoyed the feel of her fingers.

He reined in at the river so the horses could drink, and she let go of his belt, her face tinged with slight color that made her light tan skin so handsome.

He knew she was embarrassed, but he didn't bother to set her at ease, because that was the journey, as she would discover the longer she lived here. He pointed toward the muskrat mounds along the bank.

"Muskrats. Seen any before?"

She shook her head, then moved a little closer to him when he said they looked like big rats. *Must remember this*, he thought, amused.

"They live along riverbanks here and pretty much hole up for the winter."

She gave him another puzzled look.

"I knocked into one of their lodges the other day, out of curiosity. I've never seen walls so thick. That means a bad winter."

She didn't try to hide her skepticism.

"You're as unconvinced as my boss!"

"We can't call this scientific," she said a trifle tartly.

"Well, let me show you something else. Just stay here. I'll be back."

He let himself down by the water's edge and walked back among the cottonwoods, looking until he found what he wanted. "Up you get, little feller," he said as he carefully lifted a caterpillar off the tree. At the wagon, he set the little beast on the seat and watched her slide the other way.

"It's a woolly caterpillar," he said, letting it crawl onto his index finger. "Don't go all girly on me. They're upstanding little citizens. I've never seen one so woolly."

She looked less skeptical. In fact, a fine frown line worked its way between her eyes. She reached out tentatively and touched the creature. "When will it freeze here?"

"Already has. Last week."

"But that was the end of August!" She held her hand palm up and he deposited the caterpillar in it. He watched the frown deepen as she brought the caterpillar closer to her face. "It's so warm today."

He returned the caterpillar to a tree. "It'll be warm a few more days, Miss Carteret, maybe another week or two even, but we've already had our first freeze."

"You've never seen it so early?" she asked.

He shook his head. "It's going to be a bad winter, and I can't convince anyone."

"What's going to happen to all these cattle?"

"You're not supposed to ask that question," he said. "It's bad luck."

"That's silly," she retorted immediately. "I mean . . . well, I mean . . . that's silly."

"Tell Mr. Buxton for me, will you?"

They started up the opposite bank in silence, Miss Carteret with her hand on her totally impractical hat this time. He needed both hands on the reins, or he would have happily put one behind her back to steady her. She leaned forward and grasped the front of the wagon, giving a small sigh of gratitude when they were on level soil again. He pointed to a cluster of buildings—so small on the open plain—and edged the wagon in their direction.

"I don't mean to upset you, but that's your father's ranch that I won last January."

He wished he hadn't been looking at her eyes then, because he saw shame.

"Mr. Sinclair, two years ago, my father wrote his brother—my uncle—all about his wonderful ranch. He never mentioned this." She spoke so softly. "Two years! He lied to us. My uncle thought things were better, and he sent me to this wonderful ranch that now belongs to you."

She looked away, and he felt the hot embarrassment for someone else that was somehow worse than almost any other emotion. This English lady was pawning her dignity, and it ripped at his insides. He didn't know what to say, so he kept his mouth shut.

"Let's see it, then," she said after a long pause. She put her hand up to shade her forehead and take a better look. "Right now at least, I'm not feeling too sorry for myself."

It was an interesting comment, spoken clearly and with no tears in her voice. He knew then that he was looking at a lady with no expectations, and it pained him. Some chivalrous part of him wished that ladies had an easier time of it in this vale of tears than men did. Generally, woman's lot was worse, or so he had observed.

When they came to the ranch gate, he got off, and with a certain easy-walking pride, opened the gate. To his surprise, Miss Carteret slid over, took the reins, and clucked the horses through, so he could close the gate behind him. She pulled up a little shortly, but the horses didn't mind.

"Thanks for that. Didn't know you knew horses," he said as he climbed up again and took the reins from her.

"I don't know teams, but I've been watching you." She placed her hands placidly in her lap again, as if daring him to make anything of such a simple act of kindness.

The buildings weren't far from the gate, down a sheltering slope. The sodbuster or would-be rancher who had first owned the property that her father bought had known something about wind, tucking his shack a little below the constant breeze. The barn was close by. He had already told Manuel to string a rope between the two buildings, even though the Mexican had laughed. *Just you wait*, Jack thought, feeling grim again. *You'll be glad you listened to me.*

Wiping his hands on a towel, Manuel came into the yard. He was just a little Mexican, too old now for hard ranch work, but willing to sign on to watch one bull and a couple of cows and not laugh about it, as everyone else did.

"Manuel Ortega, this is Miss Carteret," Jack said, remembering the proper way to introduce a lady. "She's going to stay on the Bar Dot with her father. How's Bismarck?"

"Fat and king of the pasture," Manuel said. With a courtly little bow, he held out his hand to Lily Carteret and helped her from the wagon. "All I have inside is cold coffee, and I don't recommend it," he told her.

She laughed. "I'll settle for a glass of water, if you have one."

The three of them went into the shack, two rooms and a kitchen lean-to. There was only one tin cup, but Manuel graciously wiped off the rim with the same cloth he had used on his hands, and dipped Lily a drink from a bucket. She accepted it just as graciously and looked around the room.

She focused her attention on the wallpaper, roses on a shiny background.

"My father's home improvement."

"Yes. He also left this funny couch . . ."

"A chaise longue."

". . . and Manuel has a really nice pitcher and basin with roses."

He couldn't help but watch her expressive face, wondering if this information would break through the steely resolve she seemed so capable of, but no. She took it all in stride, though, and just glanced into the other room, which held an ornate brass bed. Manuel had just thrown his bedroll there, but she made no comment, beyond observing a whiter portion of the wall and asking if there were photographs.

Jack felt his own discomfort now. "Yes'm, two," he mumbled. "I took them down and tried to give them to Mr. Carteret, but he just gave me a strange sort of smile and reminded me that I had won the whole ranch, fair and square."

She flinched at that and tightened her lips, reminding him that even this woman with no expectations had a tender heart.

"I have them at the Bar Dot, and I'll give them to you," he said.

"I thank you for that." And then she completely betrayed herself by lowering her eyes and dabbing at them in the most casual way, perhaps thinking he might believe she was just flicking off dust. "Is there one of a beautiful woman?"

"Yes'm. You'll have it."

She gave herself a little shake, as if daring him to comment on the tears that made her brown eyes look liquid. "I would like to see Bismarck, if you please."

They walked from the house toward the barn. He couldn't help himself as he ran his hand along the rope stretched between the two buildings, testing it for tautness, wondering if Manuel was going to be equal to the winter he knew was coming.

He had to admire the barn. He had stuffed it with hay, cut from his fields when all his work was done on the Bar Dot. Mr. Buxton had unnecessarily warned him that he was foreman of the Bar Dot first, and rancher second. Jack knew that. Every penny of his salary went for hay he contracted from the few farmers in the area. No one had a good harvest that year, which meant that stunted corn, blasted by the wind, came his way too. What he couldn't cram in the barn, he and Manuel had piled into stacks and covered with canvas, anchoring them down against Wyoming wind. Would it be enough?

He gestured toward his summer-long efforts. "I am a source of real amusement to every stockman I know," he told Miss Carteret. "'Hey, reb, why don't you let that overgrown pile of beef and tallow graze with all the rest?' they joke. I keep my head down and my mouth shut. It has been my pattern."

Miss Carteret nodded. "Mine too." She put her hand on his arm, which startled him, although he liked it for the split second she did it. "After a while, people forget to tease, and you just blend in."

He nodded, impressed with Miss Carteret, and walked her to a fenced pasture, where Bismarck cropped whatever ground cover he could find. His massive head went up and he began a slow, nearly regal progress to the fence. He didn't look around, but his harem moved along in his wake, as he must have known they would.

"Goodness, does he know you?" Miss Carteret asked.

"We shared a cattle car on the train from Cheyenne. I expect he does."

Miss Carteret had draped her arms over the top fence rail. He enjoyed her smile, relieved that she didn't seem to be dwelling on the ranch that should have been her father's.

"Mr. Sinclair, if I get homesick for England, which I doubt I will, I will visit this pasture," she told him. "I've seen many cows like this one. Is he dangerous?"

"Most probably. I kept him tethered to an iron chain in the railcar, and I don't take chances now." He patted the wooden fence. "I made it stronger than most."

But there Bismarck stood, curious, with a gleam of intelligent capability in his eyes. Jack touched his big head. "His lady friends will each have a calf, come early March. Slow and sure, I'll get a herd of . . . Hairifords."

He laughed, a self-conscious sound. "If it won't ruffle your sensibilities, I'll keep calling them Herferds. No sense in giving the boys even more to laugh about."

Miss Carteret walked behind his house while he gave a few orders to Manuel, plus the promised peppermints. He questioned Manuel about the general condition of the privy, but the old man only shrugged. "It's just a privy," he said.

Jack knew Miss Carteret was too much of a lady to comment on the primitive facilities, but she surprised him. As he helped her up to the wagon seat again, she said to some imaginary person standing just beyond his left ear. "Only my father would have put a chairback in a necessary. He does like his little comforts."

Jack laughed out loud. His good humor lasted to the main road and even beyond the sight of skinny cattle over-grazing worn-out land. It might be too much to hope for, but maybe Miss Carteret really had what it took to survive what he feared was going to be a winter to remember. If she stayed that long.

Who was he kidding? Of course she would stay. He knew Clarence Carteret was not a man to plan ahead. His daughter would find out soon enough that her father probably expected her to help *him*.

It was on the tip of his tongue to warn the pretty lady beside him that if she had any money, she needed to squir-rel it away, maybe hide it in her corset. Clarence Carteret had a bad habit of thinking he would win at cards.

Jack Sinclair said nothing. His mother had raised him better than that.

CHAPTER 6

ou'll see the Bar Dot over this next rise," Jack told
Lily. "The Cheyenne L&C has five ranches in this
district, and this is the smallest. Just fifty thousand acres."

Lily knew she would have to reorder her idea of small
and large, but she had been thinking that all the way
through Nebraska and into Wyoming Territory, where
everything seemed larger, from the sky on down.

"*Just*? Thank goodness for that! I could probably take a
little stroll and not get lost on a mere fifty thousand acres."

Mr. Sinclair chuckled at her little joke. He stopped at
the rise, and there was the ranch spread out below. "That's
the big house where the Buxtons live," he said, pointing to
a smallish two-story house of regular boards, the only such
building. "Horse barn, a barn or two, bunkhouse, cookshack—we all eat there; you too, probably—and my little
place." He counted in the air with his finger. "Your father's
place is farther away, and there are corrals and more sheds
than we know what to do with." He tipped his hat back.
"You'll find any number of hounds, but they won't bother
you. I advise you to avoid the cat, a tom named Freak."

Lily felt the silliness overtook her. "A *cat*? You're all
afraid of a cat?"

"You will be too." But he was still grinning. "There's not
a mouse on the place, no small feat."

Lily shook her head over the cat. She looked at the
ranch spread below, not certain what she had expected

to find at the Bar Dot. It looked more like a bedraggled village than her idea of a ranch, gleaned from a Western novel or two she would never admit to having read. She noticed another log building nearby on the wagon road. "Over there?"

"That's a schoolhouse Mrs. Buxton demanded we build. No one uses it."

"Why ever not?"

"What would induce an Eastern schoolmarm on the search for a husband to drop everything and rush to all this splendid isolation to teach a coupla kids?"

Indeed, why? Lily thought. *I would never do it.*

He shook his head. "There it sits, too far away to be of any practical use. Mrs. Buxton wanted to make sure that whoever ended up there had plenty of cold air to breathe in and out, on the way to an education. It's healthy, she claims."

"Seriously?"

"She actually told me that." He frowned then, maybe thinking he had said too much about the people who employed him. "You'll understand better when you meet her. I'll take you around tomorrow."

And that was the end of any more confidences from the foreman. Lily brushed a stray hair from her face where the wind had teased it. So many cattle everywhere—too many. She shivered inwardly, wondering—not for the first time—why the people who made the decisions never seemed to know as much as the people they employed. Thank goodness it wasn't her problem. No one ever listened to her either.

Mr. Sinclair spoke to the horses and they started toward the odd conglomeration of buildings and corrals that made up the Bar Dot, plus one isolated schoolhouse.

No one seemed to be about, but cheery smoke poured from the cookshack chimney. Her stomach growled, too loud to be ignored.

"Beg pardon," she murmured, embarrassed.

"You'll do better here than chop suey," he told her. "I'll take you to your father's first."

"Doesn't he eat with everyone else?" she asked, suddenly unwilling to be placed in the care of a man she hadn't seen since she was fifteen.

Mr. Sinclair reined in the wagon in front of a shack no more dignified than the others. He set the brake, but made no move to get her luggage. He turned sideways on the seat and appraised her, his face troubled.

"How long's it been?" he asked.

"Nine years." She didn't know Mr. Sinclair well enough to say that the occasion was Papa's return from India, and what was supposed to have been a second or third chance to make something of himself. She was almost sixteen then, and down for a brief holiday from Miss Tilton's, which kept her out of sight and out of mind. It hadn't been much of a glimpse, either, just the sight of a slender man swaying, then collapsing into a chair. India had not been profitable. "Nine years," she repeated more softly.

"A lot can happen in nine years," the foreman said, and she knew he was hedging.

I can throw myself on this kind man's chest and sob, or I can continue to be the dignified woman I know my mother was, Lily thought. She looked Mr. Sinclair square in the eyes. "He drinks, doesn't he?"

"A lot. He's not a dangerous drunk, though, or I don't think I'd leave you here," Mr. Sinclair said, his voice flat.

"Where else would I go, sir?" she asked with some spirit. She had come this far; might as well finish. "I have five American dollars in my purse, which means the Bar Dot is my home now. If you would please get my luggage out of this wagon? I've taken up too much of your time, and you have been so kind." No need to tell him about the hundred pounds that Uncle Niles had wanted her to give to his brother for cattle shares, the last thing she would ever do, now that she knew the situation.

Still he hesitated, which touched her, even though Lily knew he had no more choice in the matter than she did. She could strive for a more pleasant tone, though. She might need an ally in the months ahead. "I have very few expectations, Mr. Sinclair. Probably no more than you do."

Her eyes chose to fill with tears then, but she didn't think this was a man much moved by tears. *I don't want your sympathy, but I do need a friend*, she thought. *Oh, I do.* "I'll be fine, Mr. Sinclair," she said, and almost meant it.

What could he do? He climbed down from the wagon, came around, and held out his hand. When she hesitated because the ground looked so far away, he grasped her waist, set her down, and then reached for her luggage.

He picked up both pieces and knocked on the door. "Mr. Carteret? I have your daughter," he called, then opened the door and set her two cases inside. "Mr. Carteret?" He shrugged.

"Miss Carteret, it's been a complete pleasure," he said. He leaned closer and she could smell his shaving lotion. "We eat at the cookshack, and I want you to meet Madeleine." He hauled out a timepiece. "There's food on the table until six tonight, and breakfast starts pretty early at five thirty."

Lily nodded, knowing she could not keep him there but wishing he did not have to leave her with someone barely more than a stranger. "Thank you," she managed to say.

He took another look at her, hesitated, and then climbed back into the wagon seat. When he gathered up the reins, she stepped closer.

"Mr. Sinclair?"

He did not try to hide his worry. Maybe the foreman on a ranch felt he was responsible for everyone.

"I promise you that I will have a plan, next time I see you."
He tipped his hat to her and was gone.

⁓

Lily took a deep breath and went into the shack. She
noted the braided rug on the floor, a table and two chairs,
and what looked like a packing crate with a lumpy cush-
ion on it, a most primitive settee. At the end of the little
room she saw a cot with folded blankets and sheets, but
not made up. Someone had tacked up a thin wire, but the
effort to stretch it to the other wall had proved too much,
apparently. The wire was there, but drooping. Two gray
blankets with "US" stamped in the center drooped too.
Perhaps that was the makeshift wall.

That will be my room, she thought, looking at the
slack wire.

She crossed the main room in only a few steps and
peered into what Mr. Sinclair had called a lean-to. "Well
named," she murmured, seeing a cookstove, counter space
for a midget, and a stand with a bucket and dipper. A
galvanized tub took up the rest of the space. She stared at
it, wondering if someone her height could ever compact
herself into such a space and bathe. It seemed unlikely.

The other door was closed. Lily stood a long moment in
front of it, wishing it would open by itself and her father,
smiling and well-dressed, would come out with a smile.
She sighed, knowing she had not told Mr. Sinclair the
whole truth. She did have expectations, and they were
breaking her heart right now.

She looked back at the outside door, wanting to rush
outside, commandeer the foreman's wagon, and go . . .
where? Using that strength of will she was only beginning to appreciate about herself, Lily forced down her
rising panic. She made herself think how little she had left
behind in England, and how she had yearned for freedom
from her uncle and his pretensions.

Here you are, Lily, she reminded herself. *You got what you wanted. Make something of it.*

Thus bolstered, she tapped on the closed door, then opened it. "Father?"

The curtains were closed, but there was enough afternoon sun to outline her father, sound asleep on a much better bed than the cot destined for her in the main room.

She removed her hat, set it on a bureau crowded with bottles, and pulled up a stool beside the bed. She sat down and regarded the man lying there so peacefully asleep, with his hands tucked under his cheek like a child. A nearly full wine glass was on the floor beside the bed.

There was no point in waking him; she would keep. Lily looked around the little room. She had taken the stool from beside a small desk. Quietly, she returned the stool to the desk and noticed a packet of letters tied with twine. She looked closer to see they were her own letters, written for years under some duress, because she could barely remember her father. Uncle Niles and the governess who had taught her manners, embroidery, and drawing had insisted she write her father two times a year. Gradually, that onerous chore to a person she barely knew had tapered off to one letter annually, and then none. *I should have written more,* she thought, stung by the slender pile.

Next to her own letters were a writing tablet, a fountain pen, and an ink bottle. *And you could have written to me,* she thought, trying to remember if he had ever sent her a letter. She started to turn away when she noticed that the wire trash receptacle was filled to the top with crumpled papers from the tablet. She thought she saw her name, so she reached for one page, straightened it, and then reached for another, and another. Across each page was written "Dearest Lily," or "My Sweet Lily," or "Dear Child."

She dug deeper. "Dear Lily, I am so delighted that you are coming to stay at my . . ." she read to herself.

She flattened out another failed letter. "Dear Daughter, Gracious, how time flies! And now you are coming . . ."

He hadn't even the courage to face his own lies. Did he think a ranch would materialize before she arrived?

"Oh, Papa," she whispered as she gathered up the pages and returned them to the waste basket. She went back to the bed and touched his shoulder, giving him a little shake. When he opened his eyes, she knelt by the bed and kissed his cheek, unsure of herself.

"I'm here, Papa. It's your Lily."

With a grunt that sounded like a protest, Clarence Carteret opened his eyes, closed them quickly, and then opened them again. "You're really here," he said. He closed his eyes once more. "It's not much, is it?" he asked, and she heard the shame in his voice.

"No, it isn't," she agreed, "but I'm here and maybe we can make something better."

He nodded but made no move to rise. Lily knelt there, uncertain, and then decided there was no time like the present to get to know her own father. She stood up, took his arm, and tugged him into a sitting position. His protest was feeble, and he sat there with elbows on knees, head in his hands. He still wouldn't look at her.

"Mr. Sinclair tells me that the cookshack is open until six and I am hungry," she said. "What do you plan to do about that?"

She had hoped he would rise to the challenge, but he continued to sit there, a beaten-down man.

"Papa?"

"I don't usually eat dinner," he said finally, his voice muffled.

"What about breakfast?"

He made a weak gesture toward the lean-to. "I have soda crackers in there for breakfast. It helps the nausea."

Lily sat beside him on the bed and linked her arm through his. "Papa, do you only eat at noon?"

He nodded. "I'm sorry," he whispered.

They sat together in silence, strangers to each other. "Do you have anything besides soda crackers?" Lily asked finally.

"There might be some cheese." He chuckled but with no amusement. "I have the wine in here."

"Well, then, don't go anywhere."

It was the smallest of quips and it brought the smallest of smiles, but Lily counted it good. "Be right back," she said and left his room. She went into the lean-to and just stood there, wondering how on earth she could help this stranger. She opened the back door and breathed deep, but got a strong whiff of corral for her efforts.

She found the soda crackers and some cheese that had hardened and was starting to crack around the edges. A handful of raisins made up the menu. The cheese was dubious, but her stomach growled again and she didn't care. A lengthy search turned up a pitiful excuse of a knife that sawed through the cheese and left an indent in her finger.

Papa was still sitting on the edge of the bed, but the level in the wine glass had declined. He shook his head at the crackers, then changed his mind when Lily gave him a fierce look.

She pulled up the stool again and ate, hungry and wanting more, but too shy to go to the cookshack. Whether she could bludgeon her father into breakfast tomorrow remained in dispute, but she knew she would be there.

The silence was awkward—two people who hadn't seen each other in years. Lily couldn't overlook the fine tremor in his right hand, even though she tried not to stare at this ruin of a man. He ate crackers and sipped from his wine glass, growing more steady with every sip.

"What do you do here, Papa?" she asked finally.

"I manage the books for Mr. Buxton." Then the old flair came back that she remembered. "I can call him Oliver, but no one else can," he boasted.

But you can't hang onto a ranch, she thought.

Finally, it was too much for Clarence Carteret. He sat there, cracker in hand, defeated finally by stale food as he had been defeated by everything else in life, from the looks of him. Silently, she took the cracker from his hand. He shook his head when she put his wine glass so far away on the bureau, but another fierce look from Lily stopped the mutiny on his weak face. He lay down again, knowing she would cover him, and she did.

"I'll see you in the morning, Papa," she said as she closed his door. No response.

She leaned against the door, tired from her heart. When someone knocked, she just stared at it for a long, stupid moment. The only person she knew in the whole United States of America was Jack Sinclair, who understood precisely what her father was. For one small moment, she wanted to throw herself on his chest and cry, but the moment passed.

She opened the door and there, indeed, was Mr. Sinclair, but he had a child with him. The little girl smiled at her and held out a sandwich wrapped in waxed paper. She took it, feeling the softness of the bread and the warmth of her smile.

"Please come in." Lily put her finger to her lips. "Mr. Carteret is asleep." She gestured to the packing crate settee as graciously as she could, banishing all thoughts of her uncle's best sitting room, because that life she had put behind her.

"May I introduce Miss Chantal Sansever?"

"You may," Lily said and held out her hand. "I'm Lily Carteret, and I am pleased to make your acquaintance."

Her eyes wide, Chantal took her hand and gave it three distinct shakes. "Jack says three shakes for ladies," she whispered.

Lily laughed, then had to turn away when Chantal put her finger to her lips in perfect imitation. "I forgot," Lily whispered. "Do sit down, please. Who do I have to thank for this sandwich?"

"My mother," Chantal whispered back. She let Mr. Sinclair lift her onto the settee. "She said you were probably too tired to come to the cookshack, so we would make allowances just this once. It's ground up roast from dinner, with a little onion and sage mixed in." She put her hands in her lap. "And that is all I am supposed to say, because I am a child." Chantal looked at Mr. Sinclair for approval, and he nodded.

"There's one more thing, isn't there?" Mr. Sinclair asked.

Chantal dug into her apron pocket and brought out a peppermint, coated with pocket lint. She frowned at the lint, blew it off, then handed it to Lily. "Jack said I had enough to share."

"I'll put it in my pocket and save it for a special occasion," Lily said softly.

"She wanted to meet you," Mr. Sinclair explained. He held out two pictures. "I said she could come along when I brought these over."

Her heart full, Lily took the pictures, one of a tall woman. She remembered the woman in fleeting ways, as if seen through gauze. "She was so beautiful," she said, running her finger lightly over the image.

"You look like her, Miss Carteret," Chantal said, then looked at Mr. Sinclair with a frown. "Is it all right for me to say that? Mama said I mustn't make a social blunder."

"It is a fine compliment, and I thank you." Lily looked at the other picture. "I've never seen this one."

"It's you, isn't it?" Chantal asked. She sighed. "I keep talking. Mr. Sinclair, you should say something instead of me because you are a grown-up."

"You're the rightful owner of these, even if the ranch is mine now," Jack said. "They've kept me company for a few months."

"You probably have your own photographs," Lily said.

"Not one. I'll miss these ladies," he told her. He looked

around the room and shook his head at the half-strung barrier. "So this is your corner of the room? I'd have thought . . ." He paused. "Well, no, this is what he would have done. Can I finish the job?"

Without waiting for a reply, Mr. Sinclair took the sagging end, stretched it taut, and then wrapped the wire around a nail that Papa must have driven before the whole business defeated him. He draped the two army blankets across the wire.

"Not too fancy, but it'll do until something better comes along."

And that will be precisely never, Lily thought. "Thank you. I am certain you are right," she said.

"I mean it, Lily," he said, his voice as firm as his expression. "Do you have a plan yet?"

She shook her head, not even trying to disguise her shame at such a father, and the greater shame at knowing everyone else knew too.

"Get one fast," he said, and it was no suggestion. "After Chantal and I leave, take a good look out that window in the lean-to. A good look. I'll see you tomorrow morning at breakfast at 5:30 and I expect you to have a plan."

"Why do you care?" she asked, keeping her voice low, angry just the same because she was embarrassed.

He indicated the pictures she held. "Because I've been tending these ladies for a few months and I've been talking to them. It gets slow here in the winter. Do it for them."

"But . . ."

He nodded to her, his equanimity restored, and held out his hand to Chantal. "Your mama will be wondering where we wandered. Good evening, Miss Carteret. Enjoy that sandwich."

She did, crying and eating, and wiping her nose, and then repeating the process until the whole sandwich was gone. When she finished, she went to the lean-to and looked out the window.

The moon had come up, which made the buildings look less ugly. She pressed her forehead against the cool glass and closed her eyes, thinking through her day that had begun with those dratted expectations, and ended with none, or almost none. She opened her eyes and looked.

Beyond the jumble of ranch buildings was that school-house. She could think of it as isolated, but she could also think of it as looking down on a little community. She only knew three people in the community, or maybe just two. Maybe her father shouldn't count.

She was a woman and knew that much wasn't expected of her. Little Chantal might see her as a lady, but she knew from painful experience that not everyone would. She could stay in this wretched little shack that represented her father's last chance. She knew that women didn't get as many chances.

She looked at the schoolhouse again. "I've never taught anyone anything in my life," she whispered to the window. "I can't."

It took her no time at all to prepare for bed. By the time she had spread out the sheets and blankets, she was starting to shiver. She lay in bed and thought of muskrats and thin cattle, and drift fences and woolly caterpillars, and of a man with a gaunt face and a scar, and a pampered Hereford. Her last thought of the day, after she had dried her eyes, was the view from the lean-to.

CHAPTER 7

～⊗⊙⊗～

*J*ack woke up even earlier than usual, staring by
habit at the space above his apple crate bureau
where he had kept the two pretty women for several
months, just because a fool was too proud to ask for his
pictures. He put his hands behind his head and lay there,
admiring them in his imagination.

"You there on the left," he said to the dignified and so
beautiful lady, "your daughter should probably be crying
her eyes out right now, but I bet she isn't." He sighed. "And
why not, you ask? Probably because she has few expectations. What happened yesterday has to be one calamity of
many, with such a father."

He imagined looking at the young girl in the other
frame, younger than little Chantal Sansever, but so
serious. "Miss Carteret, it appears that your childhood,
although spent in comparative luxury, was likely no more
pleasant than mine."

He had almost hated to surrender the pictures to Lily
Carteret, because he had become so fond of them. He had
no family, and the two women—one of color and the other
of a creamy blend—filled his heart more than he knew at
the time. They were ladies of quality but suspended in an
unkind world, because they fit no mold.

"Did I come on too strong last night, practically ordering you to get a plan, and quick?" he asked. He was a good
judge of character, learned the hard way during the War

of Yankee Aggression as he rose from private to sergeant and then to lieutenant and back to less-than-nobody after the surrender. The six hours he had spent in her company yesterday showed him a woman exercising a certain awe-inspiring calm because that was how she survived the unfairness of her life. He recognized it because it mirrored his own almost thirty-six years.

Still . . . he should never have disquieted her with his fears of the coming winter. Considering Sinclair luck, he was probably wrong anyway. *I'm not wrong*, he thought, lying there. *I know I'm not.*

Time would tell. Time would also tell if he had been a fool to sink so much money into an English bull, when fortunes were being made in these northern territories on scrub stock trailed up from Texas on yearly drives. Maybe only a fool would invest in a purebred bull, when money was being made from lesser beef.

Still . . . for someone from Georgia who had come out West in 1866 knowing next to nothing about cattle and even horses, he had learned from his hard school. Wartime experience had taught him to never say no to an opportunity, no matter how little he knew. Most important was his willingness to give his all, get up, and try again. He understood horses, and cattle weren't so bright.

Hard choices on the open range had shaped Jack Sinclair even more than the war. Marching and fighting and obeying orders hadn't required much skill. Making good decisions, even the small ones at first, had turned him into a foreman whose word was law, and who had confidence to spare.

He had thought that winning the little ranch and buying the bull had required the payment of all his bravado, but maybe he was wrong. There seemed to be a little more confidence lurking in the corner of his heart, just enough to allow the smallest thought of a home of his own, and maybe someday a wife to manage it. The thought made him glance into his front room and look at his one easy chair. "I'll need another chair," he said out loud, then laughed. *You'll need more than that*, he thought, squelching such nonsense. Some things weren't going to come his way now, especially in a territory with so few women, and even fewer of them ladies. And he wanted a lady.

"My dears," he said, "I'm glad you found a new wall."

He got dressed and stopped on his front porch, breathing deep and drawing advancing autumn into his lungs, even if his calendar said early September. He felt the momentary satisfaction he always enjoyed—looking at a well-run ranch from his doorstep. The place was buttoned down for winter, with most of the hands let go to ride the grubline and come back in the spring, when the early work began. He'd find enough to keep his four remaining hands busy. There were harnesses to mend and horses to water, doctor, and cajole. Preacher was good at duties around the big house, since the Buxtons' cook complained more and more of aching joints. There would be cattle to coax away from air holes when the snow came and covered those treacherous patches by the river. He and Indian could handle that, even those Texas cattle that took exception to their first winter in the north and tried to drift south where they remembered warmth.

Stretch and Will had already left for town to bring back barrels of apples, potatoes, and flour. Jack had told Stretch to keep an eye on Will, who had a saloon habit. He had only agreed to keep Will on through the winter because he was Mr. Buxton's cousin.

Jack looked toward the cookshack, unable to help that the habitual frown between his eyes deepened. He was a man of some imagination, but it took no creativity to remember the piercing screams from the cookshack when Oliver Buxton told Madeleine Sansever, in his usual ham-handed way, that her man had died breaking horses.

Ordinarily so careful around green horses, Jean Baptiste
Sansever had just looked away long enough to get a kick
to the head that broke his neck. Everyone in the corral
heard the snap.

After he and Preacher brought Jean to the cookshack
on a plank, Jack had stayed to hold little Chantal on his
lap as she wet his shirt with her tears. Her older sister,
Amelie, had grown even quieter in the face of her mother's agony. And Nicholas? Only twelve, Nick had taken a
gun from somewhere and killed the horse. Then he ran
away. Manuel had found him two days later, crouched in
Bismarck's hay barn, all cried out and grim.

You people are my family, Jack thought, as he walked
toward the cookshack.

Preacher and Indian were already seated at their
benches in the cookshack, digging in to porridge, elbows
on the table. "I said grace, Jack, so you can eat with a
pure heart," Preacher said in that straight-faced way of his.
"Looks like flapjacks next. God praise."

Jack raised his hand to them and went into the kitchen
where Madeleine, hair wild around her face, was stirring
down oatmeal lava. Chantal cracked another egg in the
flapjack batter and gave him her smile, the one that made
her brown eyes all squinty and never failed to melt his
heart. Amelie nodded to him as she stirred the batter, her
eyes shy but no less admiring.

Madeleine made no objection when he patted her
cheek. Madeleine had told him once that he reminded her
of her little brother, even though Jack was certain that he
was older than she. He had said that to her, and Madeleine
just shrugged in her Métis way.

"I hear she is a pretty lady," Madeleine said as she lifted
the oatmeal pot onto a trivet. She handed him a bowl.
"Chantal says Mademoiselle Carteret has skin the color of
wrapping paper. Can this be?"

"It can," he said, spooning out oatmeal and sugaring it

53

well. "I hope she'll be here for breakfast, and I hope you'll treat her nice."

"I will if she is not too good for us."

"She's not," Jack replied and hoped he was right.

Grateful that the one cow on the place was still giving milk, Jack poured cream on his oatmeal and took it into what Clarence Carteret called "the dining hall," with its benches and three long tables, testament to the number of cowhands hired on between April and most Septembers. Now the men of the Bar Dot were just crickets sawing on the hearth, sitting at half of one table. He mentally shook his head over the neatly folded blankets in the corner, where the Sansever children bedded down. Madeleine and Jean Baptiste had slept in a small room off the store-room in the back, and no one was particularly choosy in the Sansever household. Thinking about the winter to come, he eyed the dining hall for warmth. He would ask Preacher what he could do to keep out drafts. Preacher was better at indoor work anyway.

Jack sat down with his ranch hands as the door opened and Miss Carteret stepped inside, uncertainty written everywhere on her expressive face. He wondered how long she had stood outside that door, steeling herself to step inside. Hunger obviously overruled shyness. He got up.

"Good morning to you, Miss Carteret," he said, not wanting to sound hearty and phony, but hoping to convey his warmth, because he was glad to see her. "Hungry?"

She nodded. "I couldn't have managed without Chantal's sandwich. And Papa and I ate petrified cheese and crackers last night. He tells me he doesn't usually bother with breakfast."

Her voice had dropped to a whisper. He knew she was mortified, because it had to be obvious to her that every-one else knew why her father never made it to breakfast. Jack also knew he could be hearty and phony now, or he could summon his courage and just touch her hand. He remembered Sayler's Creek and the gash that his face became. His panic as he swallowed blood and choked was relieved by the firm pressure of a comrade's hand on his arm. He knew he was not alone then, and he could return the favor now, even if she was a lady.

He touched her hand. "We don't worry about Clarence Carteret. *You're* here, and the first course is oatmeal. Come into the kitchen and meet our cook, Madeleine Sansever."

"Chantal's mother?" she asked, recovering smoothly.

"The very same. She is Métis."

"Which is…"

"Someone of mixed Indian and French background. More French than Indian in her case, I think."

She pointed to his breakfast. "Your oatmeal is going to get cold."

"It'll keep. Let's find Madeleine."

She touched his arm in turn. "I have a question for Chantal, which has something to do with my plan."

"Say, about that plan, I . . ."

"You *were* too emphatic," she said in such a serene voice. "I will forgive you. I need a plan, so let's leave it at that. It's still sort of feeble."

"Plan's a plan," he said and gestured to the kitchen.

Eyes full of concentration, Chantal was mixing the pancake batter. Jack crooked his finger and she carefully set the long handled spoon on top of the bowl.

"Chantal, Miss Carteret has a question for you."

She came closer, her eyes shy. Miss Carteret knelt by the child so they were on the same level, a kind touch that impressed Jack.

"Can you read, Chantal?" Miss Carteret asked.

Chantal shook her head. "I would like to," she said so softly.

When Miss Carteret stood up and looked his way, Jack felt his face grow hot, hoping she wouldn't ask him that same question.

But she was looking beyond him to Amelie. "What is your name, my dear?"

"Amelie." The word came out so quietly. Jack would have to take Miss Carteret aside and tell her that since her father had died in the corral, Amelie, always a quiet child, had withdrawn even more.

"Would you like to read as well?" Miss Carteret asked.

Madeleine watched this exchange with real interest, her eyes lively. "They can learn, then read to me," she said, holding out her hand. "I am Madeleine Sansever. I can write a bit, but that is all. This is my kitchen, and I rule it."

Trust Madeleine to stake out her territory and make it known to another female. Jack made the proper introductions and smiled with relief when Miss Carteret held out her hand.

"I have so little skill in a kitchen that the thought of one fair terrifies me," she said, to Madeleine's obvious satisfaction, considering the width of the cook's returning smile.

"Oatmeal for you?" Madeleine handed Miss Carteret a bowl.

"She's pretty, but you mustn't stare," Chantal whispered to Jack.

Oh, glory, he hoped with all his heart that Miss Carteret was hard of hearing. The little shake to her shoulders indicated that there was nothing wrong with her ears.

Who could not stare? She wore a simple shirtwaist and skirt today. How Miss Carteret managed to confine her curly hair was a mystery to him. He hated to think what Wyoming Territory was going to do to such smooth skin, but he doubted she would remain here long enough to find out.

"Don't any of you stare or I will trip," she said as she carried the bowl into the dining hall, where he introduced her to his two hands, who rose to their feet to Jack's utter amazement. He indicated a space at their table, hoping she didn't feel the need to distance herself.

She eyed the bench a moment, then delicately slid toward Preacher, who had gone from ordinary putty beige to beet red.

"Ma'am," he managed, but that was all.

Jack had never known words to fail the man. "Preacher here always blesses the food and has a chapter and verse for nearly any situation. Preach, this is Miss Carteret."

"Ma'am." His repertoire remained the same.

Jack indicated Indian, who had returned to his oatmeal. "Indian is some part Shoshone, and Lakota, and some part French and . . ."

"Pierre Fontaine," Indian said with a nod.

". . . and he's never supplied his actual name until this very moment," Jack finished, startled at what a lovely woman could do to his ranch hands.

"It's a pleasure, Preacher and Mr. Fontaine," Miss Carteret said. She gave Jack a kindly look. "Let us cease formality, sitting here on benches in Wyoming. I am Lily. So it is Jack, Preacher, and Pierre?"

"I do believe it is," Jack replied, sitting beside her. "You'll meet Stretch and Will later. Nick's around here someplace."

She nodded and turned her attention to the oatmeal, eating with a certain delicacy not seen before in the dining hall. She shook her head at the flapjacks Chantal offered, but made no move to leave the table. Maybe it wasn't good manners to leap up before everyone was done; Jack didn't know. He forked down a dozen of Madeleine's dollar-sized flapjacks and then reminded himself that if Lily Carteret was on the Bar Dot, he was still foreman and she was his responsibility.

"You want to share your plan, uh, Lily?" he asked.

"It's a small one. I intend to teach Madeleine's girls how to read and cipher. I've never taught anyone anything in my life, but I won't do it for free. How will I ever get out of here if I do? Perhaps I had better meet the Buxtons."

"Oliver Buxton is tighter than a water-logged keg," Jack warned.

"I won't ask a lot, because I am not highly skilled," Lily replied in that precise way of hers he was coming to relish. And then she endeared herself forever with a little-girl doubt. "Do you think twenty dollars a month is too much?"

"Think bigger, Lily," he advised.

"I have no skill as a teacher," she reminded him.

"At twenty dollars a month, it's a mighty small plan."

"I know, but plans can grow, can't they?"

He saw it again, that same assessing, shrewd look he had noticed on her face when she stood in the open door of the train and surveyed the hand called Wyoming Territory that had been dealt her. He thought of his strangely won ranch, and Bismarck, and understood what she meant.

"Plans certainly can grow. Let's go meet the boss, and more important, the Mrs. Boss."

CHAPTER 8

The plan to teach had made a great deal of sense last night, especially after she checked on her father and stood a long time in his doorway, dismayed at the cozy way he had wrapped his hand around that wine bottle. Almost worse than the confirmation that her father was an alcoholic was the certainty that everyone knew.

"We all know why my father doesn't make it to dinner or breakfast," she told the foreman, trying not to inject any self-pity into her voice. "Does he do his job with any skill at all?"

"He must. Buxton hasn't thrown him off the place yet," He winced. "That was unkind of me."

"It was honest," she said, even as her insides writhed. "My father is a remittance man. He failed in Canada, he failed in India, but his biggest failure was the first one in Barbados, where he . . ." She faltered, finding it difficult to say out loud what she had known for years. ". . . married my mother."

Jack surprised her by putting his hand on her arm again, this time with enough force to stop her. "Don't say that!"

"Well, he did. She was the daughter of an apothecary and his slave."

He didn't let up the pressure on her arm. "That's not what I meant," he said, evidently determined to be as stubborn as she was, drat the man. "Don't classify yourself as part of a failure."

"And how am I not?"

His gaze didn't waver, although he did remove his hand from her arm. "There's a song out here, Lily: 'What Was Your Name in the States?' I'm no singer, but here's one verse."

He auditioned several notes as though searching for the right one, but gave up. "If I sing, you'll bolt for sure. 'Oh, what was your name in the states?'" he said. "'Was it Johnson or Thompson or Bates? Did you murder your wife and fly for your life? Oh, what was your name in the states?'"

She didn't laugh, because she understood what he meant. "Everybody gets a free pass out here?" she asked.

"Everybody," he assured her. "It's a good faith thing."

She wondered how many passes her father had gone through and then decided to believe the man so determined for her to succeed, even after such a brief acquaintance. It was a new feeling. No one had ever taken much interest in her before, and she liked it.

"Very well," she said, "although I truly do not know a thing about teaching."

He started her in motion again. "Do you like Chantal and her sister, Amelie? I'll have to tell you sometime why Amelie is so quiet."

"Yes, I like them. Who wouldn't?"

"I'm no teacher, either, but could it be that's all you really need succeed as a teacher?"

It couldn't be that simple, but when Jack Sinclair said it, Lily knew one thing: she had an ally. What had looked good last night as she stared out the window, looked good again.

"Reading, writing, and ciphers," she said, and permitted herself a little joke. "Why, I could probably even teach you how to read; that is, if you needed such instruction. Lead on, sir."

The Buxtons' dwelling was a true house, with clapboard

siding, a marvelous porch with a swing, and gangly zinnias leading up the boardwalk to the door. The summer wind had exhausted the zinnias, but at least they weren't lying down in abject submission. *It takes a strong flower to survive this territory,* Lily thought. Maybe it was true of people too. Jack Sinclair didn't look like a man with any soft connective tissue anywhere.

Lily willed herself a little taller, secure in the knowledge that her shirtwaist and skirt were well-tailored and impeccable. Uncle Niles had never skimped on her clothing allowance, although she suspected that long cotton undergarments might be more useful than her silky things.

As she walked up the step, her skirt chinked on the tread. She stopped. "See there, Jack? I took you at your word and added your lead weights to my hems."

"I am accustomed around here to having people do what I say," he replied. "Let me know if you need any more." He leaned toward her. "Ready?"

She nodded, and Jack knocked. The door was answered by a gentleman even more impeccable than she. From his dark tie and black suit to his general demeanor and bearing, she knew this man as surely as if they had met in Gloucestershire. The Buxtons had a butler.

She glanced at Jack, who was smiling at her. "Now maybe you won't be homesick," he whispered rather too close to her ear for total comfort, although she did like the sensation of his breath on her ear.

"Do come in, madam," the butler said. "I am Fothering and you are welcome to the Buxtons' humble home."

Perhaps it might have been humble in a city, but on the Bar Dot, the house stood out like a gardenia among pokeweed. The Turkish carpet was almost too much, but it did go well with the heavy dark furniture—mahogany?—and the handsome windows with stained glass in the upper panes.

"This is Miss Lily Carteret, daughter of our very own Clarence," Jack told the butler, who nodded with almost exquisite dignity. "She's from . . ."

"Bristol, Gloucestershire," Lily said.

"You ah doubly welcome, m'deah," he said. "I shall see if Mrs. Buxton is available and receiving callers. Do have a seat"—he glanced at the foreman—"if there isn't any ordure on your boots." He executed a smart turn and left them in the sitting room.

"'Ordure,'" Jack repeated. "I have been put in my place. It happens every time I come in here. I had to ask Preacher what ordure was. Don't know why Fluttering—"

"Fothering," she interrupted, trying not to smile.

"—couldn't just have said sh . . ." He paused. "Beg pardon."

Beyond a mere smile now, Lily mustered all her good manners to keep from disgracing herself with a laugh that welled up from some deep, unknown cavity. She struggled to contain herself, thinking of dark looks from her uncle and shocked looks from everyone at Miss Tilton's School, if they ever found out.

Jack Sinclair helped not at all. "You know, it's not a crime to laugh in Wyoming."

Ah, there. The moment had passed. "You do try me," she said. She almost made some comment about Fothering's somewhat unusual British Isles accent, like none she had ever heard before, but it probably wasn't her business.

The butler returned a few minutes later. "Mrs. Buxton will see you now," he said in perfect tones to any ears but hers. He indicated the stairs.

"We won't tax her," Jack said as he started for the stairs that divided the downstairs rooms. "Up you go, Lily."

He returned her questioning glance with a brief, whispered comment. "Mrs. Buxton doesn't get downstairs too often. She's a delicate thing."

And so she was. After a tap on the door, Jack opened it for Lily. He gave her a little push in the small of her back when she just stood there.

Mrs. Buxton reclined in her bed, propped up by several pillows. She wore a crocheted bed jacket with blue ribbon intertwined. She looked to Lily like the bloom of health, with a delicate complexion tinged a faint blush. Her eyes were lively and she held out her hand.

"Come closer!" she said in a voice with nothing fading away about it. "So you are our Clarence's little daughter."

Lily couldn't help herself. "I've never been guilty of being little," she said, "but, yes, I am Lily Carteret. Delighted to make your acquaintance."

Mrs. Buxton let her hands flutter to her heart as she rolled her eyes in ecstasy. "You sound even more English than my butler, and goodness knows he is all that is proper." She waved toward a corner of the room. "Come here, Luella, and make yourself known."

Lily looked toward the gesture and saw a young child with a book in her lap. They eyed each other: Lily with interest, wondering if she was the age of the Sansever girls, and Luella with something more guarded. She was dressed plainly in dark cotton with a lacy pinafore that buttoned up the front with mother of pearl buttons. Her hair was braided and pulled back so tight that Lily nearly winced for her. She was tidy and everything the little Métis girls were not. "I am delighted to meet you too," Lily said, extending her hand, which was ignored. Lily put her hands behind her back, remembering her teachers' "mustn't touch" rule when the class had made a visit to the Victoria and Albert Museum in London.

She felt a finger in the small of her back again and another gentle push forward, plus a whisper from Jack, "You have a plan."

She moved forward until Mrs. Buxton indicated a stool beside the bed. Jack moved away to sit in the window seat. Lily wished for one moment that he stood closer to her, but this was her plan.

"Lily Carteret? What a lovely name. May I call you Lily?"

"Certainly."

"And you may call me Mrs. Buxton."

I've been put into my place, Lily thought with amusement. *Better get to it.* She cleared her throat. "I'm delighted to be here in Wyoming Territory," she began, and Mrs. Buxton cut her off with a hand chop.

"No one is delighted to be in Wyoming Territory," the woman said with that sort of assertiveness that dared anyone to disagree. Lily heard something else: a brittle, nervous quality that made her wonder. "Wyoming is either hot or cold and always windy. The rain falls sideways, and everything smells of cow."

Lily shrugged. "I'm happy enough with Wyoming. Perhaps not delighted, so I stand corrected, Mrs. Buxton."

That felt like the right touch, sufficiently apologetic without sounding subservient, something she never intended to be again.

"I have a plan," Lily said. "Mr. Sinclair showed me that little schoolhouse that you built. I propose to teach whatever children around here might be interested. It will be the fundamentals of reading, writing, and ciphering." *Mainly because that is all I think I can manage*, she thought, *but you don't need to know that.*

"Are you an educationist?"

Lily shook her head. "I see a need, though, and believe I can fill it."

She glanced at Jack and was rewarded with a nod.

"I propose to teach Luella, if you are interested, and the Sansever children. I will do it for twenty-five dollars a month."

Mrs. Buxton leaned back against her pillows, still the picture of health. Her eyes narrowed, which Lily did not take as a good sign.

"Are you implying that Luella doesn't know the rudiments?" she asked in an awful tone of voice.

Mercy, she is as unpleasant as my uncle, Lily thought, startled. *But here I am, and here I will remain if Papa stays, and I haven't another plan.*

Might as well return cool with cool. "I would imagine Luella knows great deal more than the Sansever children. Think what a good example she would be." There, that sounded firm enough.

Mrs. Buxton's expression became more thoughtful. "I have a better plan: I will pay you forty dollars a month to teach Luella alone. I'd rather she didn't mingle with mixed blood children."

"It's not their fault, and the girls want to learn to read. I am afraid I will have to decline your generous offer to teach Luella alone."

Forty dollars a month, and she had just turned it down. Forty times nine months was three hundred and sixty dollars. It was enough to blast her out of the territory, it was true, but she had nowhere to go, so why did it matter?

"We are at an impasse," Mrs. Buxton said with some satisfaction. She appeared to be a woman used to having her way.

"Not really," Lily said cheerfully, starting to rise. "I have declined your offer, but I can probably teach the Sansevers for my own enjoyment. Once the men clear out of the dining hall, there is plenty of room." She glanced at Jack, who was pulling a long face as he tried to keep from laughing.

"It was grand to meet you, Mrs. Buxton." Lily stood up and held out her hand. "I do hope you feel better soon. Luella, so nice to meet you."

Apparently Mrs. Buxton didn't shake hands when she was displeased. Lily had started for the door when Mrs. Buxton called her back. A sidelong look at Jack showed one raised eyebrow, so she turned around.

"If I paid you twenty dollars a month, you could have the use of the schoolhouse and teach my daughter and the little mixed bloods. There is a condition: Luella does not sit near them." Mrs. Buxton paused a moment before delivering her final barb. "Surely you, of all people, must know what it feels like to be separated because of your condition in life."

The words stung and Lily took an involuntary step backward, only to be met with a hand at her back, pushing her forward again. It was the foreman's whole hand this time, and it was a soft touch. She swallowed down the hurt she thought she had left behind in England.

"Twenty-five, and you have my word that everyone—everyone—will learn a great deal and be a credit to you in the community."

"Done. I will not pay a penny until the spring." Mrs. Buxton looked Lily in the eyes, triumphant. "When does this school begin?"

"As soon as the boys and I can swamp it out, Mrs. Buxton," Jack said. "Give us a few days. Next Monday, Lily?"

She nodded, wanting nothing more right now than to leave this room. Mrs. Buxton's chief ailment seemed to be a crabbed and disagreeable disposition, and Lily hoped it wasn't catching. No, there was something else about the woman. What, she could not tell.

"My dear Lily, what do you propose to use for your course of study?" Mrs. Buxton seemed determined to catch her out and make her feel small.

"I plan to use whatever I can find around the Bar Dot, from whomever wishes to share. If you have any primers or . . ."

"Those are only for Luella."

"Very well. We'll manage. Good day."

She started for the door again, which looked half a pasture away. She scrunched her eyes shut when Mrs. Buxton cleared her throat again. *I will not turn around again*, she thought, desperate to leave the room.

"In your spare time, see what you can do about your disgrace of a father. I have told Mr. Buxton over and over to sack him, but still he remains. Do something."

Since the only words that came to her mind would have resulted in the loss of the job that had only been hers for five minutes, Lily said nothing. His face a perfect blank, Jack opened the door for her and closed it with a distinct click. It was the only recourse of the powerless, and something she remembered quite vividly from Bristol.

Back straight, Lily started down the stairs but sank onto a tread when her legs gave way. Jack sat beside her, their shoulders touching.

"What a horrid woman," she whispered when words formed again in her brain. "I trust she has nothing to do with the running of the place."

"Not a thing. I take my orders from Mr. Buxton, some of which I ignore, because he doesn't really know what he's doing." He looked back up the stairs. "I'm not sure why she stays in bed all the time, but I'm grateful."

"I, too! Do you think there are any books on the place?"

"We'll find everything here you need. We're ramshackle, but we might surprise you."

CHAPTER 9

~⚘~

$\mathcal{L}$ily looked down the stairs to see Fothering, his expression unblinking, the perfect butler. Maybe everyone collapsed on the stairs after a session with Mrs. Buxton.

"Could you two use a hand?" he asked so politely.

If anything, he was a diversion. Lily found herself wondering just where in the British Isles he could have sprung from. He was everything a butler should be, but oh, that accent. Maybe Jack could tell her later. Now she just wanted to get out of this house.

"Good thing she didn't order me out the back door," she muttered to Jack.

"She probably would have, but the shock of having someone deny her put her off her feed, I think," he told her. "We can leave by the front door."

Jack pointed to the closed door at the foot of the stairs. "That's the office. Shall we see if your father is at work?"

"Why not?" she said with a sigh. "It's already been a trying day, and it's only . . ." She glanced down at the watch pinned to her shirtwaist. "Eight o'clock."

Jack laughed out loud, a hearty sound that put a little more steel back into her spine. "Lily, Lily, you're starting to sound like a foreman!"

"Oh, you," she said, embarrassed.

"I'd probably have used a different word than 'trying,'" he said, which made her smile. His face grew serious then.

"He could use your help—he's probably desperate for help—but I don't think he even knows how to ask for it."

"We've never been close, but he *is* my father. How can I help him?"

"Get him to meals, listen to him." He started down the stairs with her but stopped. "You haven't really had a father, have you?"

"No. He was always somewhere else, failing." Her face burned with embarrassment. "I expect your father was better."

"He was, but he died of overwork." He was silent until they reached the main floor. "Life's hard for us small people, Lily. I can't even convince the man I work for that this is going to be a hard winter."

Jack stopped before the closed door opposite the parlor. He tapped on the door, then opened it. "Clarence? Mr. Buxton?" He opened the door wider and gestured to Lily.

Suddenly shy, she peeked into the office. Her father sat at a desk, overshadowed by a beefy-looking man in shirtsleeves and a vest ornamented with the dull gold of a watch fob. The man's eyes narrowed against the intrusion, then widened into something close to appreciation, which made Lily want to take a step back.

He looked her over carefully, a long stare that she thought rude and unmannerly. Apparently Jack did, too, because he stepped farther into the room until Mr. Buxton had no choice but to look at him instead.

"Sir, this is Miss Lily Carteret," Jack said. "She's just made a deal with Mrs. Buxton to teach your daughter and the Sansever children."

Mr. Buxton gaped at her then. "At the same time? How'd you get my stickler of a wife to agree to that?" he asked.

She glanced at her father, who gave her a warning look, the sort of look that said, "Answer carefully, or we'll both be out of here in a twinkling." Since she had no idea how the wind blew between the Buxtons, she could only rely on the most unreliable man in the room and give her father the slightest of nods.

"Mr. Buxton, she could plainly see the benefits of educating all the children on the Bar Dot. It's an American thing to do," she concluded blandly.

"But only if Luella sits by herself on the other side of the room, eh?"

Such a boorish man. "She expressed some concerns, and I assured her that all would be well," Lily replied, thinking of Chantal and Amelie's eagerness to learn, and Luella's wary look.

What could he say to that? Mr. Buxton rocked back and forth on his heels. "And what is this extravagance going to cost me?"

"Twenty-five dollars a month, Mr. Buxton," she said. "And if you or the Bar Dot could provide . . ."

Mr. Buxton slapped a hand on Clarence Carteret's shoulder. Her father cringed. "I'll pay it directly to you at the end of the term, Miss Carteret. No telling what Clarence here would do with an extra twenty-five dollars a month, eh?"

"Certainly you will pay me, since I will be earning it," Lily said, desperate now to draw the dreadful man's attention away from her father. "I would like to request another ten dollars for supplies."

"Ten dollars more?" he asked, startled. "Do you plan to put the consortium in the poorhouse?"

"Hardly, sir."

"It hasn't been a good year for beef, what with the drought."

Ten dollars, you tight-fisted fool, Lily thought, keeping her expression neutral, much as she would have with Uncle Niles. Silent, she stood her ground and wondered if there would ever come a time in her life when people wouldn't bully her. She doubted it supremely.

"Make it eight, and the boys and I will chip in four bits apiece," Jack countered.

Mr. Buxton still frowned, but Jack apparently wasn't through.

"Just think, sir, how impressed the governor will be to know that the Bar Dot is educating the territory's greatest resource, her children," Jack said. "Think what a report he'll make to the Cheyenne L&C on your behalf."

Nature intended you for a diplomatist, Lily thought with admiration.

Like most self-absorbed men, Mr. Buxton didn't appear to know when he was being worked over. Lily could almost see him preening.

"I suppose I can do that. Eight dollars for school supplies and not a cent more. Clarence, if your hand isn't shaking too bad, get the money out of the strong box!" He laughed, punched her father's shoulder for good measure, and left the room.

No one said anything for a long moment. Lily's father drew a long, shaking breath. "I hate that man," he whispered, his face pale.

"He is a tough nut, but we work for him, Clarence," Jack said. "I'll get a list from Lily and . . ."

"You should call her Miss Carteret," Clarence said, but he did so feebly, as if he doubted his ability to convince anyone of anything.

"It's all right, Father," Lily said gently. "Life is more casual here."

Clarence Carteret rubbed his eyes with both hands—a childish gesture she remembered from the few times she had seen him—as though he could scrub away unpleasantness. She knew she was looking at a man with no hope. She wondered how on earth she could bolster someone who had given up.

Meanwhile, Jack was giving her the high sign. Maybe Mr. Buxton was returning, and she already knew she didn't want to be in the same room with him again without Jack present.

"I'll be back at noon to walk you to the cookshack," she told her father.

"Usually Fothering just brings me a bowl of soup."

"That's not enough," she scolded, but gently. "I'll be back, and don't argue."

He nodded and there was something grateful in his eyes now, as if he relished the idea of someone—anyone—taking charge of him in a kindly fashion. His expression tore at her heart, the heart she had vowed to keep to herself, because she had been disappointed so many times. She wanted to kiss the top of his head, but there was Jack, watching them both.

"See you at noon, Papa," she whispered, then followed Jack Sinclair from the office.

They left the Buxton residence in silence, Lily with her head down until she realized that she was unconsciously imitating her father. She raised her head and looked Jack in the eye, swallowing her shame at such a father.

"He's a sad little man," she said, looking away.

"Life can do that," was all Jack said.

She was too shy to ask him if he would walk with her to the schoolhouse, but that seemed to have been his plan, this busy man who probably had so many more important things to do. He started toward the distant building but then stopped.

"We need reinforcements," he said. He put two fingers to his mouth and gave an earsplitting blast. She couldn't help laughing when the screen door on the cookshack banged open and Chantal and Amelie came out, Chantal running and her older sister walking more sedately.

"Madeleine might like a quiet moment," Jack said, "and the dishes are done."

She watched as they slowed down past the Buxtons'

house—perhaps Mrs. Buxton had rules—and then picked up speed. They took a wide berth around a low outbuilding, darting glances at the door sagging on leather hinges.

"Spooks and demons?" Lily joked.

"That's where Freak hangs out. Never hurts to be cautious," Jack told her.

"Honestly, the *cat*?"

He just shrugged. "He's a curious brute. If he decides to take an interest in the schoolhouse, you might see him, but only if he wants you to see him."

"I have *never* been afraid of a cat," she assured him.

"Just sayin'. Well, ladies, how about you escort your new teacher to the schoolhouse?"

With an easy familiarity that warmed Lily after Luella's wariness, Chantal took her hand. Amelie walked beside Jack, not as close as Chantal, but obviously deriving some comfort from him because the little frown left her face. Lily wondered what it was about Jack Sinclair, since she felt more confidence in his presence too. Maybe it was a knack given to the few.

Chantal skipped to keep up, so Lily slowed down. She couldn't help comparing the little child to Luella Buxton, who, at first glance, had all the advantages. Chantal's hair might have seen a comb earlier in the day, but her hair flowed free down her back. No one had yanked it back into tight braids. Her dress was too short and patched. A large patch up the back left Lily to wonder if Chantal had gotten too close to the cookstove. Obviously Madeleine Sansever was not a woman to retire a dress with a deficiency that she could mend and use another day.

Seen from a distance, the schoolhouse had appeared small. The closer they came, the larger it loomed and the greater her doubts grew. She had never taught anything in her whole life. For that matter, she couldn't think of a single person who had ever asked her advice, or even listened when she spoke, unless it was the younger students at the female academy. *What was I thinking?* she asked herself.

"What will you do when you can read?" she asked Chantal, determined not to listen to the gossip her head was trying to tell her heart.

"I will read everything I see, even labels on jars. I will read to my mama, because she just sits and rocks now." She wrinkled her face. "She misses Papa. We all do."

"A story will help?"

She nodded, then tugged on Lily's arm. "One night when no one knew it and I was feeling sad, I sat on the porch of the great house and listened to Fothering read to Luella. I felt better."

"What was it?" Lily asked.

Chantal shrugged. "Something about fairies, but it made me forget for a few minutes that I was sad." She jostled Lily gently. "But I don't believe in fairies. Do you think Luella does?"

"I don't know. You must ask her."

"Her *mama* doesn't want her to have anything to do with us," Chantal said. She explained it carefully and in a low voice, as if wanting Lily to understand without any embarrassment.

"We may have to change that," Lily said. They had stopped to talk, and Jack and Amelie up ahead had stopped too, watching them. "Let's hurry up."

"I don't know," Chantal said doubtfully, ever a realist. "But if you say so . . ."

"I do say so." Lily looked at the building that probably had some desks in it, and maybe a shelf or two. A blackboard would be nice, but her well-earned skepticism wouldn't let her guarantee much more. Suddenly, though, it didn't look so large, because in her honest way, Chantal Sansever had whittled it right down to a manageable size. Lily remembered all the books that had taken her a long way from Bristol, England, where she was lonely. She understood Chantal.

There they stood, the four of them, staring at the closed door.

"Is there a key?" Lily asked.

"Nothing's locked here," Jack said cheerfully. "If any door ever had a lock, it's been a long time. Who goes first?"

"I do," Lily said, her voice quiet. She thought of Chantal crouched on a porch to listen to a story and decided to stop feeling sorry for herself. "I'm the teacher, after all."

CHAPTER 10

～❦～

*S*he opened the door, which creaked on hinges that hadn't been oiled recently, if ever. Lily stepped inside, then moved aside when the others followed. No one said anything.

"We have a lot to do, girls," Lily said finally.

The spiders had been industrious but seemed to hold no fears for Chantal, who clapped her hands. "Is that a blackboard?" she asked, ignoring the webs that were making Lily's skin crawl. "I have heard of blackboards."

To Lily's eyes, it was as poor an excuse for a blackboard as she ever hoped to see. She glanced at Chantal and saw her eagerness. "It is a blackboard, my dear. We'll use it for ciphering and letters and the alphabet."

Chantal's satisfied sigh seemed to travel all the way to the soles of her feet. Amelie smiled, perhaps in a big-sister attempt to excuse Chantal's enthusiasm, but Lily saw the excitement in her eyes too.

Lily walked into the schoolroom and noted four desks, probably fashioned from packing crates. Each desk had a stool. A wholly inadequate teacher's desk presided over the ramshackle business. She touched the spindly chair and jumped back when it collapsed in a dusty pile.

"You broke it, Lily," Jack teased. "Let us thank Preacher's Merciful Almighty that you didn't sit on it first. Nearest doctor's in Cheyenne."

"You are a rat and a rascal." Lily gave him a long look,

which made Amelie frown and chew her lip. Jack touched the child's shoulder. "She doesn't mean it," he whispered, his eyes on Lily. "Least ways, I don't think she means it."

"Do be serious, Jack," she said. "Amelie, he's a big tease," she added, which earned a rare smile from the child.

Lily continued her trip around the classroom, doing a silent tally. No books. No chalk. No maps. Crate desks and stools that would likely leave splinters. A bucket with a dipper, teetering on someone's cast-off child's desk, probably Luella's. A hand towel last used by coal miners. The one window by the door faced south, but there were panes of glass. Several floor boards felt loose. They could be nailed down. She turned around to face the others.

"We have a classroom. Just think what is going to happen here!"

Both girls applauded, and Lily curtsied playfully. "Of course, there is much to do." She waved at the spiderwebs and shuddered when they seemed to wave back. To distract herself, she looked through the window toward the backhouse with the door flapping open.

"Jack, do you think . . . ," she began, not taking her eyes off the privy. "It's a delicate subject."

"I'll turn Preacher over to you for all necessary repairs." He crouched down by Amelie. "My dear, would you be interested in coming with me to Wisner tomorrow morning? We will have ten dollars to spend on school supplies and I will need your advice."

What a nice touch you have, Mr. Sinclair, Lily thought. She noticed Chantal's lower lip stuck out. "Chantal, you and I will keep quite busy here. Do you think we dare ask Luella to help?"

Chantal shook her head. "Fothering might." She moved closer, and Lily bent down. "That night I was on the porch? He saw me, but he didn't tell on me."

"Then I think he is your friend and will help us," Lily said. "I will depend upon you to ask him."

Chantal nodded, her eyes serious now that she had been given such responsibility. "Do you think the Buxtons might have a chair for you, since . . ."

"Miss Carteret broke hers?" Jack teased. "I wouldn't put too much faith in Mrs. Buxton providing another chair. We'll think of something, so Teacher here doesn't have to stand up all day. And I . . ."

"Jack? Mama wants my sisters."

Lily looked at the door, where stood the boy who must be Nicholas Sansever, already pointed out to her as a reluctant scholar. She knew he was twelve, but he was short for his age. What he lacked in height he more than made up for in a handsome face and impeccable carriage. She had already noticed that the Sansever girls took after their energetic mother, with her curly hair and snapping eyes. Nicholas must resemble his father.

She had also seldom seen so much disapproval on one face. "Do come in," she said with a gesture. He only backed away, as if fearing some contagion from what would be going on within, come Monday.

"Now, lad," was all Jack said, but his tone of voice had gone from humor to command. "You're to be here Monday morning too."

Nick shook his head with considerable vigor. "I'm a cowboy," he said, his eyes on Lily, as if daring her to argue. "A cowboy. Papa couldn't read."

"You will be a cowboy when I say you are, and you learn to obey orders," Jack replied. "Monday. You. Here."

The look Nick returned was no less mutinous. Jack gave him stare for stare. Nick turned away but not before growling, "All right! But I don't have to like it."

"He'll be your challenge," was Jack's comment. "I'll talk to him some more; you know, convince him of the necessity of learning something. Get along, ladies," he said to the sisters. "Your mother needs your help."

Lily stood beside Jack, watching them skip down the

slope. Chantal looked back several times, which gratified her. "Will Nick give me grief?"

"He might try. I'll work on that."

She looked around the room again, wishing she could see it through Chantal's eyes. "This isn't even a sow's ear," Lily said. "I wish I could see it as the Parnassus of learning, like Chantal does."

With a shake of his head, Jack looked out the door again. "You've just enlarged their world."

"I haven't done anything yet!" she said in protest.

"I say you have and not just for them. Look there."

Hand shading her eyes, she watched where he pointed to see her father leave the Buxtons' house. He went down the three porch steps, hand over hand on the railing, like an old man, but he had his course set on the cookshack.

"Shall we?"

Lily nodded and closed the door, wishing for a foolish second that when she opened it tomorrow morning, armed with a broom, bucket, and mop, she might see more than a room hardly better than the other shacks that littered the place. What did ranchers *do* with all these little buildings? Maybe she would learn.

They walked slowly down the hill, which gave Lily the perfect opportunity. "Why is Amelie so quiet? Does it have to do with her father's death?"

"Some," he said. "She has always been the quiet one, even from a baby. Only one who could make her smile was Jean Baptiste, and even he had to caper about and work at it." He shrugged. "Since his death . . . well, I suppose life isn't funny. The Sansevers teeter on the edge of ruin. If Madeleine wasn't such a cook, I have no doubts that Buxton would run them off."

"You'd stop him, wouldn't you?"

"I'd try." He stopped. "Lily, we're just the little people here."

Maybe the shabby classroom that Chantal and Amelie

Sansever saw as a palace was starting to turn Lily into an optimist. Time to nip this negativity in the bud.

"Little people? No. *You're* the man who owns Bismarck," she reminded him quietly.

He gave her such a look. "Tell me that now and then," he said.

ᴄ᷌ᴏ᷈

Apparently it was going to be a day of milestones. His hand shook on the spoon, but her father ate stew with the others. He did it with a certain dogged look to his face, as if determined to show everyone who knew better, just how normal he was. If he could keep up such a pretense, the least Lily could do was try to equal it.

They sat together and ate their beef and canned beans and potatoes. This dining hall was a far cry from even the breakfast room at Carteret Manor. Lily could have counted on one hand the times she had been invited to dine with guests, even though everyone in that seaport probably knew of her mother's origins. The Bar Dot was different. As her father haltingly attempted conversation, she glanced around at the others, gratified to see curiosity, but no scorn. Possibly the Bar Dot's inmates were, on the whole, kind.

As the little girls brought around Madeleine's raisin pudding, Jack introduced her to the remaining hands, as he called them.

Jack began with Will Buxton, and he left just enough hesitation to suggest to her that this obvious relative of the man in the big house was probably foisted on him and next to worthless. Amazing what Jack Sinclair could disclose without words. She said all that was proper and held out her hand, which Will shook, after a slight hesitation of his own. She was used to that, so it hardly registered.

Stretch was another matter. He wasn't much larger than Nicholas, so his nickname was evidently a joke. Or so she thought. "We call him Stretch because he can tell the best lies. You might call them stories," Jack said.

However dubious his tales, Stretch had no qualms about his handshake, which he accompanied with a little bow that made the others grin, and Chantal put her hand to her mouth, delighted.

Lily had her own questions, the ones that labeled her as the greenest amateur on the planet. "Gentlemen"—that alone brought chortles—"how is it that you can control so many cattle with so few, er, hands?"

They looked at each other, as if wondering who could do such ignorance justice, but there was no meanness. Preacher spoke up. "Ma'am, cattle stay pretty close to home in the winter," he said. "Kinda like old ladies."

"'Cept for the new ones up from Texas," Stretch chimed in. "They like to head south. We keep'um milling with the old timers, and that reassures them."

"And then in May or so, we'll have a cow gather in the district, and sort everyone out," Jack added.

"Wouldn't it be simpler to fence your land?"

The men looked at each other, and Lily sighed inwardly.

"It's too expensive to fence thousands and thousands of acres," Jack said, coming to her rescue, even though he smiled too.

"Except for Jack's *big* ranch for his pretty red bull," Will joked.

Lily was no stranger to nuance. A glance around the suddenly quiet circle suggested to her that Will Buxton didn't have the merit yet to tease the foreman.

Lily was also no stranger to filling awkward silences. She could change the subject as well as anyone.

"Gentlemen . . ." Again that chuckle. "Perhaps you have heard about the school that is opening on Monday."

They nodded, perfectly willing to move on from a subject that, from the look on Jack's face, had been chewed like cud for too long.

"We have a tiny budget and no books. Could I ask all of you for the loan of any reading material you might be willing to share?"

Will just didn't want to give up. "No French postcards?"

"None," she said firmly, not sure what he meant, but taking her cue from the frown on Jack's red face.

"I'm from Connecticut and I have farmer's almanacs," Stretch said.

"Could you use a grammar book?" Indian asked.

The others stared at him. "I'm not ignorant," he said pointedly. "Came in a missionary barrel from back East somewhere. I can read and write."

"I'd like that more than you know," she said. "Thank you, Monsieur Fontaine."

Indian grinned at her and the others stared. Evidently, this had been a day of firsts for several of the Bar Dot's residents.

And then the noon hour was over. Silent, his head down, her father had worked his way slowly through Madeleine's wonderful stew. In fact, the cook had peeked from the open door of the kitchen to see how he did, which touched Lily. When he finally finished, Madeleine pushed Chantal forward with cookies done up in a bit of waxed paper. Clarence Carteret accepted them with a smile.

"See, Papa? You've been missed," Lily said simply.

He had trouble rising, but she could stand beside him and help him to his feet without attracting too much attention. And once he was on his feet, Amelie held open the screen door. He couldn't walk fast, so Lily linked her arm through his and turned his meander into a stroll.

At the door to his office, he looked at her for the first time. "D'ye think anyone noticed?" he asked, his voice wistful.

"Papa, they were glad to see you at lunch," she assured him. "And now since I have free time until school starts next week, I'll help you here."

They spent the afternoon side by side at the desk, Lily copying whatever correspondence needed a firmer hand, and her father adding up columns, then adding them up again and again. She wondered how on earth he had kept his job. By the end of the afternoon, he could only sit and shake. To her relief, Mr. Buxton must have been busy elsewhere. His eyes kind, Fothering brought in tea at four o'clock.

She thanked him. As he turned to go, she said, "Fothering, Chantal Sansever and I are going to clean out the schoolhouse tomorrow. Could you mention to Luella that we would like her help too? It is going to be everyone's school."

He was too good a butler to appear doubtful. "I will suggest it," he assured her.

"That's all I can ask." Lily clasped her hands together. "I . . . I've never taken the lead in anything before, but I think a school should be everyone's investment."

"I am certain I can cajole Mrs. Buxton into allowing me to assist," the butler said. "As for Luella, perhaps her natural curiosity will inspire her." He stood in the door, obviously teetering back and forth about saying more. Then he succumbed. "May I say, Miss Carteret, I have difficulty believing that you have never organized anything before. You have a knack."

And then he was gone, leaving her to wonder about this knack. The thought nourished her as she walked to their shack with her father, who was so desperate for a drink that he could barely contain himself. He went directly into his room. In another moment, she heard the clink of a bottle, a massive sigh and the creak of bedsprings. Clarence Carteret, remittance man and general all-around failure, had made it through another day.

As she stood on the porch, unwilling to endure another evening like the one before, Lily noticed a stack of books and pamphlets on the bench by the front door. She came closer, impressed to see a leather-bound copy of *Ivanhoe*, with the title in gilt letters. And there was Pierre Fontaine's promised grammar, a real treasure.

She made a space and sat down with books on each side of her. She picked up *Toby Tyler or Ten Weeks with a Circus*, practically new, and a note fell out. She opened it. "Dear Miss Carteret, I'll be their tamorrah, but I can't get dirty. L," she read out loud. "Thank you, Luella."

She tucked the note in her pocket and patted it, her first reward for teaching a class that hadn't even started yet.

CHAPTER 11

Oliver Buxton made a production of counting eight
silver dollars into Jack's hand the next morning.
"That's all you'll get from the consortium," he said, sounding prissy and put-upon at the same time.

*The consortium spends more than this on one night's booze
at the Cheyenne Club, you tightwad*, Jack thought as he
smiled at his employer. "We came up with two more dollars, so we'll manage."

This didn't seem to be the answer Buxton wanted, but
Jack had long since given up understanding managers.

Clarence Carteret was already at work in the office.
Jack had secretly been impressed that Lily had bullied the
man to breakfast, and he didn't look half bad.

"That's quite a daughter you have," he went so far as to
say as he passed through.

"I never knew her," Clarence said simply. "My loss."

Wondering to himself how many lost opportunities the
man had squandered, Jack tipped his hat and went to find
Amelie.

She wore what he knew was the best of her two dresses,
and she carried a bouquet of zinnias, survivors of the
summer's heat and wind. To be sure, calling it a bouquet
was overly generous—four zinnias gasping out their last.
Amelie had given the bouquet a Gallic twist with a strand
of silvery ribbon.

He knew she could manage only a gentle tease. "Did

85

you decide to put them out of their misery?" he asked as he nodded to Madeleine, who glared at a pot of beans as though wishing she could change it into something else.

Amelie shook her head. "For my papa," she whispered, and he felt immediately lower than a snake's belly. "Mama said we would be going right past the burying ground."

"So we shall." At least he was smart enough not to fall all over himself apologizing. If anyone knew life was hard, Jean Baptiste Sansever's children did.

He had taken the ranch's smaller buckboard, the one usually reserved for consortium members because the seats were padded. Amelie saw so little luxury that he knew she would appreciate it. With a slight smile—in itself a reward—she patted the seat.

"Let's stop at the schoolhouse and see if anyone is work-ing," he said. Earlier, he had watched Chantal heading toward the school carrying a bucket and scrub brush, her hair done up in a bandana and wearing an old dress too short for her that had somehow avoided the ragbag. The determination on her face—so like Madeleine—had made him smile.

The window and door were open, giving the place the airing out it needed. Talk about sow's ears. It didn't look any better than a half dozen other unused outbuildings he should have burned down years ago. He waved to Preacher, who was putting new hinges on the outhouse door.

"Will it work?" he teased.

"I'm going to take some sandpaper to the seat," Preacher said. "The door's been open so long that the wood inside is weathered, too."

When Jack looked back at the school, Lily stood in the doorway, her hands on her hips. She somehow man-aged to look tidy, even though her hair was done up in a bandana too. Maybe it was the elegant way she carried herself as though Wyoming Territory was only going to be a temporary stop and she had grander venues in mind. Lily Carteret probably had three or four plans by now.

He set the brake but didn't get down. Through the door, he saw the tall figure of Fothering. The butler had covered a broom with cheesecloth and was swiping at cobwebs while Chantal dusted off a desk. Jack leaned across Amelie. "No Luella?" he asked Lily.

"Not yet, but I have hopes," Lily replied. She reached in her pocket and handed him a coin. "Papa's contribution. He said you call it two bits."

"If there is a bargain to be had in Wisner, we will find it, eh, Amelie?" he said as he pocketed the coin. "I have your list, and this makes ten dollars and two bits."

"We are rich," Amelie said solemnly.

"I believe we are." He nodded to Lily and spoke to the horses.

The next stop was the Bar Dot cemetery, a bedraggled patch where the zinnias would look at home. The only occupants were cowhands like Jean Baptiste, and four others done in by more horse than they could handle, or a stubborn cow. The sixth grave was even more recent than Sansever's, a pile of bones with two arrowheads and a belt buckle buried deep. He wondered if some mother back East still watched for a wandering son.

While Amelie left her little gift for her father, he took a hard look at the Bar Dot, wishing the woodpile were bigger. He had sent the others to cut more wood and he saw them down by the river. There had been protests—Will even had the nerve to point out that the wood lot was already full—but Jack was the foreman. He knew it wouldn't happen to Will, but the others didn't want the dubious freedom of riding the humiliating grubline from ranch to ranch during the winter, hoping for a handout. He had done that one winter, and that was enough.

Wisner basked in early September warmth as they

came to town. It had been a silent trip. Amelie had looked at him when he passed his own little ranch without stopping. "We'll visit Manuel and Bismarck on the way back," he assured her.

"I like Manuel," she had said, and that was their sole conversation.

Since the only game in town for them was Watkins' Superior Mercantile, he tied up the horse in front of the store. He helped down his little guest, touched to see the wonder on her face at the metropolis of Wisner. She seldom got off the Bar Dot, and he tried to see the shabby little place through her eyes.

He remembered his own childhood, a hard drill of work and hunger, growing up on a piece of land tired from years of cotton that wore out the soil, but was the only thing his father could rent. Jack never went to town. He joined up in 1863 when he was thirteen, not because he believed in states' rights or slavery but because he hated the farm. The sight of Savannah had kept him awake all night with the wonder of it. He could have told Amelie that Wisner wasn't much, but why ruin the gentle child's pleasure?

He wondered what she would make of the Superior Mercantile, which was anything but. Her eyes widened as she looked around the crowded store, smelly with smoked fish and coffee beans. Elbows on the counter, Mr. Watkins watched the whole show. "Why, Jack, twice in one week? And each time with a pretty girl? What'll that faro dealer at the Back Forty think?" he teased.

Jack put his hands over Amelie's ears. "That'll do," he said in his foreman voice. He handed over Lily's list. "We have ten dollars and two bits for school supplies. Can you help us?"

Lips pursed, Mr. Watkins surveyed the list. "So the pretty high yaller gal is a schoolteacher?" he asked, which meant that Jack's hands covered Amelie's ears again.

"Mind yourself, Watkins," he said, "or I'll . . ."

The store owner looked around elaborately. "Go to another store?" He got the hint, though, because he returned to the list. "'And if there is enough money, Franklin Colors.' Let's see what we can do."

Perhaps feeling some amends were owed, Mr. Watkins handed Amelie a basket. "You help me and there'll be something in it for you."

Jack could have told the merchant that Amelie would have helped for nothing, but the man had never seen her scrubbing pots.

"Keep her busy, Watkins. I have a plan," he said as he stood in the doorway and looked across the street to the Back Forty.

Watkins followed Jack's gaze. "Gonna drink? I can't keep Amelie busy that long!"

Jack crossed the store in a few quick strides until he leaned over the counter to speak in Watkins' ear. "Not another word, and it's not what you think."

There must have been enough menace in his voice, because Watkins nodded and quickly returned his attention to his business.

"I'll be back in five minutes, Amelie," Jack said. "Be a good girl."

He went into the saloon, a dark place that felt good after the noonday sun. There was Vivian, just reading at a table because it was early for faro.

"We haven't seen you in a while, Jack Sinclair," she said. "Saving your money for that big pretty bull?"

"He needs grain and hay more than I need to lose money in here," Jack said with a tip of his Stetson. "How are you, Vivian?"

"Finer'n frog's hair. Sit a spell."

Jack did as she asked and looked around the room. Before Wyoming started to wear him out, the saloonkeeper had tried to give the Back Forty an elegance it never attained. He looked at the fine desk in the corner. Maybe Oscar had thought his customers might be inclined to sit there and write polished letters home, something that never happened. Still the desk remained, and its equally elegant chair.

"Clarence Carteret's daughter is going to teach school on the Bar Dot and she deserves a pretty chair."

"Mrs. Buxton won't donate one to the cause of education?" Vivian joked. "Let me ask Mr. Buxton next time he's in here." She strolled over to the chair and blew the dust off the seat. "For you, one dollar. You know how Oscar likes to turn a profit."

"I don't have one dollar. Every penny is going to school supplies at the mercantile, and you know how that bandit marks up his merchandise."

"For nothing?" she asked. "Nothing's for free here, not in a saloon."

"That's what we can afford," he told her, relying on her good nature. "You're a civic-minded woman, Vivian. Oscar won't mind. Call it an investment in education."

She thought a moment, then laughed. "You sure drive a hard bargain. Take it."

He kissed her cheek, picked up the chair, and considered his remaining credit at the Back Forty. "Do you have a winter coat that you're just plum tired of looking at?

She rolled her eyes. "Does the teacher need a coat too? Jack, you're pushing it."

"I'm asking for Madeleine Sansever's girls. It's gonna be a bad winter."

He had said the magic word. With a swish of her dress, Vivian climbed the stairs. Chair in hand, he waited, confident of Vivian's kindness, even if she was ruthless at the faro table.

Vivian came down the stairs with one coat over her arm. "The best I can do," she said.

"Thanks, Vivian. You sure you can spare it?" The coat felt heavy and serviceable.

She shrugged. "Wool makes me itch. A bad winter?"

"I think so. In fact, if you have somewhere else to go, I'd advise it."

She kissed his cheek and he breathed in a faint whiff of rose talcum. "I'm still saving to open that millinery shop." She touched his hand. "You're still a good man, Jack Sinclair."

"Scat now," she teased. You'll give the Back Forty a bad reputation if we get more generous."

"Nothing's free, Viv," Jack reminded her. "You've done me a signal favor and I won't forget it."

"You like this schoolteacher?" she asked, and he heard a little edge to the question.

"As a matter of fact, I do," he replied without a blush. "You would too, though. She's trying to make a silk purse out of a sow's ear." He chuckled. "Maybe that's all anyone tries to do. It's going to be hard for her with such a father." He hefted the coat. "Madeleine Sansever will probably say a prayer for you. There isn't much between her and ruin."

Vivian nodded. She was acquainted with rocks and hard places.

He gave her a little salute and picked up the chair. He knew Lily was going to ask him where the chair came from, and he knew he'd probably tell her. He figured she had been lied to for years, and he had no plan to continue the pattern.

Watkins was tallying up the total when Jack returned. The basket rested on the counter and Amelie watched, her eyes showing her concern, as the merchant checked off each item.

"I don't think we have enough," she whispered to Jack.

"We'll have enough," he replied with a meaningful look at Watkins.

It wasn't much of a list, but Mr. Watkins tallied it again, probably more for dramatic effect than anything else. "If your schoolmarm can make do with one box of Franklin

Colors, we'll make it. Trouble is, I can only let go of one map." He leaned his elbows on the counter. "What'll it be? A map of the world or the United States?"

"I want both maps."

"Jack, you're not listening. The world map is one dollar. You'd owe me two dollars for both." When Jack said nothing, he sighed. "The world map has the US and Europe already. Granted, they're a bit small that way, but . . ."

Jack gave Amelie his whole attention. "What should we do? It's your education."

She regarded the merchant a long time, long enough for Mr. Watkins to shift his feet. Jack recognized the calculating look she gave him, because Madeleine had the same shrewd expression. He hadn't thought to see it on gentle Amelie's face, but there it was.

With a small sigh of her own, she reached into the neck of her dress and pulled out a little cross on a chain. Without a word, she undid the clasp and laid it on the counter.

Bingo, Jack thought. *I can take it from here.* "Amelie, didn't your papa give that to you?" he asked.

She lowered her eyes, silent. The next sound was Mr. Watkins taking another map from the dusty pile next to the fly strips.

"Keep your necklace, little girl," he said. "I suppose I can donate the map. It's good for business."

"The Lord'll bless you for this," he told Mr. Watkins.

"I suppose you told that to the faro dealer across the street," Watkins grumbled.

"Vivian's a good sport."

Mr. Watkins peered elaborately around him to the sidewalk where Jack had left the chair and coat. "Did those just follow you across the street when she wasn't looking?"

When Mr. Watkins finished wrapping everything, he leaned across the counter and handed Amelie a Pink

Pearl eraser, long and slim with undercut edges. "That's for your help."

Amelie's eyes widened at the gift, then she shook her head. "You already made a big donation to my education," she explained.

Jack never thought he would see Mr. Watkins at a loss, but there it was. Too bad there wasn't anyone else in the store to watch the merchant struggle to maintain his composure.

"Miss, I always pay for help and you helped. It was a promise, remember?" Mr. Watkins chuckled. "That is, unless you're certain you will never make a mistake and need it."

Amelie favored him with the kind of smile that would assure her of suitors to spare, in eight years or so, and took the eraser. "*Merci*," she whispered.

They put their purchases in the buckboard next to the chair and coat. Amelie ran her hand over the chair, with its cane seat and gilt tracery.

"I don't think Miss Carteret will break this one," Jack told her. "Try on that coat."

She did as he asked, holding her breath with the pleasure of black velvet on the collar. It sagged a bit off her shoulders and the sleeve tips nearly covered her fingers, but Jack knew Madeleine could alter it.

"I can give Chantal my old one," she said. She took off the coat as if it was made of ermine and patted it carefully between the chair and the packages. She looked around at the shabby little town, satisfaction writ large on her face. "Let's go see Bismarck."

"Not until we have lunch," Jack said.

"But you spent all the money," she reminded him.

"All the *school* money, but I have thirty cents for two plates of chop suey at the Great Wall. Besides, a gentleman doesn't ask out a lady and not pay for her lunch."

He could tell that so much largesse in one day was

almost too much. He knelt down beside her. "Amelie, just remember: Always save your lunch money for lunch."

"Will I like chop suey?"

"Miss Carteret did," he lied.

CHAPTER 12

⟨≈⟨0⟩≈⟩

To Lily's surprise, Luella Buxton showed up two hours into the Great Schoolhouse Cleanup, as Chantal called it. She stood in the doorway, watching, as Lily and Chantal swatted at spider webs.

Lily put down her broom. "Luella, I'm delighted you could join us."

"Mama said I shouldn't because the dust would make me sneeze and upset my delicate system," she said seriously. She gave a fleeting smile which transformed her solemn face for the briefest moment. "I told her I would brave it."

"We're glad you did," Lily said. "Suppose we let you stand outside on a box and wash the windows? There *is* a lot of dust in here."

"I can do that, because I am wearing my most ragged dress," Luella said. "There isn't a breeze so I will not catch cold, sicken, and die."

"Goodness," Lily said, trying not to smile, "that would be distressing." How trying it must be to be the only child of a hypochondriac.

With Fothering's help, Luella was soon washing windows. Lily watched her through the wavy glass. Luella's most ragged dress was better than Chantal's dress. Lily remembered her own childhood at Miss Tilton's School, dressed as well as the others, but kept apart because of her skin color. Everyone was polite, but no one was friendly.

My school will not be like that, Lily thought. *Heaven knows what we will learn, but we will be friends.* She shuddered as she picked the cobwebs off the broom straws, feeling not much braver than Luella but determined not to show the hard-working Chantal what a faint-hearted specimen she was.

She admired the little girl who pitched in, scrubbing and cleaning without complaint. To her delight, Chantal started to sing. It was a tune Lily recognized. In a moment, the words came back to her, so she joined in. "*Sur le Pont d'Avignon, l'on y danse, l'on y danse. Sur le Pont d'Avignon, l'on y danse tous en rond.*"

Chantal looked at Lily, her eyes bright. "Do you know the rest? Can we dance too?"

Lily glanced out the window to see Luella watching. She motioned her inside. "Chantal, let's teach this to Luella right now."

Luella hesitated in the doorway, but Lily gestured her closer until she stood close to Chantal. "Luella, we'll sing it again, but slowly this time."

They sang the catchy tune several times until Luella was tapping her foot to the rhythm. After another time, she joined in, with a voice so sweet and clear that Lily clapped her hands.

"Luella! I'm impressed!"

The child blushed, then told them to sing it again. After a few more times, Chantal taught Lily and Luella the short verses between the lively chorus. After they sang along, they put it all together, with Fothering as their appreciative audience.

"What does it mean?"

"Pont d'Avignon is a bridge in La Belle France," Chantal said. She frowned. "I don't know where it is."

"If we had a map of France, I could show you," Lily said. "I'm hoping we will have enough money for Mr. Sinclair and Amelie to get a map. Dear me, if the store in town even has such a thing."

"Beg pardon, ma'am, but I have prepared a repast, and it is the luncheon hour," Fothering said from the doorway. "Do take a moment to indulge yourselves."

"Girls, I think the spiders and mealy bugs can wait," Lily said and held her hand out. "After you."

Fothering had brought along a wicker hamper, which he opened with real flair. He snapped out a red-and-white checked tablecloth and declared they could eat *al fresco*.

"Who is Al Fresco?" Chantal asked as she smoothed down her dusty pinafore with a certain Gallic flair of her own that made Lily smile.

"I think he means we will eat outside on the grass," she explained. "I'll get Preacher, and you two help Mr. Fothering."

She saw Luella hesitate and knew the child had never been asked to help the butler.

"We need everyone," Lily said softly. "School is going to be different than home."

Luella nodded. "Mama needn't know."

While the girls took the napkins and actual silverware that Fathering handed them, Lily pondered the propriety of joining a man working on a privy and decided it was time to put England far behind. She couldn't see him, but she heard the sound of sandpaper. There he was, humming and sanding. She cleared her throat. Nothing. "Preacher?" she asked. Nothing. She touched his shoulder, and he jumped.

"Mercy, Miss Carteret," he managed to gasp out.

Trying not to smile, Lily clasped her hands in front of her. "I appreciate a man who throws himself into his work but not literally."

He smiled at her mild witticism and brushed the shavings down the hole.

"We've been invited to lunch," she said.

"Oh, not me," he said, but there was a light in his eyes that touched her heart.

"There is plenty for all," she said, hoping it was true.

"Loaves and fishes?" he joked.

To her surprise, Preacher was right. Fothering produced bread and butter cut into diamond sandwiches, and little slices of picked herring from a jar. Chantal's eyes opened wide, and Lily doubted she had ever eaten anything from a jar. Olives in a crystal bowl came next, followed by deviled eggs and raisins.

Lily glanced at Fothering, who had forgotten his butler demeanor and grinned from ear to ear as he watched the little girls eat. He must have known what she was thinking, because he leaned toward her and whispered, "I confess I raided the larder, but none of it will be missed."

"You're a wonder, sir," she whispered back.

When they finished, both girls helped Fothering repack the hamper. The two remaining deviled eggs went into the now-empty herring jar, which the butler elaborately presented to Chantal. "One for you and one for your mother."

"I will cut mine in half for Amelie," the child said. "Miss Carteret, do you think she is having as good a time as we are?"

"You can probably count on that, but I know she isn't getting deviled eggs as you did," Lily replied.

After Preacher declared the outhouse a thing of beauty and a joy forever, and took himself down the hill, Fothering left with Luella. Lily could see regret in her eyes, but she said with a straight face that she had to take a nap or Mama declared she would droop and faint. Lily and Chantal finished sweeping out the classroom. As Chantal hummed and worked, Lily realized what was happening: Both girls had begun to invest themselves in their school. Spiders and mealy bugs were part of the curriculum, and so was a bridge in France and a song.

Finally, Chantal put down her cleaning cloth with her own regret. "Mama needs my help preparing for supper," she said. "It is to be potato soup, and someone must peel."

"Very well, my dear," Lily said. "You have been of monumental help."

"Monumental?" Chantal asked, her voice dubious. "Is that good?"

"It is . . . it is monumental," Lily said with a laugh. She made a big circle with her arms. "Enormous, gigantic. That is monumental."

"Very well!" She picked up the glass jar with the two deviled eggs crowded close inside and went to the door. She stood there, then stepped back. "Freak."

Lily joined her in the doorway. There sat the cat she had heard so much about, blocking the path. His ears were ragged, and Lily wondered if they had been frozen off during a bad winter. He was probably gray and white, but he was dingy, probably unable to be the kind of cat he wanted to be, considering his surroundings. His tail had a crook in it as though he had fought a door and the door had won. He watched them and hissed for good effect, which made Chantal leap back until she was molded to Lily's legs.

"He's just a bully," Lily told the child, who obviously hadn't noticed that Lily had backed up too.

"He doesn't like us. He will sit there until I am late to help my mother."

Since she was Chantal's teacher, maybe it was time she showed a little bravery. "Chantal, would you sacrifice one of your deviled eggs?" Lily asked, keeping her eye on Freak, who looked as though he wouldn't mind settling in for a day or two, just to intimidate them.

Chantal unscrewed the jar and took out one egg. "I don't know," she said, handing it to Lily.

Lily started to sidle out the door with the peace offering, wondering if Freak ever took prisoners, when an ear-splitting yell made the cat perk up what remained of his ears, and hiss louder. The fur on his back rose to amazing height. In another second, he was gone, a gray-and-white streak.

"Was he going to hold you for ransom?"

It was Preacher, coming back up the hill with a tin in his hand. "It's safe now, little lady," he told Chantal, who ran down the hill.

Preacher came inside, tossing the tin from one hand to the other. "Thought you might need some reinforcements. I noticed him eyeing the schoolhouse when I went down. Maybe planning a frontal attack."

"Heavens, it's just a cat," Lily said, grateful the cowhand didn't know that her knees felt like jelly.

"Boy howdy, what a cat!" he said. "You should have seen him scare off a grizzly bear last winter."

She still held the deviled egg. *Maybe I need another friend*, she thought as she went outside and set the egg on a rock. "Maybe Freak could use a break from mice."

"You're too kind," Preacher said. He opened the tin. "Ol' Fothering slipped me a tin of stove black. How about I put a shine on that stove?"

"I won't argue," Lily said, grateful for his company, in case the timid offering of a deviled egg was an insult to a cat used to living rough. She swept the room as he worked. Her school was still a sow's ear, but at least it would be a clean one, come Monday.

She wanted to talk to Preacher, but her years of loneliness at Miss Tilton's, where she was merely tolerated, and other years of solitude in her uncle's manor had reinforced her difference, and she didn't know where to begin. It was easy with children, she was discovering, but this was a grown man.

Preacher made it easy for her by starting the conversation first. "My name's Wally Spears, ma'am," he said as he took a rag from his back pocket and applied it to the stove in a circular motion, working from the top down.

"Are you really a minister?" she asked.

"Ordained preacher, ma'am. Minister sounds too fancy." He worked the stove blacking into the crevices.

"I can pray and baptize sinners, marry the willing, and preach a stem-winder of a sermon that'll chastise you and keep you humble for years to come." He chuckled. "Well, not necessarily *you*, ma'am." A few more rubs, and a faraway look came into his eyes. "Yes sirree, I got the call to serve Jesus."

"Here in Wyoming?" she asked, fascinated.

"No, Alabama. Not so sure the Savior would waste his time on the quality of sinners in this territory."

She laughed. "I don't know about that, Mr. Sp—"

"Just Preacher, or you can call me Wally," he said magnanimously. He stepped back and checked his work like an artist.

"Did preaching get slow in Alabama?"

"Not precisely," he said, not looking at her. "Let's just say I needed a change of venue from some of my parishioners."

He looked so uncomfortable that Lily knew she shouldn't have asked. She thought of that song, "What Was Your Name in the States," and decided a massive change of subject would suit them both.

"Has Mr. Sinclair always been the foreman here?" she asked.

"Far as I know, but I heard from some of the boys in Cheyenne that he spent a fair share of time starving and eating out of garbage cans like the rest of us. There. It'll dry and I'll buff it."

She offered him a stool. He scrutinized it, then pulled out two hunks of sandpaper, tossing one her way.

They sanded in companionable silence. "You've heard about his bull," Preacher said finally.

"I've seen the bull." Lily flicked away the bits of wood. "Do you . . . do you think he's right about the coming winter?"

"Never known him to be wrong. Mr. Buxton doesn't give Jack enough credit." He started on another stool.

They sanded some more. Preacher cleared his throat

and she stopped. "I might be overstepping things, ma'am, but let me tell you something about Jack."

"As long as it's fit for human consumption," she joked, since he looked so solemn.

"He can't read, ma'am, but I know he'd like to."

Lily nodded, thinking of the menu in the Great Wall of China. "Would I embarrass him if I offered to teach him?"

"Probably."

"Then why did you tell me?" she asked, curious.

He shrugged and turned his attention to the stove again. "That copy of *Ivanhoe* belongs to me."

"And I thank you for the loan," she said.

"I started reading a chapter here and there out loud this winter. Jack has his own house, but he always wanted to know when I'd be reading. I finally just offered to let him take the book and read on his own time, and he gave me a vague excuse, like his eyes were tired. He can't read."

"I wish you had just read to him," Lily said.

"So do I now. As it was, he just sat there in the bunkhouse with us and looked at the book kind of hungry-like."

Preacher turned his attention back to the stove, buffing with vigor until the stove shone.

"I have a lot to do here, don't I?" Lily asked, after she finished sanding the last seat.

"Do you mean this room, or maybe all of us?" Preacher asked.

"I think you know."

CHAPTER 13

hile Lily finished sanding the last seat, Preacher gathered kindling and started a fire in the stove. "Just leave the windows open," he told her. "I have to go and help the others unload the wood they cut today. When the blacking heats, it'll start to smoke. When it burns off, it'll stop." He tipped an imaginary hat and strolled out the door.

Rolling down her sleeves, Lily looked at the rock where she had left the deviled egg, pleased to see it was gone. It shouldn't be hard to remember to bring a little something extra every day in her lunch bucket. Life couldn't be easy for a Wyoming cat. She leaned against the sill, looking down at the little place she shared with her father, wondering how to help him. And how in the world was she to let a proud man know she was aware of his secret and could help?

Maybe it was a day of epiphanies. As she looked down at the Bar Dot, Lily realized that so far, she had spent her life uninvolved with people. She had observed people from a distance, as she was doing right now. Sometimes she knew this distance had been forced upon her by others, but the blame couldn't rest there, not if she was fair. Had wariness bred wariness?

"I must reorder my thinking," she said out loud.

She had come to the United States hoping her father had finally overcome his own demons and could provide for her, his only child. The reality was that nothing had changed for her father, and likely wouldn't. Too much failure had ruined him worse than drink.

She had crossed the Atlantic hoping someone else was now in charge of her life. "How cowardly of me," she said. She had thought she wanted freedom, and here it was, scaring her.

Then she remembered the optimism with which she had stood in the door of the Cheyenne Northern and looked at Wisner. She had been disappointed with the size and shabbiness of the town, and the rough edges at the Bar Dot, but that was before this moment, when she reordered her thinking.

She looked down at the Bar Dot again. Until she developed an even better plan—"Thank you, Jack Sinclair," she murmured—the ranch would be a good place to start her self-improvement.

She watched a distant Chantal pumping water with her usual vigor. And there was the wagon piled with wood, all because a man was convinced this would be a terrible winter. Stretch was the short one; he and the Indian—no, Pierre Fontaine—were transferring the wood to a smaller cart for hauling to the wood lot where Preacher already stood, ready to help. Will Buxton stood back as she thought he probably always did, unused to toil, waiting for his orders.

She looked down at the watch pinned to her shirtwaist. Any time now, her father would leave the Buxton house and start toward his little shack. He was probably anticipating that first drink after the long dry spell of his day. She knew Madeleine was preparing their evening meal, probably working too hard so she could just fall asleep and not think about her sorrow without her man beside her.

Who knew about the Buxtons? Lily smiled to think of Luella, probably whip smart and quite aware that her mother was a hypochondriac of enormous proportions, but bending to her mother's will, at least for now. Lily knew she didn't care much for Oliver Buxton, who had the air of a bully about him. She had seen it when he had leaned over her father at his desk, showing his power over one of God's weakest creations.

She watched a horse and rider loping behind the wood lot. She knew nothing about Nicholas Sansever yet, except that both his sisters had assured her that he had no interest in school. He would probably come to her classroom ready to hate everything about it. She knew he was a wounded soul, suffering the loss of his father too.

She heard horses in harness and stepped into the schoolyard to see who was coming on the wagon road. She smiled to see Amelie leaning against the foreman, probably asleep. Amelie held what looked like a coat on her lap, and Lily wondered what Jack had been up to in Wisner.

He spoke to his horses and they stopped, which woke Amelie. Jack helped her down from the buckboard, and they gathered brown paper packages.

"Success?" she asked, coming closer and feeling shy because she knew more about him now than she had this morning.

"Absolutely. We didn't have quite enough money, because Watkins tacks on a bundle and calls it freight. But I got everything, or close enough to most."

"Close enough to most?" she asked. "What a delightful turn of phrase. Is it Southern?"

"Mostly it's me," Jack said. "My ma would have said, 'Sumpin is sumpin, sumpin ain't nuppin.' Would you have even understood that?"

"Doubtful, but I like it too."

He laughed. "I convinced Mr. Watkins that as a prominent merchant of considerable renown in these parts—the *only* merchant, I didn't add—he owed it to territory education to toss in a map of the world, since he had one." He made a face. "Of course, he didn't tell me it's an advertisement for bitters too."

"But it's a map," Amelie reminded him.

Lily took the packages he handed her and hurried into the classroom, eager to see what he had purchased, even though she knew what she had asked for. Maybe it was the fun of opening packages. Amelie brought in another armful and one more, setting them on her desk.

"And this."

She turned around as Jack stood in the door with a lovely cane-bottom chair, all gilt and elegant. "My goodness," she said when she could talk. "I know you couldn't afford that from our ten dollars and fifty cents, and you had better not have used your own money."

"Just say thank you like a lady," he teased and set it down. "Try it out."

She did, delighted, even though she worried. "Seriously, Jack, you had better not have spent a penny of Bismarck's hay money for this chair."

"And what if I did? It's my money," he said, then softened it. "I didn't spend a penny." He leaned closer. "I'll tell you how I got it after Amelie leaves."

"A scandalous story?" she teased.

"It can wait," he whispered back.

Amelie took the slates out of their brown paper. "Mr. Sinclair bought one too many. He says it's the hospitable way to do things, supposing someone new comes to school."

Lily chuckled over the world map, which featured a fairy relying heavily on the proper folds in her gown to remain clothed. "'Braxton Bitters,'" she read out loud. "'Improving digestion from Arabia to Argentina.'" Jack rolled his eyes.

Amelie stayed right at her elbow as though reliving her adventure with every package that Lily unwrapped. "Mr. Watkins let me help and look what he gave me when we finished!"

She held up the Pink Pearl with a flourish that reminded Lily of the more-dramatic Chantal. "I can make as many mistakes as I want," Amelie said. "I will share it with Chantal and Nicholas."

"They might be a little envious," Jack warned her.

"We will take turns carrying it to school," Amelie said.

"That will be the most beloved eraser in the history of . . . of erasers," Lily assured her. She touched the coat that Amelie wore. "This is something new!"

"Jack said it came from a kind lady, but I wasn't to pry."

"Ooh, more secrets!" Lily replied.

Jack took out his timepiece and gave it a lengthy scrutiny. "Amelie, I promised your mother you would be home in time to help with the evening meal. Look here."

Amelie looked and became the responsible child again. She put her eraser in the pocket of her coat, patted it, and held out her hand most formally to the foreman. He shook it with equal finesse.

"I had a lovely time today, and thank you for the chop suey," she said.

"I did too, Miss Sansever," he replied. "Hurry along now."

She darted for the door, but then stopped to look around for the first time at the swept room, the beautifully blacked stove, and the seats all smooth. "This is the loveliest place, Miss Carteret," she said with such feeling that Lily had to look away to collect herself. With a wave of her hand, she started down the hill. In a moment, she was skipping.

"Hmm. I've been calling this room merely an improved sow's ear," Lily said to excuse her emotion.

"You're not ten and desperate to learn," Jack told her. "Remember: sumpin is sumpin." He sat down at one of the desks and gestured for her to seat herself again. "Let us begin with the chair."

He did not shock her. Lily had already gathered that Wyoming Territory could be a desperately lonely place for a man. His obvious familiarity with Vivian the faro dealer was understandable. And considering that he won his ranch in a card game, not surprising. That bit of news was easy enough to reorder. She had no claim on Jack Sinclair, so she listened with real amusement to his expert handling of a faro dealer.

When Jack could see that she wasn't horrified with the implication, he relaxed. "Then I got bold and asked Vivian if she had an extra coat. Never hurts to ask. It's a little big, but Madeleine can work it over. Amelie kept stroking the velvet collar."

Jack looked around the room with the same pleasure Amelie had shown. "She liked chop suey better than you did. She even told Wing Li about your school." He stood up. "Which reminds me." He stuck his hand in the pocket of his linen duster and pulled out a paper fan. "Mr. Li told me to give this to you. It's red, so he said it'll bring you luck."

Touched, Lily accepted the paper fan, just a cheap notion with painted flowers, and suddenly saw the lesson in it.

"Jack, do you think Mr. Li would come out here some time to tell my students about China?"

"Why not try?" He stood up. "Now we have to close the door on so much splendor and adjourn for supper. Madeleine hates to be kept waiting. What do you want me to do with all the brown paper?"

"Fold it and I'll set the dictionary on it. Tomorrow the girls and I can draw the alphabet and cut out the letters. Numbers too."

He did as she said, while she closed the windows and made sure the fire was out in the stove that had started the day as a wretched castoff and ended it in buffed and shining splendor. She looked around with pleasure. The room was far too humble still, but she was already imagining the ABCs in brown paper, and the maps. Maybe she could color more clothing on the Braxton Bitters nymph.

Jack gave her a hand up into the buckboard and

pointed to the clump of cottonwoods. "Don't look now, but we're being observed by Freak," he whispered out of the side of his mouth.

"I left him a deviled egg today," she said. "I guess he isn't too choosy, because it's not still on the rock."

"I'm impressed!" He looked at her with admiration. "Everybody has to eat. Just don't expect to make a friend there."

"I don't plan to, but I would like it if Freak wouldn't hiss at us as we pass by and scare the girls."

He slowed the buckboard. "I should tell you: Madeleine asked me to see if I could tease out what's bothering Amelie."

"And? If you are half as persuasive with little girls as you are with a faro dealer, I expect you succeeded."

"I did, and I'll dump it in your lap, Teacher." He turned slightly to face her. "Amelie's worried that her mama will need help with the noon meal while she and Chantal are in school. She's thinking about not going to school or leaving school at eleven each day."

"She can't!" Lily exclaimed. "She told you this?"

"Not me. She's too shy." He chuckled. "We stopped at my ranch and while I was talking to Manuel, she got nose to nose with Bismarck—"

"Oh, heavens."

"—on her side of the fence—don't worry!—and told *him*. She did that last spring after her father died. There's something about animals . . . Maybe Herferds are better listeners than others, and Amelie knows the difference," he joked. "I wouldn't put much stock in Freak, though." He slapped the reins. "Think about Amelie's dilemma, Schoolmarm, and see what you come up with."

Lily nodded. She glanced at Jack. *Thank goodness you don't need anything from me*, she thought.

CHAPTER 14

*Y*ou know Lily won't mind," Jack told his sliver of a shaving mirror as he washed his face and picked up his Bible. He looked around his room for something else the school might be able to use and found a pamphlet given to him during the war. Pamphlets with thin paper usually ended up in the privy or as fire starters. If Lily could use it, all the better.

No point in putting on airs with Lily Carteret, not after what he'd told her in the schoolroom this afternoon. Maybe she saw his efforts with a chair and a coat as indications of his resourcefulness, rather than evidence of his love of gambling.

It hardly mattered. He was here doing a job he was paid for, and she was probably here until she found a way to leave. He already knew he would miss her when the time came. He already noticed that the Sansever girls had begun to gravitate toward her.

Others had noticed too. With his coffee cup, Preacher had pointed to Chantal, who was circulating with the second pan of biscuits. "We used to get first pick, boss," he said. "What do you bet Amelie will make Lily her first stop with the pie too?"

"Never bet on a sure thing, Preach," Jack had replied. "I'm okay with that." He chuckled. "Maybe the girls'll like us better again when the homework starts!"

"I doubt it. Have you noticed that Lily is the kind of

person you don't mind doing things for?" He nudged Jack. "Think what a great foreman she'd make."

He asked himself again why he thought Lily needed a visit tonight. He knew Lily Carteret was capable, but he didn't think she knew her own inner strength yet. In his twenty years in the territory, so hard at first but easing some now, he had seen the weather, the Indians, and the loneliness break people. The Indians were mostly guests of the US government on reservations now, but the loneliness and weather remained as potent barriers to settlement.

He thought Wyoming was hardest on the women, who seemed to need other women around to talk to and learn from. He couldn't help but consider Mrs. Buxton, increasingly jumpy and strange. Had she always been that way, or was life here weighing on her admittedly fragile mind?

He had never thought of women as weaker than men, just different. Someone like Lily Carteret was different in more ways than most. He had developed his own love for Wyoming Territory; maybe he wanted her to like it too. And so he would visit.

She seemed glad to see him, kindly ushering him in. She took his hat and set it on the table, and he looked around, amused to see the little changes that now showed a woman's touch.

She had hung up the two photographs that had kept him company for several months. He noticed a clean towel by the basin and pitcher, and a new bar of soap. She had stuffed a few flowers into a bitters bottle, flowers he recognized from the Buxtons' yard. He pointed to them and she nodded.

"I plucked a few. I don't think anyone noticed," she said.

He saw a jumble of books and pamphlets on the drop-leaf table and added his donation. "Just a Bible and a pamphlet someone gave me. Nothing much. Looks like you already have a Bible."

"I can use another one," she assured him. "Papa, look who has come to visit us."

Jack hadn't even noticed Clarence Carteret sitting there so silent. "Good evening, suh," he said.

"Ah, yes." That was Clarence: always about a beat behind. He was pale and sweating, but he sat there, as if he knew he owed something to his daughter, even if he wasn't quite certain what it was.

"I've been telling Papa about my day, and Freak, even," Lily said. "Do have a seat."

Maybe that was why he came to visit. He liked the little elegancies about her, from the accent on the second syllable of *Papa*, to her well-bred tidiness—not a hair out of place. He had never seen anyone like her.

"Would you like some tea?" she asked. "I do appreciate that you found me some in town."

"All Wing Li had was green tea; at least, that sounds like what he was saying," he told her, pleased that she liked the little packet he had left by her plate in the dining hall.

"We enjoy it, don't we, Papa?"

Her father nodded, but he was sweating, and he kept looking toward the closed door to his room.

She got them each a cup and sat down next to her father. She plucked the book from the little shelf above the packing crate settee, and he recognized it as the book that Preacher had been reading out loud last winter. It was a wonderful story about Crusaders and a Jew and his daughter. He couldn't remember the name.

"I've been reading *Ivanhoe* to him at night. We're on chapter seven. Do you mind?"

"No, ma'am, not at all."

Before she began, she did a little rundown on the earlier chapters, and it was just as he remembered. "You might have read it somewhere before," she said. "If you'd rather I didn't read . . ."

"It's no bother," he assured her again, wanting the story,

even if it was only one chapter. She had no idea how much he wanted the story.

She cleared her throat and began. "'The condition of the English nation was at this time sufficiently miserable. King Richard was absent a prisoner . . .'"

Jack closed his eyes with the sheer pleasure of her proper English voice, so much better than Preacher's Alabama twang. Even if he never heard another chapter of *Ivanhoe*, he planned to store up this memory of the night a lovely Englishwoman read out loud.

He was scarcely aware of the passage of time as Lily read chapter seven. She used different voices, depending on the characters. He knew she would read to her little students that way, and he envied them already. They would have her special gifts for five or six hours every day.

"'. . . leaving the Jew to the derision of those around him, and himself receiving as much applause from the spectators as if he had done some honest and honourable action.'"

Please don't stop, he thought as she put her finger in the book to mark the place.

"I think my Papa is ready for bed," she said, keeping her voice neutral, as if that would make the sight of Clarence Carteret sweating and shivering more bearable.

"Should I help him?" Jack asked in a low voice.

"No. He'll make it."

She stood up and kissed her father. "I think you should go to bed now."

Clarence nodded, and with a great sigh, he pulled himself erect with some effort and went to his room without a word, closing the door quietly. Jack tried to ignore it, but he heard the sound of a bottle against a glass almost immediately.

Lily looked so young just then, as she glanced down at her watch and then right into his eyes without flinching. "Another half hour tonight," she said simply.

"I'd better go," he said, remembering his rusty manners. Trouble was, Lily's eyes filled with tears, and he realized that his abrupt departure would signal something he never intended—that he was ashamed and couldn't wait to distance himself.

"No," he said decisively and sat down again. "I'd like another cup of tea. That is, if you don't mind."

"Not at all," she said, and he heard the relief in her voice.

She came back from the lean-to kitchen with his cup refilled and handed it to him. The starch was back in her spine again, and he knew his damage hadn't been irreparable.

"I should have some biscuits or tea cakes, but I'm no cook," she confessed. "I never learned. Do you think Madeleine might have time for lessons this winter?"

He took a sip and doubted that he would ever get used to tea. "Perfect. Time hangs heavy in the winter. Just ask her."

Cooking may not have been her forte, but Lily Carteret had impressive skills as a hostess. He wasn't sure how it happened, but he found himself telling her about his childhood near Valdosta, Georgia, just scraping by on a farm so poor that one meal a day was the rule. He could have lied and made it sound better. How would she have known? If he couldn't lie about his association with faro tables, what would have been the point in lying about the poverty of his youth?

"The war started and I signed up," he said. "I am probably the only Confederate soldier who put on weight on rebel rations." He chuckled, and not from embarrassment. "Told you we were poor!"

He didn't fight any battles for her, but he did describe the rapid retreat into the Virginia countryside, and the final battle, when everyone was hungry and discouraged beyond imagination. "That's where I got this," he said, pointing to the scar by his mouth. "And thus ended my army career. And now I will go," he said, shaking his head over the offer of more tea. Mercy, how did anyone drink more than one cup of the stuff and not have to pee?

They shook hands, and it felt formal, where before the evening had been friendly.

"I'll read another chapter tomorrow night," she said. "You know, if you're not too busy."

"I'll be here," he told her. He put on his hat and touched his finger to the brim. "You have the girls lined up for duty tomorrow?"

"I do. We're going to cut out letters and numbers from the brown paper Mr. Watkins so kindly gave us—freight notwithstanding."

He laughed out loud at that, then glanced at the closed door.

"Never mind," she said. "He's past hearing." She squared her shoulders, which touched his heart, and opened the door to the outside. "Madeleine is going to dip the letters and numbers in some starch. She says it will make them sturdy."

He nodded to her and she closed the door. He stood there a moment, wondering about the bravery of women, then remembered his overtaxed bladder and made tracks.

⁂

Lily took the cups and saucers into the lean-to and then allowed herself the luxury of forgetting about them. The days of maids around to do those things were long gone, but it was nice to imagine it for a moment. The dishes would still be there in the morning.

She put *Ivanhoe* back on the shelf, smiling as she remembered the delight in Jack's eyes while she read. How could a person go through life and never read? Somehow she would find a way to teach him this winter. Like he said, time hangs heavy.

She thumbed through the Bible he had loaned her. She had three now, and there would be a use. Some of the

Psalms made easy reading for her beginning readers. She picked up the pamphlet he had left, and felt the blood drain from her face.

"'The mixing of the races is an abomination to the Almighty,'" she read silently, horrified until she remembered that Jack Sinclair, trusted foreman on the Bar Dot, ambitious rancher, and owner of a magnificent Hereford bull, was illiterate. Poor man! He would die a thousand deaths if he knew just what it was he had given her. At least, she thought he would, but she didn't know him well, and he *was* a Southerner, after all. Both ideas rattled around in her brain until she told them to stop.

No, Lily, he is merely a man who cannot read, she thought as she thumbed through the poorly printed screed. She put it in her trunk, but it could just have easily gone in the stove. She hoped he didn't hold with such sentiments as expressed in the pamphlet, because she was coming to like Jack Sinclair.

CHAPTER 15

⁌↬◦↫⁌

$\mathcal{L}$ily remembered to take some scraps of fatback for Freak the next morning. She set it on the rock and went inside to take a pencil to the brown paper and begin the letters. By the time the Sansever sisters arrived after their kitchen duties, the fatback was gone. She didn't know if the cat had appropriated it, or some other creature, but Chantal mentioned that Freak was seated near the safety of the tree line, washing his face with his paw, something she had never seen before. Perhaps he was tidying up after breakfast.

The first dilemma of the day was solved by Fothering, in his usual unflappable way. He watched Amelie struggling to cut out one brown-paper letter with Lily's embroidery scissors and said, "One moment," as he held up one finger.

He returned a few minutes later with a pair of dressmaker shears and the sole comment, "Mrs. Buxton hasn't used these in years."

Luella trailed along behind with another pair of scissors, which she stated were hers, and only hers. Chantal frowned at her but returned to her task of darkening the letters. Lily had penciled them in lightly, mainly to give Chantal a chore.

In the middle of the morning, Jack and Nicholas arrived with a wood box and a load of wood. When the wood box was placed to Jack's satisfaction near the stove but not too near, he directed Nick to stack the rest outside.

"Nick will bring more later," he said, his hand on the boy's shoulder. He gave it a little shake. "Nick, you'll be here in school with your sisters."

"Too old," Nick said.

"Twelve's too old for school?" Jack asked. "That's a pity, because I don't hire anyone who can't read and write."

"You hired my pa," Nick argued.

Touched, Lily saw Nick Sansever for what he was, a boy with too many responsibilities thrust on him, maybe even before the death of his father. She said nothing.

"He had a skill I needed," Jack replied. "I mean what I say."

"I don't have to like it," the boy said, looking at Lily this time, daring her to say anything.

"No, you don't," she agreed. "All I require is that you do not stop anyone else from learning."

What could he say to that? Nick shrugged and left the room.

"He's old for his age," Lily said in a low voice, her eyes on his sisters, outlining and cutting.

"I recognize me in him," Jack said. "I had a war to fight, which made me some sort of hero in my own eyes, at least. And you should have seen the admiration on my little brother's when I got a three-day furlough once! Nick needs to be a hero. I'm open to suggestions."

He shook his head and followed the boy out the door.

Fothering must have heard the sharp exchange. He stood in the doorway and watched them leave. She joined him.

"What would *you* do?" she asked the butler.

"Perhaps we could arrange for Nick to rescue you from a burning building," Fothering said with a completely straight face. "Or from Indians, except they seldom cooperate in a meaningful fashion."

Lily gasped in surprise, then started to laugh. She laughed so hard that she had to sit down. The girls looked at her, great questions in their eyes. When she could speak, she managed to choke out, "Fothering told me a great taradiddle."

Their questioning expressions turned to puzzlement.

"You don't have that word here?" she asked.

"Is it French?" Luella asked.

Both Sansever girls shook their heads.

"Taradiddle. Taradiddle. I supposed it would be a great fable," Lily said, not daring to give the butler more than a glance.

"Fothering never, ever jokes," Luella assured her. "He doesn't believe in nonsense."

Fothering gave his head a sorrowful shake. "Miss Luella, sometimes I am overcome with levity."

"You are a rascal, Fothering," Lily whispered. "I wouldn't have thought it."

"Only now and then," he told her, making no attempt to hide his smile this time. "You *will* think of something, my dear Miss Carteret, because you are the teacher."

Not yet, she thought. *I don't even know what I'm doing.* She looked around, then whispered, "Fothering, you are kind to say that. Tell me something."

"Anything within reason," he said.

"I have not been able to place your accent, try as I might. Kindly tell me where, in all of England, you are from?"

He looked around too, and there was no mistaking the humor in his eyes. "That part of England which is closest to Cleveland, Ohio."

She opened her mouth in amazement, but she had the good sense to clap her hand over it to keep from exploding in whoops again, so undignified in an almost-teacher.

"Simple, Miss Carteret: they wanted a butler and I needed a job. I trust my naughty little secret is safe with you?"

"I will be as silent as the grave," she assured him with all solemnity. Then she spoiled it by asking, "Is Fothering your real name? It does sound butlerish, but now I have to ask."

He leaned close. "Sam Foster. I was working my way West and ran out of money in Omaha. The Buxtons were advertising for an English butler, and here I am. That was ten years ago."

"Since we are confiding, I am hoping to get enough money this year to head for greener pastures."

"And where might that be, miss, if I may ask?" he asked, so proper again.

"I have no idea, but I'll find it," she assured him.

The girls were busy. "Jack says Wyoming Territory can change people," she said. "Did it change you?"

His answer was prompt, so she knew he had considered the matter. "I have a good job and singularly few responsibilities. I suppose I like Wyoming for that."

"What has it done for Jack?" she asked quietly. He had been on her mind since last night, and it couldn't hurt to ask.

"He is a good rider and a leader," Fothering said, after some thought. "I think Wyoming has made him hard and used to being alone."

"That's a little sad."

What will it do to me? she wondered as the day ended and she stood in the doorway, watching Amelie and Chantal carry the letters to their mother, who would dip them in starch and make them stalwart little soldiers enlisted to fight the war against ignorance.

Luella and Fothering had left after another picnic basket luncheon that Lily strongly suspected Mrs. Buxton had no knowledge of. She also suspected that Fothering did pretty much as he pleased in a household where the lady stayed upstairs and played sick.

All through supper, she thought about Fothering's assessment of Jack as hard and lonely. Sitting with her father, who seemed to be eating better, she watched the foreman out of the corner of her eye. He sat with his hands, but they were all silent, which made her wonder if that was an American idiosyncrasy. Miss Tilton's had coached its young ladies in the art of conversation, with emphasis on dinner parties.

With quiet amusement, she remembered the dinner-table rules: only safe subjects such as the weather or certain literary works—never that upstart Browning. When ten minutes were spent in this improving fashion with the diner to one's left, one looked to the diner to one's right and began again. It had seemed ridiculous to Lily then, and even more now, as silence reigned.

She could talk to her father of the weather, but what did one say about the constant wind? She had already noted that the food was unvarying: in the evening, soup or stew of pleasing variety, as long as it was beef. Madeleine's scones—no, biscuits here—were a fluffy delight, and she had discovered a fondness for choke-cherry jelly. Hash would follow a day or two of a beef roast, and it was better eaten with ketchup. Nobody complained.

The Buxtons had their own cook. Lily decided to ask Fothering what the menu in the big house was like. Fothering neé Sam Foster, that is. The thought made her smile.

"Something amuses you, Lily?" her father asked.

Lily looked at her father with real delight. Rather than keep his head down over his plate, he had asked her question.

"I was just thinking how strange it is to have a butler in Wyoming."

Clarence Carteret nodded and gave a dry little chuckle, as if he was unused to amusement any more. "Do you know, I have been trying to place his accent, but it escapes me."

She yearned to be able to tell her father about the butler's naughty little secret, but she had promised. "I have wondered too. Should we ask him someday?"

"When I feel better."

It was his usual answer to any of her questions, but at least he had spoken.

She had stored up her conversation for their house, when she tried to keep her father from the bottle. She had already exhausted her commentary about the two photographs that Jack Sinclair had returned to her. She could talk about cutting the alphabets from brown wrapping paper. And then what? This shell of a man was her father, and she didn't know what to do with him.

To her relief, someone knocked on the door and she recognized the knock this time: three firm raps. Jack Sinclair wanted another chapter of *Ivanhoe*.

She opened the door and laughed when he held up a steaming cup of coffee. "Last cup of the night. Lily, I'm no tea drinker."

He set down the cup and pulled out a packet wrapped in waxed paper. "I should've left this with you today when we brought the wood." He opened the packet and pulled out a little sliver of wood soaked in something that made her nose wrinkle.

"Splinters soaked in coal oil," he explained. "When you lay the fire in the morning, put this underneath your kindling and light it with a match." He rewrapped the packet and laid it on the table.

"I've never started a fire," she said. "Papa does it here in the house."

"Don't look so serious, Lily! I can teach the teacher a few things. You won't need a fire for a month or so. There's time."

He just stood there then and glanced toward the book-shelf, waiting for her to ask him to sit down, waiting for another chapter, but too polite to ask. It was a nicety she hadn't suspected.

"Have a seat, sir," she told him. "I was just planning to read to Papa."

He made himself comfortable on the settee, and Lily opened to the next chapter. Since Papa had chosen the rocking chair, she sat next to Jack.

Chapter eight was the joust between the Disinherited Knight and a host of others. Halfway through, Jack put his hand across the page. "They're tough on horses," he said, then took his hand away. "But don't stop reading."

When she finished the chapter, Jack objected. "You really can't stop there, you know," he said. "Another chapter?"

To Lily's chagrin, her father whimpered at Jack's question. "I really need to go to bed," he said, his voice plaintive. His little apology was worse. "You know . . . you know how early morning comes around here. G'night."

When Clarence veered off toward the lean-to, Jack got up and pointed him to his bedroom door, opening it and standing there until she could see her father sitting on his bed within easy reach of his bottle. She closed her eyes in shame.

Jack sat down again. "Lily, someone a whole lot wiser than I am told me that everyone is mostly trying to do his best. Or her best, I suppose."

"That's his best?" she asked, incredulous.

"Could be. Read another chapter." He smiled at her and nudged her shoulder. "C'mon. You know you want to. Chapter nine." He put his hands behind his head and closed his eyes, perfectly ready to head back to the jousting field.

∽

"That's enough for one night," she said when the chapter ended. "Don't argue."

He gave her a "who, me?" look, but reached for his coat. And then he was all business again. "Given any thought to Amelie's predicament?"

"Certainly," she replied, all business too. "I'll ask Madeleine if adjourning school from eleven to one is enough time for the girls to help with the main meal."

"That'll rile Mrs. Buxton," he said, putting on his Stetson.

"I'll tell her that Luella will get that eleven to twelve hour with me, all by herself. It's what she wants, anyway."

"Sounds like a plan, Lily. You're getting good at plans."

He opened the door and his head went back in surprise. Alarmed, Lily wondered what had happened.

"My goodness, it's snowing," she said as she moved closer to stand beside him. "Look how big and beautiful the flakes are!"

She heard the breath go out of him in a big sigh. "Lily, it's only the middle of September."

She reached out her hand. The snow fell so softly, so lightly, like petals. Already, the ugliness of the ranch was disappearing under a light blanket of white. "It is pretty, and it'll melt tomorrow, won't it?"

"It had better," he said, his voice grim.

She could tell he was agitated, so he must not have realized what he was doing then. That's the only way Lily could account for his hand on her shoulder. She doubted he wanted comfort, because she knew he was a hard man. His hand felt more like protection to her. She may have been the smallest, most unimportant cog in the machinery of the Bar Dot—heavens, Chantal and Amelie were more useful than she was—but it was as though the foreman had added her to his list of responsibilities.

She looked at the snow with new eyes, then at Jack's face. His jaw was set and he frowned.

"It'll melt. You know it will," she said.

He walked away with no good-bye.

"Chapter ten tomorrow?" she called after him.

No answer.

CHAPTER 16

❦

*J*ack Sinclair was as good as his word. In the morning he showed her how to lay a fire in the schoolroom stove using the coal oil splinter. Lily had arrived at the school first, mainly so she had time to put another piece of fatback on the rock for Freak. The snow was already melting, so she brushed off what remained and set down the tempting scrap.

She stood in the doorway, hoping to see the cat. She waited to the end of her patience, then went inside the room and looked around with some satisfaction. She had tacked up the maps yesterday, which hid some of the deficiency in the log walls, and the occasional gaps where she could look out.

To honor Mrs. Buxton's strange request, Lily arranged three desks in front for the Sansevers, and one behind for Luella. She didn't like it, because it reminded her of Miss Tilton's School.

She admired the chair that Jack had scrounged for her at the Back Forty. It was by far the most elegant item in the room. For one fanciful moment, she pictured herself with a whip and the chair, defending herself from lions, as she had seen in a visiting circus in Bristol. The solitary lion had been a wheezy old gent who made a single, perfunctory swipe with his paw at the chair before he returned to slumber, to the boos and stamps of the audience.

Speaking of lions. She went to the door and noted that

the fatback was gone. She looked toward the tree line and there he was, observing her out of what she thought was only one eye. Freak glared at her and stalked back into the trees and vanished, camouflaged by the tawny prairie grass.

"It's not polite to eat and run," she called to Freak.

Lily shook her head at her own folly and decided to let Freak be Freak. She could leave some daily tidbit—it could be anything—but expecting any affection in return was beyond the cat's capacity, obviously.

"It's your loss, Freak," she said. "I know precisely where cats like to be scratched."

No answer, and just as well, because Jack Sinclair and his Sansever shadows were halfway to the school, the girls skipping along with all the energy of youth. Pierre Fontaine came, too, moving more slowly because he carried a large bundle.

Lily watched with interest, stepping back when Pierre came into the classroom and plopped what looked like a buffalo robe over two of the desks. He pointed with his lips and a toss of his head to the wall without maps. "I'll hang this here," he explained.

"Talking to yourself, Lily?" Jack asked.

"Your hearing is far too acute," she said, feeling her face grow warm.

"Huh, nothing cute about the boss," Indian said.

"*Acute*, as in sharp," Lily replied. She threw up her hands. "All right! You caught me talking to Freak, who snatches food and doesn't hang around for conversation."

Indian's lips twitched. "At least Jack don't have chewed off ears and one eye. Not yet, anyhows."

He and Jack spread out the buffalo robe and turned it over, exposing a spiral of pictures. She could make out single figures, and horses, and what looked like fire and guns.

"Oh, my," Lily said. "What is this?"

"*Waniyetu wowapi*," Indian said and looked at Jack.

"We call'um winter counts. Where do you want it, Indian? Help us out, girls."

Amelie and Chantal obliged by pushing over a desk so Indian could stand on it. He had strung a small length of rope through two holes in the robe. Jack handed him a nail, he pounded into the wall. He pounded in another one, until he was satisfied they would hold the weight of the robe.

"The Indians around here tell yearly time from winter to winter," Jack said as Indian jumped down. "What is it? One event for each year?"

"Yes," Indian said. He pointed to the center of the spiral, and what looked like a child with a white horse. "There is a *tiyospaye*, the counter, you would say, who decides what is the most important happening."

"A boy and a horse, Pierre?" Lily asked, enchanted by the simplicity and beauty of the artwork on her ugly wall.

"A white horse. Very special, very rare," he replied and gave Jack a meaningful look. "I like that you call me Pierre."

"It's your name."

"Remember that, boss," he said to Jack, and it sounded like no suggestion.

Lily traced the horse with her finger, then turned to Pierre. "Are you the winter count keeper now?"

The Indian shrugged. "My great-grandfather started this, then my mother's father. He died at the Greasy Grass, so it came to me because I didn't go to the rez. No one wants to keep track of anything on the rez."

Lily looked at the final drawing, a lone buffalo, but thin. "Is this the count for this year?" she asked.

"Last year. I only saw one buffalo on the plain where many used to roam. I have not decided on this year yet because we have not reached winter. When I decide, I will come to your classroom and paint it. Would you mind?"

"We'll be honored to keep your winter count at the Bar Dot School," Lily said.

"Is that what we are?" Chantal asked.

"I believe so." Lily touched both girls on the shoulder. "If you could find an old board around here, and maybe some black paint, I could print that on the board. You could paint it, and maybe we could get Pierre here to nail it over the door."

The girls looked at Pierre, their eyes eager. Pierre nodded. "Let's go find an old board."

Jack waved them off and he looked at the winter count. "Hope you don't mind, but once Ind . . . Pierre gets an idea, he runs with it."

"It's wonderful, and it's giving me an idea. Could you get me some muslin or canvas?"

"Sure. What for?"

"My students could make their own winter counts."

"Bravo, Lily," he replied. Then he pointed to the packet of coal oil-soaked slivers on her desk. "First things first, though."

He laid an economical fire in the potbelly stove, using a balled-up bit of wrapping paper left over from yesterday's alphabet, followed by the coal oil sliver and then a little tent of kindling. Next came a larger tepee of medium-sized wood, followed by a log. He struck a match on the stove and set it by the paper and sliver. In a matter of seconds the fire caught. He stood to open the damper in the stovepipe, then closed the door.

"I'll tell Nick to keep the fire going for you. He can empty the ashes too."

He stood there and looked around the room, as though assessing it for solidity. He tapped the window and shook his head. "Don't like these gaps in the logs. And a south-facing window. Who ever thought that was smart?" he murmured, as though talking to himself.

"I don't understand," Lily said.

He tapped the window a little harder this time, as if holding it responsible for failure. "You can't see the blizzards coming from the northwest. Do me a favor. If it's a cloudy day, just go outside now and then and look to the north."

The potbellied stove had begun to heat the room, but Lily rubbed her arms from a sudden chill. "Then what?"

"If you see a big cloud moving fast, you grab the kids and run to the Buxtons, because it's closest."

"And if I don't look in time?"

"Stay where you are. I'll come and get you."

He said it with confidence and that capability she already suspected everyone on the Bar Dot took for granted. But there was a worry line between his eyes that she hadn't noticed before, at least, not before the surprise of last night's snow.

"Chapter ten tonight," she said, wanting to change the subject, because he was starting to frighten her.

"We'll see," he replied, which wasn't the answer she wanted, not with the uneasy feeling that had started in her heart and seemed to spiral out like a winter count. "I'm going out with all the hands today for some more firewood. They hate it, so I'd better go along. We'll see about tonight. Close the damper on that stove and it'll go out. It's getting too warm."

He touched his hand to his forehead, then put on his hat and left without another word. She stood in the door, enjoying her vantage point of the Bar Dot, wishing she could see it through Jack Sinclair's eyes. Cattle grazed everywhere. Jack had said there were too many.

She recalled the garrulous old rip who had sat next to her across Nebraska. Most people had at least asked her permission to sit, but he just plopped himself down. Maybe it was a perquisite of old age. She had tried to lose herself in her book, but he was having none of that. As the Union Pacific swayed from side to side and clacked along, he described "them early days out here, missy," the ones where the buffler grass was as tall as his horse's underbelly.

She looked around now, seeing grass cropped into nothing. Swirls of dust rose fitfully, then died. She tried to imagine the place in winter and had no point of reference. Winter in Bristol was a genteel matter, mostly more rain than usual that brought out the musty odor of wet wool on small children and the scent of burning leaves. When it did snow, the flakes seemed to toss about in the wind briefly and then settled on the grass, more picturesque than inconvenient.

The old fellow on the train had eventually worn himself out with words and slumbered all the way to the Grand Island Depot, where he woke when the conductor shook him and stomped off. Lily wished now she had asked him about winter.

CHAPTER 17

*S*chool began in the snow on Monday morning. *This is not a bad omen*, she told herself as she opened the door and took a deep breath, and another. She was no expert, but the snow had probably been falling most of the night. Looking around to make sure she was unobserved, Lily scooped up a handful and packed it into a ball. She threw it hard against the never-used hitching post in their yard and let out a cry of triumph when it connected and splattered, setting an observational crow scattering, with harsh words of his own.

"Splendid, daughter."

She turned around to see her father in the doorway, pulling on his gloves.

"My throwing skills will keep us safe from marauders and road agents as long as there is snow," she teased back, delighted at his interest.

He came down the step toward her and offered his arm, as he had done lately. He had managed forty-five minutes in the front room last night, which had made Jack Sinclair whisper, "Bravo, suh," when he finally retired.

Sinclair must have been on her father's mind, too, as they strolled through the ankle-deep snow to the cook-shack. "I don't think Jack will be delighted, however. I've certainly never seen the snow this early."

The foreman sat by himself in the dining hall, his lips on the coffee cup, his elbows on the table, the picture of discontent. Lily watched how he roused himself when Chantal came to him shyly, holding a bowl of mush. "You're a gracious lady," he said to her. "Is that a new bow in your hair?"

She twirled around so he could get the full effect. "Excellent in every way," he praised her. "Where did you come by such a bow?"

She moved closer, but Lily could still hear her. "Amelie told me *you* bought it when you went to town."

"I believe I did," he said. "I asked Mr. Watkins if he had a bow for a little girl starting school today."

At least you didn't get it from the faro dealer, Lily thought, amused.

"Miss Carteret, are you wearing anything new today since it is the first day of school?" Chantal asked.

"As a matter of fact, I am, but I shan't show you," she said.

"Please, Miss Carteret," Chantal begged.

"Yes, please, Miss Carteret," Jack teased.

At least you don't look so down in the dumps, Lily thought, even as she felt her face grow warm. "Since I must . . ." Lily carefully pulled up her shirt to reveal her sturdiest pair of shoes, the kind for standing on all day in front of a classroom.

"Smart and practical," Jack said.

"No, not these old things," she said. Wondering at the wisdom of this, she pulled her skirt a little higher to show off her new blue and white striped stockings. She had coveted them in the ladies' emporium in Bristol, and they were her first purchase with her miniscule quarterly allowance that Uncle Carteret parceled out with an eyedropper.

Chantal sighed with pleasure. Jack turned away, his shoulders shaking. Even her father smiled.

He was still smiling as they left the cookshack. Amelie handed Lily a waxed paper packet with bread and butter for her lunch, and a handful of dried apricots twisted into a clean handkerchief.

Chantal and Amelie skipped along ahead of her toward the school, their brother trailing along behind, his hands deep in his pockets, head down, sentenced to a term of school. Papa had tucked her arm through his again, maybe to steady himself, or maybe just because he wanted to. Lily preferred to think it was the latter.

"Tell me, Papa, why did you name me Lily?" she asked. "I'm going to ask my students about their names, because we are going to learn to write them today."

A cloud seemed to cross his face, but it passed so quickly she might have imagined it. "Your mother loved flowers, and her first choice was Lily."

"I've always liked Lily Carteret," she said.

Clarence sighed, as he often did, when owning a deficiency. "You probably don't even know that your middle name is Rose. I thought you were as pretty as an English rose."

She tugged him to a stop, her arm through his, and kissed his cheek. "That's quite the loveliest story ever."

"I should have told you sooner," he said, and she heard the regret.

"Now is good, Papa. Wish me luck today."

"I have, every day of your life," he said simply, and he gave her a small salute as he squared his shoulders and mounted the steps to his office in the Buxton house.

She stood there, transfixed, hoping for some childish reason that he would turn around before he went inside. When he did, her already full heart overflowed.

❧

The day was easily ordered. Luella sat by herself on the back row, so the Sansevers lined up in the first row. Lily had fashioned a roster out of a partly used ledger from the Bar Dot, Cheyenne Land & Cattle Company, courtesy of Clarence Carteret, and called roll, which made even Nicholas smile.

"There are only four of us, Miss Carteret," he said. "Can't you just look and see?"

"We're forming good, regular habits," she answered. "Who knows? Someday you may be sitting in a large lecture hall at a great university, where you will be required to answer with a resounding 'In attendance!' Let's begin it here."

No one had any objections, not even Nick. Maybe the idea of a university lecture hall appealed even to beginning cowhands.

Remembering Miss Tilton's pattern, she followed roll with a psalm. "Once we learn to read, we can take turns choosing a verse or two from the Bible."

Luella raised her hand. "I can read right now," she declared and looked around, pleased with herself.

"Then I will enlist your aid in helping me with the alphabet, our building block to Great Things," Lily said.

She handed each child a slate, slate pencil, and a cleaning rag. "We will be learning our alphabet and numbers on our slates, which we can erase, as needs be," she explained. "We will save true greatness for paper and pencil."

"I like true greatness," Chantal said softly.

"So do I," Lily said. She looked around her homely little classroom, with maps on one wall and a Lakota winter count on the other. True to Madeleine's promise, the starched letters looked alert and sharp, thumbtacked just above the blackboard, which someone had sanded to an amazing smoothness and then repainted. She suspected Preacher, but it could just as easily have been Jack or even Pierre Fontaine. Maybe everyone was going to become invested in her modest temple of education here in the middle of nowhere.

They worked diligently toward true greatness until eleven o'clock, when Lily quietly dismissed the Sansever children to help their mother. Nick left with a whoop and on a dead run, while his sisters followed. She watched them a moment, touched when the sisters joined hands and started skipping. *A sister would have been nice*, she thought. She turned to face Luella, who looked vaguely dissatisfied.

"Well now, it is the two of us until noon, when I believe Fothering plans to escort you home for luncheon. Shall we go over some simple words, since I know you are farther along than the others?"

"Nothing too strenuous," the child said. "Mama says I am delicate."

And I'm the czar of Russia, Lily thought, hiding her smile. "Let me put a few letters on my slate, and you see how many three-letter words you can make."

"That shouldn't wear me out," Luella said with that matter-of-fact simplicity Lily was coming to enjoy. "Mama said she would have Cook prepare a fortifying luncheon for me with time to lie down."

"Excellent," Lily said, thinking of Amelie and Chantal setting the tables and mashing potatoes and washing dishes, hurrying to keep up and finish, so they could pursue true greatness.

While Luella worked, Lily printed "TRUE GREATNESS" on some cardboard that Preacher had brought to the school last week. She outlined the letters and got out the one box of Franklin Colors that Jack had been able to afford. The children could take turns filling in the letters when they returned.

Luella outdid herself, creating three-letter words until she ran out of room on her slate. There was no mistaking her glow of pride when she handed over the slate with a little flourish.

"This is fine work, indeed," Lily praised her.

Luella leaned toward her and whispered, "I'm really not fragile, but Mama thinks I am."

"Your mama is concerned for your well-being," Lily said, wondering how a child like Luella could ever thrive in the hot house environment on the Buxton's second floor. Then she remembered her own upbringing and knew anything was possible.

When Fothering arrived to escort Luella to luncheon, he left her a slice of bread fried in bacon fat for Freak. "This should prove well-nigh irresistible to that miserable beast," he said with all the dignity of his office.

"You needn't support Freak's bad habits if you don't wish to," Lily said as she followed them out to put the offering on the rock.

"He amuses me," Fothering said in his top-lofty way, but ruined it with a Sam Foster wink.

Pleased, Lily sat at her desk and ate her bread and butter, finishing it off with a dipper of water from the pail inside the door, and the apricots. The snow had long melted and the air was brisk but warming. She would probably leave the door open for afternoon class.

As she sat at her desk, looking over the afternoon schedule, she heard the smallest of sounds and looked up to see Freak edging his way into the classroom. She sat still, almost holding her breath as the cat made a circuit of the room, flattening himself against the walls, as though he dared her to notice him. When he finished, he stalked out with as much majesty as a cat with chewed up ears and one eye could.

"That was unexpected, Freak," she said as he sauntered away. "Do you hanker after true greatness yourself?"

෴

She tackled numbers after the children returned, using twenty more or less even sticks that Pierre Fontaine had left for her at the table where she and her father usually ate. His note—*The Bos told me to mak thees*—in a careful hand, told her about his own skill level. What made them special were the little beads he had strung together and attached to each stick with a thumbtack.

Nick had done his best all morning to look bored, but the beaded sticks caught his attention. The sticks quickly became numbers on his slate as he copied the numbers she wrote on the board. After only the barest instruction, he leaned over to help Amelie. *Well, well,* Lily thought.

Then it was back to letters. She wrote their names on the blackboard in chalk and turned to face the class. "I will give you paper and pencils to trace your name. Tonight I want you to ask your mothers why you were named Luella, Chantal, Amelie, and Nicholas," she said, pointing to each child.

The children wrote their names, with Amelie taking out her pink pearl eraser to erase and start over.

"I have one of those too," Luella said and took hers out of the colorful pencil box she had set so conspicuously on her desk.

Amelie nodded. Lily hid her smile when Chantal pouted, because she didn't have one.

Better deflect a mutiny. "When you finish with your names, Chantal will hand out a color of your choice and we will make 'True Greatness' our motto. Preacher found us this cardboard."

"Motto?" Amelie asked.

"Something that inspires you to do your best," Lily explained. "We'll find a tall person to tack this over the blackboard and leave it there all year."

"Could we add other mottoes when we learn to read?" she asked.

"As many as we want." She glanced at her watch on her shirtwaist. "We had better hurry with your names so we can color."

Chantal raised her hand next. "Miss Carteret, would you write your name on the board too? Maybe your father would like to see your name tonight."

"I believe I will do that," Lily said and wrote Lily Rose on the blackboard. "There now."

They worked quietly and then selected one color from Chantal's fistful of Franklin Colors. Since her desk was the largest, Lily moved her books and spread out "True Greatness." They efficiently colored in the words she had outlined.

"If we border it with black around each letter, they will stand out more," Nick suggested.

"Excellent idea," Lily said, and she smiled when Nick flashed a grin her way, pleased with himself.

Where did the time go? Lily looked up to see Fothering standing in the door. She gestured him in. "See what we have done? Children, hold up our motto."

They did. Hand to his chin, the butler studied it, stepping back for a better view.

"Superior," he pronounced, which brought out more smiles. "You are tall, but I am taller. Miss Carteret, might you wish me to affix it to a conspicuous place in your classroom?"

"The more conspicuous, the better."

"Here, then," he said, pointing to the middle of the room, directly over the blackboard.

Pierre Fontaine had left a nail yesterday, after attaching the winter count. Chantal giggled when Fothering took off his shoe, stood on Lily's chair, and nailed the motto to the wall.

"*That* is a motto to be proud of," he said with a sweep of his hand. The gesture turned into an elaborate bow, which made even quiet Amelie put her hand to her mouth. "Miss Carteret, you are to be commended."

She laughed and dismissed the children. "Take your names home and remember what I said: Find out why you were named thus."

"My goodness, what a day," Lily said under her breath as the children, all of them guided by Fothering, walked down the hill, that improving walk that had convinced Mrs. Buxton to put the school such a distance from the other buildings. At least she built a school, Lily reasoned.

She looked around. Freak was nowhere in sight, but she already knew he wasn't impressed with crowds. She heard a horse coming from the north and stepped around the corner of the school to see who it was.

Jack Sinclair tipped his hat to her. He looked considerably more pleasant than he had that morning. The snow was gone, and she already knew he was the sort of man who couldn't sit idle for long.

"Have a moment?" she called.

He did, dismounting and coming into the classroom. His eyes went to the school motto.

"True Greatness," she said, touched to see how his eyes followed the two words he could not read. "It's our motto for the year. We have plans to learn to read and cipher and explore whatever else we happen onto."

"Is it going to work, Lily?"

"It is," she said with a nod.

He looked at the desks with their slates set just so, as she had requested. He pointed to Chantal's slate. "Nice flowers."

"They were supposed to wipe them off before they . . ." She stopped and put her hand to her cheek. Chantal had carefully printed Lily Rose on her slate and drawn two flowers. She doubted Chantal had ever seen a lily or a rose, but she knew zinnias, lined up against the cookshack like prisoners waiting to be shot and bent double by the wind, but zinnias nevertheless.

"It's my whole name," she said, her voice soft. "Papa told me this morning that my middle name is Rose." She looked at the foreman. "Is Jack your only name?"

"It's John James Sinclair. I was part of a twin that died. He was going to be James, so I got both names when they figured I was going to live."

She had been on the Bar Dot long enough to

learn a few things. "Tell me, do you have a brand for Bismarck?"

"I do, indeed." He picked up the clean slate from Amelie's desk and drew a circle, with two Js back to back. "Circle Double J. Ind . . . Pierre did it for me. I registered it last spring in Cheyenne. Some folks call my place the Double J, but I like Sinclair Ranch."

She took a piece of paper and printed his name. "There you are: John James Sinclair, and Jack underneath." She drew the brand too.

He took the paper from her and studied it; then he looked at her with that level gaze that allowed no wiggle room. He swallowed, but his gaze never wavered. "You know I can't read, don't you?"

"Do you want to learn?" she asked quietly.

"More than just about anything."

"Maybe instead of *Ivanhoe*, I could teach you," she said.

"Maybe both?"

"You drive a hard bargain, Mr. Sinclair," she said. Lily went to the apple crate that Fothering had tacked up to hold her paltry supplies and took out the extra slate. She handed it to him.

"Amelie told me that you bought one too many."

"I did it on purpose," he told her. "I just didn't know how to ask you. I'm too old for school." He took the slate pencil she handed him and stuck it behind his ear. The slate went under his arm. He went to the door and looked back, his eyes going to the motto.

"Here's a down-home, straight-from-Georgia expression for you, Lily: 'Chile, if you don't just beat all.'"

"What does it mean?"

"True Greatness, what else? See you tonight."

CHAPTER 18

School was new to all of them. They settled into a routine that felt strange at first—Nick still dragged his feet into class—but grew into a comfort that Lily felt in her bones. As her simple lessons gave structure to the four children in her charge, they gave Lily a purpose too. After the second day, when her students returned with stories of how they got their names, and even Nick seemed animated, she knew she would succeed.

Then came the third day, when the whole thing fell apart.

The morning began as the others: a reading of a psalm, and then the opportunity for class members to report on whatever interested them. Since she had been routinely ignored at Miss Tilton's and never close to her classmates, Lily wanted to make up that deficiency in the Bar Dot School.

True greatness struggled that third morning after Amelie had shyly mentioned she had found two yolks in one of the eggs she cracked for flapjacks.

"That *is* interesting, Amelie. Next time you get one of those, show me, will you?" Lily said. She looked around. "Any other events of note?"

Some red flag in her brain made her suddenly want to overlook the thundercloud that had settled on Luella's face. Were her braids finally too tight? Lily could not ignore the upraised hand. "Yes, my dear?"

Her lips pinched as tight as her braids, she looked

at the others. "One of you has purloined my Pink Pearl Eraser," she declared.

Her announcement was met with stares. Nick spoke up. "What on earth does that mean?"

Luella gave a put-upon sigh of indignation. "One of you ignorant Indians, or French, or whatever you are has stolen my Pink Pearl Eraser! I left it here on my desk and it is gone."

The stares turned into frowns. Lily knew she had to intervene.

"Luella, you must have misplaced it. No one would . . ."

"Chantal stole it," Luella interrupted. "She is envious that I have an eraser."

Chantal's mouth opened in shock, and her face drained of color.

"See? I told you!" Luella said. "That is the look of guilt!"

Chantal put her head down on her desk and sobbed.

Lily leaped to her feet. "Luella, that is quite enough," she said, struggling to keep her voice low when she wanted to grab the girl and shake her. "Chantal would never steal anything."

Sublimely confident, Luella folded her arms and stared hard at the sobbing child. "I stand by my accusation. If she will produce the eraser, I will consider the matter closed. I am being supremely magnanimous."

You're being a cruel little prig, Lily thought, at a loss. "That will be entirely enough, Luella," she said. She put her arm around Chantal. "You would never do such a thing."

Chantal shook her head, but the sobs continued.

"A thief and a liar," Luella said, digging a deeper rut through the previous calm of the little classroom. "I will tell my father and he will turn off Madeleine Sansever immediately."

Amelie gasped and turned as white as her little sister. Nick leaped to his feet, his fists balled.

Lily grabbed him, but he was strong. Using all her own

strength, she pinned his arms at his sides. "Stop, Nick! The eraser has merely been misplaced and we will find it. Luella, one more word and you will leave this classroom. Chantal, dry your tears."

Lily held her breath, wondering what she would do if Luella chose to ignore her. There was no need to feign indignation on her part. She drew herself up as tall as she could, which was tall enough, and kept her grip firm on Nick until she felt his shoulders sag and the tension leave his body.

Luella held her peace, staring straight ahead, her lips still tight together. She raised her chin and narrowed her eyes, announcing with her body language that her father was going to hear of this massive injustice. Lily's heart sank. *Please, please let that eraser be at her house*, she prayed, she who had never petitioned the Almighty because she didn't think He played fair.

"There now. We will continue with our letters this morning," she said finally. "Luella, take a good look at home tonight. I will go through the classroom carefully." *And find what?* she asked herself with some exasperation. *We have so little in this room. Where could the eraser be?* "There is probably a simple explanation for the disappearance of your eraser."

Chantal dried her tears. Nick sat down. Luella continued to stare straight ahead as though the sight of the Sansevers was abhorrent to her. Lily saw the fear in Amelie's eyes as Luella's threat sank home. Lily suspected that Mr. Buxton was entirely capable of doing what Luella said.

The day seemed years long, especially the hour that Lily spent alone with Luella while the Sansevers hurried to help their mother. When Luella opened her mouth, her eyes still full of ill-use, Lily put up one finger. "Not a word about this," she said. "You and I are here to study and that is all."

Luella glanced toward Chantal's desk. "We could look . . ."

"We will not. Now, let us see how many words you can create by adding letters to i-n-e." With a hand that shook, Lily wrote the three letters on Luella's slate. "You're a bright child and you can read already. Surprise me with two-syllable words, if you can."

When Fothering came to fetch Luella for lunch, Lily whispered in his ear what had happened as Luella walked ahead. "I don't know what to do. If she tells her father . . ."

The butler patted her shoulder. "Miss Carteret, she may tell her father, but I can assure you he pays little attention to what anyone says." He peered at her in such a kindly way that she wanted to burst into years like Chantal earlier and sob it out on his chest. "We'll get through this."

She nodded, feeling her own ruin and disgrace as a teacher settling around her ankles like a petticoat with a broken gathering cord. Three days into teaching and she had already failed.

‿◌◌◌

Somehow they all struggled through that miserable day, Nick the portrait of gloom, and Chantal and Amelie with fear in their eyes. Luella was calm and superior, and the Pink Pearl was nowhere in sight. At the end of the day, Amelie approached Luella with her own eraser in hand. She held it out to Luella, who stomped out, muttering about a used eraser that wasn't as good as her own.

Lily held up through dinner in the dining hall. When Jack came to their shack for his reading lesson and a chapter of *Ivanhoe*, she nearly sent him away, pleading a headache, which was no lie. He took one long look at her, and that was all she needed. Horrified with herself, she burst into tears. Humiliated, she tried to turn away but he took her arm and pulled her close, his hand on her hair, much as he had probably comforted the Sansever girls when their father died.

"What in the world is wrong?" he whispered into her ear. "Madeleine is looking nearly haunted, and the girls have been crying, even though they won't admit it." He handed her his handkerchief. "Blow your nose and tell me."

She did as he said. Jack had a way about him that demanded obedience without even exerting the dubious tool of a raised voice. He released her and she sat down. He sat close beside her but not touching. Her father retreated to his room.

Between gulps, she told him about the whole, horrible day. "Jack, I know Chantal is disappointed that she doesn't have an eraser, but she would never do that. I . . . I even thought maybe Nick might do something to sabotage the school, but . . ."

"Oh no," Jack said, his voice grim. "I made it perfectly plain to him that there would be school or I would not hire him. Did you look for the eraser?"

"Everywhere," she said, her nose deep in the handkerchief again. "After they left, I searched the little space under each desk where they can keep things. Luella's pencil case was in hers, but the others don't have anything."

Jack leaned forward, his elbows on his knees. "I'm at a loss," he told her.

"All I can do is carry on," she said.

"Luella wouldn't . . ."

"No, I am certain she would not," Lily said with conviction. "She was genuinely upset."

He sighed. "I'll ask the hands if they're playing a prank."

Her heart dreary and weighed down, Lily turned for comfort to the alphabet. She had written out the alphabet—upper- and lowercase letters—on a piece of cardboard. She sounded out each letter, which only reminded her how frustrating English could be.

"Sometimes C is hard, as in *cat*," she said, pointing to the letter. "Sometimes it is soft, as in *cease*. Sometimes it has a *ch* sound, as in *chaps*."

"We pronounce 'um shaps here." He grinned at her. "What do you say in England?"

She socked his arm. "We don't say the word there. Don't tease me."

"But it's fun when you get all huffy," he teased. "I recommend Sit Walter Scott now, because you're getting cranky and I have a pranking streak."

"I am n . . ." She stopped. "I probably am."

He picked up *Ivanhoe* and opened to the bookmark. She moved from the table to sit beside him on the settee.

He pointed at the page. "Huh. Chapter." He nudged her shoulder. "I know it's not shapter."

She couldn't help but laugh, and maybe she had her own pranking streak. She never would have suspected such a thing before Wyoming. "Shapter Twelve."

He pointed at the heading. "Chapter," he repeated "Ch, ch. Ta Waw."

"Put it together."

"Twa. Twelve."

"There's hope for you. 'Morning rose in unclouded splendor, and ere the sun was much above the horizon . . .'"

❦

In the morning over breakfast, Jack assured her that the cowhands weren't playing tricks on the schoolmarm.

"You believe them?" she asked, grasping at straws because she was at her wit's end over the eraser.

"Completely. They don't lie," he said. "Indian—you know, he likes Pierre now—wanted to know if anything else was missing."

She hadn't considered that. "I . . . I don't think so. I'll take a good look today." She sighed. "Provided anyone is in my classroom."

"I can't vouch for Luella, but the Sansevers will be there. I talked to Madeleine about this, and she is worried."

"So am I," Lily said simply.

On their walk to the Buxtons, Lily told her father what had happened. "I don't know what to do, Papa," she said. He stopped and looked at the Buxton's house as though it was the last place on earth he wanted to be.

"You'll think of something," he said and gave her a wistful smile. "Your mother was resourceful and you do remind me of her."

I have enough worries, she thought. She kissed his cheek, and continued walking that improving half mile that Madame Buxton, the imaginary invalid, had decreed for good health.

She was early, so she looked around the room she had already searched, hoping something would materialize and solve the dilemma of that dratted Pink Pearl eraser. She remembered what Pierre had asked Jack, so she changed her approach, trying to see if something else was missing.

Nothing. She stared at her desk, bare as usual, because her own teachers had instilled in her the virtue of a tidy desk at the end of the day. Something *was* missing, but she couldn't place it. "Bother it," she said out loud and opened the long drawer in her desk. There they were. She had planned to tack up the papers on which her students had printed their names so carefully. She reached in the little box of thumbtacks and remembered that she had put four thumbtacks on her desk last night to remind her to put up the papers in the morning.

She stared hard at her desk again, then looked under it, wondering if she had knocked off the little silvery tacks. Nothing again. With a sigh, she took out four more tacks and put up the papers. Amelie Lavinia, named after a favorite aunt. Chantal Celeste, named after another aunt.

Nicholas only, because he was born on the feast day of Saint Nicholas, December 6. Luella Lorna, because her grandmamas were Louise and Ella, and Mama liked *Lorna Doone: A Romance of Exmoor*, a book she read "during her anticipation," as Luella so primly put it.

The day dragged on, and not because there were any accusations this time. Luella had made life immeasurably worse. She had come into the classroom head held high and flounced to her seat. Lily watched as Chantal and Amelie snuck worried glances in her direction as they wondered what had happened at the Buxton house last night.

Luella knew what they were thinking, not so much because she was devious, but because she was smart and understood how the world worked. "I didn't say a word to anyone last night," she announced, without looking around. "Maybe I will tonight."

And that was all: the beginning of a thick, ugly silence that weighed them down. After lunch, Lily attempted some relief by instituting what had always been the best part of her day at Miss Tilton's.

She took a book from her top drawer, a much-read book, if the wear was any indication, that Stretch had given to her. The cover was of thick cardboard that he must have taped to keep the pages together. She held it up.

"Luella, since you have a little more skill with words, what is the title?"

Luella smiled and smoothed her tightly braided hair, preening with her superiority. She opened her mouth, then frowned. "I can read some of the words."

"Excellent! Read the ones you can read."

She squinted, and Lily made a mental note to try to convince her to sit on the front row.

"'Street Life in New York,'" she read.

"Very good. It is *Ragged Dick: Or Street Life in New York with the Boot Blacks*," Lily said.

"I am dubious," Luella said. "Is *this* an improving work?"

"I doubt it," Lily replied. "I think it will be fun. Listen, my dears."

She read one chapter, then two, and the atmosphere in the classroom relaxed. They wanted to protest when she put Stretch's bookmark with the Indian beads on a rawhide string in place. "More tomorrow. Now it's time for ciphering. I'll write these on the board and you copy them on your slates."

She wrote rapidly, beginning simply, because everyone knew so little about numbers, including Luella. When she finished, sat down, and said "Begin," the students applied themselves diligently. "Five minutes," she said, then unpinned her watch and set it on the desk, resolving to ask around tonight at supper for an alarm clock.

She stopped them at five minutes, pleased with the results. Luella had finished all but three, and Anna and Amelie followed with all but four. She looked at Nick's slate, pleased to see he had finished them all, and they were correct.

Encouraged, she wrote more numbers on the board, with the same results. Nick raised his hand. "Can you put three numbers instead of two numbers?"

She did. After a few minutes, Luella put down her slate pencil, her expression put-upon and abused. The Sansever girls shook their heads. Nick held up his slate with a flourish and she saw the pride in his eyes.

"Well done, Nick," she said quietly. "How did you do this?"

"I lined up some knives and forks from the kitchen last night and figured it out."

୧∞ꕯ

She told Jack and her father that night about Nick's accomplishment. Jack nodded, pride in his eyes as if Nick were his own boy. Her father smiled. "Train him well, Lily, and I'll let him tote the numbers for Mr.

Buxton," he said. It was the gentlest of teases, but it touched her heart.

"While I set the girls to working on their letters, I put up more numbers and timed him," she said as her own enthusiasm grew. "They were just small numbers, you know, just one plus three plus eight, but he finished in less than two minutes."

She touched the place on her shirtwaist where she pinned her watch and looked down in dismay. "I left my watch in the classroom," she said. She sucked in her breath. "I've got to run."

The night air was chilly, and she could see her breath, but Lily didn't bother with her shawl. She ran from the house, and Jack followed.

"Slow down. Ground's uneven," he said as a preliminary to taking her hand.

Please, please, please let it be there, she thought as she hurried the healthy half mile to the empty school.

She knew she should have grabbed the table lamp before she ran from her house, but there was enough moonlight to show her a bare desk. Even *Ragged Dick* was gone. No. She dropped to her knees as Jack watched and found the book on the floor in front of her desk. She sat back, dismayed. The little bead bookmark was nowhere in sight.

She could barely keep back the tears, but she had cried all over the foreman last night, and she didn't intend to do that again in her lifetime. Deep breath. "Jack, ask your hands again. Someone is giving us grief and I don't know why."

CHAPTER 19

*J*ack went even further at breakfast. He stood up in the dining hall and announced to his hands, the Sansevers, Lily, and her father that someone was playing a mean trick on the schoolmarm and it had to stop.

"She's lost her watch now, and that little beaded bookmark of yours, Stretch," he said.

Stretch shook his head in disgust. "I paid a whole dollar for that cuz somebody told me it belonged to Sitting Bull."

Pierre laughed. "The Lakota will tell a white man anything."

Stretch glared at him.

"And four thumbtacks yesterday," Lily added, remembering. "I can't have this. How can I know when we should change from reading to ciphering, or learning our letters? I need my watch. Oh, please."

All she saw were puzzled looks. Almost all. Pierre was regarding her with a frown, his lips pursed.

"Do you know something?" she asked point-blank.

"I might," he told her. He glanced at Jack, and the two men nodded.

In her anxiety, Lily wanted to pluck at his sleeve and hop up and down, but she was twenty-five years old and that would never do. She hated that her distress showed on her face, but she could see her one road off the Bar Dot dribbling away. Mr. Buxton would fire Madeleine over an eraser and the Sansevers would go heaven knows where.

Luella would reign supreme, and Mrs. Buxton would probably veto the teacher. She had thought to make something of herself in Wyoming Territory, but all she was making of herself was a fool.

Pierre must have seen it all on her face because he patted her shoulder. "You worry too much. Do something for me."

"Anything, if you can help me," she pleaded.

"Leave some more thumb tacks on your desk tonight."

"What?" she asked, mystified.

"And maybe a dime, if you have one."

That was about all the money she had. Lily nodded, past even wondering what on earth the Indian was going to do.

"Don't take too much of her money," Jack said, his voice lighthearted. Drat the man, but he was impervious to her upcoming ruin. "If you do, she won't even be able to buy half a plate of chop suey from Wing Li."

The two men chuckled. She tried to scrunch up her eyes, but it was too late. Lily felt the tears slide down her cheeks. She wasn't sure if she cried from fear or anger or helplessness or even sorrow that nothing was going to go right for her. She was her father's daughter.

She turned away, but they had seen her tears. She stood there in silence, listening to the clatter of crockery in the kitchen, where Madeline was hard at work, even though her world might be crumbling around her too. *I am giving up too soon*, Lily thought, embarrassed, as she listened to the sound of a woman with everything to lose, working. *Pierre Fontaine is trying to help me and I am giving up. Shame on me.*

She took a deep breath and left the dining hall, not stopping for her father. She walked in silence up the hill, determined to teach.

⌒∞⌒

"We shouldn't have laughed at her, boss," Pierre said.

"No. She's a little finely drawn right now," Jack agreed.

"Do you think she'll leave out them tacks and maybe a dime? Gotta have bait."

"She'll do it." Jack felt the heat rise from his neck and wished he had the Indian's dark complexion. "I should have said something. She's going to worry all day."

Pierre shook his head. "Nah, she isn't. I think she's mostly just angry at us now. That'll keep her going." He pointed with his lips toward the kitchen. "That's the worried one. Maybe I should tell her what I'm going to do."

"You just want more coffee with a half pound of sugar in it. It beats all how much sugar you Indians crave."

"That too." He tipped his hat to Jack. "See ya on the range. Same place?"

"Yep. Too many LC beeves hanging around. Time to move'um back, if McMurdy and his boys won't come get them."

Lily did look angry, Jack decided as he watched her walk up the slope, her shoulders set and her stride more purposeful than usual. She had a pleasant sway to her hips that he probably could have watched a little longer, except that the boys were getting ready to ride, and he couldn't afford the luxury of standing there mooning over a pretty lady who probably would have thrashed him into next Thursday because he had laughed at her predicament. *Time to toughen up, missy*, he thought. *Tears won't cut it.*

They would have cut it, he decided a few hours later as they chivvied LC cows away from Bar Dot land. If he had been alone, he would have tried to soothe her agitation. Still, Lily Carteret could use a heavy dose of patience. When nothing was going right was the time to hunker down like a prairie chicken and ride out the storm.

Of course, it had taken him several years of near starvation and raw deals as he slowly learned the cattle business.

He rode a little apart from his crew, remembering those bad days after the war, when former rebels were fair game. It had led to beatings in alleys until he learned to keep his mouth shut.

He owed part of his hard-earned wisdom to a sheriff who had found him bleeding and hungry in one of those alleys. The man had prodded him with his boot just to make sure he was alive, then picked him up, slung him over his shoulder, and plopped him down on a cot in the jail.

"No, no, you're not under arrest," the lawman had told Jack when he groaned and came around. "It's cold out and you're not fit for it. I'll leave the cell door open. You can leave when you please."

Jack felt only gratitude for the warmth. He was unprepared for the bowl of thick stew and two rolls—merciful heaven, two!—that the sheriff left without comment. He ate like a wolf and then slept all night under a blanket. He couldn't even remember the last time he had slept in an actual building.

By morning, Jack had sorted himself out and knew this good time couldn't last forever. He had made his way from the cells to the room where the sheriff sat, playing solitaire. When the man saw him, he folded the cards and leaned back in his chair, the better to take a good look.

Jack had thanked him for the food and the bed for the night. It was snowing lightly, but he knew he had to leave. Laramie wasn't running a charity hotel, after all. He started for the door, but the sheriff had stopped him. He scribbled a note, folded it, and handed it to Jack.

"There's a ranch two miles west of here, the T Bar, my brother Tom's place," the sheriff said. "He'll put you up and teach you something, if I say so."

Jack had thanked him again. Two miles in the snow

wouldn't be pretty, but he had walked much farther for Stonewall Jackson. He had stopped at the door. "If you don't mind, suh, why're you doing this?"

The man had chuckled, sort of like he and Pierre had chuckled at Lily. "Tom and I are from Virginia, but we don't advertise it. Get rid of that chip on your shoulder. We lost the war, and it's over."

He had leaned across the desk then, looked Jack in the eye, and handed out the foundation of Jack's Western education. "Lad, you can only make so many bad decisions before they either kill you or you learn something."

Jack didn't reckon that Lily had made too many bad decisions. Maybe it *was* different for women, because he knew she hadn't been given a fair shake in life. Still, he hoped she learned something, and quick, because he was finding her more interesting by the day.

The Indian caught up with him an hour later, as they were trailing LC cattle north to their own range. He looked around. "Too many cattle, and pretty much as thin as ours."

Jack nodded and looked where Stretch was pointing. "It's LC hands," he said, after they came closer. "Wondered when we'd see them."

He recognized the rancher, Mike McMurdy, and loped to his side. The man was full of apology and excuse, something he was famous for, but Jack listened patiently. What he heard chilled him.

"We've been in the saddle for days, and my boys are tired," the rancher said. "We can't keep'um from moving south. It's like they know something."

"They do," Jack said. "You have a big herd of Texas cattle, don't you?"

McMurdy nodded and gave a dry laugh. "They all want to go back to the Lone Star State." He swore long and fluently. "What's up, Jack?"

"A winter like we've never seen before, and they know

it." He raised both hands when the man started to speak. "I don't know how they know, but they do!"

"So they're going to drift, no matter what?"

"They are." Jack hated to say it, hated to give voice to his deep fear, but there it was. "They're not smart, but they know more'n we do."

Again that dry chuckle, followed by increased fluency in words so choice that Jack nearly felt his ears singe.

"My advice to you is move'um north as best you can. I don't want your Texas cattle in Bar Dot herds."

"We could use fences."

"No doubt, but a bit late to save us. G'day to you."

They parted company. Jack sat by himself, looking to the northwest where only a few idle clouds drifted by. It was a picture-perfect September, but the cattle milled in little bunches, looking northwest too. At some cow signal, they turned and continued their relentless slog south.

The men of the Bar Dot spent the day with the LC boys, coaxing cattle against their will. Other brands began to show up, and more cowhands. By midafternoon, the herds were finally separated and moving north again, but it was a surly and mean bunch of cattle thwarted in their instincts.

By the time the shadows changed and stretched, the men had done all they could. Tomorrow the same struggle would begin again. A disgruntled bunch themselves, the Bar Dot men rode south toward stables and food. The satisfaction Jack felt to see their own herds placidly grazing and chewing was short-lived, because he knew cattle were ruled by consensus. When the new Texas herds broke for the southern plains again, as he knew they would, they would sweep all before them.

He knew he needed a diversion and hoped Lily wasn't too distracted by her own worries to read another chapter. Funny how a story about knights and the Crusades could take a body out of his own worries. What magic did words play in compelling him to care about Rebecca and the Old Jew?

It had to be more than that. He enjoyed the way Lily read, her accent so clipped and precise, each word an obedient little soldier. For a few years after he left the South, he had missed the leisurely way words just took their sweet time. The harder he worked and the busier he got, he had less patience for such time wasted. Lily's accent suited him right down to the ground.

They rode past the school long after she had adjourned for the day, but the door was open so he dismounted and motioned to the Indian to join him. They walked toward the open door. The grass stirred and Indian leaped back when Freak came at him, hissing. Jack laughed, at the same time glad it was Pierre and not him.

The Indian clapped his hands and waved his Stetson. Freak backed away before turning around with a vast amount of disdain and vanishing into the cottonwoods.

"Do you think he scares the kids every morning?" Pierre asked, keeping his voice low as if afraid Freak would hear and respond in his inimitable way.

"Nope. Looks to me like he was protecting Lily."

Pierre gave him a look and stared at the sun. "Sunstroke getting your brain, boss?"

Jack went inside, where Lily sat at her desk. Her hands were folded and she stared down at them, a woman at her wit's end. She looked up and he saw all the misery, but no tears this time. Maybe she was a quicker learner than he had been.

"Chantal and Amelie are so frightened of what Luella might do that they can barely study," she said. She looked beyond him to the Indian. "Pierre, here are my thumbtacks and my dime."

"That's all I need. I'm going to come back and just sit here by the door, all quiet like."

"If this is dangerous, I'd . . . I'd rather you didn't," she told him.

"I'll be fine. I'm a tough Indian."

✑

Jack had to give her credit. With a certain steely resolve that he nearly envied, Lily coached him in sounding out small words. *Bat* and *cat* became *battle* and *cattle*, and he began to see the possibilities.

Through it all, Clarence Carteret sat in the rocking chair, watching his daughter with pride. He seemed more at ease, to Jack's eyes, and Lily said as much, when he finally surrendered to his vices and retired.

"I think it was an hour this time," she whispered, and then the worried look returned. "I'm not certain because I don't have a watch. Maybe I'm just looking for improvement so hard that I'm unrealistic."

"It was an hour this time," he told her, not certain either. He knew she needed good news, and that was enough for him.

"Chapter thirteen," she said, taking the book from the shelf by the two photographs.

She held it, and he knew her heart wasn't in the tale tonight, so he pointed to the pictures instead, noticing that someone had polished the frames until they shone.

"Don't bother with *Ivanhoe* tonight," he said, even though he yearned to hear more. "Tell me about your mother. Do you remember her?"

"Oh, yes," she said and returned the book to the shelf. She outlined her mother's figure in the frame. "We left Barbados when I was five. I . . ."

She stopped as someone tapped on the door, just a light tap, but Jack knew who it was. She opened the door and there was Pierre, grinning and holding up her watch.

CHAPTER 20

ily reached for the timepiece, her heart so full of gratitude and relief that she couldn't speak. She motioned Pierre inside, but he took her hand and placed the Pink Pearl eraser in her palm, curling her fingers around it.

Her knees were doing funny things, so Jack led her to the settee and sat her down.

"Who? How?"

"I left the thumbtacks behind," Pierre said. "Couldn't swipe the whole stash, not after he worked so hard to get it."

"He?"

Pierre turned to the foreman. "Who, how, and he?" he asked, his voice most solemn. "I speak more English than that."

The best she could manage was a nervous giggle. Her hands shook until Jack grasped them in his hands, warming them as a side effect.

While she sat on the settee, her hands held and warmed, Pierre went gracefully to his haunches so he could look in her eyes. "It was a Little Man of the Prairie, a pack rat," he told her. "I was puzzled until you mentioned tacks. They love shiny things." He shrugged. "'Course, the eraser fooled me. Maybe he wanted a change."

"I don't even begin to understand this," Lily said. She moved her fingers and Jack released them.

"Get a lamp. I'll show you." Pierre stood up as effortlessly as he had sat down and left the house.

Lily grabbed the lamp on the table, which Jack kindly took from her because her hands were still shaking.

"I'd hate to have you start a range fire and make our situation even worse," he said.

The schoolroom looked just as she had left it, except that Pierre must have moved one of the stools to the shadows by the door.

"I just sat there and waited," he said. "Sure enough." He pointed to the opposite corner of the room, where Lily had noticed a hole in the floorboard.

"That's it?"

"Yep."

Pierre lifted the board and Jack held the lamp closer. "There's plenty of room for the Little Man, but I pried it up, and the one next to it, so I could take a good look. See?"

Lily leaned closer.

"Go ahead and kneel down," Pierre told her. "He's long gone, at least for now."

"I am *not* reassured," she said, and the men laughed. "Very well."

Apprehensive at first, not eager to see a rat staring back, she knelt and peered into the opening. In a moment, her natural curiosity took over. "It's a nest, isn't it?"

"Nest, food pantry, treasure room, what you will," Pierre said. He moved some of the grass and bits of cloth aside. "Look."

Lily laughed to see hairpins that she knew were hers. "That little dickens! I repinned my hair during lunch only two days ago, because it was warm. Oh, and look!" She took out a little bell, and another, and rang them.

"Hawk bells," Pierre said. "People of my nation put them on their special clothes. Dig around and you'll probably find some beads."

She did, seeing beads of all sizes. And there was

the beaded string Stretch had used as a bookmark for *Ragged Dick*. She took it out. "Do you think . . . Did Sitting Bull . . . ?"

Both men shook their heads, grinning.

"So, Miss Lily, your little criminal is a pack rat." Pierre picked up a shiny nib from a pen. "I think he's been robbing the Bar Dot blind for years and stashing everything here, where it was quiet. Tell me: Did you find a pebble on your desk where you left your watch?"

"My goodness, now that you mention it . . ."

"The Little Men are sociable and they like to trade," Jack said. "I got two pebbles for a nickel-plated timepiece once."

"And there were little bits of grain or grass where the thumbtacks used to be," she said. "I wish I had thought to mention that to you."

"We'd have known right away and spared you some anxiety," Jack said. Something must have caught his eye because he gently pulled aside more bedding to reveal a cuff link. The gold gleamed dull and real, and Pierre whistled.

"Looks like he thieved in one of the consortium member's room," Jack said. He chuckled and covered it up again. "No loss."

Both men looked at her then, and she knew what they were going to ask. Lily shook her head. "No. Other than what we know is ours, we'll leave the rest here. Don't kill the Little Man."

"That, my dear, is the right answer," Jack said. "He's just doing what pack rats do."

Lily still held her watch. She pinned it to her shirtwaist and pocketed the eraser. Stretch's bookmark went back to the business of marking *Ragged Dick*, but she put the book in her drawer this time.

"Pierre, could you come to my class tomorrow morning? I'll return Luella's dratted eraser and we'll show them the hole. I'd like you to tell them about pack rats.

Could you draw one on the board for me? We'll turn it into a lesson."

"Can I, boss?"

"Sure. We'll just be pushing back the Quarter Circle cattle that we pushed back yesterday. You'll have more fun here." He looked around the room. "We'd all have more fun here, because I really think Miss Carteret is a teacher." He gave her a look that she knew she would remember. "It just took a plan to tease that out."

∽

Maybe it'll be a very good lesson, Lily thought the next morning as she prepared for school. "I wonder, Luella, if you are up for an apology?" she murmured.

She had taken the time last night, after Jack and Pierre returned her home, to walk back to the Buxtons, knock quietly on the door, and speak to Fothering, who sighed with relief. At her request, he promised not to say anything to Luella.

As she walked her father to work and continued up the hill, Lily couldn't help patting her little watch, grateful it wasn't gone forever. She carried an alarm clock that Fothering had loaned her. It was far too large for even an ambitious pack rat like theirs to stuff down any hole.

School began in the usual way with Luella looking more glum than typical. Lily wanted to think that her accusation and the resulting disruption to the classroom was preying on the girl's mind, but who knew the mind of a child, especially one used to being the center of attention? She sucked in her breath and looked down at her desk as a new idea pelted like a bit of hail. Or maybe a child wanting attention she didn't get at home.

Lily was writing short words on the board for her students to copy when Pierre Fontaine knocked on the open door. She was pleased to notice that he had shaved and his braided hair flowed free this time. Maybe he had even washed it for the special occasion when *he* would be the teacher.

"Children, you might have noticed that I have my watch back." Lily reached in her desk and took out the Pink Pearl, handing it to an open-mouthed Luella. "Mr. Fontaine solved our mystery and found the thief. Sir?"

The Indian was no showman. He walked to the corner of the room. He motioned to the students, who clustered around him. When he pulled back the two boards, everyone said, "Ahhh."

The nest was unoccupied, which made Lily wonder if the Little Man had abandoned his cache. Just as interested as she had been last night, she watched as Pierre told her students about pack rats: their habits, their nests, and their little lives as tidy citizens of the mountains and plains, and occasional burglars.

"He means no harm, but he loves shiny things," Pierre explained as he took out the rat's treasures, from thumbtacks to the one gold cuff link, to bits of metal that might have gleamed and tempted him or an ancestor years ago. He replaced them and sitting on the floor with her students sitting around him, he answered their questions.

Nick had a question for Lily. "Are . . . are we just going to leave him there?"

"What do you children think?" she asked in return. "He's only doing what Little Men do."

Nick looked at his sisters and Luella and everyone nodded. "Maybe we could just leave him alone." His eyes showed his concern. "Mr. Fontaine, will he come back?"

"I believe he will, if he feels you mean no harm," the Indian replied.

"We could test that by leaving something for him, couldn't we, Miss Carteret?" Nick asked.

They all looked at her and she couldn't help her laughter. After all, she was no professional, and what good were stern looks and solemnity? "I won't use my watch for bait."

They laughed. "I can, um, acquire a thimble," Luella offered. She smiled for the first time in a long time. Her braids were so tight that her eyes seemed to disappear. "*I'll* be the one purloining."

"I'll leave that to your conscience," Lily teased in turn. "We have more thumbtacks."

The children nodded. Chantal leaned against Pierre's arm and looked up at him. "Does the Little Man sleep through the winter?"

"No, he does not," Pierre told her. "If you could find seeds and grasses, he would hide those away too." He touched Chantal's head and stood up. "And I should go to work." He nodded to Lily. "After I draw the Little Man on your dark-painted wall."

Without any urging, the children returned to their places and watched as Pierre drew on the blackboard a rodent with large ears that had as much body as fluffy tail. Lily gulped, not certain she wanted a rat roaming under the floor in her classroom. A glance at the interest on all the children's faces told her that, yes, she did.

As the children drew their own pack rats on paper, she looked at the beautiful buffalo hide winter count that Pierre had loaned to her classroom of True Greatness. "D'ye think, sir, that I can convince your boss to permit you to tell my children about winter counts?"

"It'll take no convincing," the Indian said in his straightforward way. "I've noticed that he's happy to help you."

"He's interested in education," Lily said, even as her face felt warm.

"That too," he replied with a smile.

Heavens, Lily, stop talking, she scolded herself. She walked Pierre to the classroom door. She held out her hand and he shook it. His handshake was light and delicate, telling her that Indian men did not usually touch anyone's hands like that.

"Thank you," she said. "You're a good teacher, Pierre Fontaine."

"Not as good as you."

"Oh, I . . ."

"Just look at them," he said simply and released her hand. "See you later, Teacher."

Lily watched him head back down the hill, noticing at the same time that Freak the scary cat was watching him too. When Pierre grew smaller and smaller, Freak came closer, his eyes still on the retreating figure. For the smallest moment—she quickly dismissed the notion—Lily wondered if Freak had decided to be her protector.

She threw up her hands and went back into the classroom, walking around to watch her children. Oh, they were hers. How did that happen? Nick wasn't much of an artist, but Luella's effort looked remarkably like the Little Man of the Prairie that Pierre had drawn. Lily couldn't help a little shiver, hoping that the pack rat would confine *his* education to after hours, when the school was empty.

When the children finished, she asked, "Should we pin them up here or take them home?"

"Here, I think," Nick said, reminding her that he had the makings of a leader already. He cocked his head a little to one side, looking like his mama. "If we tell you the words, could you write a little something to go along with the pictures?"

"I can," she said. "Perhaps we could just pull our desks together closer to mine, and we'll all decide what to say." She looked at Luella. "Luella is a little farther along with writing. Should we let her write our final version for the wall?"

The Sansevers all nodded. Lily looked at Luella, surprised to see the tears in her eyes. "Is that satisfactory with you, Luella?" she asked, unsure of herself.

Luella nodded, then took a deep breath and stood

beside her desk. She looked directly at the blackboard first, then at Chantal. "I owe you an apology, Chantal," she said, her voice tight with emotion. "You didn't steal my eraser. I am sorry."

A child of impulse, Chantal reached out and touched Luella's hand, and her eyes filled with tears too. "That's all right." She dabbed at her eyes. "Would you like to sit on the front row with us?"

Luella nodded. Nick stood up, bowed to her, and pulled her heavy desk closer to the rest of them, while Lily surveyed the effect. "I like this, but let's go a little farther," she said. "Let's move our desks into a u-shape and I'll move my desk closer."

Without a word, her children did as she said. When they were all seated again, shy Amelie raised her hand.

"Yes, my dear?" Lily asked. Maybe she shouldn't say "my dear," but she was not really a teacher, so what did it matter? No one seemed to mind.

"I think we will learn better this way," Amelie said.

"I believe you are right," Lily said, swallowing the boulder in her throat. "Now, let us decide what we want to say about our Little Man."

The afternoon's lesson plan went out the window as a better one took over. By the time the school day ended, Luella's neatly printed statement about the pack rat was tacked to the wall opposite Pierre's winter count and surrounded by five pictures, Lily's included.

There was only time to make one last assignment. "Mr. Fontaine said that pack rats don't hibernate. Let's think about what little bits of food he might like. We could bring him something every day or so for him to hide."

The children decided that raisins and seeds might be best. Nick suggested coffee beans, but his classmates firmly vetoed this victual. "Mama has lentils and there are oats," Amelie said. "Coffee beans would keep him awake, Nick."

The others giggled, and Nick had to smile too.

"Maybe he's English like Miss Carteret and likes loose tea," Chantal teased, her eyes on Lily.

Nick threw back his head and laughed. Chantal and Amelie looked at each other. Lily wondered what had just happened, but she had no trouble teasing back. She put her hands on Luella's shoulders. "What do you think, Luella? Loose tea or coffee beans?"

"Tea," Luella said decisively. She leaned back ever so slightly against Lily and sighed, as though a great load had been lifted from her young shoulders. Or if not lifted, at least rearranged to become more manageable.

What other burdens do you carry, Luella? Lily asked herself, wondering how solitary the child's life really was, once the school day was over. She would have to ask Fothering. Whatever he said, Lily knew there were ways, good ways, to give the lonely child the attention she craved. Maybe teaching with True Greatness was going to require at least as much understanding of her children as the alphabet and numbers. Only a week ago, such a thought would have terrified Lily. Now she welcomed it.

CHAPTER 21

֍

"What a day," Lily said softly as she said good afternoon to her students and watched them march away, Nick leading the little parade with Luella right behind. Satisfied as never before, she turned around and surveyed the classroom, making sure all objects that would snare the Little Man's interest were safely tucked in her desk drawers. Knowing he must have had a difficult two days, she took two hairpins from her chignon and left them on her desk as a peace offering.

She closed the door quietly behind her and looked to the tree line. Freak stood there, his tail twitching. He took a step forward, thought better of it, and retreated.

"Never mind, I say," she told him. "We have all year. Just leave the pack rat alone, do you hear?"

He narrowed his eyes as if to say, "You're talking to a cat, imbecile."

Lily took her time. The September sun felt good on her face, but there was no denying the chill underlying the sun's warmth, like the suddenly colder current in a shallow stream. She sauntered past the cookshack, where the door stood open.

When Madeleine saw her, Lily waved. The widow blew her a kiss, but that wasn't enough. As Lily watched, Madeleine wiped her hands on her apron and ran out the door, her arms held open wide. She grabbed Lily in an unexpected embrace, rocking her from side to side, speaking in French.

"My French isn't so good," Lily said as she hugged the woman back.

Madeleine just held her in her arms. "Chantal and Amelie told me."

"About Luella's apology?"

"*Oui*, but my dear, even better: Nicholas laughed." Madeleine's face grew serious. "He has not laughed since . . . you know."

Lily took a deep breath. "Then this was a good day for all of us."

Over her protests, Madeleine gave Lily an extra helping of mashed potatoes that night at supper, which she divided with her father. As she chatted with him, it was her turn for her mind to wander. She glanced at Pierre Fontaine, sitting next to Jack. He sat cross-legged on the bench, which suggested to her that the Indian wasn't totally resigned to his cowboy world. She wanted to ask Jack where he had come from.

On the way west, she had looked with interest on a handful of Indians riding in the same railcar, accompanied by white men in dark suits and a man who looked neither one nor the other, in a suit but wearing moccasins. Her curiosity overcame her shyness—after all, wasn't she neither one nor the other?—so she said thank you when he held a café door open for her at one of the stops for meals. She held back a bit and found herself at the lunch counter at the same time he was.

"Excuse me, sir, but where are these Indians going?" she had managed to whisper as the harried server practically flung cheese sandwiches with some sort of mystery meat at them and held out her hand for a dime. Never mind that Lily had whispered for tea and toast.

He had looked at her with interest of his own when he heard her unfamiliar accent, and with his lips, indicated a bench outside the crowded café. Shy and wondering if she had just violated some fearsome taboo of travel, she sat with him as he looked at his sandwich with vague displeasure. He took a bite and rolled his eyes. "At least it is food," he had said, which made her smile. "Or something like," he added, which made her chuckle.

"They are Lakota," he told her as she ate, "back from a visit to the great white father's house."

When he could tell she did not understand, he tried again. "Washington and big fat man name of Cleaverland."

"My goodness, the president of the United States," she had said, having gleaned some information from an old newspaper someone had left behind on a train seat. "Did they have a good visit?"

He shrugged. "Someone stole their souls and took pictures, and Cleaverland and his men talked a lot, but nothing will change."

That thought wasn't going to digest any better than the sandwich. "They are going home now?"

He had smiled faintly at that question. "Never home. Back to a little piece of land they don't much like."

"And you? Where do you go?"

"Same place. I am the man who tells the white men and the Lakota what the other is saying."

"You are the interpreter?"

He had nodded and gave her a shrewd look, one that she knew took in her olive skin and West African features, mingled with French and what have you. "You are like me—you have a foot in two worlds."

The train whistle had sounded then and the conductor started swinging his lantern and shouting, "Booard! Booard!" Lily left her half-eaten sandwich on the bench, even though she was certain not even a stray dog would be that hungry.

Without missing a step, the interpreter scooped up her left-behind food and tucked it in his overcoat. "You never know when you might be hungry for nearly anything," he said with no embarrassment. He had returned to his section of the train compartment and she to hers. He had looked at her a few more times before the entourage got off at Ogalala, and tipped his hat when they left. She thought about him a long while and wished there was some way to have made more of his acquaintance. A foot in both worlds.

◈

Jack put on a clean shirt that night for his visit to the Carteret's shack. He had shaved two days ago, but it never hurt to revisit that sun-wrinkled face he knew so well and do some more efficient resurfacing.

Same old face, right down to that still-impressive scar. Jack rubbed his chin, pleased that at least the thing didn't hurt. He debated a moustache and discarded it again. Better to do nothing. After all, she had seen his face for a few weeks now.

And he had seen hers. She reminded him of the pretty half-daughters of the nearest plantation owner, their mother a woman of color who worked in the plantation kitchen. Everyone knew about it, even the planter's wife, but there they were, a fact of Southern life.

His own kind—the sharecropping, white trash kind—were none too particular about a little color in their own background, except his father, who wouldn't countenance such things. He had warned Jack a time or two, but died a few years before Jack reached that age when he might have gone looking for a wife, had not a war intervened. The matter became moot then, as he struggled to fight and stay alive in a war he didn't care much about, except that it took him from the desperation of that poor farm in Georgia. He hadn't regretted leaving it or the South.

He had no doubt that Lily Carteret was several genteel cuts above him, no matter the shade of her complexion. Her father was a gentleman, even though he was a remittance man and an alcoholic. The back of the photo of Lily's mother that had been in his possession for several months had the stamp of a studio in Bridgetown, Barbados. Mrs. Carteret had been an islander, where mixes and matches through a century or two had produced the world's most lovely women, in Jack's estimation. Ah, well. Lily didn't mind him, and they could surely be friends.

He flattered himself that Lily had been watching for him, because the door opened before he even raised his hand to knock. Her excitement was palpable, but she took his hat politely and motioned to the packing crate settee as elegantly as if he sat in an English parlor. But her eyes! How lively they were, how wide and beautifully brown.

"I gather the day went well," he said, once he sat down. "The Little Man of the Prairie didn't frighten anyone?"

"Oh, heavens, we're just hoping that the whole kerfuffle didn't frighten him away."

He said hello to her father, who was sitting in the rocking chair with a back issue of the *Cheyenne Tribune* open. Clarence Carteret nodded his own greeting and returned to the paper he had probably read half a dozen times already, if the creases were any indication. At least he was sober and awake.

Lily sat beside Jack, turned a little and facing him, her enthusiasm so charming. "Jack, we created a whole lesson around the pack rat, and everyone is committed to supplying him with food." She sighed. "I hope he'll be back."

"Time will tell," he said, and it sounded so perfectly insipid that he wanted to roll his eyes.

"What was even better, Luella apologized to Chantal for accusing her of theft. That takes courage." She looked at him, those lovely eyes troubled. "I stopped to talk to Fothering, and he told me that she is mostly ignored at the Buxton house."

Clarence was now asleep in his chair, but she moved a little closer, as if she feared that legions were lined up outside with an ear to the thin wall. "Perhaps this is rude of me, but what on earth is wrong with Mrs. Buxton that she cares not to mother her only child?"

He had no enlightenment for her, but he knew from experience it wasn't a normal family. As he wondered how much to tell her, he couldn't overlook Lily's inquiring eyes. He felt his face grow warm, which only reminded him that his was no poker face, even if he had won her father's ranch on the turn of a card.

"What are you not saying?" she asked.

"I . . . I think she just likes to be sick," he managed.

Lily's own expression told him that she wasn't satisfied with his lame answer. He could say more, that Mrs. Buxton just seemed to be bored and suffered her own lack of attention from Mr. Buxton. Beyond that, he knew he would never tell Lily about the time he answered a summons to her bedroom, ostensibly for a shopping list in town, and found her ready for a diversion he wasn't inclined to provide. In fact, he couldn't leave the room fast enough. When Jack mentioned the matter that night to Preacher, his hand had said something about Potiphar's wife.

"She's bored," Jack said in his official foreman tone of voice that discouraged further discussion.

To his relief, Lily nodded. " 'Tis a pity she can't see that Luella just wants some love and attention." She became all businesslike. "Now, sir, let us forge ahead to two syllable words."

They did, moving to the table. He carefully copied the random collection of letters at the top of his slate and made words. When he finished, she looked over his slate. As he had hoped, she paused at the word *yall*, then tapped the slate with her fingernail.

"That is not a word, Jack."

"Sure it is," he told her, not trying to hide his smile. "I say it all the time. '*Yall* hurry up shoveling out that, uh . . . that, uh. . ."

"Manure?" she offered helpfully, her eyes lively. "*Yall* is still not a word."

"Y'all. I am from Georgia and that's what we say. You've heard me."

She folded her hands and eyed him. "Very well! I will concede that *yall* is a word, but let us add an apostrophe here. Now I will allow it, even though it's only one syllable, and you are beyond that. Y'all."

They looked at each other and burst into laughter, which made Clarence Carteret start from his doze and looked at them, owl-like.

"I'm sorry, Papa," Lily said. "He's being funny."

Clarence put down his paper and narrowed his eyes. "Behave yourself, Mr. Sinclair," he said, and then his lips twitched.

The three of them laughed, after which Clarence stood up, kissed Lily on the top of her head, and said, "Good night, y'all," as he went to his bedroom.

Lily looked so pleased that Jack could not resist. "Sir, no, I'm afraid that when you are addressing two or more people, it is most properly 'all y'all.'"

Clarence just shook his head and laughed as he closed his door. Jack glanced back at Lily, who seemed to be struggling. "What happened?" he asked softly, not wanting to disturb her further.

"He made a joke," she said simply and dabbed at her eyes.

"Bravo, Lily," he said. "You're good for him."

"Am I?" She sounded so hopeful and suddenly as young as Chantal.

He nodded and pointed to *Ivanhoe* because he really wanted to cuddle her on his lap, and that would never do in a million years. "You are. Now, chapter twenty, is it?"

She read the chapter, pausing now and then to point at small words. "Your turn," she would say, and he read too. It was a small thing, but he felt his whole body expand with the pleasure of reading.

He didn't want the chapter to end. *Ivanhoe* seemed a bit wordy to him, but Sir Walter could have added another page or two of something, anything, just so he could listen to Lily read. Jack couldn't help but wonder if Nick Sansever had fallen in love with her yet. Good thing he, Jack Sinclair, was just a friend.

Nick. That reminded him. After she closed the book and returned it to the shelf, he stood and wondered just how brave he was. She handed him his hat.

"I have to tell you something, Lily," he said. "Madeleine was in tears when she told me how delighted she was that Nick had laughed in your class today. Chantal told her." He managed a self-conscience laugh of his own. "Why do women cry when they are happy?"

"I am convinced we are an entirely different species," she joked in turn, then her eyes grew serious. "They've suffered so from their father's death."

"Y'all are so right," he said, hoping to see her smile again. He took a deep breath. "This is from Madeleine. Just so you know. She told me to give you a kiss on each cheek as her thanks."

He thought she might step back in surprise, but Lily was equal to the task. She stepped forward without any hesitation he could notice and turned her cheek to him. He put a hand on each shoulder, but lightly, and kissed one cheek and the other. She smelled of rose water.

"Good night. I hope the Little Man shows up," he said in farewell.

It had been a long day of turning back other ranchers' cattle, but Jack still had a hard time falling to sleep that night.

CHAPTER 22

For two days, the Bar Dot Temple of Education looked for the Little Man. Anxious eyes met hers every morning, and all Lily could do was shrug her shoulders.

"What if we scared him away?" Luella asked finally, probably putting voice to the other children's fears too.

"I haven't given up yet," Lily said, "and I don't expect you to, either. Now, let us address our attention to these sums."

There was no denying Luella's anxiety during that hour when she was alone with Lily while the Sansevers helped their mother. The child winced, squirmed, and squinted while trying to read a story from the simple grammar text Pierre had loaned the school.

Lily put down the book. "Luella, do you need to visit the backhouse?" she asked.

Tears sprouted in the girl's eyes. "It's my braids," she whispered. "Mama makes them so *tight*."

Without a word, Lily motioned her closer and promptly untied the braids, which made Luella give a small sigh of relief. Her relief was quickly followed by a frown. "Mama will notice when I go home."

"Not if I rebraid them at the end of this hour, before Fothering takes you home for lunch."

"You're certain?" Luella asked, her voice so wary.

"I am," Lily said in her firmest teacher voice. "What on earth would happen if she noticed?"

"Nothing," Luella said quickly, too quickly. She sheltered her face in her hands.

Lily knelt down. "Luella," was all she said, but the child needed nothing more.

"She pinches me," Luella whispered. With a hand that shook, she rolled up her sleeve to show a row of black-and-blue welts.

Lily sucked in her breath, speechless for a moment. "Th . . . those are more than pinches," she managed to say finally. She stared at Luella's arm, noting the dried-up welts, older marks that had turned into scars.

With that calm that had already amazed Lily, the girl looked her in the eyes. "I try to please her, but I don't, for some reason."

Lily cupped her hands around Luella's face. "You please me," she said. "You are a wonderful student and such a help."

"Is it enough?" Luella asked, anxious.

"It is enough."

∞

"I'm worried," she told Jack that night, when he came over for his lesson and more *Ivanhoe*. "Luella says her mother pinches her, but they are nearly gouges. Is something wrong with Mrs. Buxton?"

The foreman waited a long time before he spoke, but Lily was used to that. He wasn't a man to waste words. She watched his face, but then looked away, because he seemed embarrassed about something.

"There *is* something wrong with her," he said finally and with obvious reluctance. "Beyond that I'm not prepared to say."

But you know a lot more, don't you? she thought. "How can I protect Luella?" she asked instead.

"I'll talk to Fothering, but I think he is already doing all he can to protect her," Jack said. "Perhaps we can talk the Buxtons into letting her spend more time with Chantal and Amelie." His expression turned wry. "Maybe under the pretext that she is helping them with their alphabet and ciphering. Come with me?"

"Now?"

"As good a time as any."

Her father had already closed his door. Lily pulled a shawl around her shoulders and walked with Jack to the Buxtons. She was seldom outside after dark, and the cold surprised her. She glanced at Jack's set, determined look, something she noticed more and more through each day. Each day he looked more concerned, and she was adding to his burden. She put her hand on his arm and he stopped.

"Look, I can do this myself," she said, even as some part of her hoped he would shake his head. "You're tired. I can talk to the Buxtons."

"I expect you can," he said, which made her heart plummet. "But, Lily, every single person here is my responsibility, and I don't take it lightly."

"Isn't Mr. Buxton the manager?" she asked, confused.

"He can fiddle with a ledger, but he doesn't know cows, and that is our business." He smiled then, a genuine smile that took some of the worry from his eyes, but not all, to her chagrin. "Come on. Let me help. I'm going to anyway."

"Oh, I . . ."

He put his hands on her shoulders. For one irrational moment, Lily wondered if he was going to kiss each cheek again. "Lookie here, Miss Carteret: You've been carrying a lot of burdens all your life, I suspect."

"So have you," she protested, but feebly, because she suddenly didn't want to haul one more heavy load by herself.

"We both have. You will agree to this?"

She nodded.

"Good! After all, I am paid seventy-five dollars a month

to carry burdens." He touched her forehead with his. "And, boy howdy, you are a light burden. Come on."

⤫

He knew he could leave it to Lily because she *was* a light burden; that was no joke. "You're the teacher," he said as he knocked. "I'll back you."

She gave him a grateful smile, then took a deep breath. She held it so long that he nudged her.

"Breathe, Lily, and that's *not* a suggestion."

Fothering opened the door. He gave them both a long, appraising look, and Jack knew the old prissy pot was dying to know what was up. He had to applaud the butler's demeanor, which remained mostly unaltered.

"I'd like to speak with Mrs. Buxton," Lily said. If her voice sounded a little higher than usual, Jack doubted Fothering noticed. "Please tell her I have such good news about Luella."

"Very well, my dear," the butler said, sounding most congenial. Lily had obviously wrapped him around her finger too, which impressed Jack. "Kindly wait in the parlor a moment."

As Fothering made his stately way up the stairs, Jack leaned closer and whispered, "What good news?"

"I'll think of something quite soon," she whispered back. "You taught me to plan. Hush and let me consider the matter."

Amused, he did as she said. When Fothering came back downstairs, she raised her chin. "Ready," she whispered.

"Mrs. Buxton will see you now," the butler said. "She had a putrid sore throat and palpitations, but she says there are no lengths to which she would not go for her child." He delivered the message with a straight face and only the slightest twitch of his lips.

"I'll keep it short, Fothering," she said.

He opened the door and ushered them in. Jack was

relieved to note that at least the woman on death's door didn't remind him of Potiphar's wife. He glanced at Lily, who had somehow managed to draw herself up even more, appearing almost elegant, even in calico.

There was no hanging back. Lily moved forward so gracefully, almost regally—and slap him sideways and call him a fool if she didn't manage to sound even more English than usual. As he watched the little tableau, he began to understand that Lily Carteret had probably been coexisting with fools all her life. Maybe he should take lessons.

To Jack's surprise, Lily sat on the edge of Mrs. Buxton's bed and took her hand.

"You have such a wonderful daughter, Mrs. Buxton," she said, beginning what he suspected was going to be a masterful campaign. "So courteous and such a good example for the Sansever children."

So that was it. Jack made a mental promise to never reveal any of this conversation to Madeleine, whose stalwart children needed no good example.

"We all try," Mrs. Buxton said, patting her heart.

"I have such a favor to ask," Lily said. Without asking, she picked up a little bottle of cologne and a handkerchief more lace than substance, dabbed the cologne on the useless square of cloth, and gently touched Mrs. Buxton's temple. "There you are."

"What would you like?" Mrs. Buxton asked as she practically wriggled like a puppy with this attention.

"I would love for Lily to spend some time each evening in the cookshack with the Sansever children, helping them with their numbers and letters."

Jack groaned inwardly. *There goes* my *time with Lily*, he thought.

"Never," Mrs. Buxton said, the steel back in her voice, and sounding not even slightly infirm. "Is it *safe* there?"

"As safe as houses," Lily replied, her voice so soothing.

"Luella already has the skills of a teacher. This will only hone them."

"My daughter will never have to grub about and earn her living," Mrs. Buxton said. Jack couldn't help wincing at such a slap to Lily.

"Certainly not! I would never suggest that," Lily murmured. "I was thinking what good she will do someday as a conscientious member of society pledged to helping those much less fortunate."

"If you put it that way . . . ," Mrs. Buxton said after a lengthy pause, in which Lily dabbed her wrists with the cologne. "What can it hurt? You will be there to supervise, I trust?" She frowned and looked surprisingly like Mr. Buxton all of a sudden. "This will not mean any increase in your salary."

Lily did her own bit of masterful fluttering. "Heavens! I would never even suggest such a thing. Luella's good works go far beyond anything as crass as . . . as remuneration."

He wasn't totally sure what the word meant, but the way Lily said it, the word sounded like something he had scraped off the bottom of his boot only this morning.

"Very well," Mrs. Buxton said. "Tomorrow, after we have family dinner here? I'll send her with Fothering around seven."

"Perfect." Lily rose as gracefully as she had sat down. "I apologize for taking up so much of your time on what is, I fear, a bed of pain. You're such a brave lady."

Jack left the room first, always happy to be away from a place that smelled of camphor and something suspiciously like small beer. He watched, impressed, as Lily paused in the doorway.

"I wonder, do I ask too much . . . could you send Luella with some scraps of yarn, if you have any to spare? We have a little class project."

"I will put Fothering on it," Mrs. Buxton said. "And now, just close the door quietly. I have such a pain in my head."

They said nothing on the stairs. Jack knew he would burst out laughing if he even looked at Lily.

Fothering waited for them at the bottom of the stairs, his eyebrows raised. "Success, my dear Lily?" he asked.

"Yes. We're going to see that Luella spends more time away from this . . . this place," she said, her voice still even, but with an underlying intensity that made Jack promise himself that he would never cross her. "I wonder . . . could I say good night to her? Is her room upstairs? I should have asked sooner."

"It's down here, just a small room," Fothering said, showing her the way.

She knocked and went inside, closing the door behind her.

"I couldn't help but overhear from my vantage point on the landing," Fothering said. "Miss Carteret has certain powers of management."

Jack laughed into his hand. "You old rip! I'll bet you had your ear pressed against the door."

Fothering raised both eyebrows. With unholy glee, Jack observed that the older man did not issue any denial. He did turn serious as he walked Jack to the front of the house and out of earshot of anyone inclined to listen.

"This is not a happy home," he said.

"I didn't think it was, and neither does Lily," Jack replied, knowing to trust the man. "She plans to keep Luella involved and out of here each evening."

He saw relief on the butler's face and knew Lily had done the right thing. *You're no burden at all*, he thought.

CHAPTER 23

⟬☙0☙⟭

*M*rs. Buxton remembered the yarn, which meant that Luella, smiling in triumph, brought a small skein to the Temple of Education in the morning. Lily assigned the children to unroll the ball and cut the yarn into four-inch pieces while she wrote sums on the blackboard and tried not to worry that the Little Man still hadn't returned.

"Maybe he wants more than the two hairpins on your desk," Nick said as he unwound the yarn ball and the girls snipped off the sections.

"That's why we're doing this," Lily said, putting down her chalk. "I talked to Mr. Fontaine last night and he suggested yarn for nesting material." She smiled at her charges. "We'll tempt the Little Man with luxury. It is beautiful yarn, Luella."

The girl beamed with pleasure.

When they finished, a lively discussion followed. Nick argued the merits of piling it up in one place, while Chantal advocated a little yarn in each corner. Amelie agreed with her brother and Lily sided with Chantal. Lily gestured to Luella.

"We will let you break the tie, Luella, since you brought the yarn."

"Let's do this," Luella said. The child sounded assured as if she made decisions every day. "Let's pile some yarn by the hole, as Nick and Amelie want, and then a little in each corner, as Chantal and Miss Carteret want." She looked at Lily, seeking approval.

"That is a brilliant stroke," Lily said. "Do you realize what we have done? This is a compromise." She turned and wrote the word on the board underneath the numbers. "C-o-m-p-r-o-m-i-s-e. That means we have each given a little so everyone is satisfied."

Chantal raised her hand. "Since Nick is so good at ciphering, I could give him some of my numbers to add in columns. He will be happy and so will I."

The children giggled.

"But I will not be happy," Lily said. She looked at her students. "What else could we do?"

Everyone was silent, considering the matter. Lily added some wood to the pot-bellied stove. The wind was picking up and she felt a chill. She glanced out the window beside the winter count, dismayed to see the cottonwoods bending and swaying. Did the wind never stop in Wyoming Territory? She would have to ask Jack.

Luella raised her hand. "I could help Nick with his letters while he is helping Chantal with her numbers." Her face fell. "But that is not compromise."

"True," Lily said. "It is something else. Do any of you know?"

Amelie's eyes were bright, but Lily knew how shy she was. Lily cupped her hand around her mouth as she had seen actors do to deliver an aside to an audience. "Look you, I think Amelie knows."

"Tell us, Amelie," Luella urged.

"We would be cooperating," Amelie said softly, glancing at Lily.

"Yes, we would," Lily agreed, touched. "We can all help each other." She clapped her hands. "But first, let us distribute the yarn for the Little Man."

They did as she said, but they were sober about it, careful to mound a tempting yarn pile at the doorway to the pack rat's home, and then a little bit in each corner. She saw their fear that he was gone for good.

Lily added another pine log to the stove, making a mental note to ask the men to bring up more wood. She looked at her students and their gloomy faces. "He'll be back, I just know it," she told them.

"Maybe he is sulking because we bothered his home," Chantal said.

Amelie opened her mouth to speak, then closed it.

"Yes, my dear?" Lily said, prompting the shy child.

"I say a prayer every night," she replied, then looked around to make sure no one thought that was silly.

"We could all do that," Luella said. "Do you think God cares about pack rats?"

Lily nodded. "I remember reading something in Matthew about the Lord Almighty being mindful of sparrows that fall."

"That's well and good for sparrows, but this is a pack rat," Luella said, ever practical.

"I think He means all little things, not just sparrows," Lily said, trying not to smile.

The children considered that. "Does he keep a look out for us?" Chantal asked. She frowned. "My father died and he was more important than a sparrow."

Lily was sitting on Amelie's stool while the children had spread around the yarn. She held her arms open for Chantal, who crowded in close. "He looks out for us," she said, even as her eyes started to fill. She had never met Jean Baptiste Sansever, but she knew his children. "Sometimes things happen, and that is life."

"It's not fair," Nick said as he moved closer too, no longer a boy trying to seem older than he was.

"No, it isn't," Lily agreed, thinking of the mother she barely remembered, except for the softness of her brown hands and her soothing voice. "I . . . I still miss my mother, but I decided a long time ago that I would be very good, because she would want that." She reached for Nick's hand and he did not pull away. He leaned against her shoulder, and her arm went around his waist.

"He knows we're here in search of True Greatness in the Temple of Education," Lily told them. "In Wyoming Territory, America."

When they chuckled, she knew the moment had passed. She glanced at the board, where the morning's ciphering lesson languished.

"My goodness! We had better get busy," she said, standing up to stand by the board. "Slates out, everyone."

They did as she said, students once more, and not children searching the mysteries of life and death and reluctant pack rats.

Trust Luella to make a comment. "We're not learning much this morning, are we?" she asked.

"I believe we have learned a great deal, Luella," Lily replied. "Here we go now: three plus four equals . . ."

"Seven!"

ᘓᘓ

"They fear we frightened off the Little Man," Lily told Pierre that afternoon, after the children had marched down the hill in what had become their everyday pattern. He had walked up, giving her a little nod as she stood in the doorway, watching her charges as she always did, and keeping an eye out for Freak. When she glanced toward the cottonwoods, Pierre looked too.

"Do you ever just stand still and wait for Freak?" he asked.

"Quite often. He'll come out from the trees, but that is about all for now." She felt her face grow warm, wondering what he would think of this next piece of information. "I've started called him Francis instead of Freak. It seems more polite."

So much for stoic Indians. Pierre threw back his head

and laughed loud and long. His laughter was irresistible and made her smile.

"How would *you* like to be called Freak?" she asked, when she thought he was through. "You already know how we feel about True Greatness at the Bar Dot School. We look for the best in everything, not just children."

He smiled at her then, and she saw nothing but admiration in eyes as dark as her own. "Francis it is then." He reached in his vest pocket and pulled out a twist of paraffin paper. He unwrapped it, exposing what looked like meat pellets.

"I like to trap rabbits and chipmunks now and then." He touched a little beaded bag on the leather thong around his neck. "I make medicine bags with the hides, and I dry the meat. Here."

He handed her the paper of meat. "Set it on the rock for . . ." His lips twitched, but he managed. ". . . for Francis."

She accepted the dried meat as politely as she could, whooping inside when she imagined what starchy Miss Tilton would think, if she could see her less-than-star pupil. Lily set the meat on the rock for Francis and turned back to Pierre.

"Thank you, Pierre." She stared down at her shoes a moment, still caught up in the peculiarity of this social situation. "Give me some advice: What if Francis decides to come closer and be my friend?"

He considered the matter more seriously than she thought the problem warranted. "I think he will not, because cats never do what you want." He chuckled. "If he does, pet him carefully."

"You're mostly no help," she joked.

"As Jack would tell you, free advice is worth what you pay for it." He stood there in thought again, but she was getting used to his pauses. Maybe that was the Indian way. She waited.

"Jack said you're ready for me to talk to your children about winter counts."

"I do. What I want is to have each of them start a winter count. We'll do it by months instead of years."

He nodded his approval. "I like it. For the next two days, we are moving cattle." He made a disgusted sound and looked up at the cloudless sky. "Pushing cattle, more like, because they know something is coming."

Lily felt again the little chill she remembered from the river bank when Jack showed her the thick muskrat lodge. "How do animals know?"

He shrugged. "Will Friday be all right for you? Jack said I can have some canvas in the tack room that you can use for the counts."

"What, you cannot find me four middling-sized buffalo hides?" she teased.

"I cannot even find you buffalo now," he replied, deadly serious, and with sadness in his eyes. "They are all gone, and the people are on reservations, eating flour, lard, and thin beef."

"There isn't much in the world that is fair, is there?" she asked, understanding him perfectly.

"Very little." He looked toward the trees, nodded, and lowered his voice. "I think I see Francis." He tipped his Stetson to her. "I'll go." He took off his hat, which sent the cat farther back into the trees and underbrush. "Lily, thank you for calling me Pierre, and not Indian."

"It's your name," she said simply. She looked at him. "Do you have another name? A . . . a Lakota name?"

"My mother's family call me Blue Hat." He held up his hand, evidently seeing the question in her eyes. "I'll tell you sometime."

"Say it in Lakota."

He did, guttural sounds that she knew she couldn't reproduce easily. "I'll stick with Pierre," she told him.

"Blue Hat is all right too." He started down the hill,

walking backward to watch her. "Maybe you will get a name before this winter is over."

"I'd like it to be 'Teacher,' since that is what I have become."

"No word for that in Lakota," he said. "Besides, it's not up to you. Maybe it'll be She Who Pets Wildcats."

"Oh, you!"

He started up the hill again until he was close. "I promise you it will be right and true."

Lily nodded, feeling as shy as Amelie. "Does Jack Sinclair have a name?"

"Oh, yes. His name is Determined."

"There's a Lakota word for *determined*?" she asked, skeptical.

"Well, no. It is 'He Stands With Feet Planted.'"

Lily nodded. *I can see that*, she thought, impressed.

"If a better name comes along, I will know."

She felt that chill again and clasped her hands together. "I think you're telling me that this winter is going to change us."

He didn't reply. Maybe she was wrong to ask such a question. What did she know about Indian ways? Pierre looked at the sky and held his hand up to the wind that blew stronger now from the north and west.

"There will be snow by morning."

She couldn't help the catch in her throat. Drat him and Jack for frightening her with vague suspicions. And what did muskrats and woolly caterpillars know, anyway? He noticed her agitation, because he touched her arm so lightly.

"Just a little snow this time."

Lily nodded. His finger went to her frown line and he shook his head.

"Do not worry. A man named Determined doesn't bend and fold. If you want to worry—Lakota women do that too—worry for the other ranchers."

"Maybe I'll worry for Francis and the Little Man of the Prairie," she said, hoping to lighten the moment.

He looked toward the trees and there was the cat, his tail twitching. "He wants me to leave. And the Little Man? He'll be back."

"You're so certain?"

"I am. What rat in his right mind would leave such a place as you have created here?"

"Thank you, Pierre."

He tipped his hat again and started walking Mrs. Buxton's healthy distance from the school house to the main buildings of the Bar Dot. She started to worry a wisp of hair that had escaped her bun, wishing that some magic hand would suddenly pick up the school and move it closer to the ranch.

"I am an idiot," she said out loud, but not loud enough for the retreating Indian to hear, she thought.

"Far from it," he said, waving his hand behind him.

Shaking her head, she went inside the school, peering out the window as she swept the floor, pleased to see Francis on the rock, making short work of the dried meat. She watched, pleased, as he groomed himself.

Letting our guard down, are we, Francis? she thought as she put the broom in the corner by Little Man's front door. She stood there a moment, wishing a rat to appear, of all things. Then she put her shawl around her and closed the door with a decisive click, irritated with pouting pack rats.

At the sound, Francis leaped from the rock. She waited for him to vanish into the tree line, but he held his ground, eyeing her. She took a step toward the cat and he backed up, flattening his ears.

"That attitude will not do," she told him. "Good night. Kindly sweeten up by morning, since you just had a free meal you didn't have to work for." She laughed, which made his ears go up. "And I am talking to cats."

CHAPTER 24

ⅈly thought her father might object to her evening plans that involved him, but he did not. She
explained the matter to him over supper, Madeleine's
usual beef and beans, livened this time by dried apple pie.

The special occasion was a cookshack full of hands
from other ranches, everyone hungry and expectant. Their
eyes serious with the task of refilling bowls and lugging
around the heavy coffee pot, Amelie and Chantal hurried
from table to table.

Lily wondered why the extra hands were there. Like all
cattlemen, they ate with no commentary beyond thank
yous to the girls, and pass this or that to their fellow diners.
Steel forks clinked on heavy white china and someone had
a nagging cough.

"Papa, do you know I had a lesson once in proper dinner
conversation?" she told her father in a low voice.

He smiled at her, that smile she saw more and more
often, and ducked his head close to hers. "Would have
been a true waste here, eh?" he whispered.

"Do you know . . . do you have any idea why these men
are here?" she asked.

"I might. Jack came to the office this morning to tell Mr.
Buxton that several ranchers had agreed to join together
to gather their drifting cattle," he told her and reached for
another slice of bread as Amelie hurried by.

You are eating better, she thought, grateful, and almost

let his words pass her by. "He *told* Mr. Buxton?" she asked, paying attention again. "How did he fare?"

"Mr. Buxton called him a fearmonger, among other things which I will not repeat," her father whispered. "They went at it hammer and tongs, and I am surprised Jack wasn't told to draw his wages, as they say here. Jack didn't back down." He gave a disgusted snort. "All Mr. Buxton wanted to know was that it wasn't going to cost him anything."

Lily thought of her afternoon conversation with Pierre. He Stands With Feet Planted didn't seem to fear unemployment. She remembered her brief visit to his little ranch and her introduction to Bismarck, and how Jack draped his arms over the corral fence and watched his three-cow herd with shy pride. "I think he really likes cows, Papa. He cares."

She looked around at the men of the Bar Dot. Pierre sat close to Jack, listening to a conversation growing more intense by the minute. Stretch had his own little circle of friends, laughing and smoking. Preacher had tipped his chair back, perhaps the better to hear several conversations, while Will Buxton sat alone playing solitaire, belonging nowhere.

She saw exhaustion on many faces and a certain uneasiness that had no real name. Over conversation, she heard the wind outside, rattling the panes of glass as though wanting to join the gathering too. If there had not been so many warm bodies in the room, it might have felt colder. She was already not looking forward to their walk back to Papa's quarters.

"Would you mind staying here a while?" she asked her father. "Nick Sansever is doing so well with his addition and subtraction. He is ahead of the others, and I wonder if you would help him along with multiplication. Just for a little while."

He considered her request. "It will be noisy here," he said, but it was a feeble objection.

"Just for an hour. And look, here is Fothering with Luella," she said as the door opened and the wind blew them in. "She will help the Sansever girls with their alphabet."

"How can I say no?" her father teased. "Are you managing me?"

"I suppose I am," she said, grateful for his light tone. "I was thinking, a few nights a week . . ." She nudged her father's shoulder, then kissed his cheek. "And here is Nick with his slate."

"I wonder how he knew?" Papa gave her an arch look and then loosened his cravat, that article of clothing that set him off as a stranger in a strange land of cows and ranchers. The dingy cravat was as shabby as his collar, but it touched Lily's heart to see his own brave struggle to stand his ground and remain a gentleman. "Thank you, Papa. Just one hour."

She went to the girls, who had gathered at a table closest to the kitchen. In a few minutes, Luella and Chantal and Amelie had their heads together over small words. Pleased, she watched them, enjoying Luella's confidence.

"And who, miss, are you?"

The gravelly voice boomed out over all the talk, and all conversation ceased. Lily turned away, uncertain. She put her hand on Luella's shoulder, because the girl had half risen from the bench, startled. "Just keep working," Lily whispered. "I doubt he means any harm." She pointed at Amelie's slate. "Very good. If you add an E you have . . ."

"I mean *you*, Miss High Yaller. Putting on airs?"

Mortified, she heard a chair hit the floor and another scrape back, and then Jack's familiar voice, except there was menace in it. "That's enough, Mr. Ledbetter."

"Just wondering, that's all."

Lily turned around. Ledbetter was a big man, taller than some, but no taller than she was. He looked like the others with his shirt that had probably been white in better days, a vest probably greasy enough to stand on its own, and jeans. He needed a haircut and a shave like the others, and he was regarding her with more than interest. He looked her up and down.

"I am Miss Carteret, the schoolteacher here," she said, suddenly finding a purpose for those lessons in precise diction she had learned in Bristol.

"She is my daughter," her father said as he stood beside her, swaying a little because he was never steady.

"On purpose?" the big man said and threw back his head to laugh.

"Here now . . . ," her father began.

"I, sir, am a gentleman's daughter," Lily said.

"How in tarnation can that be? You're a—"

The click of a hammer pulled back stopped the man right there.

"Just one more word, Ledbetter," Jack said. "You rubbed my last nerve."

Lily deliberately stepped in front of the man who had taunted her, the man who was now ghostly in complexion. "I am not worth a life. Not over this."

"Oh, you are. What's it to be, Ledbetter? If I don't get you tonight, since this *lady*"—he said it with emphasis—". . . this lady is far kinder than you are, I'll get you later. Count on it."

"It won't happen again," the man said behind her, his voice so high and strangled that some of the other men chuckled. He put on his hat. "Past my bedtime," he said as he started for the door. "Bunkhouse?"

"If they'll have you there," Jack said, easing back the hammer and holstering his gun. "If they won't, there's a tack room next to the horse barn."

Ledbetter nodded and left. Everyone in the room seemed to take a deep breath. The children went back to their studies. His own face pale, Fothering took her arm.

"That was a bit too much like the old West," he said as he sat her down. "My dear, would you care for some tea?"

"I would," she told him, hoping her own voice was in its proper register. She clasped her hands to stop their shaking and looked around the room at the cowhands, the ones she knew and the strangers. "I must confess, gentlemen." Chuckles here and there. "No, gentlemen," she insisted, but mildly. "When I knew I was coming to Wyoming, America, I read what I hear is called a dime-store novel."

Stretch slapped his forehead. "I'm crushed you would stoop so low!"

Everyone laughed, and the air seemed to start circulating again.

"Which one?" Preacher asked.

"Let me see . . . it had an obnoxious title," she replied, going along with the more friendly tide now. "Oh, how could I forget? It rejoiced in the name of *The Train Robbers, or Lucy in Peril*."

More laughter.

"It was set in Texas."

Groans followed the laughter.

"What did you learn?" This from Pierre, who had just slid what looked like a filleting knife back into its beaded pouch.

She looked around again at friendlier faces and understood just what she had learned. She stood taller. "I learned that the West is colorful, and that . . ."—her voice faltered—". . . that cowboys are kind to ladies."

"Have to be, ma'am," said a cheerful voice. "Scarcer'un hen's teeth. By the way, I know Buxton is a skinflint. I'll double whatever he's paying you to teach *my* kids."

"I'm not really a teacher," she said.

The cheerful man—he must have been a rancher, rather than a hand—looked around at the children, who had returned to their tasks. "You could'a fooled me." He tipped his hat to Lily. "If you change your mind, my ranch is the Bar Lazy M and I'm Pete Marquardt. I'm off for your bunkhouse, Sinclair."

"No need," Jack said. "I have room at my little place. You know where it is."

The rancher opened the door, and a gust of wind nearly blew the knob out of his hand. "Woo-wee! Colder'n a well digger's . . ." Marquardt closed the door behind him.

Fothering stood up. "What say you, Luella? Might this be an opportune time to leave?"

Lily thought the butler looked as though he expected an argument. "Morning comes early, Luella, and the Temple of Education awaits," she added.

The child nodded. She looked at Fothering, then at Lily and declared in her forthright way, "A few weeks ago, I probably would have said that I will catch my death in this cold and surely die before the week is out." She appeared genuinely puzzled. "What happened?"

Lily exchanged a glance with the butler. "Perhaps you are discovering how resilient you are."

"Resilient?" Luella asked. "Define it, please, for my benefit."

"Strong and mighty, but able to bend," Lily told her promptly, trying not to smile at Luella's quaint ways. "It's an excellent quality in Wyoming ladies, so I am learning."

The men in the room laughed. Some returned to their cards, and others poured more coffee. Jack grinned at her, relaxing again.

Pierre got to his feet. "Fothering, let me walk with you. Between the two of us, we'll keep Luella from blowing away."

"I would greatly appreciate it," Luella said. "Mr. Fontaine, *will* the Little Man return?"

"He is probably in your classroom already," Pierre said as he shrugged into his coat. "It's a cold night." He smiled at Lily. "He has probably pouted enough."

"I thought that's what he was doing," Chantal said. She

fingered one of Luella's braids. "Thank you for helping us."

"Thank you for forgiving me," Luella said softly. "See you tomorrow."

After they left, Lily turned to her father. "Papa, perhaps we should go now."

Papa looked up from Nick's slate. "Wait a while, my dear. Nick and I are not quite done, are we, lad?"

"Not yet, Miss Carteret," Nick said. "Just a few more minutes."

"He's doing so well, I would hate to stop right now," Clarence Carteret said. He smiled then, and his smile took her breath away. "Oh, please, Miss Carteret," he teased.

Lily let her breath out slowly, wondering—perhaps like Luella—what had happened. This felt surprisingly like a tender mercy, except that it had been years since she had petitioned the Almighty for anything since she knew He wasn't all that interested in little girls of partial color stuck in boarding schools.

"I can wait, Papa," she said.

"No need," Jack said, standing up. "I'll be your escort." He looked around. "I have room for two more of you bandits, if you don't mind Marquardt's snoring. There's a reason why no one likes to sleep near him at cow gathers."

Two men stood up. "Ready, Lily?" Jack asked.

She nodded, already bracing herself for the wind outside.

"Put your head down," Jack said outside. He held her arm with one hand and his hat with the other. One of the cowhands linked her other arm through his, and the second man walked in front of her, trying to block some of the wind that roared down from the north and west, always from the north and west.

Although she had also learned how to carry on a conversation to gentlemen walking home a lady, Lily knew that everything she said would be snatched from her mouth, so she was silent.

"I'll get her the rest of the way," Jack shouted over the wind as they passed his quarters. He stopped a minute, looking at his roof. Then he pulled her closer and continued the short distance to Papa's place, where the wind, impatient to enter, rattled the doorknob. When he opened the door, the wind blew her in. Jack followed her and shut the door, after leaning against it.

"I'd hate to run into that wind in January," he told her. "You all right?"

"Certainly. It's only wind. I may need more lead shot for my skirts," she replied. *And I will never tell you what else I need*, she thought. Her English undergarments were no match for Wyoming, but she didn't see a remedy for that dilemma from the foreman of the Bar Dot. Maybe Madeleine would have a suggestion before her legs fell off.

"Well, then, good night." Jack pulled his Stetson down more firmly. "We'll be gone for the next few days pushing cattle." He leaned against the door and regarded her seriously. "Lily, this winter is already unfolding like I thought it would."

Yes, he had told her, but it frightened her anyway. "Pierre said it would snow tomorrow."

"I wouldn't doubt him. He's staying here, so you'll have your winter count lesson."

"Surely you need him," she protested. "I wouldn't dream of letting my puny plans stop him from important work. The winter count can wait."

"No. Some of the boys don't like Indian cowhands, and I don't take chances. He stays."

Lily nodded. She took off her coat. "I understand that better than you know."

"Thought you might. Sorry about that fool in the cookshack."

She shrugged. "It's happened before and it'll happen again." She did have a bone to pick with him. The wind had made her forget for a moment. "Don't you ever take a chance like that again! He could have killed you."

"He's a bully, and I know bullies. All hat and no cow-hand," Jack said with a shrug. "It won't happen again. Not on the Bar Dot, and not while I'm in charge. 'Night, Miss Carteret."

"Have we been reading too much *Ivanhoe* and Unknown Knight?" she joked, wanting to lighten the moment because he looked so serious, and heaven knows he had enough burdens already. "Do I have a champion?"

He nodded and waited a long moment before he replied, almost as if mulling around whether to say anything at all. "I decided *that* at some point after you got off the train and maybe before we ate chop suey at the Great Wall. Don't sell yourself short. Chapter twenty-four when I get back? Good night."

CHAPTER 25

There was snow in the morning, just as Pierre had predicted. Lily watched it fall so lightly, now that the wind was probably blowing its way across Nebraska, or maybe one of those states farther east that she couldn't name.

She held up her mittened hand so the flakes fell on the dark wool. Enchanted, she stared at the little dots of white, each one with its own design. They melted soon enough. She could probably scare up more paper from Papa's office so her children could draw snowflakes. Each one would have to be different. She wished she knew why snow did that.

That was the problem with teaching, she decided, as she waved to Fothering and laughed to see Luella on his back as he trudged up the hill through the ankle-deep snow. *The more I learn, the more I want to know*, she thought, waiting for them. *My children probably think I know everything, but I don't.*

The Sansever children were already there and practically leaping about in their excitement.

"The Little Man is back!" Chantal said. She started to dance around the room. She grabbed Luella's hand when Fothering set her down. "Look! The yarn is gone."

Hand in hand, the two girls—no, friends now—ran to the corner. They knelt and tried to peer into the tiny hole, which made Lily turn away in laughter. She walked to her desk, nodding to see the hairpins gone too. The Little Man had left a pebble in exchange, which Pierre had said he might do.

Nick's smile was as broad as his sisters' when he came in with more wood, tracking in snow. Lily swept it out the door while he thundered the logs in the woodbox by the stove, where Fothering had just finished lighting a fire. Soon the room was warm enough for the children to take off their coats. Lily noticed that Amelie was now wearing the coat Jack had procured from the faro dealer. Madeleine must have cut it down because the sleeves were perfect.

"Your mother did a lovely job altering the coat," Lily told Amelie, who blushed.

"*Ma maman* can do nearly anything," she whispered. "And look, my old coat fits Chantal just right." Amelie paused, perhaps wondering if she should say anything else.

"Go on, my dear," Lily said.

"Did someone ever give you hand-me-downs?" Amelie asked.

"So that's what they are called here? No, my clothing was always new," Lily told her. No matter what her uncle had felt about his younger brother's ill-advised marriage to an island lady, he had never shied from putting the best of everything on her back. Madeleine had remarked only last week that her clothes were so well made.

"Your uncle was a wealthy man," Amelie said.

"He still is," Lily said.

Chantal had been listening. "Then why is your father . . . Ow! Amelie, you don't need to poke me."

"Maybe we are asking private questions," Amelie told her little sister. "I'm sorry for her prying, Miss Carteret."

"Not at all," Lily said. She realized how little she had told the children about herself. Papa had probably said nothing. Maybe it wouldn't hurt to tell them where she came from, especially after the tense scene in the cook-shack last night.

She knew Pierre was coming to the school in a little while, after the riders left to work the cattle that were so relentlessly moving south. She had watched Jack this morning during breakfast. He had a perpetual frown line now that she feared would only deepen as winter came. "We're trying to convince Texas cows that they can't trail over the next rise or the next, and find warmth along the Nueces or the Brazos rivers," was how he put it. "Cows are not so smart."

He had given her shoulder a little squeeze as he passed her table where she sat with her father. His hand still on her shoulder, he had leaned closer. "That man who harassed you last night? Someone gave him an amazing black eye."

"It had better not have been you or Pierre," she warned.

"We're pure as the driven snow," he said.

"Since when?" she retorted without thinking.

He lifted his hand from her shoulder. "I mean it, Lily. You have more champions than you realize. Don't know how it happened, but word is spreading about the Bar Dot School."

She had basked a moment in the security she felt when Jack was around, or Pierre. Maybe every girl needed an Unknown Knight or two. She felt suddenly self-conscious as he stood so close to her, so she looked around, hoping no one noticed. Her father was finishing his coffee, correcting Nick's late night math. Everyone else was gone, except for Pierre, who looked at her with a half smile of his own.

"Champions?" she teased, hoping to lighten the moment. "Every lady needs one! Thank merciful providence that I didn't decide to read *Tom Brown's Schooldays* to you, instead of *Ivanhoe*." There. That was friendly and nothing more.

"I was your champion before *Ivanhoe*," he said and put on his Stetson.

◦∞◦

"Miss Carteret, you are not paying attention to us."

Lily laughed and turned her focus to Luella. "And I apologize. Amelie said something made me think that you might like to know more about me."

Nick raised his hand. "I do, but it's more than that." His eyes were troubled. "That man in the cookshack was rude to you."

"He was," Lily agreed, wondering in her heart if everything in life belonged in a classroom for discussion. "You know I am darker than you, but my father is light." She went to the wall where the map of the world hung, complete with the Braxton Bitters nymph in her diaphanous robes. She pointed to the Caribbean Sea and touched the small island in the Lesser Antilles that still held such a chunk of her heart. She pointed to England and located Bristol.

The children squinted to see, so she called them forward. Besides, it was getting colder, and they could warm themselves closer to the stove.

"My father is the youngest son of a prominent family here in Bristol," she explained, tapping the map. "Since he could not inherit his father's estate, he went here to manage a sugarcane plantation." She ran her finger from England to Caribbean waters to Barbados.

"Sugarcane?" Chantal asked.

"It grows in tall stalks and tastes sweet. That's one way sugar is made," Lily explained. "Papa met my mother there. She was the daughter of an apothecary." Lily held up her hand before Luella had a chance to raise hers. "What is an apothecary? My grandpapa made potions and pills to cure people of their illnesses. He was from Spain. My grandmama was the daughter of a former slave and a French plantation owner."

"Slavery?" Amelie asked, her eyes wide.

"Yes. My *abuelo*—my grandpapa—actually freed my

grandmama. They married, and my mother was born about a year later."

"You're pretty," Luella said in her forthright way. "Was your mother pretty too?"

"She was beautiful," Lily said simply. "I'll bring a photograph of her tomorrow."

"Is she in England?" Amelie asked. She looked down. "This isn't going to end well, is it?"

Her heart went out to the quiet child who held back so much. Lily picked up her chair from behind her desk and set it in front of the students. She wondered if she had been hiding behind her desk, not feeling confident, unsure of herself. The moment had come and gone, and she knew it would never return.

She heard a small sound in the corner, and there was Pierre. He had come in so quietly, and now he was squatting by the door. He nodded to her, encouraging her to continue.

"No, it isn't, Amelie," she said, her voice soft. "It's a sad story. Mama died in Barbados of yellow fever. It comes and goes on the islands, and it came to her."

Amelie's head went down on her desk. Lily rested her hand on the child's hair. "It came to me too, but I survived. I was five." She glanced at Pierre. "What this means is that I can never get yellow fever."

She couldn't sit still. A few strides took her to the blackboard and she wrote i-m-m-u-n-e in big letters. "Immune. This means I can never get yellow fever."

"If it comes to the territory, you'll be safe," Luella said.

Lily couldn't help her smile, and it relieved her heart. "Yes! Of course, yellow fever doesn't come here." She sat down among her children again. "None of you need to fear it."

"What happened then?" a voice asked from the corner.

The children looked around in surprise and relaxed to see Pierre.

For a small moment, she wanted to be angry with him for forcing more of the story, but it passed; he was right. Besides, Nick wanted her to explain someone like the man last night.

"My father and I went to England, where I shivered in the cold and cried because I wanted to go home," she told her little audience. "My Uncle Niles sent me to a very nice school nearby and saw that I had beautiful clothes." She sighed. "But I didn't look like the other girls and they made fun of me. Called me names, like that man last night. I tried to ignore them, but it hurt." She glanced over her shoulder at the word on the blackboard. "*Immune* means to be protected from something. We are never immune from hurtful words, so it's best never to say them in the first place."

"If I see him again, I will fight him," Nick said, barely suppressing his anger.

She touched both his hands that were balled into fists on his desk. "No." She felt her face grow warm. "I have plenty of champions. All I need you to do is study and learn and promise me that you will never say hurtful things about people's color."

The boy held out his arm and rolled up his shirt sleeve. He looked at her, and she unfastened the little mother of pearl buttons at her wrist. She pushed up her sleeve and turned her forearm up, too, next to his.

"You're not much darker than I am, not at all," Nick said. He watched her face, and Lily could see what a fine-looking man he would be someday. "I think Luella is whiter than we are."

The little girl rolled up her sleeve and moved closer. "True," she said, "but you know, I'm not really white, not like teeth or snow."

"What are we then?" Lily asked, loving these children in the Temple of Education with all her heart.

The children looked at their arms. "Maybe beige,"

Amelie suggested. She glanced back at the Indian. "Mr. Fontaine, what do you think?"

Pierre rolled up his flannel sleeve. "I am a little lighter than Miss Carteret. My mother was Lakota and my father was a French fur trader, with maybe a little Ojibwa." He rolled his sleeve down. "You are beige. Miss Carteret and I will be tan like a buffalo hide. This one." He pointed to the winter count with its spiral and colorful figures.

What a perfect change of subject, Lily thought with admiration. She rolled down her sleeve and had Chantal fasten the two buttons at her wrist.

"Mr. Fontaine is here to tell us about winter count," Lily said. "We can make our own, because I think he found some canvas."

"Jack Sinclair found it," Pierre said. He opened a stiff, vividly painted hide shaped roughly like a box, but flat. "This is *parfleche*, Miss Carteret. I store things here." He pulled out five squares of canvas, each about the length of a yardstick. "One for you too."

"Tell us first, and then we will do as you wish," Lily said.

He stood beside the buffalo hide, touching it lovingly, smoothing his hand over the ever-widening spiral. "We tell time in stories," he said. "We begin at the beginning." He pointed to the center of the spiral. "Every year, after we are in our tepees and winter is roaring outside and trying to get in, the elders decide what is the most remarkable thing that happened all year. The winter count keeper draws it." He gestured to the children. "Come close and tell me what you see. You too, Miss Carteret."

Forceful as always, Luella went nearly nose to nose with the winter count. She put her finger on spotted people lying down. "What's this?"

"A visit from smallpox, brought upriver to Fort Union Trading Post. Many died," he said. "You would call that year 1837."

Nick pointed to a picture nearer the outer ring of the

spiral of blue-coated men falling from their horses and body parts here and there.

"You might call it the Little Bighorn. We call it the Greasy Grass battle," Pierre told him. He moved his finger to the next portion, which had a flag Lily recognized.

"That's the English flag, the crosses of St. George and St. Andrew," she said to her children. "And look: tepees."

"A year after Greasy Grass, Sitting Bull and his nation crossed to the Grandmother's Land, Canada."

Amelie, ever the observer, pointed to several scenes with the same drawing. "Here, here, and here."

Pierre tapped the blank space on the hide, the next spot to draw on, for 1886. "I might add that here, too. It means long winters."

Lily rubbed her arms, looking at the representations of snow and the bare trees bending. She looked closer on one of the later drawings, which had the snow, plus two thin figures with tears gushing from their eyes.

"Winter and a starving time," Nick said simply.

CHAPTER 26

You know, Pierre, I should feel some guilt at abandoning my entire day's plan, but this was better," Lily said as she sat on the doorstep after school with the Indian, who had returned from adding more nails to roofs, his orders from Jack Sinclair before he rode off the place. "Month by month instead of year by year is perfect."

"Chantal is only six," Pierre said. "Think how small would be her winter count of what she remembers. And your idea of May to May was best. It still gives them much to think about."

Too much, she thought, drawing up her knees to rest her chin on them. It was vastly unladylike, but she was tired. She turned to Pierre. "The Sansevers each drew such sad pictures for March! Come, I'll show you."

He followed her into the classroom, looking where she pointed at the individual winter counts spread on each desk. His smile looked wistful to Lily as he ran his finger above each sad picture, as if to touch it would invite ruin. "But look how true to character, Lily. Nick has drawn Jean falling off a horse; Amelie's picture is a headstone; and here is a little girl in tears for Chantal." He looked away and Lily saw his shoulders rise and fall. "We all cried except Amelie."

"She does hold things inside," Lily said as she traced the outline of the tombstone.

"What is this?" Pierre asked, touching Luella's February.

"Two arms with red dots? She does have an imagination, but we didn't have smallpox last winter."

"It's not that simple," Lily told him, wondering how much to say and fearing to betray the child. "You mustn't say anything, but her mother pinches Luella's arms and leaves welts." She touched the little picture of pain. "Could it be that *our* winter counts are ways to say things we cannot say?"

Pierre took several audible breaths, then touched June on Luella's winter count, which showed a girl in braids gathering flowers. "We have pretty wildflowers." He moved back to the Sansever drawings for June and tapped Chantal's drawing of a girl washing many dishes. "It was the cow gather, and there were so many consortium members going from ranch to ranch. Jack even drafted Preacher and Stretch to help Madeleine and the children in the kitchen. You should have heard them complain!"

"My dears lead different lives on a ranch where they are so close," Lily said.

"They *are* your dears, aren't they?" he asked.

Lily nodded, unable to speak. She went to the board to erase i-m-m-u-n-e, which had stayed there through a perfunctory arithmetic lesson shortened so everyone could return to their winter counts. "I didn't plan for them to become my dears," she said, happy that he couldn't see her face. "It's only been a few weeks! How does this happen so fast?"

She heard his chuckle. "I know I'm being silly," she said.

"No, not that. This picture you drew in . . . in August. Jack will be impressed."

She turned around to see him pointing at the big animal with the white forehead and red body. "I cannot draw cattle, and it's rude to laugh," she told him, which only made him laugh more.

"Maybe I'm amazed that Bismarck was more important

to you than anything else," he said. He shrugged. "But that is winter count: people notice different things."

"You should have seen him with his arms on the fence, just staring at Bismarck," Lily said, putting down the eraser Stretch has made for her out of an old chamois he claimed was just lying around. "You know how determined he can look. He's staked everything on that bull."

"I know. Remember that his name is He Stands With Feet Planted." He pointed to Lily's September. "There are two more days in this month and you have already filled it in?" He looked at her, delight on his face. "That's me drawing the Little Man of the Prairie!" He looked closer. "My nose is not that big."

"'People notice different things,'" she echoed. "It happened to me too. Look here at Luella's drawing, and Nick's, and . . . oh, what they have done."

She pressed the bridge of her nose to stop any tears as Pierre tapped each little picture of her in September, a tall and slender woman with big brown eyes, round like a child's, and tan skin. Nick's Lily was drawing numbers. Chantal's Lily knelt by Little Man's hole to look in. Amelie's Lily was laughing. Luella's Lily was unbraiding her hair.

"You really got down on hands and knees to look in the hole?" Pierre said.

"I really did," she confessed.

"You worry too much. I told you the Little Man would return."

"You were right. This afternoon we put out a sliver of a mirror for grooming purposes, and some wheat from Madeleine."

"Would you mind if I bring her here to see her children's winter counts?"

"If it doesn't make her too sad," Lily replied warily.

"No harm in tears for a good man," he said. "Also, she's your best source for wheat. Which reminds me: Freak. . ."

"Francis," she corrected.

"Francis followed me here, just sort of gliding along the tree line like he does. If it were warmer, I'd tell you to sit on the rock and wait." He shrugged. "Cats."

He left with a wave of his hand over his shoulder. Lily watched him go into the side door of the cookshack. Thinking he wanted to show Madeleine the winter counts by himself, she put on her coat, wished it were warmer, and tied a muffler around her neck. She stood by the Little Man's hole and left a few bread crumbs she had remembered to stuff in her pocket after breakfast.

"Thanks for coming back," she told the hole. "Look out for Francis."

She closed the door behind her and stretched her shoulders, feeling pleasantly tired. She walked to the wagon road that ran past the school and gazed at the empty prairie. The dried grass made a whooshing sound, reminding her of small pebbles in a rattle. She knew it was only a few miles to her father's former property—Jack's now—and four miles to Wisner. Maybe if the weather held this weekend, she would walk to the little ranch with the fences and take a look at Bismarck by herself. She wondered if Manuel got lonely, with no more company than an impressive bull and his pregnant harem.

Lily had decided that tomorrow, after completing the lessons so neglected today, she would ask the children what they thought about writing a letter to Mr. Wing Li at the Great Wall of China café, inviting him to the Bar Dot Temple of Education to tell them about China. They were nearly through with Alger's little pot boiler about Ragged Dick the shoeshine boy. She knew Stretch was from Connecticut, somewhere back there by New York City. Maybe he could be prevailed upon to tell the children—her children—about big cities.

There would be more class tonight in the cookshack, all to keep Luella a little safer, and Nick moving ahead on his math, and her father occupied. She looked in the direction the men had gone this morning, but the prairie horizon remained empty. She saw mountains in the distance, big brooding things with snow already on top from last night's storm.

The snow at the ranch had melted during the day, where the sun had struck it. Snow remained only in the more shaded areas. And there was Francis, peering at her. She patted her pocket and felt the piece of cheese in paraffin paper that she had forgotten about yesterday. She unwrapped the cheese and held it in her outstretched hand.

Nothing. She waited, her hand out, holding her breath as he started toward her. Two hesitant steps, then one back, and then three forward, standing sideways with the ruff on his back high.

"It's just cheese and you probably won't even like it," she told Francis. "Don't get so exercised. It's rag manners."

His ears went back and then forward as he dropped the pose that surely intimidated little creatures like the pack rat. She could have reached out and touched him, but she held still, remembering Pierre's words.

As she watched, holding her breath now, Francis delicately took the cheese from her palm. She waited for him to bolt for the tree line, but he rubbed his cheek against her hand for a split second. Up close, his battered and frostbitten ears were testimony to a hard life. His one eye was big and green and beautiful.

Another rub, and then he was gone. "My goodness," she said. She looked down the road again, wishing for Jack to materialize. She would share the news about Francis with her father over supper, and the children tomorrow, but she wanted more than anything for Jack to know. Why, she wasn't sure, except that he would probably say something stringent and pithy in his slow-talking way, and she liked the cadence of his Southern speech.

She kept her eyes on the road a little longer as she closed

her eyes and sent a silent message to the foreman. *I am planning every day now, Jack*, she thought. *True Greatness requires it.*

❧

Jack pushed back his Stetson and tried not to glare with envy at Will, Stretch, and Preacher, who still looked lively after three days of pushing around cattle that didn't want to be pushed around. As they passed through Wisner, Will and Stretch had tried to talk him into stopping at the saloon, but he vetoed their plea. "Praise the Lord," Preacher had said, looking heavenward with what could only be called a smirk on his face.

"Gents, Oscar has standards at the Back Forty, and to put no bark on it, we stink," he said. "I'll let you loose early enough tomorrow night."

I do need a bath, he thought. The range was so dry that generous helpings of dust had been their appetizer and main course. That was bad enough, but the dust also settled in crooks and crevasses unused to such indignity. He hoped he wouldn't see Lily or Madeleine before that bath, because he was walking funny. He knew that Lily's impression of cowboys in the American West had been informed by the larger-than-life heroes in dime novels. He doubted those cowboys ever had painful crotch problems.

"What you grinning about, boss?" Preacher asked.

"Nothing much. Just thinking about what a jolt it must have been for Lily Carteret to find out what real cowhands are like."

"What? You mean that we smell bad and should've taken along our toothbrushes?" Preacher joked in turn.

"Yep. That." Jack pointed west. "We're takin' a detour to my ranch."

Stretch groaned. "We can't visit the saloon in Wisner, but we have to look at your bull?"

"Healthier and cheaper for you," Jack replied, laughing when the others groaned.

As he rode onto his property and hallooed for Manuel, Jack found himself wondering, as he always did, whether Manuel preferred company or not. Manuel had been a sheepherder since his childhood in Mexico, a lonely occupation. Jack had come across him in Cheyenne, out of work and hungry, and happy to find a simple-enough job for his old bones, since he admitted to at least seventy years, but looked older.

It was short visit, just long enough for his cowhands to shake out their kinks and throw in a few more barbs about vast ill usage. With Manuel's slight help, Jack unloaded a hundred-weight bag of potatoes and more pinto beans from the light wagon holding their own food and bedrolls for the past three days. He stacked them against the other bag of potatoes and beans in the board shack with the elegant wallpaper. Hands on hips, Jack stared at Manuel's supplies—onions, green coffee beans, sugar—without which Manuel had stated firmly that he would not work.

"You have enough cornmeal for tortillas?" he asked the old man.

"*Si*, and flour too."

They walked to the corral together in silence, to be met by Bismarck himself, who seemed to enjoy an audience. Jack's cowhands were already leaning on the sturdy fence, admiring the bovine lover as he stared back at him, his massive jaws working.

To Jack's surprise, Will Buxton appeared the most interested. "These two cows you bred him with—will their calves look like Bismarck?"

"That's my hope," Jack said. "The closer cow there has some Herferd in her already. I'm hoping for heifers, naturally. I'll breed them to Bismarck too, and we'll see what we see."

"It's better beef?"

"Will, it is far beyond what we bring up from Texas. In a few years, I can guarantee you a great steak." *The trick is getting through the next few years*, Jack thought. *But you don't need to know that, Will.*

"No quick profit now, eh?" Will asked, sounding annoyingly like his uncle, who thought he ran the Bar Dot.

"That's the gamble," Jack said, hoping he didn't sound too short. It wouldn't do to irritate someone named Buxton, even though Jack had no idea how close the connection was. Mr. Buxton had a knack for keeping his employees off kilter and concerned for their own future. Trust him to set a spy among them to keep everyone reeling. "Once people start tasting the difference between Herferd beef and scrub cattle, you'll see."

"Providing your uh, herd, survives this fearsome winter you say is coming," Will said, with a prissy sort of smile that might have resulted in a mere cowhand without the Buxton name being invited to change employment. "Three cattle and a fearsome winter, or so you say."

Jack swallowed his irritation because he didn't have a choice. "It's coming, Will," he said quietly.

Chapter 27

With a wry look on his generally inscrutable face, Pierre met them by the empty schoolhouse, sitting so casually with a leg crossed over his saddle, a better horseman than any of them, with or without a saddle.

"The Big Boss wants to see you right away," he told Jack with no preamble.

"I'm pretty rank," Jack said.

Pierre shrugged. Jack doubted that pleasing bosses was ever in the Indian's greater plan.

"He might mind if I sit within smelling distance of him," Jack said as he motioned the others forward and rode with Pierre. "Everything all right here?"

"The Little Man of the Prairie returned to his home in the school, and there was general rejoicing, as Lily would put it," Pierre said.

"She has a funny way of expressing herself," Jack said. *I'd rather listen to her than anyone else I know*, he thought.

"I'd rather listen to her than anyone else I know," Pierre said. "Everything sounds better when she says it."

"Clarence Buxton has that same accent," Jack replied, laughing inside at himself and men in general. "You feel that way about *him*?"

They both laughed. *So that's how it is*, he thought, with a glance at his top hand and friend. He tried to visualize Pierre Fontaine as a lady might. Beyond noting long eyelashes and a certainty dignity of carriage, Jack came up dry.

When he arrived at the Buxton house, he waved off Pierre and looped his reins through the hitching post. Fothering answered the door.

"My, aren't we a sight for sore eyes," the butler said. "If you look this fraught, how did the bovine fraternity fare?"

Jack smiled, used to Fothering. He was reminded of something Preacher had read from the New Testament when they hunkered down a night or two ago in slush and mud.

"'A double-minded man is unstable in all his ways,'" he quoted to Fothering. "That's somewhere in James. It pretty well fits cows too. Slap me if the whole bovine fraternity on the northern range isn't dead set on moving south."

"What can you do about that?" Fothering asked.

Jack gave him a long look, knowing that the butler had asked a question Buxton would probably never even think of. "If it's the winter I am expecting, not a single thing. They'll drift south until they freeze to the ground, fall into air holes, or land in the rivers. If we have even half our herd left come spring, I'll be amazed."

They stood in silence for a moment until Fothering knocked on the office door.

"Send him in," came the voice within. Trouble was, with Oliver Buxton you never knew whether he was angry or calm or downright wrathful. It all sounded the same.

Hope he has the windows wide open, Jack thought and then brightened. *If not, then it would be a short interview, no matter what the problem.*

"Well?" was all Buxton asked. He didn't gesture toward a chair, but Jack told himself he didn't want to sit down anyway, not after days in the saddle.

At his own desk, Clarence Carteret gave Jack a sympathetic smile, one not in Buxton's line of sight.

"We pushed 'um back and wondered how on earth we're going to manage this winter."

"I can't believe that the other ranchers around here actually agree with you about this winter," Buxton said, brushing off the catastrophe to come with a dismissing chop of his hand.

Believe, you ninny, Jack thought. "The signs are all there." He glanced out the window. "Never seen snow this early on the mountains, and it was snowing here when we left." He slapped his gloves from one hand to the other, which was better than beaning Mr. Buxton with them. "We did what we could with the men we have. Now, if you don't mind, I really need—"

"Just a moment, Sinclair," Buxton said. He indicated Clarence. "I should have mentioned this sooner. I had cash here ready to pay the commissioning agents' fee for the cattle that we *didn't* sell this fall."

He gave Jack a look that blamed him for the drought and the overgrazing, but Jack maintained his neutral face, the one reserved for the boss and consortium members.

"Got a telegram from Cheyenne while you were away. Seems four or five of the consortium members want that money in a Cheyenne bank as soon as possible. There's wind of a big deal in Texas for more cattle."

"Mr. Buxton, this range can't even support what we have right n—"

"I don't pay you to comment on consortium business." Buxton bit off every word and threw them at him like pellets. "I'm sending Clarence to Cheyenne with the cash. I want you to go with him and make sure it ends up in the consortium office and not on some poker table."

You could have said that in private, Jack thought as acute embarrassment for Clarence washed over him like stinging nettles.

"I'd go, but Mrs. Buxton is certain she is dying this week." He glared at Jack as though daring any commentary.

"You can trust Clarence," Jack said quietly. "I have too much to do here, and so do my hands. I can get him on the Cheyenne Northern, telegraph ahead, and have someone from the consortium meet him at the depot. Nothing simpler."

"I hadn't thought of that."

Of course not, you pea brain, Jack thought. *One more year here, one more year. Bismarck, do your duty.* The idea of his placid Hereford servicing a territory-full of heifers, just so he could quit the Bar Dot one minute sooner made Jack smile.

"What is so amusing, Sinclair?"

Might as well be honest about part of the matter. "Sir, that's not a smile, it's a grimace. I've been riding in grit and dust and my crotch is killing me. If I don't get to a tin tub soon . . ."

Buxton laughed and waved a dismissal. He looked at his clerk. "All right, Carteret. We'll trust you by yourself. Two days from now?"

Clarence sat there with considerable dignity, more than Jack had noticed in a long while. "I won't disappoint you, sir," he said.

"You had better not," Buxton said with more menace than Jack knew was necessary, when addressing a wounded gentleman like Clarence Carteret. But that was business.

"Go on, both of you," Buxton said. "As I said, Mrs. Buxton is dying."

Unsure what to say to that remark, Jack touched a hand to his forehead and beat Clarence to the door. "I don't mind confessing that Buxton unnerves me, at times," he remarked to Lily's father when they were both across the porch and down the steps. He untied his horse but walked alongside Clarence.

"You're probably in a great hurry," Clarence said with a half smile of his own. "I won't think you rude if you ride ahead."

"Nah. Maybe walking is better. Can't be worse, anyway," Jack said. He gazed into the distance for a moment. "I'm not certain if there is a more tactless man in the entire territory than our boss. You have to put up with that every day?"

"On a bad day." Again there was that ghost of a smile. "Perhaps Mrs. Buxton has the right idea."

"I had no idea you were a wit," Jack said when he finished laughing.

The sigh that came from Clarence Carteret could have put out a lighthouse lamp. "There is a great deal no one knows about me. I even used to be a caring father and a good husband." It was his turn to look away. "The highway of life exacts a toll."

"I've noticed," Jack said dryly. He brightened, thinking of Lily. "You have a fine daughter, and that's something."

"I do," Clarence said with quiet pride. "It *is* something. This will surprise you, Jack: Although I look like a man with many regrets . . ."

"Oh, I'm—"

"No, it's true. I know what I am," Clarence said, his voice scarcely audible. "I have only one regret. There! I can see I surprised you."

"Well, yes," Jack admitted.

"It is this: After my dear wife died of yellow fever, and after Lily survived, she and I should have stayed right there in Barbados. I had a job working as a clerk for a plantation owner. Nothing grand, but I was good at it and Lily was happy."

"You went back to England? On purpose?"

Clarence nodded. "And everything went wrong. I know I am a weak man, but in Barbados I had work and a little home and a five-year-old child who was the joy of our lives."

"Why'd you go?"

They were getting close to the stable now, so Jack stopped.

"You don't have time for this," Clarence said, the meek man again.

"I do. Why'd you go?"

Clarence waited to gather his serenity, or so it seemed to Jack. He looked the foreman in the eyes. "My brother promised me a brighter future if I would go to India to manage some family business. He snatched Lily away and put her in a boarding school and sent me to India."

"You should have taken her along," Jack said, wondering how difficult it would be to part from a child, the only particle remaining after the death of Clarence's wife.

"She was still weak from yellow fever, and I thought it best." Clarence gave a harsh laugh that he adroitly turned into a cough. "My brother thought it best, rather. Like a fool, I bowed to his will since he controlled the family purse."

"Wha . . . what happened in India?" Jack asked, wondering if he really wanted to know.

"I missed Lily with ever fiber of my heart, and I started to drink. I wallowed in alcohol and fair ruined the family business until others took it over and sent me home." He spoke calmly, but Jack heard the underlining shame and disappointment in his voice.

"I'm sorry for you," he said, and it sounded so lame to his ears. "Did he send you somewhere else?"

"I was given a few weeks to visit with Lily—she was ten then—and sent to Canada to a smaller family business." He wrinkled his nose. "A fish processing plant somewhere in the interior, where I drank more. After that I was sent to Scotland on more business, which I made a muddle of. Are you seeing a pattern?"

In a hurry as always, Madeleine walked by with her daughters, all of them struggling with bags of coffee and flour. Jack handed his reins to Clarence and lent a hand. When he returned, Clarence was still standing there.

He handed Jack the reins. "My brother gave up then, and I became a remittance man. I was banished to Wyoming Territory, told to buy a ranch, and stock it with cattle. I would get a quarterly check deposited in the nearest bank." He raised his eyes to Jack's. "You know the rest, I think."

"I know you bought the property, but I don't remember seeing cattle on it."

"No, you wouldn't have. I drank away the cattle money, and then I lost the ranch to you in a stupid card game. Jack, I disgust myself."

What could he say? Jack hesitated a moment, then put his hand on Clarence's shoulder and gave it a squeeze. Tears started in the older man's eyes. He gave a rueful laugh.

"Listen to me, going on about my petty problems, all of which I brought on myself! You fought a war and I don't hear complaints from you."

Jack kept his hand on Clarence's shoulder, drawing him closer. "I think everyone fights a war, Clarence. Mine was just easier to see than yours." He looked up. "Hey, guess who's coming to take you home?"

Clarence looked up and Jack saw all the love in his eyes as Lily waved and walked toward them. "She's the best thing that I ever did," he whispered. "I know her life is hard too, but she is a great lady."

"No argument from me," Jack said with a smile of his own. "Say, uh, Clarence, we've all sort of noticed how you've been perking up lately. Seems to me like you might be turning the corner on your . . . your difficulties."

"People have noticed?" Clarence asked, and his eyes had a hopeful glint to them now, a sort of quiet pride.

"Preacher was saying to me only yesterday—he talks and keeps us awake on long drives—he was saying that you're walking steady and your color is better." Jack patted Clarence's shoulder. "And my goodness, you seem to have found a kindred spirit with numbers in Nick Sansever. I think you're a teacher too."

Clarence's smile widened. "He's a bright lad! I've been thinking: Lily says you're always after her to have a plan. I have a little plan of my own. When I get to Cheyenne, I'll see if I can act on it."

"Care to share?"

"Not yet. It's just an idea right now." He patted Jack in turn. "You've been kind to listen to my ramblings. I never talked about any of this before."

Maybe you should have, Jack thought, wondering at the sorrow people bring on themselves.

He stepped back as Lily took her father by the arm and kissed his forehead. "I was wondering if you found yourself trapped between ledgers, Papa," she teased. It was a gentle joke, the kind of joshing that a parent might use on a child.

Jack saw clearly how the relationship had changed. Lily had taken charge of her father in such a loving way that he doubted Clarence had a clue. He *was* a weak man, one who needed structure and guidance, much as a child would. Jack tipped his hat to Lily and moved toward the horse barn, trying not to walk funny.

As for me, that would never do, he thought, watching them walk away, close together and bumping shoulders the way people who loved each other did. He had been in charge so long that he didn't know any other way to act, but a weak man might look with relief on being corralled and guided by someone stronger.

Smiling to himself, he curried his horse, grained him, and then turned him into a loose box to forage and rest from three relentless days of hard work. A half hour later, after giving Nick and his sisters a dime apiece to haul hot water to the shed that subbed as a bathing room, he stuffed as much of himself as he could into the community tin tub and sank into the water. Stretch probably had some calamine lotion to daub on his sorer parts.

So Clarence Carteret had a plan too? One imp in his brain tugged at him to be wary because weak men can't be trusted. The other one clasped hands above his head in a victory salute. Before he closed his eyes in the bliss of warm water lapping at his aches, Jack wasn't certain which imp to heed.

CHAPTER 28

In the classic fashion of man proposing and God disposing, Jack didn't need to escort Clarence to Wisner after all.

Lily had packed her father's bag, frowning over frayed collars and shirts that had suffered from Wyoming's hard water. If they were able to move somewhere else after school ended in May—provided she could save every cent of her princely salary—maybe they could find a town with actual stores and a Chinese laundry.

As they hurried to the cookshack for breakfast, Lily noticed the air had turned chillier. The wind blew in fits, puffs, and bellows from the northwest, and practically threw them into the dining hall.

Jack was sitting with a stranger, a genial-looking fellow who shoveled in Madeleine's admittedly excellent flap-jacks like a man who hadn't been near breakfast in weeks. Jack gestured to them and they came closer. He stood up.

"Clarence, this is . . . this is . . ." He leaned toward the man wielding his fork with such dexterity.

"Ed Parker," he said. He tipped his loaded fork in salute. "She's some cook."

"Ed is going to Wisner and he said he'd take you along too, if you're agreeable," Jack said. "There's so much to do here."

Ed eyed Lily's father. "Got room on the wagon, if you're not picky about sitting with a scoundrel." He laughed, showing off flapjacks and blackened teeth.

"I haven't been picky in years," Clarence assured him. "Let me have breakfast first, and then I'll go back to my house and get my bag."

Parker nodded and directed his interest to two new flapjacks that Amelie put on his plate. Jack joined them at their table, nodding to Chantal when she refilled his coffee mug.

"Says he comes from Marquardt's outfit, but I don't know him. If you'd rather wait a day, I can probably free up Preacher."

Clarence shook his head. "Mr. Buxton made it amply plain that he wanted this money in consortium hands as soon as feasible." He sighed. "They want to buy even more Texas cattle for next year's drive north."

"Jeez Louise," Jack said in disgust. "Thanks, Clarence, for agreeing to this. You too, Ed." He leaned closer to Clarence. "Did Buxton give you any money to stay at a hotel?"

"He never does," Clarence replied, so serene that Lily had a sudden urge to shake him. *Papa, it's one thing to be proud, but another thing to be meek*, she wanted to tell him, but he had been pummeled enough by events and time. He didn't need his newly found daughter berating him.

"I'll take care of him," she told Jack, more sharply than she should have, because both men looked at her in surprise.

"I was going to offer to—"

"No need, Jack. I have a little money set by," she said, wincing inwardly because she knew better than to interrupt good-intentioned people, even when she knew Jack Sinclair had her father's welfare at heart.

Jack reddened, and Clarence put his hand on her arm. "He didn't mean anything by it, daughter."

"I'm sorry. It's just that your boss is a stingy fellow," she said, perhaps louder than she should have, because Will

Buxton glanced her way with a frown. "And I'm making it worse," she finished in a whisper. "Forgive me?"

Jack nodded, but she could tell she had wounded him. She nearly said it: *Someone has to come to my father's defense and it should be me*, but she choked the words back in time and nodded instead, miserable, because she liked Jack Sinclair, liked him a lot. Now he would think she was a shrew and a busybody. She mumbled something about seeing her father back at the house and left the cookshack.

The air was definitely cooler. Maybe she could work up her nerve soon and ask Madeleine where a lady might find warmer undergarments in this windscow of a territory.

Lily stood still. "Stop it," she murmured. What had happened to her appreciation of the territory, and her admiration for her little students? Blown by the wind, she suddenly realized how much she loved her father. "Papa, I just want to smooth your tattered way," she said to the wind, which obligingly carried her words east.

She hurried to her house and dug around for some cheese and crackers in the lean-to kitchen. Too embarrassed to return to the cookshack for breakfast, she gathered it into a napkin, along with some bread crusts for the Little Man of the Prairie. She reminded herself that she had asked her children to think of a name for the pack rat.

Looking as cold as she felt, Papa opened the door.

"Papa, I'm sorry," she began. "I just . . . I just." She took a deep breath. "I just love you, and I fear I try too hard to be your champion. Forgive me?"

He answered by opening his arms. She moved into his embrace, relieved and happier than she remembered in years. Clarence Carteret was no protector, and he never would be. He was her father and she loved him. She thought of all the years they could have been tramping the world together, and she mourned the lost moments, even as she cherished their future, whatever it looked like.

How could she say all that? She tapped his shoulder. "You're my papa," she said simply.

"I wish I had sent for you sooner. Ah, well. We have time now."

"I have a little money," she told him, going to her trunk, which she had covered with a tablecloth dredged up from some cubbyhole and turned into a bedside table. She removed the tablecloth and the copy of *Ben-Hur* that she was reading at night, after Jack reshelved *Ivanhoe* (always with regret), and left. She had earlier hidden her uncle's money in her extra corset, fearing that her father would scavenge through the trunk.

It was all there. She sat back on her heels. "Uncle Niles gave me fifty pounds," she lied. "He wanted me to invest it in your cattle herd for him. I had it changed into dollars." She counted out ten dollars and looked him in the eyes. "That should buy a nice room and meals." She took a deep breath and plunged ahead. "I won't give you more because I'd rather you weren't tempted to spend it . . . inappropriately."

There. She sounded like the parent to the child, but he made no objection. His fingers closed around the greenbacks. "I won't need all this for any room in Cheyenne, but I'd like to buy you something nice. What do you need?"

Sweet man, sweet, sweet man. She laughed and held her hand out, and he pulled her to her feet. "Papa, you'll be embarrassed, but what I really think I need are what they call union suits for ladies. I don't have anything warm to wear, you know, under everything."

Papa scratched his chin. "A dry goods store here might have what you need."

Blushing, she wrote her measurements on a card and tucked it in his pocket. "If you have time, and you're not too embarrassed, I'd appreciate it."

"I have time for you," he said, putting on his coat again. "Walk me as far as the Buxtons'. Mr. Parker said he'd meet me there in an hour." He waved the ten dollars and then pocketed it. "Fifty pounds, eh? Niles has no idea what cattle cost."

He laughed, the first genuine laugh Lily had heard in years, maybe even since Barbados, when they were all so happy. "Hang onto the rest, my dearest. Maybe you can invest in Jack's cattle herd because it's a modest sum. You know, keep it on the, ah, family ranch. I'll never tell Niles."

She smiled back, pleased to hear him laughing about what she knew must have been a sore point with him. "Maybe it'll buy a salt block for Bismarck."

"One or two thousand! Don't forget: I know salt blocks because I account for all the Bar Dot's business."

"So you do, Papa, and you're good at it."

It touched Lily to see how he basked in even the smallest compliment. He had heard so few in his life. "Maybe you can teach Nick how to do double entry bookkeeping—you know, for those moments when he isn't breaking broncs."

"I could do that, Lily. When I get back."

Arm in arm they walked up the hill, struggling against the wind together. "Papa, wherever we go next year, let's find a place with no wind," she said, shouting to be heard.

"I hear that San Francisco is nice," he shouted back.

Just then, the wind stopped, and his words carried so far that Fothering, helping Luella, looked behind him in surprise.

Lily and her father laughed. "San Francisco, then, in 1887," she said.

He stood still, as if struck by something important. She gave him an inquiring look.

"Daughter, only a few months ago, I would have said, 'I'll drink a toast to that.'"

"But not now?"

"No. I don't know if you are aware, but I've been

imbibing less and less." He took a deep breath, and she saw the pride in his face. "Last night, I didn't drink anything."

She hadn't been aware and couldn't help the tears in her eyes. Papa kindly wiped them away with the end of his muffler. "San Francisco in 1887," he told her softly. "You can count on me."

Lily walked him to the Buxtons' porch and kissed his cheek. She tightened his muffler, and wished he had a hat made of something warm. At least Wisner was only four miles, and then he would be on the train, chugging to Cheyenne. With Papa gone, maybe it wouldn't do to have Jack come to her house tonight for a reading lesson and *Ivanhoe*. When she was helping the children in the dining hall tonight, she could take him aside and apologize for speaking sharply.

"Write when you get work, Papa," she teased.

Papa waved and gave her a thumbs-up—so American and so vulgar, and she loved it. Fothering and Luella waited for her, and she continued up the hill with them.

"I heard the mention of San Francisco," Fothering said. "Making plans, are we?"

"We are, indeed," she said.

He sent Luella skipping ahead. "Maybe you would like a butler in San Francisco. Mrs. Buxton is ever more certain daily that she is going to die. She's even starting to cling to Luella, which is unnerving in the extreme. Poor child doesn't know what to do." He turned to face her, hanging tight to his hat. "You have no idea what a refuge school is for Luella."

Suddenly, Lily knew that even if she was never paid a penny for her efforts at the Bar Dot Temple of Education, her cup of purpose already flowed over the rim. "I think it is a refuge for most of us," she assured him. "As for needing a butler: would you like to live somewhere and not have to resort to an English accent? Papa and I won't require it."

He leaned closer and spoke in his Ohio accent. "Lily, you're a spiffy gal."

Nick had already started a fire in the stove. Usually there was a cheery warmth by now, but the wind had a bite to it so strong this morning that even the winter count robe fluttered from the darts of cold air that forced themselves through the gaps in the log walls.

"Better get more wood from outside," she said, taking off her coat, then thinking she might just want to leave it on. No, that would hardly be professional, even in a tiny little classroom in the middle of nowhere. Still, she might keep it close on the back of her chair today.

Nick put two fingers to his forehead in salute and went outside. He carried in two armfuls, and then it was time to call the class to order and contemplate True Greatness, once they decided on a name for the Little Man of the Prairie.

Chantal raised her hand. "Miss Carteret, I think I saw the Little Man peeking out of the hole yesterday."

"Do you know, I think I did too," Lily said. "All the more reason to name a fellow class member."

Trust Luella to be literal. "Miss Carteret, what can he possibly learn from us?"

"Maybe the bigger issue is what are we learning from him?" she asked in turn, even as she wondered if real teachers found more of their lessons outside of the arithmetic and reading.

A thoughtful silence followed, then Amelie slowly raised her hand. "That maybe we should be kind to those smaller than we are?"

The children nodded.

"Let's put these on the blackboard," Lily said as she stood up and turned to the board. "I like that one. What else?"

"That if you steal something, you'd better leave a pebble behind?" Luella offered, then covered her mouth and laughed.

They all laughed. "Let's turn this to our advantage," Lily said. "How about, 'If you want to borrow something, please ask.'"

It was Nick's turn. "Maybe sometimes you don't know who your friends really are. He was afraid, and he didn't need to be."

Up it went on the board. "This is good. Now we need to name our Little Man of the Prairie."

More thought. "We don't know if he is a boy or a girl," Chantal said and blushed.

"We don't," Lily agreed. "For the sake of argument, let's say he is a boy."

"Edward?" Luella asked. "I like the name."

"St. Dismas," Nick said. "He is the patron saint of thieves."

More giggles. Lily wrote the name on the board, wondering what educationists would think of her class naming a pack rat. She turned to face her students. "We'll think about this. Now it is time for your arithmetic." She nodded to Nick. "I have asked Professor Sansever here to show us how to add and carry numbers." She held out the chalk to him, and he took it, his face full of purpose.

Lily walked to the back of the room as he went to the board, cleared his throat, and began his simple discussion. *If my father could see you*, she thought with pride.

She glanced out the window to see Mr. Parker and her father in the buckboard nearing the top of the incline, and remembered the letter for Mr. Li. "Pardon me, Nick, but I need to take our letter to Mr. Li to my father. He can take it by the Great Wall Café."

Nick waited while she fished the letter from her desk, the one signed by all her students inviting him to visit their class and tell them all about China. She nodded to Nick to continue, and she hurried outside in time to flag down Mr. Parker.

She handed the letter to her father, who promised to deliver it in person to the Chinaman in the Great Wall. "Don't let him talk you into chop suey, Papa," she said and blew him a kiss. "It isn't that fortifying."

Smiling to herself, she returned to the classroom, after reminding herself to bring her wool shawl tomorrow. That would look more professional than a coat worn indoors.

⁓

The morning passed with surprising speed, as all mornings seemed to in the Temple of Education. Chantal added the name Carol to the blackboard, reasoning that it could be a man or a woman's name. Luella changed Edward to Ned because she liked nicknames, and Nick stood firm with St. Dismas.

She had her children clear their slates and turned to the blackboard again. "Spelling words," she said as she printed. "Copy each word three times and . . ."

That was odd. Sudden movement caught her eye as the winter count buffalo robe began to flap. The morning had been growing steadily colder, and she had gotten used to the slight motion of the winter count robe. She glanced at the robe and watched it move faster, standing out from the poorly chinked wall. *Wind, wind, go away*, she thought, *come again another day*. But now the wind was moaning almost like a living thing. She felt the airs on her arms rise.

The students were copying her words, unmindful of the wind, until the room began to darken. Chantal looked up, startled, then Amelie and Luella. Nick was on his feet, uneasiness written all over his face. Only great force of will kept Lily from crying out when the building began to shake with the fury of a storm, and not just any storm.

She hurried to the only window, a south-facing one, and watched in wide-eyed horror as their little world vanished behind a curtain of snow. They could have been in the middle of Mongolia, colored pink on their world map, which was fluttering too.

Lily thought of her father, grateful he was probably in Wisner by now. She thought of Jack Sinclair and the other men and hoped they had taken shelter. Her thoughts returned to Jack. "You were right," she whispered, knowing she would never be heard above the wind.

CHAPTER 29

ᕼᕼᕼ

*L*ily glanced at the half-empty woodbox and then looked away, so the children wouldn't see the worry written on her face. She wished with all her heart that Nick had managed to bring in more wood before school started. She stared out the window as the children clustered around her.

"I can't see my house," Luella said. Her lips started to tremble.

"We can't see *anything*," Nick added. He glanced at Luella. "Don't cry. It's just snow, and you've seen snow." He hesitated, put his arm around her, gave her a quick pat, and let her go.

They all looked at her, and Lily felt the fear leave her body because she was the grown-up and they needed her as much as they had ever needed anyone in their lives. They knew it; she knew it. Every slight and hurt vanished as she turned into a woman grown. No matter where life led after this, she would never be the same again.

Lily took several deep breaths as the wind roared and shook the schoolhouse like a cat with a mouse in its jaws. Luella jumped in fright, and Chantal and Amelie drew closer together until their arms circled each other's waist. Then Amelie did a wondrous thing and held out her free arm for Luella, who quickly turned them into a trio.

"Girls, I want you to put on your coats and pull your chairs close to the stove. Nick, will you add more wood?"

He did as she asked, and his worried glance at the wood box was a mirror image of her own, only minutes ago. "That's probably enough for now," he told her, leaving several good-sized pieces in the box.

The room had turned into a weird twilight, which would have frightened her even more, had she not just experienced the epiphany of her life. She managed a chuckle. "Image this, my dears: we have enough light for me to read to you!"

"Miss Carteret, we are going to starve to death!" Luella burst out, with all the melodrama that Lily remembered from her interviews with Mrs. Buxton.

Lily rested her hands on Luella's shoulders, dismayed to feel her tremble. "It won't come to that," she said. "I have some bread and cheese. All we really need is water, and it will be a simple matter to heat snow on the stove."

"In what?" Chantal asked, sounding more curious than doubtful.

Lily pointed to the enamel pitcher and basin on the table by the door, and the flour sack towel that Madeleine had contributed when school began. "Nick or I can fill them both just by standing in the open door, and we will have all the water we need." She patted her slim belly. "As for me, I can always stand to take off a pound or two. No one is going to starve, Luella."

The building shook again, and this time snow pounded against the north and west sides. It swung to the east, as if testing every corner to find a way inside. The one south-facing window had already rimed over with ice as the temperature steadily dropped.

Nick gestured to her and she joined him by the door. His was an old man's face in a young boy's body. "This blizzard could last three days," he whispered. "I've never seen one like it so early." He cleared his throat, as if he had arrived at a decision. "We should hold hands and leave this place right now. We can get as far as the Buxton place, and they might not mind if we all stayed there." He gave a Gallic shrug. "If they do, well, maybe Fothering can help us."

She heard the doubt in his voice, as though the ranch's manager would have no qualms about sending her and the Sansevers on to their own quarters. Time to stop this right now.

"Nick, we'll never know, because no one is leaving the school until the storm is over."

"We can't stay here," he contradicted.

"We *will* stay here," she assured him.

He scowled at her, the sullen Nick she remembered from the first few days of school. He took several resolute steps toward his sisters, the issue decided in his mind. "Chantal and Amelie, come with me *now*."

The sisters looked at Lily and then at Nick. Chantal started to rise slowly, and Lily felt her heart sink. She knew she could stop the girls, but Nick was wiry and quick, and already pulling on his coat, his mind made up. If he went by himself, something told her that he would never survive.

"No. You are all staying here."

He shook his head and held out his hand for Chantal, who still stood there in a half crouch. "We'll just walk a straight line and we'll make it. How many times have we walked this way?"

Before Lily could stop him, he wrenched the door open. Although the door opened inward, the combined force of the wind and snow nearly separated the door from its hinges. Lily sprang to the door, slamming it shut with all the strength in her arms. In less than a few seconds, snow covered her body. She leaned against the closed door.

"No! You can't walk a straight line in this wind! No one can."

Nick eyed her, equally stubborn. His voice took on a

wheedling quality. "Mama will worry about us, and you don't want her to worry, Miss Carteret. It's a quarter mile down the slope and we've walked it for three weeks now. Then it's just another quarter mile to the cookshack. Come on, Chantal." He gestured again.

Chantal stood up, and so did Amelie, but only to force her sister into the chair and storm toward her brother, her usually gentle demeanor at odds with the sudden fire in her eyes. She pushed him off his feet and he stared up at her, looking as astonished as Lily felt. This was a different Amelie.

"Nicholas Sansever, we're not budging and neither are you!" Amelie had to speak up to be heard about the storm, but there was nothing but determination on her pale face. "Miss Carteret knows what she is doing, and you are just a child!"

It seemed as though even the snow held its breath for a moment, the silence weird and other-worldly. Lily shivered, and not from the cold.

"I . . . I'm older than you," Nick finally muttered, but the fight had gone out of him. Lily tried to touch his shoulder to reassure him, but he shook her off and stalked to the corner.

"Let him alone for a few minutes, Miss Carteret," Amelie said. "He'll come around." She ducked her head, shy again, now that the crisis had passed. She whispered, "Maybe you can give him something useful and heroic to do." He voice softened further. "Boys are like that."

"I think men are too," Lily said, forgetting the storm for a moment, a co-conspirator with a child. "I'll think of something, but right now, let's sit close together and read. Let's see—we're on chapter ten of Ragged Dick, aren't we?"

Lily pulled her chair close to the stove. The metal monster that had seemed so large on the first day of school seemed tiny now, a stove for a doll's house, as it struggled to heat the room. She opened the well-worn paperback, wishing she had thought to bring mittens this morning. She glanced around. Only Luella had mittens. Chantal and Amelie had shoved their hands deep into their coat pockets. "Here we are. "'Dick's ready identification of the rogue who had cheated the countryman, surprised Frank . . .'"

She had read only a few pages, speaking up to be heard above the wind, when Nick joined them, pulling his chair close to Amelie. His sister smiled at him, all turmoil forgotten in the generosity of her nature. She held his hand and pulled it into her more commodious coat pocket. He smiled back, and a look of affection passed between the brother and sister.

We are in this together, Lily thought, gratitude outweighing her fears.

She read four chapters, leaving Dick to confront Mickey Maguire, another street bully, when Luella raised her hand. "Yes, my dear?"

"Where do you think everyone is?" Luella asked.

"My father is likely on his way to Cheyenne on the train, your parents are probably hunkered down in your house with Fothering, and Madeleine is probably scolding the cowhands for tracking snow into her dining room," Lily said.

The children chuckled as she hoped they would. *And we are here alone*, Lily thought, *as alone as if we were in the middle of the Arctic.*

"You . . . you don't think anyone is out of doors in this, do you?" Chantal asked.

"Heavens, no! When the snow and the wind stop, I feel confident that Jack and Pierre will come and get us." Lily nearly said "rescue," but changed her mind. No need to alarm them further. "Nick, could you put another log in the stove?"

He looked at the now-empty woodbox and shook his head. "None left."

Chantal puckered up and started to cry, which meant Luella joined her. Amelie's face was solemn, her eyes apprehensive.

Lily wished her brain wasn't starting to feel so sluggish. She stood up and motioned the girls to sit closer together as she walked with Nick to the window, where nothing could be seen. "We have to get more wood from outside," she said.

He nodded. "Pierre moved the box closer, but it's still at the end of this side of the school."

"I know."

She stared at Pierre's buffalo robe winter count and slapped her forehead. "I'm a dunce. Nick, help me lift this off the wall."

Amelie brought her chair and Lily stood on it as all the children held the heavy robe from below, bearing the weight so she could lift the short rope he had used to hang the robe from the nails. She nearly fell from the chair as the robe came loose, but the children were there to catch it. Little Chantal ended up on the floor.

Lily detached the rope, wishing it were longer, and set it aside. "All right! Girls, I want you to wrap this robe around you, hair side in. Just sit close together. Ah, yes. I do believe there will be room for Nick and me too, but we have something else to do."

The girls did as she said. They dragged the winter count close to the stove that was barely warm. Amelie was the tallest, so she took charge, positioning the robe so everyone had cover.

"Excellent. Now, Amelie, I want you and Chantal to teach Luella all those verses of 'Sur le Pont.' She knows some of them already." She took a deep breath. "Nick is going to be our hero and go for wood."

She must have said it with confidence she barely felt, because Amelie nodded. In a minute they were singing. She turned to Nick. "Will you get wood for us? It's dangerous, but I'm going to tie a rope around you, and tie you to me."

He nodded, no words necessary. Maybe that was how heroes behaved. Lily didn't know.

"I'm going to tie the rope around your waist."

She tied it over his coat, dismayed to see that only two feet of rope extended. They looked at each other for a long moment as the wind howled and snarled. She looked back at the wall where the winter count had hung, promising herself that if they got out of this fix alive, she would keep coiled rope and a woodpile *inside* the classroom.

Her gaze fell on the canvas winter counts that her lovely children had created only a week ago, with Pierre's help. She walked closer, admiring the months her students had already filled in, chronicling their courageous lives in a wonderful way. She turned around, decisive now because she saw a way through this current dilemma. Likely there would be others before the storm ended, so she would take them one at a time and not borrow trouble.

"My dears, we are going to have to cut your winter counts into strips to make a longer rope for Nick. I'm going to tie the other end around my waist and stay inside. If something happens, we can all pull him back inside."

If she had thought there would be objection, she saw none, beyond the initial disappointment to see their work made into a rope. "I am almost certain we can prevail upon Mr. Sinclair to find us more canvas, so we can reproduce our winter counts."

Lily removed the canvas winter counts from the wall, made snips with her scissors, and ripped the winter counts into strips. "I'm not good with knots," she said when there was a pile of canvas on her desk.

Chantal took charge, deftly knotting each strip to the next. "Papa taught me a square knot," she said. "A bowline and sheepshank too, if we ever need them."

Amelie nodded, pride on her face. "Papa could do anything." Her face fell. "Except stay alive."

"He would be immensely proud of you," Lily said quietly. "Ah. That is a good spelling word." With fingers getting cold and stiff, she printed *immensely* on the blackboard.

She tugged on the growing canvas rope as Amelie deftly knotted one end to another until the makeshift lifeline stretched across the classroom. Nick smiled to see the results and tied a square knot, uniting the end of the canvas rope with his hemp rope. He gave Lily a triumphant smile and looped the canvas end around her and tied a slip knot this time.

"That's Papa's bowline," he said. "You can slip it out if you need to."

The girls all looked at Nick. Luella unwound the long woolen muffler from her head and neck and wrapped it around his head. He knotted it and tucked the ends into the front of his ragged coat, then crammed his knit cap over the muffler, until only his eyes were visible. Luella's mittens went on his hands next.

Lily stood at the door, her hand on the knob. "Just hug the wall and don't try to take too much at once."

He nodded to her and she opened the door, hanging onto it and trying to catch her breath as the wind whistled in with the snow and blinded her. Lily wiped her face and held the door close without chafing the canvas lifeline. *Just hurry,* she thought over and over, until he banged on the door and fell into the room, propelled by the wind. As he lay there gasping, Amelie and Chantal darted forward to grab the logs. Luella wiped the snow from his eyes with her pinafore, and Lily pulled the muffler tighter.

With her help, Nick stood up and went back outside. Six times he made the trip, only two logs each trip, which irritated him. On the seventh trip, the rope separated.

CHAPTER 30

⟨≈◦≈⟩

*L*ily fell down when the tension left the rope. She scrambled to her feet and wrenched open the door.

"Miss Carteret, you need a muffler!" Luella called. She sounded so far away, even though Lily only stood outside the open door.

"No time," she muttered and clutched the wall, head down, as the storm tried to dislodge her. "Luella, hang onto the end of this canvas," she called. "When I tug on it, you three pull for all you're worth."

She slowly moved along the log wall, yelling for Nick and wishing for a handhold, anything to grab. The logs were smooth with ice and she went to her knees.

Struggling to her feet, Lily stepped back involuntarily. One step and two, and then she couldn't even see the schoolhouse, even though it couldn't have been more than a yard away. She shoved her panic back into that corner of her brain where it had been pacing around all day and threw herself against what she hoped was the wall. Nothing. She tried again and this time her forehead banged against the logs.

Relief forced the blood back to her face, warming her for a minute. Deep breaths only hurt her lungs, so she took shallow ones, fighting with herself not to breathe too fast and faint. She edged along the wall and then fell over Nick.

He lay facedown in the snow, which had already mounded over his body. Drawing on all her strength, Lily

244

wrenched him from the snow, sobbing with even more relief when he clung to her, alive but so cold.

She tugged on the rope, then tugged again when nothing seemed to happen. "Please, please," she said under her breath, and sighed when she felt a returning tug from the little girls. Her arm around Nick, she tugged him along, then took heart when he seemed to move forward under his own steam.

It seemed like forever, but the door opened and they fell inside. Without a word, Amelie turned her brother over on his back and jerked the muffler from his face. He muttered his complaint, then opened his eyes.

"You scared us," Chantal said, her eyes huge in her face.

Lily closed the door and leaned against it, silent with more gratitude than she could ever remember. The room was cold, but all was orderly. The girls had stacked the wood Nick had managed to bring inside into an orderly pyramid by the stove. She watched as his sisters and Luella walked Nick to the winter count buffalo robe and gently bullied him into sitting in the middle of it.

"There now," Luella said, looking both capable and young, which touched Lily to her heart's core. "You're next, Miss Carteret."

"Not until I find that hatchet," she said. "We're going to need it."

Luella looked around, her eyes puzzled. "The pieces of wood Nick brought in are already small enough. Why do you need a hatchet?"

"We're going to have to burn the chairs and desks," Lily said quietly, not wanting to frighten them but needing their full attention. She pulled on her coat and grabbed Luella's muffler.

Luella gulped, but she did not fail Lily. "Amelie and Chantal, we're going to stand at the door for Miss Carteret, because she has to find the hatchet outside. Hurry now," she said, every inch a leader.

When the girls were in place by the door, Lily opened it and threw herself into the storm. The gentle pressure on the remaining canvas rope gave her heart and she bowed her head and moved along the wall. The wood pile seemed miles away and she couldn't see it. She should have reached it by now, which made her heart pound harder. She forced herself to remain calm, reminding herself that nothing was as it seemed. The world was white and she might have been in a giant cocoon, dunked in the world's coldest river. She was barely moving against the unbridled energy of wind and snow; no wonder she hadn't reached the wood yet.

Lily struck the wood with the toe of her shoe. She just grasped the snow-covered logs, relieved at their solidity, then tried to remember where Pierre had left the hatchet. She wanted to give up as wind whipped at her skirts and sent them sailing nearly over her head, despite the lead shot that she had sewed into the hem. She scolded herself for being too shy to ask Madeleine about long underwear, remembering a time that seemed so distant now when she had felt a little vain about her hand-sewn silk drawers.

In her frustration, she pounded on the logs, then moved around to the other side, kneeling down to dig in snow that was already waist deep. With a cry of delight that forced sharp pellets of ice into her mouth, she felt the snowy outline of the hatchet. Her fingers could barely bend, but she tugged it from the snow and started back to the schoolroom door.

She knew her whole body was coated with snow now, and the weight began to drag her down. Panicking, she tugged hard on the rope, then calmed herself when she felt the answering tug on her waist. She closed her eyes and inched along, then opened them and stared south toward the rest of the Bar Dot.

She should never have looked, because there was nothing to see. They were alone.

Funny how the classroom felt like a refuge, once they slammed the door with their combined energy. She sank to the floor and closed her eyes, grateful beyond measure.

"Miss Carteret?"

Chantal unwound Luella's muffler that Lily and Nick had both borrowed. Amelie held her arms out for Lily's coat, then shook off the snow, with Luella's help. They trundled her back into it when they finished and led her to the stove.

Not only had the girls stacked the wood, but they had mounded snow in the pitcher and basin and crowded them onto the stove, where they melted. Everyone had big drink of lukewarm water that tasted of autumn's leaves and good earth. The color was back in Nick's cheeks and he basked in praise from the ladies at the Temple of Education. When her own hands thawed, Lily parceled out thin slices of bread, cut with Nick's pocket knife.

"I'm going to pretend that mine is slathered in butter then sprinkled with cinnamon and sugar," Luella said. "You can pretend that too, if you'd like," she generously offered Lily.

"I believe I shall," Lily said, accepting a slice from Nick.

They debated whether to eat Lily's cheese and voted to save it for supper, with a three to two majority.

"That won't leave anything for breakfast," Amelie reminded them after the vote. "I think we should save it for breakfast tomorrow."

A re-vote yielded a different answer and Lily put the cheese in her desk drawer. They bundled themselves into the buffalo robe, after agreeing that the people on each end would take turns in the middle every twenty minutes. Lily was about to begin chapter fourteen when Chantal raised her hand.

"Yes, my dear?"

"Miss Carteret, do you think the Little Man of the Prairie is safe?"

Her eyes were anxious and Nick came to his little sister's rescue. "He's probably sound asleep and wrapped tight in all that yarn Luella provided," he said. His cheeks went pink. "Luella, thanks for loaning me your muffler. I was warm."

"Happy to," Luella said, her voice gruff.

The Little Man. It seemed to Lily that years had passed since that morning, when she had told her father that they would choose a name for the pack rat today. She wondered if the snow had stalled the Cheyenne Northern. At least there would be plenty of coal if worse came to worse and the passengers had to use it to keep warm. He would probably be stuck in Cheyenne until the tracks cleared. Lily wished she had given him more than ten dollars for lodging and meals.

Since she was on the edge of the buffalo robe, Lily went to her desk and pulled out the *Police Gazette*—bright pink, scurrilous, vulgar, utterly fascinating in a naughty way, and probably an even greater distraction than Ragged Dick and his steady rise to fame and fortune in New York City. After making sure that the page she wanted didn't contain any buxom women in chains, she looked around at her class.

"As I recall, Luella wants to name the Little Man Ned, and Nick favors St. Dismas." Lily held up the *Gazette*, one of the more questionable bits of educational material she had received for the school from someone, probably Stretch. "Let me read you this." She cleared her throat, wondering why it was sore and then remembered how loud she had screamed for Nick. The storm raged as she read the article about the Wyoming Kid, who robbed trains, stages, and ordinary citizens on the streets of Laramie, leaving behind a little note of thanks scrawled on expensive-looking stationery. She left out the paragraphs about his soiled doves in brothels from Sheridan to Cheyenne, and his sad, but defiant appointment with a hangman's noose.

"I think we should name our pack rat the Wyoming Kid," she concluded, folding the newspaper. "The Little Man always leaves us something, just like the Kid, and he is a thief too."

Her students exchanged glances. Nick laughed, looking young and more like the twelve-year-old he was, but still a hero who went for the wood; the boy who loved arithmetic, but who probably shouldered even more cares than she knew about.

"*I* like it," he said, and the girls nodded.

"When times are better, maybe we can make a little signpost next to his hole that says, 'The Wyoming Kid,' in big letters," Luella added, tracing out imaginary script with her hand in the cold air.

"Very well," Lily said. She rolled up the *Police Gazette*. "We'll stick this in the stove the next time we put in a log."

She thought she was being offhand and casual, but Chantal, astute Chantal, saw through the whole thing. She snuggled closer to her sister, and her voice was low. "Are we going to have to burn *everything* to stay alive, Miss Carteret?"

"We won't miss the *Police Gazette*," Lily said firmly. "We'll let the desks go next, because we're going to huddle close tonight and see how long . . ." She stopped. ". . . and keep each other warm." There was no point in trying to fool these wise-to-Wyoming children.

"I'd really like it if Mr. Sinclair found us," Amelie said, her voice wistful.

"So would I," Lily said, and never meant anything more in her life. Jack was a man with a capable air, the kind of man who could probably make the worst moment more bearable. Besides, she hadn't finished teaching him how to read, and there was *Ivanhoe*, with love and duty hanging in the balance in old England.

She was silent a long moment, then Nick prodded her. Her educationists back in Bristol would have thought it a rude thing to do, but she knew Nick better than they did. "Yes?"

"Miss Carteret, you said we are to change places every twenty minutes so those on the edge can get warm in the center. You've been on your outside edge for a long, long time, so it's time to trade places with me." He was firm, fair and right.

"Very well," Lily said, glad to move into the center of the robe again, since she was starting to shiver. "Now I think we need to find out what happens to Ragged Dick, who is trying to become respectable."

She read as the storm raged and the room grew colder and colder. Every syllable brought a puff of steam to her lips, which made Chantal clap her hands and exclaim, "We can see a story in the air!"

After two more chapters, when Ragged Dick continued his reformation and became known as Richard Hunter, Esquire, Lily forced herself to stand in the frigid room. "All right, everyone. Let's get up and march."

Amelie shook her head, but Nick pulled her to her feet and pushed her in front of him. He was rough and she gave him a hurt look, until he kissed her cheek and said softly, "March." Lily took Chantal's cold fingers in her own and marched with her up and down, then across the room. She looked back to see Nick squiring Amelie and Luella, who giggled.

"Stomp, stomp, stomp," Lily ordered, clapping hands that felt like frozen sticks. "You're the British Army marching across Spain to defeat Napoleon. We can't stop until we reach Toulouse, France. March!"

They marched while Lily ducked outdoors for more snow to melt on the stove, hanging onto the door frame and scooping in snow that was breast high now. The blizzard showed no signs of letting up. If anything, the wind shrieked louder. If the door didn't opened inward, she knew she would not be able to open it at all. *What do I do?* she asked herself as she crammed snow in the pitcher and basin. *Ask them to remember their favorite summer day? Think of a time when sweat rolled down their faces? When there were flowers to pick, and bees moved from blossom to blossom?*

She closed the door with some effort and set the snow to melting. While the children marched, Lily grasped the hatchet and whacked apart her beautiful chair from the Back Forty Saloon. The children stopped and stared, mouths open.

"We're going to keep warm, one way or the other," she told them as she wielded the hatchet and wished she had learned something practical at Miss Tilton's, like cutting wood or making food appear where there was none. "March now."

When she had reduced the dainty chair to wooden bones, Nick took the hatchet from her and more expertly dismantled his own stool and then Amelie's. He picked up Chantal's stool and gestured with the blade down. "If you hold it like this, Miss Carteret, you'll get a cleaner cut. Try it."

She did, and Nick gave her a thumbs-up. Between the two of them, the remaining stools turned into lifesaving fuel for the stove. Next he tackled the woodbox itself, his eyes calm and full of concentration.

"Now *that's* a lot of wood," he said out loud.

"I think we need to chop up one of the desks before it gets dark," Lily said.

He moved closer to her and spoke softly so the girls could not hear. "Do you think we will live through the night?"

"I have every hope," she replied, beating back that fear again. Did she sound positive enough? Brave?

"I expect you're right," Nick said, in his own rational way. "Let's grow the fire a bit. If the room is warm enough when we go to sleep, we'll do better."

He added chair legs until a slightly larger perimeter around the stove felt almost warm. Chantal lost her pinched look.

"Very well, my dears. Let us finish this story of Ragged Dick before it grows too dark."

The room was deep in shadow when she finished. "And there you have it," she said, closing the book. "Ragged Dick is now Richard Hunter, Esquire. He has a new suit of clothes and the admiration of his employer."

She looked at her students, who lived in a world far removed from that of an ambitious boot black. They were slowly freezing in the Temple of Education, hoping to survive until morning, when the grind of another day of a blizzard would continue. No one complained, not these children who understood hard times and disappointment as well as she did.

"I have much to be grateful for," she said out loud, and the others smiled.

Lily's watch told her that the hour was not much advanced beyond four in the afternoon, but the room was dark, except for the weird, glowing light that came from rapidly falling snow. The snow sounded faint, and she thought for a moment that it had stopped, until she realized that snow had completely covered the schoolhouse. So be it.

"The room is nicely warm now," she lied. "We should try to sleep."

The words had barely left her mouth to hang in the air when a series of bumps jolted the back wall of the school house, the side facing north. Luella gasped and Chantal started to whimper.

Lily's heart plummeted as she wondered what diabolical trick the wind was trying to play on them now. Wasn't it enough that they were cold and hungry and *already* frightened?

Two more bumps, and then a soft lowing, a sad sound, the sound of animals in trouble.

"Nick, what is it?" she whispered, pulling Chantal, weeping openly, onto her lap.

"It's cattle. Remember what Jack said about cattle drifting south? They're banging up against the back of the building."

"Mercy! Can we do anything?"

"No. Not if we want to live." He spoke firmly but reached for Lily as he shivered, as frightened as the others. She reminded herself that even heroes have their limits.

Somehow, all four of them had managed to squeeze themselves close to her. Lily reached her arms around them all. "We're going to . . ."

She stopped, hearing another sound. Something was scratching on the door. She reminded herself to breathe as she listened.

There it was again, a scratch scratch, pause, and then another scratch.

"Something's out there," Nick said, and he did not sound like a hero.

Suddenly, Lily knew what it was. "I'm going to the door, children," she said. "Move a bit and let me up."

Her teeth chattered as she left the warm nest of her children and hurried to the door. Bracing herself, she opened it, and reached down to touch frozen ear stumps—souvenir of earlier winters—and then a rough coat. He hissed, but to Lily's ears, it was a half-hearted effort. She petted the cat again, amazed that he allowed her touch. Would Francis a.k.a. Freak let her pick him up? She slowly put her hand under his belly, which produced no objection.

"Children, we have a visitor. Make some room."

CHAPTER 31

⟜⟨◊⟩⟞

*F*rancis sniffed the little bit of warm water that Luella took from the stove. She approached the cat with considerable trepidation, which ended quickly when Francis lapped at the water until it was gone. He startled Lily by curling in her lap and settling down. In another moment he was purring.

"Stars and garters, I never expected to see Freak —"

"Francis," Lily prompted.

"Francis turning into a star boarder," Luella concluded.

"I suppose anyone can change," Amelie added.

"If we get really hungry . . ." Nick began, and let the thought dangle.

Chantal started to laugh. "You'd have to catch him, and I don't think you could! Luella's right: Francis is our star boarder."

Nick eyed the cat from a cautious distance. "Why did he have to come into our schoolhouse?"

"Maybe he's never seen a storm like this one, either," Lily said. She set her hand down slowly on the little vagabond, driven to the dubious comforts of the Temple of Education because she had been kind enough to leave bits of food on a rock. "We all just need a little kindness."

No one questioned her puny wisdom, maybe because it was as true as anything she knew. Lily put her arms around Chantal and Amelie and drew them close to her in the dark. She thought of her uncle, who could have helped her father better by nurturing him, instead of sending him into world exile, accompanied by a quarterly check to keep away, a reminder of his worthlessness to the family. She thought of her own mistrust of her father, her hesitation to give him even ten dollars to buy a little comfort in Cheyenne, fearing he would spend it on liquor. True, he seemed to be changing, but why couldn't she have seen that for herself? When he returned, things would be different, and they would make plans for San Francisco.

Chantal gasped when the milling cattle bumped against the schoolhouse walls, not just the back wall, but on all sides now. How many were there? Lily, who seldom prayed, prayed that the men of the Bar Dot were warm inside the bunkhouse, and not out in the storm, searching for straying cattle.

"I wish they could come in, like Francis," Chantal whispered, her voice drowsy.

"So do I, my dear," Lily whispered back, and kissed the top of the child's head. Probably teachers weren't supposed to do things like that, but she wasn't a real teacher, so how could it matter?

"What are we going to do tomorrow? We don't have enough desks to keep the fire going all day."

Trust Luella to be forthright. "We'll think of something, my dear," Lily told her. She reached around Chantal to touch the child's shoulder. Luella leaned her cheek toward Lily's hand. Lily felt for Nick's shoulder on her other side, and he did the same thing.

"Nick, it's up to you and me to keep the fire going tonight," she told him, wishing he could just be the lad he was, and not someone forced to shoulder the burden she carried. "Can you and I take turns sleeping?"

"We can," he told her, "but Miss Carteret, I think you will be awake all night anyway, because you love us."

It was simply said. Lily knew that if her life ended that cold night, as the wind howled like doomed spirits on All

Hallow's Eve, she would have hardly a regret, because Nick had found her out.

✑

Nick was right. She stayed awake all night, watching the fire as the children slept and Francis purred in her lap. They kept each other warm and they lived. She knew there were two more desks to dismantle, and then her desk. The little bookcase might buy them another half hour. After that, who could say?

As the night wore on, the cattle grew quieter. She knew they were still there, because every now and then, the schoolhouse shook as they pushed against it. Even lowly beasts wanted to live another moment. She remembered her mother's death from yellow fever. They lay sick in the same room as servants fanned their hot bodies. She remembered the intensity of her mother's gaze as she looked at Lily, her only child. Lily had wanted to tell Mama one more time that she loved her, but the fever seemed to press down like a wet blanket, smothering them both.

"I loved you, Mother," she said softly into Chantal's hair. "Papa, keep being strong after we are all gone."

As the night wore on, even the wind seemed to tire. Long stretches passed in a supernatural sort of silence. She wondered if the moon had fought its way through clouds, because the room was strangely bright. She thought she could see out of their one window. Surely that couldn't be, but it was. The wind had blown away some of the snow. Maybe if someone were to search for the schoolhouse now, it wouldn't be buried in drifts.

Then the wind blew from a different quarter, as though trying to wear them down, and the drifts filled the window again. She closed her eyes, wondering how sixty seconds took so long to make a minute, and how sixty minutes struggled to become an hour. Time behaved so strangely in a storm.

They kept each other warm and they outlasted the storm. By morning—6:00 a.m., according to her watch—the storm had worn itself out. Snow still fell, but it fell softly and in a straight line, not blown sideways.

She took no comfort in the silence, since the blizzard left behind a bone-cracking cold that clamped down, until she knew that they needed more than wood from a couple of desks.

In sudden panic, she wiggled her toes, welcoming the pain because that meant blood still flowed there. Her legs ached from cold, but at least they ached. If she survived this next ordeal, she planned to cast away all modesty and beg for . . . for . . . what did they call them? . . . long johns.

In the low light, she squinted at the sleeping children, studying them for waxy spots of frozen skin. Everyone breathed evenly. They might have been in their own beds, and she hated to wake them. She looked down at Francis in her lap, who was looking up at her, with that scowl suggesting she did not measure up. Maybe it wasn't a scowl, really. His battle-scarred face spoke of spats and quarrels and hard living. *We probably all look like that inside*, Lily thought.

She couldn't understand all this wisdom that seemed to be arriving as she slowly froze to death. She had heard from an old pensioned veteran who had survived the Crimean War that his entire life flashed before him at Balaclava when the Russians counterattacked. *And what do I get but wisdom too late*, she thought, discouraged.

As the room lightened, she told herself not to look at the calendar, then looked at it anyway. She began to shiver as she stared at the date—Saturday, October 2. It gave her no satisfaction whatsoever that Jack Sinclair was right in his prediction that this would be a terrible winter.

She knew the stove needed to be replenished, but she just stared at it, as though she could only concentrate on one whole thought at a time. Her brain was getting stupid, and she just sat there.

God bless Nick Sansever. As she stared from the stove to the calendar and back, he rustled out of the warm cocoon of Pierre Fontaine's winter count robe. On stiff legs, he put two more sticks of desk into the stove. He held the stove's door open and looked at her.

"Miss Carteret, you put in the next two."

"But I . . ." *Don't want to move?* she thought. "Very well. Francis, you have to move." She shook the irate cat from her lap and staggered to her feet.

The girls' neat pyramid of wood was nearly gone. Two desk legs and part of the woodbox remained. Lily picked up the desk legs, ordering her stiff fingers to curl around the wood. In they went, and Nick closed the stove door with something resembling a flourish.

"We'll have to chop up another desk," he said. "You or me?"

He wasn't going to let her quit. Lily felt the blood flow into her legs and arms. She held out her hand and he gave her the hatchet handle first.

"Chop what you can, and I'll do the rest."

"Then we will have cheese," she said, pointing to the drawer where the single slice of longhorn cheese remained. "Remember what I told you last week?"

Hatchet poised, Nick thought a moment. "That breakfast is the most important meal of the day?"

They laughed together.

❦

Jack Sinclair decided there was no dignity and barely any mobility to two pairs of socks, moccasins, knee-length Dutch wool socks, overshoes, two suits of underwear, pants and overalls, and a wool army issue shirt he had bought from a furtive fellow in Wisner who was probably a deserter. The wool gloves inside wool mittens and his blanket-lined overcoat cut the cold, but just barely.

Without Will Buxton's sealskin cap pulled low over his forehead and Preacher's muffler tying the fetching ensemble together, he doubt he would have survived the nearly half mile on foot to the schoolhouse.

He couldn't find his own snowshoes, but Pierre brought his out from under his bed in the bunkhouse and told him not to lose them.

"Do you realize that if I fall down, I'll be as helpless as a turtle on its back?" had been Jack's observation to his dressers. He couldn't help but think of Ivanhoe preparing for a tourney. At least he didn't have to shrug himself into chain mail too.

Pierre just glared at him in his Lakota way that suffered no fools, gladly or otherwise. Jack already knew Pierre's opinion of complainers, so he buttoned his lip. They had weathered the blizzard in the bunkhouse, then cut a trail to the nearby cookshack when the snow slacked off after midnight. The first order of business had been to tie a rope from the bunkhouse to the cookshack for future wintertime strolls. The second had been to wipe Madeleine's eyes, nicely command her to blow her nose, hug her tight, then assure her that Lily Carteret was as sound as a roast and would never have sent the children to find their way home through the storm. Jack hoped that was the case, anyway.

Since the distance was not so far, Pierre said he would go to the horse barn and look for Stretch, whom Jack had sent, before the storm hit, to muck out the stalls. None of them had made any comment during that long day and night about Stretch, beyond the Preacher's observation that Stretch generally had common sense, and why should a storm prove the exception?

He sent Will Buxton and Preacher to brush off and take firewood to the cookshack. "What about the bunkhouse too?" Will had asked. Will always had a comment, which was starting to get on Jack's nerves, not that he could do anything about the boss's nephew or cousin or whatever he was.

"Just the cookshack right now," Jack said. He had other plans, but he wanted to keep them to himself for a while. No need for Will to think he had to know every little detail. Buxton he was, but the boss he wasn't.

To add to his already considerable bulk, Madeleine handed him a canvas sack with four loaves of bread and a small sack with dried apples. "That's in case another storm comes up and you can't get away from the schoolhouse."

The anxiety in her eyes humbled him. She had already lost her husband last spring. Any more arithmetic of death could break even a stalwart like Madeleine Sansever. "I have some extra blankets," he told her. "When I get your children back, you can use it to line their coats."

She nodded, then seemed to remember something. She held up a finger and he waited while she went into the lean-to bedroom she shared with her children. She came back with what look like a woman's union suit, wearing a blush on cheeks that didn't usually blush.

He knew Madeleine had probably heard it all, and maybe even done it all, but she still had trouble meeting his eyes. Her voice was scarcely above a whisper, so he revised his opinion of her rough and tumble ways. "I have been washing some of Lily Carteret's clothing, and . . ." She paused and went redder. ". . . and I've been washing her underthings too. They're just frivolous bits of silk and lace. She needs these." She thrust the garments at him and then looked away, which was probably a good idea, because he was having a moment's pause at "bits of silk and lace."

"I'm on it, Maddie," he told her as he took the union suit and stuffed it on top of the bread. That probably wasn't the appropriate turn of phrase for so delicate a subject, but he had said it. He slipped the loop of the sack over his coat and started toward the schoolhouse.

He couldn't help cursing a little when he passed the Buxtons' house, top heavy with snow now. Why in blue blazes had that woman insisted on the school so far away? So what if children would benefit from a healthy walk in brisk air? What had made him chuckle to himself and shake his head at the foibles of his betters made him frown now, and pray that those children—and their novice-to-Wyoming teacher—were still alive.

Even with Pierre's snowshoes, better than his own, the going was still difficult. The fickle winds had blown snow this way and that into fantastic drifts. He sank to his waist several times, which made his heart sink too. Chantal was so small. Could he get her through the snow to the cookshack?

This and other worries left his mind when he saw what had become of some of the Bar Dot cattle. Laboring along on Pierre's snow shoes, he kept his eyes ahead until he got the hang of the easy stride. When he felt more competent, he looked around, wondering about the odd mounds of snow, which seemed to be everywhere.

Curious, he veered from his route and approached the nearest mound. He gave it a push, and felt no give. He pressed again. Nothing. He began to brush off the snow, his heart jumping about in his throat as he finally came to a woolly, matted coat. Faster now, he brushed away the snow. The sight that met his eyes made him gasp and step back.

It was a steer, one of the Bar Dot herd, with its head down as though grazing, but more likely just trying to buttress itself against the pelting snow. The animal's breath must have created a frozen pipeline to the ground, holding the steer's head in its icy grip. It had asphyxiated, then frozen solid as snow packed itself around the beast as it struggled to breathe ice, then surrendered.

"Dear God in heaven, please don't let me find more like this," he whispered, even though he knew that each of these mounds contained a dead cow.

The sight so unnerved Jack that he hurried forward even faster, not looking from side to side anymore, because he didn't want to see the ruin of the Bar Dot. After what seemed like forever, he saw the school on its little slope beside the wagon road. Smoke seemed to be coming from the chimney, which relieved his heart. Drifts had nearly buried the small building, Lily's Temple of Education with True Greatness as its credo. Snow had packed and scoured the building, with impossible drifts predictably against the north and west sides.

Everywhere were the mounds of cattle, at least he hoped they were cattle, and not little bodies of children and their teacher who had thought to walk to safety. It was something someone unfamiliar to the territory might attempt. Jack swallowed hard, blinking back tears that he knew would only freeze on his face. He couldn't remember the last time he had cried.

Snow piled against the door, so he started to shovel, faster and faster until his breath condensed and froze on his face, creating a mask like the one that had killed the cattle. He forced himself to stop and slow his breathing, as he swiped at his own icy death mask. He wasn't a man to panic, except that he was, apparently.

He took a deep and appreciative breath, listened, and felt the greatest relief since Appomattox, when the Yankees had handed out rations to ranks of starving Johnny Rebs, he among them. He was only fifteen and hadn't eaten in a week of rapid march and skirmishes.

The children were singing and stomping. He shouldered open the door and stood there in so much gratitude that he couldn't form words.

He had heard the Sansever girls sing "Sur le Pont" several times, but this was a militant version as they marched in a circle and stomped their feet. And there was Freak the cat in the corner, observing and giving him a sour look.

Lovely Lily Carteret, her eyes like two coals in her head, stopped marching and put her hands on her hips, regarding him as if he were dense and stupid, which he thought was surprisingly accurate. Still, her voice was sweet. Maybe she thought she needed to cajole an idiot.

"Really, Jack, please close the door. We only have one desk left to burn."

Chapter 32

_J_ack resisted his first impulse just to gather them all in his arms, but it didn't matter, because Chantal and Amelie flung themselves at him. Luella followed, but Nick just stood there, giving him a grave look that told Jack all he needed to know about the last twenty-four hours. He could hardly bear to look at Lily, who obviously had not slept and who wore responsibility on her shoulders like a Portland cement cloak.

"Thank you for coming," she said with that well-bred British accent of hers, as though he had dropped in to pay his respects, drink tea, and eat little cakes. She ruined the effect of normalcy by suddenly pursing her lips tight together, which pulled her eyebrows closer and made her look more five than twenty-five. She took a deep breath that ended in a sob, so he knew who needed his attention right away.

He kissed Chantal, Amelie, and Luella in turn, set them aside, closed the door as their teacher had asked so politely, then went directly to her, his arms open wide. She threw herself against him, which was a feat in itself, since he was so heavily clothed. She didn't cry, but she shook so hard that he knew if he didn't hold her close, she would fly to pieces like an old wagon driven too hard.

Jack heard a snarl and felt a sudden heavy weight against his leg. Startled, he looked down to see Freak hanging onto his many layers of clothing, trying to murder him, most likely, because this was no ordinary cat. He let go of Lily to brush off the little monster, but Lily beat him to it. He stared as she bent down and gently extricated Freak, all the while admonishing him.

"There is no call for such behavior," she said, "and don't you put your ears back like that!"

"His ears are pretty much gone," Jack said. "How can you tell? Boy howdy, you have a bodyguard."

Lily gave her bodyguard a little swat on his hinder parts and he slunk away to the corner, facing in and twitching what remained of his tail. Luella burst into laughter, and so did the others. He listened, heard no hysteria, and realized that bruised and battered as it looked, all was well in the Temple of Education. He turned back to Lily.

"I'm sorry I couldn't come sooner," he said.

"We're grateful you came at all."

He remembered something he had to do. He went to the door, threw it open, drew his .45, squeezed off two shots, and closed the door. Lily had clamped her hands to her ears.

"I told the hands I'd fire two shots if all y'all were all okay," he explained as he worked his well-padded arm over to reholster the gun. "They'll be here in a bit to help out. Meanwhile . . ." Jack unlimbered the cloth bag and tucked Madeleine's undergarments under one arm. He took out the bread and dried apples and handed them to Nick.

Jack understood immediately what had happened in the past twenty-four hours when Nick gave the food to Lily. There was no question who was in charge in that classroom, even through what he imagined was a terrifying ordeal. It was frightening enough in the bunkhouse, and they were all grown men.

Lily set the food on the remaining desk and her students gathered close. "Here now."

She handed each child a loaf of bread. Jack felt his tears start again when each child broke off a goodly hunk and handed it to Lily. They all ate silently, dipping into the dried apples, no one taking too much at once. These were children who had learned a terrible lesson in a mere twenty-four hours—Luella, for sure. Jack thought the Sansevers already knew the lesson.

Lily ate one of the portions the children had given her, then took another to the corner, where Freak the cat sulked. "Here you are, you little beast," she said in a most loving tone, setting the bread by his lashing tail. As he listened to her, Jack knew he'd give the earth to have any woman give him such a tender endearment. The thought made him smile, which hurt his cold face.

As the children sat together by the stove, Jack decided to put his arm around Lily's shoulders whether she wanted him to or not. "I'm impressed," he said, which sounded so stupid when it came out of his mouth.

She must not have minded. "I've never been so frightened in my life."

She kept shivering, and he remembered Madeleine's little gift. "Here. Madeleine thinks you might need these." He handed her the two-piece undergarments, wondering if she would slap him across the chops.

Lily took the underwear with a huge sigh. Her light tan complexion sported two pink spots, so he knew she was embarrassed. She was also unwilling to look this gift horse in the mouth, because she told him to turn around and stand between her and the children, who were concentrating on the food. He did as she said and waited as she pulled on the drawers.

And waited. She tapped him on the shoulder. "Pardon me, but my hands are too cold to unlace my shoes. Could you . . . ?"

He could and did, sitting her down on the remaining desk. He removed his mittens and gloves, and unlaced her shoes. She had well-shaped feet, but her shoes were impractical. He wasn't sure what he could do about that.

"Here." She handed him the bottoms, her face even redder. "Just get them started. I'm so cold that I can't do it."

That admission was all he needed to snap him back into his foreman duties. He knew he was responsible for everyone on the Bar Dot, because Oliver Buxton just didn't understand the rules. He pulled the bottoms on Lily without a blush or a qualm, because she was part of his stewardship. The only issue was safety and survival.

He pulled them all the way up over her ridiculous lacy underwear which he could feel, but did not see, because he kept his eyes on a spot on the map of Europe just west of England. She didn't protest when he felt along her waist until he found the cords, and tied them firmly, but not too tight. He put his hands back where they belonged and helped her tug down her dress.

"That'll help," he told her. "You and I are about the same height, and I have another pair I'm not wearing. I'll give them to you and you'd better keep them on. It's too cold to risk your legs." He tucked the flannel top into her overcoat pocket and pulled on his gloves. "You can put it on later."

She accepted all this attention and wisdom in the spirit in which he offered it, which eased his heart. She looked him in the eyes and said simply, "Thank you." Her eyes showed how desperately tired she was, how depleted, from a test that not all would have passed.

She ate another hunk of bread. She held another out to him and he took it, hungry too. "Do we wait for the others?" she asked.

They were both sitting on the last desk now. He leaned closer and spoke in her ear. "Stretch never made it to the bunkhouse. I sent Preacher and Will to haul more firewood to the cookshack, and Pierre to look for Stretch."

"Lost?" she asked, her eyes wide. "Oh, I hope not. It was a dreadful storm."

"He was in the horse barn to muck out the stalls. I hope he stayed there."

She leaned close this time. "Nick wanted to take his sisters and leave," she whispered. "I was almost tempted because I didn't know what to do." She shuddered, which gave him a perfect excuse to put his arm around her again.

"You did everything right in here."

"I had help," she told him simply, and looked toward Amelie. "She refused to leave and told him to do as I said."

"Amelie?" he asked, surprised and speaking louder than he intended. Amelie heard her name and looked his way, kind and charitable in her silent way. He blew her a kiss, and she blushed.

"She was forceful and he listened," Lily whispered. "I do not intend to ever underestimate her."

And I will never underestimate you, he thought. This first blizzard could have ended so badly for the Temple of Education, but it did not. He had long thought of himself as the most capable person on the Bar Dot, with Pierre running him a close second. Now there was a third.

She looked around and sighed. "Now our lovely class-room is gone."

Jack was prepared to tell her firmly, if he needed to, that there would be no more school in a building that was too far from the main ranch quarters. She beat him to it, which relieved his heart. As much as he didn't mind meting out bad news when warranted to his cowhands, he had no wish to disappoint someone as fine as Lily Carteret.

"We can't continue here," she said. "I won't have the children so far from help. Will you think of something else?"

He nodded and stood up, then held out his hand for her. "Most certainly. Right now, up you get. We need this last desk turned into firewood. You or me, Nick?"

Nick took the hatchet and began his destruction of the last desk. He chopped clumsily, his hands stiff with cold. Disappointment on his face, Nick handed the hatchet to

Jack, who finished the job. He was liberal with the wood in the stove, and soon the room was nearly bearable. The children seemed to relax. In a few minutes, Chantal came to Lily and whispered in her ear. Lily nodded and the two of them went to a corner of the room. He watched, curious, then looked away when Lily spread her skirts and Chantal went behind her.

"We solved this problem early in the storm," Lily said, with no embarrassment.

When Chantal finished, it was Amelie's turn, and then Luella's. "What do *you* do?" Jack whispered to Nick, who was also looking away.

"Just open the door a crack and let fly," the boy said. "It's easier for us men."

Jack chuckled. When everyone was back near the stove, Lily asked her students to sing "Sur le Pont," for their rescuer. He applauded when they finished, and he remained an appreciative audience as they sang "Silent Night" and "O Come All Ye Faithful."

"We learned several songs last night," Lily explained. "I am already planning a Christmas party." She looked toward the window that was a solid block of ice. "Who knew that it would look like Christmas on October 2?" She gave him a solemn look. "You knew."

⌒∽⌒

An hour passed and another. As Jack began to wonder if he should have been more frugal with that final desk, someone banged on the door. Informing him that it was her turn to be the door monitor, Luella opened the door and ushered in Preacher and Will, bundled to their eyebrows and snow covered.

"Need a little help with your classroom, Miss Carteret?" Preacher teased.

Lily was sitting cross-legged with her students on Pierre's winter count, which Jack knew had saved their lives, that and the wisdom to burn the desks. "They're a rowdy lot," she teased back, which made her students look at each other and grin. Chantal lay with her head on Lily's thigh, and Luella sat close on her other side.

"We were just biding our time until more knights in shining armor arrived," she said. "It appears that our wish is granted, gentlemen. Do help us tidy things."

Jack couldn't help smiling. Lily had that effect on the average cowhand, and probably vagabonds and rustlers, for all he knew. They all looked at her expectantly.

Lily clasped her hands in front of her and took a deep breath. "My dears, it seems that we must close the Bar Dot School."

Amelie burst into tears. Jack had wondered when the sum of two terrifying days would sink in, and here it was before him. He shouldn't have worried. Lily wrapped Amelie in a fierce embrace and held her. She looked over the child's head to her other students, who looked equally solemn, with Chantal sniffing back tears.

"My darlings, here is the wonderful thing about schools: they don't disappear just because the building does! We'll take the school with us." She kissed Amelie's cheek. In true Gallic fashion, the child turned her other cheek toward Lily, who laughed and kissed that one too. "Now then, let us gather our books and slates and whatever papers we have. Preacher, will you roll up our maps?"

Everyone did as she said. Soon there was a small pile on the winter count, the painted surface showing, now that the furry side had done its duty and kept the children alive. Lily stuffed the chalk in her coat pocket and walked slowly around the room, near tears herself. Jack tried to see it through her eyes, a magic place where children learned. He vaguely remembered his Georgia childhood, planting cotton, chopping cotton, and getting beaten for mistaking weeds for the tender plants. Black and white, bond and free, they hoed through humid summers where the air was heavy enough to drink, then harvested, dragging huge burlap sacks behind.

There had been no Temple of Education for him. As he watched more favored children carry books and slates down the dirt track toward the Methodist school, he had told himself that learning was for sissies, even as he yearned to walk with them. His envy showed only once, and his father had beaten him for that too. He hadn't understood that beating then, but he did now: his father had wanted to learn as much as his oldest son.

He watched as Preacher and Will bundled up the buffalo robe and tied it with what looked like a canvas rope, knotted over and over, that they had found just outside the door.

Lily stood beside him. "We ripped up our own winter counts and tied them together to make a rope. Nick and I bound ourselves together and went for wood."

"I can find more canvas," he told her, grateful all over again at the common sense and courage of the woman beside him.

She nodded. "I hated to do that, but we had to survive."

Will surprised him by shouldering the heavy bundle without being asked. Maybe there was hope for such a useless cowhand, after all.

Still the children stood in the nearly empty room.

"You can set up shop again in a corner of the dining hall," he told them, which brought smiles, but not for long.

"We can't just leave the Wyoming Kid," Luella said.

"The what?" he asked, amused.

"We named our pack rat the Wyoming Kid," Lily explained. "Oh, dear."

No one moved. Without a word, Lily put the rest of her loaf of bread and the remaining dried apples by the Little Man of the Prairie's hole.

"That's not enough for a whole winter," Luella said mournfully.

Lily took her hand. "We'll have to trust that The Kid is wise and capable and tough." She gave Luella's hand in hers a little shake. "Like you, my child. We have to leave now."

"What about Freak?" Jack said.

"Francis," Lily told him.

The cat sat near the barely warm stove, watching them. Lily held out her hand—Jack had given her his too-large mittens—and spoke softly. "Francis, I have to close the door."

"He can't understand you," Luella said.

The cat was still no fool. He looked at them all with vast disdain and made his way slowly toward Lily.

"He'll do you damage," Jack warned as she picked up the feral stray who had taken refuge in the Temple of Education.

"No, he won't," she contradicted. "We kept each other warm last night. There now, Francis. Be a good cat." She settled the bedraggled veteran of many winters along her arm and tucked him close to her side. He growled deep in his throat, which only made her say, "Oh, you." Jack closed the door and they started down the slope, walking past dead cattle, snow-covered and anchored to frozen ground, killed by their frantic efforts to breathe.

Nick stared at the mounds. The wind had picked up as evening approached, uncovering some of the cattle. Chantal cried out in fright, so Preacher swooped her up and settled her on his shoulders. "Eyes ahead," he told her. "You're safe."

Jack came last, his eyes open for stragglers. They slipped and slid toward the ranch buildings, all of them looking puny and ready to collapse, and this was only the first storm.

Fothering was watching for them as they came close to the Buxton house, bearing its heavy weight of snow on the roof. He met them at what used to be the picket fence, but which was now just another mound of snow.

Jack felt no surprise at Luella's reluctance to turn loose of Lily's hand. "We have to hurry inside," Fothering told her, his eyes kind. "Your mother is hungry for the sight of you."

As if to emphasize his words, Mrs. Buxton began to wail from her upstairs bedroom, Chantal and Amelie looked at each other in alarm, then in sympathy at Luella.

"We'll have school again quite soon," Lily said in a soothing voice. She waved to Luella as the child turned around to watch her.

"I'd hate to live there," Jack muttered to Lily.

"Surely it isn't all that terrible," Lily replied, but he heard no conviction in her low voice.

Pierre joined them as they passed the horse barn. He shook his head at Jack. No Stretch.

They trudged to the cookshack. Like thirsty horses heading toward the water trough, Amelie and Nick broke into a run. Chantal started to clamber down from Preacher's shoulders, so he helped her. The kitchen door opened and with cries of delight, Madeleine welcomed in her little brood. Her arms around her little ones, she raised one hand to gesture them all toward her. Preacher and Will started in her direction.

Might as well broach the matter with Lily right now, especially as she was looking at the other buildings, trying to discern which one was the house she shared with Clarence Carteret. He took her arm when she started toward what he knew was an old tack shed, and not her house.

"Lily, it's too far to your house from the rest of the buildings."

"Yes, but I . . ."

"I've already moved into the bunkhouse. You and your

father will be in my old place. It's closer and I won't have an argument."

From the look of exhaustion on her face, an argument was the last thing Lily seemed to be entertaining. She nodded. "All I want to do is sleep."

"Did you stay up all night, feeding the fire?"

She nodded again. "Mostly I want to be warm. Will I have to wait until spring for that?"

"I fear so," he told her. This was no woman to lie to.

"Very well. I do need to my clothes, and there's *Ivanhoe*."

Jack took Lily's hand. "We haven't had time to shovel, so just be careful."

Silent, they crossed the open space between the horse barn and the old tack shed to the Carteret's place. Jack whistled softly under his breath. The first blizzard of 1886 had caved in the tack shed's feeble roof. "That was the first building here in '69, so Mr. Buxton claims," he said.

He tugged on Lily's hand because he could see she was flagging. "Tell you what," he started, "how about you just tell me what you want and I'll go ahead and . . ."

He had turned to talk to her, kept walking, and staggered sideways into a small mound of snow. He dragged her down with him, and they both foundered against what felt like a log at first, but which a horrible feeling told him it wasn't. He let go of Lily and pawed into the mound.

He should have waited until Lily had her clothes and was safe in the cookshack before investigating. A few more swipes of snow, and there lay Stretch.

CHAPTER 33

⚜

*J*ack knew he was no gentleman, but the gentleman in him tried to thrust Lily behind him to spare her the sight of his cowhand from Connecticut, mouth ajar in a twisted scream, his frozen hands clutching his open shirt, as if to rip it off.

They both stared down at the dead man. Lily started to breathe faster and faster. Jack took her gently by the neck and gave her a little shake. "Deep breaths, Lily," he ordered, and she obeyed.

He was almost afraid to look at the woman who was even now trying to burrow into his armpit, which was no easy task, because he was wearing nearly everything warm that he owned. He looked into her eyes, and she continued to amaze him. Behind the obvious fear was something he had not expected—compassion, and it seemed to be directed at him and not the frozen man.

"Jack, do what you need to. If you want to take me to my house, I can get my clothes ready. I'll just wait there for you or someone." She tried to smile but failed singularly.

It was a generous offer that touched his heart, because he knew she meant it. She probably already knew what a practical man he was.

"I can't do a thing for Stretch right now, and you're cold, tired, and hungry. Keep walking."

Her little shack was as cold inside as outside, but at least the wind wasn't blowing snow through it. He opened her portmanteau as she looked around. Then she put in books first before clothing because that was Lily. He helped her, because she was starting to shiver noticeably.

The pictures went in next, followed by petticoats and underwear—glory, it *was* silk—and shoes. She closed the lid and pulled out a smaller suitcase from under her bed. Her corsets and dresses went in, and nightgowns—again that silky material. Working as quickly as she could, she spread out a blanket on the floor and bundled in all of her bedding and her father's.

"I don't feel very good, so it's enough for now."

As he thought about it later, in the relative warmth of the cookshack, that was the first time he ever heard Lily Carteret complain. She had no interest in food, even though he knew she was hungry. He took her straight to his two-room shack, sat her down, removed her shoes while she shivered uncontrollably, and told her to get in bed, clothes and all. He pulled the blankets high around her neck and went for help.

When he returned with two pigs and Amelie, Pierre and Preacher were already digging in the snow, trying to free Stretch, frozen solid and welded to the ground. Jack walked on Amelie's other side so she couldn't see what they were doing, but she knew.

"Did he suffer?" she asked.

"I sincerely doubt it," he lied. "He probably just lay down and went to sleep."

Amelie nodded, satisfied. It was probably going to be his best lie of the winter.

෴

Why wouldn't people leave her alone? Lily had voiced her objections forcefully, but no one listened. Obviously nothing had changed from Bristol to the Bar Dot. She didn't want to sit up, but Jack insisted.

Amelie stood beside him, her eyes serious. "Do what he says," she said in the same firm voice she had used on Nick.

Dutifully, Lily held out one arm and then the other, until she found herself down to that union suit he had helped her into in the schoolhouse.

"Stop!" she ordered, and he stopped. She stared him in the eyes. "You are not to take my clothes off," she told him.

"Wasn't planning to," he said with a grin. He said something else which she chose to ignore and then stated, "You're a knucklehead."

Amelie giggled.

He was holding out another pair of those long johns. "Raise your foot like a good girl," he said. "Other one now. Stand up."

Standing up made her list to one side and then the other, so he sat her down quickly. The top went on next, then her nightgown over everything. "Foot up." He slid on wool socks. "Other one."

She closed her eyes, shaking so violently now that her stomach hurt. He gave her a little push and she flopped on her side, nearly asleep again. Now if everyone would leave her alone . . . Something warm and hard pressed against her back.

"It's a pig," Jack said. "No, not that kind. It's iron and it holds hot water. It's padded with a towel. I have one more pig. There. Amelie, your turn. Hop up and keep your teacher warm."

Lily relaxed as Amelie got between the covers, nestling down with a contented sigh of her own as they spooned together, stomach to back. Already Jack's voice was farther and farther away, rattling on about "eat later," "get warm," and "we might add Chantal."

He pulled the coverlets higher on both of them, then rested his hands on Lily's neck, rubbing it gently. "Sakes, you're tighter'n a drumhead." His warm hands went to her shoulders and he massaged them, which coincided with her last memory of the day.

Or nearly so. At some point, something light jumped on the bed, turned around a few times, and settled by her feet. She reached out a hand, but Francis lay too far away.

She woke hours later because she was hungry, and finally warm, even though the room was not. Amelie must have left her, but Lily remembered where she was and what had happened. She looked for Francis, but the cat was gone.

There were others in the room. She looked around, startled to see Jack, Pierre, and Preacher. Will Buxton stood there too, but on the side, not mingling. *I need to talk to him about that*, she thought, even though she realized how irrational that was. She had learned something both terrible and wonderful during their ordeal in the school: they all needed to work together.

"Are you warm now?" Jack asked. "Amelie went back to her mother, but I can get another hot pig."

"I'm warm, and I thank you," Lily told him. She propped herself on one elbow, wondering about the delegation crowding the small room.

"Food first," Jack said, and he gave her a sandwich consisting mainly of bread and cheese, with a smidge of butter only.

She took it but looked at the others. "It really isn't polite for me to eat when no one else is."

"Lily," was all Jack said, but she got the message. The sandwich went down faster than anyone at Miss Tilton's would have approved of.

"Much better." Lily sat up. She had never worn so many clothes to bed in her life, but she still felt awkward with her audience. "And now?"

"I just want you to know the lay of the land."

She didn't understand that expression, and Pierre must have noticed. "How things are," he said, and she nodded.

"We've strung rope from my house here to the bunk-house, the cookshack, and then to the barns. We're not going to be caught flatfooted again."

The men nodded. Lily looked from grim face to grim face.

"We've put Stretch in an unused shed," Jack explained. "Can't bury him because the ground is frozen." Lily plainly saw the strain of the last few days on his face. "We can't even straighten him up."

Lily shuddered. The foreman minced no words, but at least Amelie wasn't there.

"Everyone else is accounted for." He gave a dry snort. "Mr. Buxton's biggest worry seems to be that his cook has declared she is leaving on the next train from Wisner as soon as we can get her there."

"The cattle?" she asked.

He shook his head. "The ones around the buildings? All dead. I doubt Buxton's cook will like this, but our first task is to saddle up and see what we find."

"That doesn't sound safe."

"It isn't. What I want from you is to continue the school here in my house. The children are upset." He sat on the edge of her bed, surprising her again. His eyes were so serious, and he leaned close as though speaking only to her. "I need you to keep teaching, even with the school gone." He gestured to Pierre's winter count, still folded and containing everything they had rescued from the Temple of Education. "We're going to have a rough go of it, but the children. . ." He stopped, swallowed, and looked away.

She took his hand. "Is it Sunday?"

He nodded. His emotion touched her heart.

"We'll begin tomorrow." She looked over his shoulder to Pierre. "Could you possibly get the True Greatness sign from the school?"

"You'll have it."

"I want it nailed over the door."

Jack dabbed at his eyes and smiled at her, his equanimity restored. "You don't need a sign to have true greatness, Lily."

She released his hand and folded her hands in her lap, thinking of the incongruity of sitting there in a nightgown and two layers of long johns with men all around. "We might need to be reminded this winter."

Pierre was the last man to leave. Before he closed the door, Jack set what looked liked dried beef on the floor. "For the cat under your bed," he told her as he left.

ॐ

The men rode out the next morning, each of them bundled with every article of clothing they owned. Lily wondered that the horses could bear the weight. Before they left, Jack had made sure she could get from his house to the cookshack, walking with her. The men had shoveled paths between the buildings, and the snow on either side stood knee deep. The wind had created huge drifts against the north and west sides of the buildings.

The Sansever children sat with her as they ate breakfast. She observed their faces, all of them older now, maybe even feeling, as she did, the weight of their situation. Jack wanted her to provide the normalcy they needed, so it was no time for her to show her own fears.

Before he left the cookshack, he just stood there, staring at the room with its table and benches. Lily held her breath, wondering if he was already deciding what they would have to burn here. While the children carried the dishes to the sink, she went to him, just wanting a private word—or, if she was honest, some reassurance.

He must have known that. Maybe her face wasn't as calm as she had hoped. He put his arm around her shoulders. "Lily, you did everything right in the schoolroom," he told her, speaking softly, truly for her ears alone this time. "You had never been in a situation like that and you didn't panic."

"Oh, I did," she whispered back. "I almost decided to let the children go."

His grip tightened. "What stopped you?"

She considered his question, thinking back to that long moment when the snow swirled everywhere and Nick was urging her to let them leave before the snow deepened. Suddenly, she knew what it was, and she struggled against it, not because the idea wasn't appealing, but because it opened her up to more honesty than she had ever admitted to in her life.

"What?" he asked again, almost as if he already knew but insisting she say it.

"I loved them too much to take even the tiniest chance," she managed to say. The only thing left to do was rest her head against his chest for a small moment. "We would live together or die together. I . . . I've spent my life avoiding hurt, and now I want to care. This is harder."

He was silent, just hugging her shoulders, nothing more.

She had her own question. "Why does that matter so much right now, when there are far bigger worries?"

"Tell you later, if I have to," he said, releasing her. He didn't look at her again as he tied his Stetson down with what looked like Luella's muffler.

Irritating man, she thought, but she couldn't help her own smile to hear him whistling after he closed the door.

CHAPTER 34

*L*ily and her children spent the day turning the front room of Jack Sinclair's two-room shack into another Temple of Education. Before he rode out with the others, Pierre found the bedraggled cardboard True Greatness sign and shook his head. He came back an hour later with True Greatness painted on a wooden slab and nailed that in place instead, all without saying a word.

Quietly at first, but then with smiles and finally laughter, Amelie, Chantal, and Nick swept the floor, conferred together about what to do for desks, and hatched a plan of their own, which impressed their teacher.

"Jack's table here isn't much," Nick said, eyeing the little drop-leaf table with something close to scorn. "It's not even good enough for you, Miss Carteret."

"We'll worry about that later," she told him, secretly pleased. "Do you have any thoughts about desks for all of you? That's probably the larger issue."

"We think we can get the men to move over one of the tables from the cookshack, and a bench," Amelie said.

"We can burn it too, if we have to," Chantal chimed in, then burst into tears.

"Oh, my dear one," Lily said, scooping up the child and holding her close. Chantal sobbed into her shoulder as she sat down with her on Jack's wobbly settee. She looked at the worry in Amelie's eyes, and the way Nick clenched his jaw, and gestured them close. Soon the four of them crowded together on the settee as Chantal wept for them all. When the moment passed, they continued preparing their new classroom.

Luella and Fothering came with lunch—cheese sandwiches and dried apples. By the time the men rode back to the ranch buildings late that afternoon, everything was ready for them to move in a table and bench.

She hated to ask anything of the men, whose exhaustion was palpable, but they went right to work after a nod from Jack, who followed the table with a bench balanced on his shoulder. When they returned to the cookshack, he was smiling.

"My place never looked so good," he told her, as he peeled off layer after layer of outer clothes and left them in a heap on the floor by the other men's clothes. "Good to get down to shirtsleeves again. Sure is hard to . . ." He stopped, remembering his audience as his face reddened. "Let me say, basic functions are more of a challenge, wrapped up thoroughly." He brightened. "That sounded almost elegant, Miss Carteret," he joked. "You're good for all of us rough types."

Over beef stew, he told Lily about their search for cattle. Pierre kept the narrative going when Jack stopped to eat, and Preacher filled in where needed. The children listened, wide-eyed, and even Madeleine left her beloved domain to sit with Chantal on her lap and shake her head over stories of air holes where cattle had fallen in, and great mounds of snow where the cattle had gathered together for defense against the blizzard.

"Some of them are still alive," Jack said. "We searched as far as we could, and so did the other ranchers. We have a slight advantage on the Bar Dot because we seem to have more sheltering slopes where the beeves could hunker down. We'll bring more of them closer tomorrow." He stopped and drank deep from Madeleine's good coffee. "Two days of that and we'll see." He looked around. "How'd school go, Amelie?"

"Miss Carteret said we were perfectly excellent in our preparation."

Jack raised his eyebrows and glanced at Lily. "I believe you have quoted your teacher exactly. Only Miss C would say that." He held out his cup. "Any more of that, Madeleine?"

She filled his cup, scolding all the while that it would keep him up.

"Not a chance. I'll be out before I hit the pillow." Jack looked at his men. "I never knew a better crew than this one," he told the room at large, then looked at Will Buxton. "Will here found twenty cattle all by himself." He raised his cup in salute.

Lily watched the pleasure in Will Buxton's tired eyes. She looked around and saw True Greatness everywhere.

❦

School began in the morning with spelling words on a makeshift blackboard made of tin, probably a remnant from the larger piece that rested underneath Madeleine's cookstove. It had appeared mysteriously in Jack's front room, left there during the night by someone determined not to waken her in the back room. She had her suspicions. Written on the tin sheet, its edges carefully turned under for safety, was "Teach me good judgment and knowledge, Psalm 119:66."

"Preacher, what are you doing here in Wyoming?" she asked the tin sheet.

Before they left for another cold day, Pierre nailed his winter count to the wall and announced to her children that he had a handful of wheat to leave for the Wyoming Kid. More dried beef found its way by the inside door. She left it there, wondering if Francis would leave his place of safety under Jack's bed. By noon, the cat was curled in Amelie's lap.

The men told the same story that night at supper, giving Lily and Madeleine a glimpse of the tragedy unfolding, precisely as Jack had predicted. They had found more cattle and trailed them closer, but other ranchers had horror stories of their own.

"It's only October, and barely that," Preacher said.

"Could you pray us good weather?" Chantal asked.

Preacher shook his head. "I don't think it works that way," he told her. "I think sometimes the Lord has to deal with what He has before Him, when it comes to weather, same's us."

"No miracles?" Amelie asked.

He regarded the child for a long time. "I'm starting to think the Almighty expects us to do everything we can first."

"And then?" Nick asked.

"We wait and look for His mercy."

The miracle is we are still alive, Lily thought, too shy to speak.

Silence settled over the group, broken when Lily took *Ivanhoe* out of a pocket in the apron Madeleine had loaned her. She ruffled the pages. "Jack and I are on chapter sixteen, but we'll start over. Bring the lamp closer, Nick, please."

✿

It snowed the next day, which meant that Fothering and Luella had to flounder through fresh snow, arriving just as Lily finished the spelling test. Her classmates waited while Luella took the test. The men rode south toward Wisner, coming back with enough cattle to make Jack's pinched look of disappointment leave his face.

"We've lost a lot, but not everything," he told her after *Ivanhoe* as he walked her and Amelie back to his house. Madeleine had decided that her girls would take turns staying with Lily, which calmed her heart. Lily assured her children that she would be fine when her father returned from Cheyenne, which made Chantal frown.

"We *like* to stay with you," Chantal said. "It is a rare treat."

Jack laughed at that and nudged Lily. "They sound more like you every day." He nudged her again, but gentler, making it almost a caress. "I have to tell you, as I ride and cuss and rope cattle out of air holes and deep snow, I still think about that first day, when you asked me if I tend cattle, like they were delicate creatures needing me."

"They are," she told him and nudged gently in turn.

༄

The Buxtons' cook forced the issue of a trip to Wisner, declaring that if she did not leave immediately, she would do herself damage. Oliver Buxton must have believed the old biddy, because he issued his own ultimatum in a rare visit to the bunkhouse the next morning. Jack groaned inwardly as his boss looked around the cluttered room, taking in the unmade beds and jumbled clothes, disdain all over his face.

"Take my cook to Wisner and stick her on the train," he told Jack.

"Can't get through with the buckboard or wagon yet," Jack said. "She'll have to go on horseback."

Mr. Buxton gave his gallows smile. "I hope she suffers!" He stopped at the door. "Get any mail. There should be a telegram from the consortium secretary and maybe one from Clarence, so you'll know when to get him."

After a long look at the northwest sky, Jack rode out with Pierre and Winnie the cook, who complained loud and long about her transportation. Jack listened as long as he thought polite, then stopped her with a chop of his hand.

"Miss Winnie, if you want to leave now, this is how is happens. Well?"

The hefty cook glared at the saddled horse as if willing it to turn into the Union Pacific Railroad. When nothing happened, she let Jack heave her into the saddle, no mean feat. He tied stuffed carpetbags behind each saddle, and they started for Wisner. Pierre took a detour at the schoolhouse, deserted and bereft with no students, and left grain for the Little Man, a.k.a. the Wyoming Kid. The cook was not amused.

Jack and Pierre rode abreast, partly to break the way for the cook's long-suffering horse, and partly to avoid conversation. She complained anyway, going on and on about Mrs. Buxton's weird crochets and lengthy arguments between the Buxtons, all of which ended with door slamming and tears, which usually advanced into hysteria.

"I'm amazed Luella isn't stranger than we already know about," Jack whispered to Pierre, who only grunted and kept his eyes ahead.

When they passed the drifts by the road to his own ranch, Jack resisted a powerful urge to turn in and see how Manuel and Bismarck had fared. He could see the cabin in the distance, but no smoke climbed from the chimney. *Now what?* he asked himself, imagining his old hand dead and Bismarck failing.

"Don't borrow trouble. We have enough," Pierre commented.

"How did you . . . ?"

"Jack, I know you."

Wisner looked bedraggled and defeated, with snow mounded everywhere, testimony to as severe a time as the one they weathered on the Bar Dot, except the snow here was turning black with smoke from the train and wood and coal fires.

Still muttering about her cavalier treatment, Winnie brushed before them into the depot and plunked down her money for Cheyenne.

"One way or round trip, ma'am?"

Winnie leaned over the counter and the clerk reared back, terrified. "One. Way," she declared in a voice impossible to misunderstand.

"Jack."

Vivian from the Back Forty sat on the bench closest to the pot-bellied stove. Jack noted her luggage and handsome traveling coat, and couldn't help wishing there was such a coat for Chantal.

"Taking my advice?" he asked, sitting beside her.

"I am. I've saved enough and I'm going home."

"Which is?"

"Moberly, Missouri. If you're ever through there, you'll see a millinery shop with my name on it. Time to leave faro behind." She held her hand out, and he shook it. "You were always a gentleman."

"No, I wasn't."

She tightened her grip, then released his hand. "Don't sell yourself short, Jack Sinclair."

He nodded and followed an amused Pierre out the door. "I don't even know her last name," he said outside. "I played cards there off and on for five years, and I never asked."

Thoughtful, he picked his way across the slushy street to the post office and asked for Bar Dot mail. The clerk found the pigeonhole and handed him newspapers, mail for Mr. Buxton, and a telegram. He stared at it. "Should I open it?" he asked Pierre. "Suppose there needs to be a reply."

"Go ahead," Pierre said. "Not that you need *my* permission."

Jack slit the thin envelope and pulled out the message. He started to hand it to Pierre to read, but the Indian pushed it back.

"You've been learning with Lily. At least, I think that's what you do in the evenings," Pierre teased. "You try first."

Jack looked at the telegram, thinking, not for the first

time, how ironic that a mixed breed Indian could read better than he did. He cleared his throat. He knew these letters. He could even string them together. "Wh . . . wh . . . where." That was it, and the next work was simple. "Is." He knew the third word, but he felt a chill that had nothing to do with cold and snow. "Carteret?"

The two men looked at each other.

"We have a problem," Pierre said quietly. "It's a big one."

CHAPTER 35

*J*ack swore so fluently that the mail clerk told him to leave. He banged the door behind him for good measure but felt only embarrassment, followed by a fierce anger he had not felt in years.

"That old scoundrel!" he said, looking at the telegram again to see if the words had changed. "How could he *do* this to Lily?"

Without a word, he crossed the street again to the depot. Vivian looked up from the book she was reading, and the cook glowered at him. He rapped his hand on the counter and the clerk returned to the window.

"Did you sell a ticket to Cheyenne to Clarence Carteret last week?" Jack demanded. "A tall, thin, Englishman? Works at the Bar Dot?"

"I did. It was the day of the blizzard and by the eternal, it was snowing so hard."

"The train made it to Cheyenne?"

The clerk laughed. "Eventually! That four-hour trip took two days."

Two extra days was still plenty of time for Clarence Carteret to hand the money over to the consortium secretary. Jack looked at the telegram again. How could the man do this? And how in the world could he, Jack Sinclair, tell Lily?

"Did he say anything, you know, anything to you?"

"Besides just the business of a ticket?" the clerk asked. "I remember that he looked at the ticket, chuckled, and told me that come spring, he'd be heading to San Francisco."

"That was it?"

"Yes, indeedy. The depot was filling up with folks doing their dead-level best to get out of Wisner, but I remember that. Anything else, Jack?"

"No, nothing," he mumbled. He nodded to Vivian again and shoved the telegram in his pocket.

Pierre stood on the boardwalk, looking at the sky. "Clouds gathering. If you want to stop and see your expensive bull, we'd better ride."

Jack nodded. He made Pierre wait while he ducked into the emporium for a sack of beans and a quart bottle of lemon juice, which he had Watkins wrap in several layers of cardboard and brown paper. He tied it securely to his saddle and strapped the beans to the riderless horse. Six more skeins of gray yarn took care of the rest of his cash. Pierre crammed them in his saddlebags.

They rode north in silence, both of them watching the gathering clouds. He had grown used to the snowy mounds with cattle underneath, but here and there, the drifts had blown themselves out, shifting the blankets of cruel snow and exposing death on the hoof. *How could Clarence do this to Lily?* kept echoing through his brain, even as he stared at death all around. He tried to think of some reason that Clarence wouldn't have deposited the money, and there was only one reason. *How could he do this to Lily?* he thought, and the words went round and round.

If anything could salvage the day, his reception at the Double J did not fail him. Grim and silent, he rode toward Manuel's cabin, where no chimney smoke wound its way toward the clouds. They dismounted at the cabin and he knocked, then opened the door. Nothing. He was past cursing, so he walked from one wallpapered room to the next and stopped in surprise.

The bedding was nowhere in sight. He looked into the

lean-to kitchen, two weeks ago cluttered with dishes and sacks of food, enough to last a careful man all winter. It was bare.

"I can't take it," he said out loud, heartsick. He couldn't remember a day this bad since the surrender.

He went outside, dreading one more minute on his property. Pierre was already sauntering toward the barn, a low-slung affair ideal for his bull and girlfriends. Jack had planned to enlarge it next year, but what was the use now? Maybe Manuel was a scoundrel too, and Bismarck was gone.

Pierre stood just inside the small door next to the closed barn doors. He waved Jack closer, but there was nothing urgent in the motion. Of course, it wasn't Pierre's bull missing or dead, was it?

"*Jefe, jefe,* calm yourself! I decided to move."

Manuel's cheerful voice greeted Jack as he ducked through the low door. Only a month ago they had knocked together a roomy stall for Bismarck and company. Manuel had moved himself into a smaller stall and roofed the little enclosure with wood from a farther enclosure. Jack stooped to look inside to see bedding, a chair and table, sacks of beans, and all those onions in the corner.

In a rocking chair, Manuel sat close to Bismarck's pen, knitting. He had found a square iron stove from somewhere and there it sat, giving off plenty of heat. Jack just shook his head, amazed at the resourcefulness of one old man.

"Uh, where did you get the stove? And how in thunder did you move it here?"

Manuel stuck his knitting needles through the ball of yarn. Clever man, his knitting covered his legs. He gestured over his shoulder. "It was there in the corner. I hitched up Bismarck. He is kind to me."

Jack stared in amazement, picturing the stately progress from one end of the barn to the other. He doubted

Bismarck even broke a sweat. "He's your friend," he told Manuel. "I don't have to tell you to be extremely careful with fire in here."

"No, you don't, *señor*, but I understand why you do," Manuel said. "Bismarck cost you very dear."

"It's more than that," Jack replied, shy to say it, but so grateful that one thing had gone right today. "You're my friend too. If it comes down to life or death, I value your life more."

Manuel gave a philosophical shrug. "If the wood gives out, I have lots of straw to burn. We will outlast winter, and you will have calves. *Adios* now. There will be snow tonight." He looked down at his knitting. "And I have work to do."

"I may have trouble returning, if the snow is too deep and it is cold," Jack said, reluctant to leave. Everything he wanted was here in this barn. Well, almost everything.

"I have never minded solitude, *señor*," Manuel said gently. "Think of the years I herded sheep." He looked around at the barn and the cattle, contentment on his face. "This is enough."

The snow came sooner than nightfall, but there were no blizzard winds. They rode silently, each man to his thoughts, with the Indian's probably more productive, no matter what he was thinking. *How in the world do I tell her* warred with *If I see you, Clarence Carteret, I will murder you.*

By the time they reached the schoolhouse, that first landmark of the Bar Dot, darkness had fallen and the snow was beginning to drift.

"You going to Buxton first?" Pierre asked.

"He'll keep. I'm going to talk to Lily."

"I wish you had good news."

"So do I. D'you know, I was becoming genuinely fond of Clarence Carteret."

He curried Sunny Boy in silence, then turned the tired horse into a stall and added more hay than he probably should have, considering. One hand on the rope, he walked behind Pierre, who branched off to the cook-shack. Jack could just make out a light on in his old quarters. Hand still on the rope, he drew frigid air into his lungs and patted his pocket with the telegram.

Lily opened the door with a smile. "We were starting to worry about you. Come in," she said.

He looked around the front room, now the school, with the winter count, maps a little worse for wear from their trip from the old school to the new one, and the table and bench that took up most of the space. He could see beyond the room into his bedroom. He wondered if she made the bed every day. She had hung her precious pictures in there. On the small table by the bed was a photo of her father. It took all his willpower not to rush in there and throw the thing into the snow.

He sat at the table moved from the cookshack, noting that someone had drawn lines to separate each student's area. They had created a classroom, a little refuge from what he knew with vast uneasiness was going to be a tough winter. All was orderly and calm. He felt his shoulders relax.

"We are careful about our space," Lily said. "It might matter a great deal when we are snowed in."

She spoke with calm practicality, her words so precise. He loved the sound of Lily.

"It might come to that," he said, at a loss of where to begin.

He hesitated, heartsick at what he had to do, when all he wanted to do was sit with her in his old house and pretend they shared it—as simple as that. He could imagine that he lived there again, and he didn't have to leave once he had delivered his fearsome message. He could comfort her and share the misery, not leaving her to stare down the long, solitary corridors of her disappointed hopes.

He pulled out the telegram, watching her eyes as he pushed it toward her as she sat across the table from him.

She picked it up, read it, and gasped. He kept his eyes on her face, but she refused to look at him. He didn't even hear her breathing; maybe she wasn't.

"Lily," he said, mainly to start her drawing breath again.

She still did not look up. "I am so ashamed," she said finally. She put her arms on the table and rested her head on them, a woman mortified and stunned by such betrayal. He almost wished Clarence had begun no reformation, because Lily would be in less pain right now. He hesitated only a moment, then rested his hand on her head. He felt her shake.

"What will Mr. Buxton do?" she whispered. "Tell me truly."

Keeping his hand on her head, wishing the space between them was smaller, he said, "He will order you off the place."

"I have nowhere to go, and little money to do it with."

"You asked me what he would do, and that's it. But I will remind him that you are teaching his only child, and you are desperately needed."

"He won't care."

"No, he won't, but Mrs. Buxton will, and she has the power to make him miserable."

Lily looked up at that. She sat up. "Do you approach her, or I?"

"Both of us."

She gave a little sigh at his words, and he felt in his bones how desperately tired she was of trying to bend events in her life by herself. Maybe he was tired of it too. He reached across the table and took her head in both of his hands.

"We'll do this together."

"When?"

"Now."

CHAPTER 36

*J*ack waited in the front room while Lily pulled on the extra long johns and wool socks that Preacher had left for her. She had less trouble buttoning her dress over all the excess underwear than she expected, which told her she was losing weight. The worst of the winter still loomed ahead, and Madeleine had already put them on shorter rations, probably at the foreman's suggestion.

Lily tried to think of anything except her father, but all she could think of was the man who had left last week, smiling and happy, the man who had deserted her over and over again. This was the last time, she vowed to herself as she stood there, hands clenched.

She covered her mouth, but her anguish came out anyway, half a sob and half a cry of fury.

"Lily?" Jack asked on the other side of the closed door. "Lily?"

She took several deep breaths, determined not to be a further burden to an already overburdened man. "I'm fine."

"No, you're not."

Drat the man. Why couldn't he be superficial like her uncle? If she had told Uncle Niles she was fine, he would have searched no deeper because it was the answer he sought. She yanked open the door.

"Actually, I have seldom been worse," she said, wiping

angrily at traitor tears she hated to feel, because they showed how thoroughly Clarence Carteret had rummaged through every hope she possessed. Her voice softened. There was no need to disturb this kind man only trying to help. "Really, Jack, I'll get over this. I have before."

He nodded, troubled because she was troubled, which touched her heart down to its dusty center. He held out his hand and she put her hand in his, craving nothing more than a touch that told her she was not alone.

He managed a smile, the philosophical kind. "You have a long winter ahead to decide what you will do, come spring."

"Provided Mr. Buxton doesn't turn me out in fifteen minutes."

"Let's find out."

Snow pelted them as they slipped and slid from building to building, guided by the ropes the men had strung earlier. Deep twilight had come and gone, leaving an eerie light created by falling snow. She tugged on Jack's hand, and he obliged her by slowing down and inclining his head toward hers.

"Do you know, I really enjoyed that very first snowfall," she said. "It was a novelty to me."

He laughed and clapped an arm around her shoulder.

He had to tug her up the two steps to the Buxtons' porch. Fothering may not have been a real English butler, but he held the door open before Jack even knocked.

"We need to see the Big Boss," Jack said.

Fothering looked from one to the other. "What has happened?"

"How . . . how do you know anything is wrong?" Lily asked.

"My dear delightful Lily, no one goes outside in this weather. Tell me, please."

Jack showed him the telegram. Fothering's eyes narrowed. "Lily, you can do better than this father."

"I know, but this is *my* dilemma," she said.

"*Our* dilemma," Fothering corrected. Ever proper, he turned to Jack. "You already have a plan, don't you?"

"Not much of one," Jack admitted. "I'll take any suggestions."

"Something will come to me," Fothering assured him. Then he bowed and went his serene way to find Mr. Buxton.

"If Bismarck ever makes me a wealthy man, I want a butler," Jack said.

Fothering returned quickly and gestured to them. "Courage, dears," he whispered as he opened the door.

ᴄ∞

Jack had been in Oliver Buxton's office many times, often bearing good news, sometimes to be yelled at for some misdemeanor, but more likely to receive stupid orders from a man who didn't know the first thing about cows. Never before had he cared so much about the outcome of an encounter with his employer. He had always known he could walk away from the Bar Dot and find work, because his reputation guaranteed him a job anywhere in the territory. This was different; this was Lily. Women existed at the whim of men, even in this territory where they had the vote.

Silent, he handed Buxton the telegram and waited for the explosion.

Not surprisingly, Buxton did exactly what Jack had done in Cheyenne. He cursed with a fluency that made Lily take a step back, her eyes troubled. Jack did nothing to stop the foul language that spewed from his employer's now beet-red face, simply because he did not want to call any more attention to Lily's presence, which he knew would be the man's next target. He moved closer to Lily, not quite touching shoulders with her, because he dreaded what Buxton would say about that. Better to keep this as professional as possible.

When he ran out of filthy words, Buxton turned to look at Lily. His eyes narrow and mean, he raked her up and down as she stood there, head high, remembering to breathe now and then, her own face a curious mottled color that made Jack wonder if he ought to slide a chair behind her.

Silence. Lily swallowed. Buxton just stared at her, dissecting her down to the marrow. Jack felt his throat go dry. Somehow, the silence was worse than the swearing.

"Get. Off. This. Ranch." Buxton delivered his ultimatum in a low voice more menacing than shouts.

Jack watched Lily, ready to intervene, because the air fairly crackled with Buxton's animosity. What he saw amazed him, humbled him, and assured him that forever after he would know that women were strong.

"I have nowhere to go and I am your daughter's teacher," Lily said. Her voice was no louder than Buxton's, and she did not plead. She calmly stated the issue, making no apology because nothing that had happened was her fault, even if Buxton's venomous helping of vitriol had accused her of everything her father was.

If he had expected her to grovel, Buxton must have been sadly disappointed. He stared at her. "Leave."

Without a word, Lily Carteret turned on her heel and left, closing the door quietly behind her. Anyone less polite would have slammed it into the next room.

As Buxton staggered to his chair and sank into it, Jack listened to the sound of Lily and Fothering conversing quietly in the hall. In another moment, he heard footsteps on the stairs, Lily's and Fothering's. He began to breathe again himself. He had underestimated Lily's courage in facing someone as hopping mad as Oliver Buxton, and he had no intention of underestimating Fothering. Without an invitation he sat down in the chair opposite Buxton's desk and waited.

He didn't wait long. Buxton flinched and ran his hands across his face when Mrs. Buxton began to scream. Jack felt the hairs on his neck rise as the scream turned into hysteria. He felt sudden pity for Luella, who had to live in this house that had probably never been a home. He looked at Buxton, seeing a man in torment, someone who had probably turned his wife into the fragile woman she was, or at least had a major hand in the matter. The tragedy was, Buxton probably had no idea of his own culpability.

The hysteria died finally, subsiding into noisy tears, then sobs, then the sad weeping that seeped though the ceiling and almost rained down on them in the room below. Jack said nothing.

He heard footsteps then, a man's tread. Fothering must have left Lily to console a woman so mentally fragile that she couldn't be left alone.

Fothering tapped on the door and opened it. Sedate as always, he approached Buxton's desk and said with no emotion, "Mrs. Buxton is not dealing well with the news of Miss Carteret's dismissal."

"And what else is new?" Buxton said with vast sarcasm.

"This, sir," Fothering replied. "I am tendering my resignation and will leave on the same train with Miss Carteret, should you choose not to require her services as a most excellent teacher."

Good show, Jack thought, with admiration and actual hope.

All color left Buxton's face with this calm announcement. "You wouldn't," he said. The threat had gone out of him.

"Alas, I just did." The sorrow on Fothering's face seemed almost genuine. "Take heart, though. That will leave you, Mrs. Buxton, and Luella with a maid who will learn to cook any day now, providing her reading improves. Excuse me, sir, but I should go pack." He executed a perfect turn and started for the door.

"Don't be so hasty, Fothering," Buxton said, a beaten man. "You will, uh, remain here if Miss Carteret is allowed to continue teaching?"

"I will consider it, sir," Fothering said with more aplomb than found in entire small countries. He put his hands behind his back. "Sir, it's a harsh thing to visit the sins of the father on the daughter."

Careful, Fothering, Jack thought and held his breath.

But Oliver Buxton was beaten, and he knew it. "Very well," he said, his voice a perfect monotone as he looked at neither of them. "Until spring, and then she goes."

Fothering bowed. "Excellent, Mr. Buxton! By then, I am certain the maid will know how to cook. Excuse me, and I will give the good news to your wife and Miss Carteret."

Buxton leaned back in his chair, his face a study in bewilderment, as though wondering where everything went wrong. More steps on the stairs and Lily came into the room with Fothering this time. She looked to Jack like a woman on her last nerve, but she stood there as calm and dignified as the butler.

Buxton stared at her again until Jack stirred in his chair, bothered by the man's insolence. Slowly Buxton raised his finger and shook it at her.

"If I learn that you and you father are in cahoots about this two thousand dollars—two thousand dollars!— there'll be room in that prison in Laramie for you too!"

"I am here to teach," she said. "By spring, I will have other plans."

Buxton deliberately turned his chair around and faced the wall. Lily slowly let out her breath and left the room. She was on her knees in the foyer, head touching the braid rug, when Jack and Fothering closed the office door behind them.

Jack helped her to her feet. "I thought you were about done for in there," he said. "Can you stand on your own?"

She flashed him a rare and lovely smile that made his heart stop for one cosmic moment in a universe that had not always been kind to him, either. "I'm not standing on my own, anymore, am I?"

"Nope," he said, then was too shy to say anything else.

Fothering cleared his throat and handed back their coats, mufflers, hats, mittens, and everything needed to survive in brutal cold between the Buxton's house and Jack's place. Jack helped Lily into her coat and felt his own equilibrium return. "Suppose he had called your bluff, Fothering?"

"Who says it was a bluff?" Fothering asked in turn as cool as the best card shark Jack had ever gambled with at a table. "It's been overlong since I visited my home."

"All the way to England?"

Fothering and Lily looked at each other. "Cleveland, Ohio," he said, and Lily giggled. He held out his hand. "Sam Foster's the name."

Jack gaped at them both, especially since Fothering's English accent had disappeared. He opened and closed his mouth, feeling like a trout tossed onto the bank.

"Be generous, Jack," Fothering said. "I've heard your tales about starving out here and working piecemeal to squeak by. Surely you don't think you're the first man to tweak matters to suit his situation?"

"I won't ever again, um, Foster? Fothering?"

"Let's keep it Fothering until such time as I do blow the dust of this wretched sty off my impeccably shined shoes and, uh, beat it for greener pastures." He unlimbered so much as to kiss Lily's cheek. "It's late. Good night."

Jack helped Lily down the steps. The snow came down harder, but the pellets of ice chips had turned into big flakes, the kind that might have interested him when he was a child. He watched, amused, as Lily studied the snowflakes on her dark coat. How snow could still be a wonder to her, he couldn't imagine.

He plucked out some courage from a forgotten source. "You're not alone, Lily."

Again that sunny smile. How was a man proof against that?

"I know."

CHAPTER 37

᠁

$\mathcal{I}$n the fraught and frigid weeks that followed, Jack asked himself many times how one person—Lily Carteret—could be so cheerful about the prospect of makeshift school in a ramshackle classroom, with cold air seeping in and wind moaning like a cat in heat. Somehow she was, and everyone on the Bar Dot knew it, except the Buxtons. Everyone benefited, including the Buxtons— Luella, at least.

Jack had some small idea what it cost Lily to move ahead, even though her faith in her father had crumbled into the dust. He only hoped that her faith in men in general hadn't evaporated after such betrayal. More than almost anything, he wanted to offer her a shoulder to cry on, but he hadn't the courage. He could only guess what it cost her each morning to make her way cheerfully to the cookshack, hand over hand on the rope, even when it wasn't snowing, and then teach all day.

As he lay awake in the bunkhouse, tossing, turning, and cursing his inability to help the one person who probably needed more kindness than them all, he wondered how her nights passed, alone. He understood solitude and knew that too much of it could turn a person inward and bitter. True, Francis the cat had taken a liking to Lily, but the independent little beast was not a cuddlesome creature. *Am I?* he dared to ask himself when the other guys around him were snoring.

He doubted it. The life he led wasn't designed to create sympathetic men.

He asked her about Francis—a harmless topic—over mush and coffee one morning, when the wind howled and the snow blew sideways. "Is Francis a good enough companion?"

"You would be amazed," Lily replied, her eyes crinkling in good humor. "He crawls to the foot of your bed and stays there."

He wished later she had said "the bed" instead of "your bed." He decided that the advanced age of thirty-five was proof against nothing. He was a young man still, at least until ten hours in the saddle with cold boring into his head like an auger convinced him that not even a young man could survive such torment forever.

The cattle suffered beyond belief, drifting in bunches, dying together. In Jack's mind, because he really was sympathetic, even sadder were the solitary deaths, a cow wandering off, trying to put cold and snow behind her, perhaps with a memory of the plains of Texas. How did anyone know what a cow thought? Did a cow even think?

The worst horror came at the rivers, where somehow the forces of nature created air pockets where bank met water. After a blizzard just before Thanksgiving—Madeleine crossed off each day on her calendar—the Bar Dot crew and McMurdy's LC hands came across scores of cattle trapped in snow that had melted slightly, then frozen again into ice.

Jack roped one cow, getting an easy loop over its neck because the trapped animal could only look at him with hopeless eyes. Another loop from Pierre, and they started to pull. The cow bellowed in pain, and they flinched at the gruesome sound and sight of hooves separating from legs as they pulled. They watched in horror as the cow tried to stagger away on bloody stumps, still turned south toward warmth so far away, hopeful when hope was gone.

Without a word, Jack shot the cow and it sank onto bloody snow, free at last.

The other hands pulled out their rifles and shot all the cows mired in the air pockets, which earned Jack a blistering ream-out from Mr. Buxton when he reported the day's work to him. Jack listened, his heart sore, and then just walked out of the office as Mr. Buxton screamed, "You can't just walk away from me!"

He could and did. Only one thing could possibly ease his pain and he was beyond propriety now. Jack wallowed through snow to his old house, knocked on the door, and came inside before Lily even had time to admit him. She sat on his old sofa, a book in her hands, her eyes wide at his intrusion. He flung the book aside, dropped to his knees, and sobbed his misery into her lap. When he managed between gasps to tell her what he had seen at the riverbank, she cried too, her hand gentle on his head.

"Forgive me," he said finally, when he was seated beside her, handkerchief to his nose and eyes, which seemed to run in tandem. Glory, how appealing was that? "I just couldn't manage another minute of this winter."

Manage, manage? It was only November. He railed then against the sins of the ranchers visited upon the helpless cattle, his voice rising to be heard above the wind, and she just listened, tears on her face. He stopped, mortified. "These are just animals," he said, his voice a bare whisper because his throat hurt now. "You're probably in more pain than I am."

He watched her lovely face, the face where so many nations had played a role in creating such beauty. He saw nothing in her eyes but great compassion for him, and it humbled him right to the ground.

"In pain? I would be, if you hadn't given me a school and children to love like my own." It was quietly said, but he could hear her even above the roar of the storm.

Jack had described the whole incident to Preacher later

that night as they lay in their sterile bunks. He had heard the rustle of paper, then Preacher's voice, "First Kings, nineteen, twelve: 'And after the earthquake a fire; but the Lord was not in the fire: and after the fire a still small voice.'"

The thought of Lily's still, small voice sent him to sleep with something resembling peace. Maybe a theologian would consider his comparison of a mere woman's voice to deity as blasphemy of the grossest sort, but it hadn't bothered Preacher.

All the men of the Bar Dot were used to the grinding sameness of Wyoming winters of watching cattle, getting them out of trouble, and patrolling for the ones that drifted. The winter of 1886–87 was a different sort of grind, because they knew their efforts were hopeless. The storms were too strong and cold, the snow too deep for foraging, the range overcrowded. Jack endured another mighty scold from Mr. Buxton when he told him their efforts were futile and he was only endangering the men who rode.

Stretch's death—probably because, unlike Lily, he panicked—was bad enough. Now the stories began to circulate of cowhands dead who had been forced by bosses to ride into blizzards to search and rescue cattle. He duly reported them to Buxton, who just as duly discounted them all as rumor until the morning two LC hands rode up in the teeth of a blizzard, seeking shelter, and bearing two frozen dead men strapped on behind their saddles.

Jack led them directly to Mr. Buxton's warm office in his house, flung open the door, actually took his boss by the arm, and dragged him outside to see the bodies, frozen into u-shapes. Mr. Buxton shook off his arm and stormed back inside, muttering what sounded like, "Sinclair, you'll draw your pay tomorrow."

"Go ahead, Mr. Buxton," he had said. "Do what you must." Then he helped his friends to the tack shed where they had stored Stretch. It had required the effort of all the few Bar Dot hands to get the bodies off the horses and into the shed. The two survivors spent the night in the already overcrowded bunkhouse. No Bar Dot hand made a single comment about the tears they heard when the LC men must have thought everyone was asleep. It could have been them frozen and waiting burial in the spring.

Jack needn't have worried. When he worked his way through snow and wind to the Buxton's the next day to either get his orders for the day or his pay, Buxton made no comment about his threat.

"What'll you have us do today, Mr. Buxton?" he asked.

"Stay close to home," Mr. Buxton said, without looking up from papers he shuffled from one pile to the other. "Save the riding for a clear day."

Since the boss seemed to be a mellow mood, he decided to raise a subject that had been on his mind since Lily had received the gut punch about her scoundrel father. For one day too many, he had watched her droop, flag, then rally and teach, at what personal price he didn't know.

He leaned against the doorsill. "Mr. Buxton, would you consider letting Luella stay in my old place with Miss Carteret? Fothering could get her to you on weekends. It'd be safer for Luella and I think Miss Carteret would enjoy the company of an evening."

Mr. Buxton looked him in the eyes finally. He raised his eyebrows in obvious thought and nodded. "I'm in agreement. I'll tell Mrs. Buxton."

"You don't think she'll mind?"

Buxton ran his hand over his face and then exposed a bleakness in his eyes that exceeded anything Lily could have come up with, even on a bad day. He began to understand his employer and felt a small surge of pity, which passed.

"My wife is troubled," Buxton said, biting off each word as if dragging them from his throat hand over hand. That seemed to be all the honesty he could manage, and he turned back to his useless paperwork, dismissing Jack.

Luella couldn't pack fast enough. Fothering helped.

"Wish I could take you along, Fothering," Jack said as Fothering handed up Luella to him to perch on the front of his saddle, and then her bag of clothes.

"I'm needed here," the butler said with little conviction. "You're doing a good thing, Jack." He stepped back and regarded the foreman. "What rank did you achieve in the Civil War?"

The question surprised Jack, coming at him out of the blue. "I started as a private at age thirteen, then moved up the ranks. I was commissioned a lieutenant about three weeks before Appomattox. Why?"

"If the war had lasted long enough, you'd have been a major general," Fothering said. "You're a leader. 'Bye, Luella. You be good to Miss Carteret."

Flattered, Jack waved and walked his horse carefully through drifts to his old house. School was about to begin, but he came inside anyway with Luella, carrying her bag. He nodded to the Sansever children and tugged Lily aside while Luella took her spot on the bench.

"I asked Mr. Buxton to let Luella stay with you during the week." He leaned closer to whisper, "It's not good there at the Buxtons."

Lily nodded, her eyes on her students.

"It's not good for you to be alone, either. Stuff can fester if there's only you."

She turned to look at him then, and her lips were so close to his that they both backed up. Chantal giggled, and he felt his face turn into a flame. He took her farther into the corner of the small front room.

"I'm not doing this right, but I never should have done what I did a few nights ago."

"Don't trouble yourself about that, Jack," she whispered, back. "Please don't." She chuckled. "Everyone needs a shoulder to cry on or maybe a lap. Go on, now, it's time for class."

She followed him out the door and closed it behind her. The sky was so blue and crackling cold and the snow so bright that he winced, thinking of the frigid day ahead.

He stood there, wanting to say more, but unsure of what would be right. And while he wondered, Lily kissed his cheek and hurried back inside.

Chapter 38

❦

*T*hanksgiving was going to be just another day on the calendar, even though Lily's children introduced her to pilgrims and turkey and starving times. In turn, she told them about Harvest Home festivals in England, and sugar cane harvests in Barbados. Trouble was, this turned everyone's thoughts to food, so the day before Thanksgiving was not a profitable one in the Temple of Education as snow flew outside.

"Rolls with butter," Luella said, and Chantal sighed.

"Turkey, for sure," Nick said.

"Pumpkin pie with rum sauce," Amelie added. "What about you, Miss Carteret?"

What about me? Lily thought. *I crave trifle and three kinds of cake and marzipan.* "I have enough right now," she said, and correctly interpreted the skeptical looks from four children. "I do!"

Strangely, she did, and so she told Jack that night when he came over to sit with her, as he did every night, now that Luella was here. She didn't question his presence any more, understanding that he felt comfortable to be with her as long as they weren't alone. Son of a tenant farmer, he had remarked to her more than once that he was no gentleman, except that he was. Sometimes he said very little while she helped Luella with her more advanced studies, and then shooed the child off to bed with a trusty iron pig wrapped in a towel that was getting singed in the middle.

"Miss Carteret does this so when she comes to bed, there will be a warm spot for her," Luella solemnly announced one night, which made Jack smile.

He didn't laugh any more. Sometimes Lily thought he only smiled because she expected it of him. When the door was closed, she sat beside him and continued reading *Ivanhoe* out loud, stopping now and then to make him read a few stumbling sentences. Hard to imagine that someone could break into a sweat in such a cold room, all from reading, but he did.

She noticed how it relaxed him when she read, so she read more and more each night. She read to everyone during dinner each night in the dining room, then read the same chapters again with Jack alone. She had suggested that they start another book, but he shook his head at that.

"I think we need to ration our books," he told her. "It's going to be a long winter."

She wasn't even sure he heard anything when she read, because his eyes were either closed, or they were open as he stared at the wall, miles away in his mind. His eyes were closed tonight, so she stopped reading, set the book aside, and just rested her head on his shoulder.

He started and opened his eyes, then slowly put his arm around her. After an hour, he got up, went through the process of piling on two shapeless sweaters, his coat, mittens, muffler, and hat, and then left without a word. It took the cold to finally drive her to bed that night, long after she should have been asleep.

Thanksgiving Day blew in with snow. As Lily stood at the obscured window and shivered, she wondered at her foolishness in thinking the snow beautiful. The days when she had enjoyed the sight of it softly falling seemed to belong to another century.

Everyone had already agreed to wait until noon to eat their usual roast and beans, so Lily and Luella munched

on crackers at the house and Luella drew turkeys and pilgrims on a strip of building tape.

"I'll run it down the center of the table," she said. "That
will make the roast special."

There had been no word from the Buxtons that Luella
was to join them in their house for Thanksgiving, and the
child never mentioned it. Lily sat close and watched Luella
draw, remembering her own loneliness. There hadn't been
a Miss Carteret for her.

"Might I draw too?" she asked, and Luella handed her a
pencil. Together they finished the runner, rolled it up, and
were bundled up when Jack knocked on the door for them.

"Hang tight onto the rope," he shouted over the roar of
the wind.

Slowly, hand over hand on the rope, they made their
way to the cookshack, each step harder than the last until
Lily, exhausted from the effort, wanted to turn around
and crawl back in her bed. She could pull up the covers
and wait for spring.

When she thought she couldn't manage another step,
the door opened and welcoming hands pulled them inside.

Lily let Chantal and Amelie unwind her muffler and
help her from her coat. As she grew accustomed to the
relative warmth, she sniffed the air. Oh, it couldn't be. She
sniffed again, then looked around in amazement.

Madeleine had scrounged up a tablecloth from some
dark recess. It covered the longer table that was set with
the usual steel utensils and thick china plates. A great
slab of pork rested on her largest platter, flanked on each
side by the usual beans, and applesauce made from dried
apples and spiced with cinnamon and nutmeg.

Lily stared and came closer. She knew her eyes had to
be playing tricks, but there it was, pork with crackling bits
of fat. She looked at the men of the Bar Dot, who were all
smiles. "Where in the world did this come from?" she asked.

"The Lord giveth," Preacher said.

"Come now," she said, and he gave her a wounded look. "Pigs just don't drop out of the sky!"

Even Jack had to laugh. "We came across this pig last week, trudging along with some cattle."

"Whose cattle?" she asked.

"Someone's," Pierre said vaguely. "And wouldn't you know, *Monsieur le Cochon* stopped right in front of my horse. What was I to do?"

"Ask around, I hope," Lily said as she came closer and breathed in the fragrance. Steam rose from the mound of pork. *But don't ask too hard*, she thought, delighted.

"I did ask around," Pierre insisted. He took her arm and guided her to the bench.

"*Really?*"

"He did," Jack assured her with a straight face. "I was there and heard it all. Pierre stood in the middle of the pasture, looked around, cupped his hand to his mouth, and whispered, 'Anyone belong to this pig?' We didn't hear a thing." He drew in a deep lungful of fragrance. "We couldn't just leave it there all friendless. Happy Thanksgiving, Lily. Let's have a better one next year."

Lily tried unsuccessfully to wipe the corner of her mouth without being noticed. She dabbed at her eyes with even less success. Madeleine beamed at her from the doorway to the kitchen. Lily looked around at her friends and her students, feeling more blessed than at any time in her life.

"Wait." Luella held up her hand and unrolled the Thanksgiving table runner she and Lily had made. She stepped back, pleased.

"I really think someone should ask a blessing," Lily said.

Jack gestured to Preacher. Touched, Lily noticed that Jack wore a white shirt, instead of the two wool shirts she had seen him in for the last month since the first blizzard. In fact everyone had put on clean shirts.

Preacher stepped forward until he stood right in front

of the pork. His eyes grew serious, and he took him time looking at each one of them. "For what we are about to receive, may the Lord make us truly thankful. Amen. I never meant anything more," he concluded simply.

With a scraping of benches, they all sat down except Madeleine, who darted into the kitchen and returned with nine biscuits, small, to be sure, but biscuits. Lily watched the Sansever children eye the fluffy bits of goodness with their light brown tops. She knew there wasn't any butter, but there suddenly Madeleine whipped out a little lump of yellow heaven from behind her back.

"I've been saving it." She handed the plate with the biscuits to Chantal. "Take one, *mon cherie.*"

Chantal shook her head and passed on the plate. Amelie did the same, and then Luella, even though her eyes lingered on the biscuits. Jack held up his hand.

"That's enough," he said, his voice firm. "There are nine biscuits and each of you is eating one. Start over, Chantal."

She did, gave him a grin, and sent the plate around until it was empty. The beans went around next and then the pork, luscious slabs of pork, heavenly and greasy.

"Shouldn't we save some of it?" Luella asked, doubtful.

"Not today," Jack said. "I sent Will over to the Buxtons with a nice share for their table. Madeleine saved the bones and marrow to flavor our beans this week. We're going to stuff ourselves until it's gone, and I won't have an argument."

It was quietly said. Lily wondered if he ever raised his voice and decided it wasn't necessary. Leaders were like that, she decided as she took her tiny share of the butter, doled it onto the little biscuit, and then turned her attention to the pork. She ate the fat first, hungry for it, aware that the beef they had been eating, while plentiful, had been lean with no fat. She hadn't realized how much she craved fat until it was there before her on her plate. The others did the same thing, then, in near silence, they demolished the pig that had appeared from nowhere.

When everyone sat there, stunned, Madeleine handed around the applesauce, which vanished too, settling inside on top of Thanksgiving pork.

"I told Preacher he could have a minute with a little Holy Writ," Jack said. "Preacher?"

The young man from Alabama took out his Bible. "There are lots of verses about Thanksgiving, but this is the one we need." He cleared his throat, and spoke with some command, maybe remembering an earlier pulpit. "It's from Thessalonians, one of Paul's letters. 'Rejoice evermore. Pray without ceasing. In every thing give thanks.'" He shut the Bible and looked at Jack. "Sir, I thought maybe each of us could go around the table and mention one thing we're thankful for."

"Good idea. You start, Wally."

Preacher grinned at him. "You haven't used my name in a long time."

"It's your name."

Preacher nodded. He started to speak, but the wind picked up suddenly, as if trying to remind them that all wasn't well, not by a long shot. "Christ could calm the wind," he said wistfully. He looked at the table, every bowl and plate clean. "I was going to say I'm thankful for food, but I'm mostly thankful for all of you."

Lily swallowed the lump in her throat. She thought of the fancy dinners at her uncle's manor, the ones she had been invited to attend, and all the courses picked over, a bite here and there, and then returned to the kitchen. She had never wondered where that leftover food had ended up, but now she did. One of those fancy dinners would have fed them for a week.

She felt the lump grow as she remembered crackers and dried cheese with her father, and wondered if he thought of her this day. Her heart went to the Little Man of the Prairie and his bits of seed and grass. She glanced at Francis, who had eaten his own pork and sat in the doorway between kitchen and dining room, cleaning his face.

"I'm thankful for friends too," Pierre was saying now. He fingered the medicine bag around his neck. "Are we all going to be boring and say the same thing?"

Everyone nodded.

"I have something else," Luella said, blushing a little when everyone turned to look at her. Lily had brushed her hair into soft pigtails, the tight braids a thing of the past. "I am thankful for the Temple of Education."

"Oh," Lily said, swallowing a bigger lump than pork.

"And *Ivanhoe*," Jack chimed in, which made her suddenly feel the need to examine her fingernails.

"My children," from Madeleine as she reached for them.

"Plans," Lily said, which made Jack smile and give her a slow wink.

The door banged open, and Will Buxton stood there. He shut the door and leaned against it, as though trying to barricade them from the world outside.

"I . . . we thought you'd be at the Buxtons' all afternoon," Jack said. "I hope you ate."

"I did, but I'd rather be here. Is there room?"

Preacher moved closer to Pierre. "Here you are, friend."

Will looked up at that, gratified. He sat right in the middle of the bench, not on the edge or the outside. He breathed a long sigh of something that sounded like relief, and Lily was thankful she had not been invited to the Buxtons' for dinner.

Chantal cleared her throat and looked at Lily. "Now?" she asked.

Lily nodded. The children got up and stood close together. Lily looked into each dear face: Nick so reluctant at first, but Nick, her hero at the woodpile. Luella, probably bearing more burdens than any of them, but stalwart. Chantal, so sweet and lively, but who drew a gravestone on her March winter count. Amelie, so quiet, but with heart, depth, and grit that Lily was only beginning to understand. They were her students, her children, her comrades in the classroom. Somewhere deep in her heart she knew that they would never learn as much from her as she had learned from them. She nodded again and gave them a note.

"'Come, ye thankful people, come. Raise the song of harvest home,'" they sang, each line centuries old and cherished, but never sung with more meaning than right now, on this isolated ranch in the middle of something that could yet prove greater than them all. "'All is safely gathered in, e'er the winter storms begin.'"

The wind roared and slammed against the building and their voices rose to meet the challenge. "'God, our maker, doth provide, for our wants to be supplied.'" Pierre's pork, Madeleine's little bit of hidden butter. "'Come to God's own temple, come, raise the song of harvest home.'"

CHAPTER 39

༄༅༦༠ཀ

*T*he pattern of riding and hunting for lost cattle did not take the holiday season into account, but Jack had known it would not. As he shivered and swore and forced himself to endure endless days in the saddle, he thought of earlier years when he was learning his trade and was cut loose to ride the humiliating grubline. As bad as this was, he wasn't begging at ranch houses for food in exchange for chores or wondering if his horse could hold out too.

Besides, there was Lily to ride home to, even if she didn't know it. The night he had dropped to his knees and cried out his heart with his head in her lap hadn't furnished sufficient humiliation for him to stop seeing her. He couldn't stop. There was something about her serenity, even in this terrible time, that drew him like a filing to a magnet.

He knew roughly when Luella went to bed. He tried to show up a little before, because Luella always gave him a hearty greeting. In her bossy way, she would take his hand and make him sit beside her on the bench in his former front room, the room that had now become the Temple of Education. She'd put one of her books in front of him and demand that he read to her.

"Just a sentence or two" became "just a paragraph now," and then as December neared its middle, "Just this one page." His halting efforts became fewer as he came to understand words and sentences. He finally reached the night when the story itself began to make infinite sense. Everything started to string together, and he discovered the fun of reading.

"Say, Lily," he had said, looking over Luella's head to the lovely brown lady who usually sat on his sprung sofa, her feet tucked under her, because she was always cold, this daughter of Barbados. "I think I like this."

"Of course you do. Luella has graciously let us borrow more of her books. Tomorrow we will begin *Toby Tyler, or Ten Weeks with the Circus*."

Once Luella was in bed, tucked in with a prayer, a hug, and then another hug—something he doubted that her own mother ever provided—Lily came back to his sofa, picked up *Ivanhoe*, and began where they had left off.

She tried to get him to read, now that she knew he could, but he refused. They nearly had an argument over that, and he knew what she looked like when displeased: lips twisted to one side and eyes small. He explained to her why she was to read *Ivanhoe*, and the look disappeared.

"That's it," he concluded with a touch—just a touch— of his foreman's voice. "Your English accent is the best part of my day. I want to hear it. I sound like a Georgia cracker. You sound like a queen of England. Trust me; it's better."

She had glared at him but succumbed. "It's just the way I talk."

"I know, I know. That's what I want." He folded his arms and waited for her to capitulate, which she did, after tapping him on the head with the book.

She could always tell when the day had been so bad that not even her voice as she read could take away his pain. Then she would stop reading, put in the bookmark, and set the book aside. "Tell me what happened," she said, and he did, usually in fits and starts, and then with an outpouring of his exhaustion, sorrow, and true pain, about watching animals suffer and having no way to prevent it.

He told her about watching cattle wander and die against the drift fences that were supposed to contain the majority of the district's cattle. "We ride the fence on a normal winter, and chivvy them back," he said, taking a running jump before leaping into the horrors of the day. "Different ranches send different hands. We usually ride with the LC, since they're closest."

"Why is it called LC?" she had asked. Brands interested her.

"McMurdy's wife is named Elsie," he said. "Come spring, I'll take you up there to meet her. She's a great cook. Better'n Madeleine, but you didn't hear that from me."

There now, he had softened himself and set her at ease a bit. He told her what the Bar Dot boys and the LC hands had found that day by the drift fence, the main one located south of the Bar Dot. He described the cattle piled against the fence so deep, frozen and dead, that the cattle behind walked over them and kept struggling south into the whiteness that extended for a thousand miles. "They'll die against someone else's fence," he said and couldn't help his shudder. No need to tell her how many of them staggered on hoofless stumps or describe the low moan of dying cattle. He knew he would hear the sound in his dreams for the rest of his life.

If he felt either brave enough or miserable enough, he put his head on her shoulder. Her arm invariably went around him, and they sat together like that until the room was too cold, and he had to leave, even though it was the last thing he wanted to do.

Whether it was the last thing she wanted him to do, he did not know. He suspected it might be but did not force the issue. This winter was proving to be more complicated and problematic than any he had lived through since Petersburg and the works before Richmond in 1865. Throwing his heart into the ring would have only been one more challenge. Or so he thought.

A little bit of sky in the face of endless winter surfaced in mid-December, when the earth struggled to warm itself. One night a chinook blew through their valley, bringing warming southern winds that melted some of the snow and brought the blue sky.

Even the children seemed more cheerful over breakfast. Chantal kept going to the window, where the ice had melted, just for the pleasure of looking out, until her mother had to remind her to take the coffee pot around again.

He looked at his ranch hands. Even Will knew what was coming.

"Well, boys, let's cowboy up and use every inch of this weather."

He told Madeleine and Lily not to worry if they weren't home tonight. "Likely we'll be close to the LC and we'll bunk there," he said, accepting a sack of hot potatoes for lunch, and more of the everlasting raisins Madeleine had insisted on getting early in the summer.

"What will you do?" Lily asked, reminding him that she knew so little about cows and ranching.

"McCurdy said he knew of a draw where there might still be some live cattle. We'll check it out and trail them toward the LC," he told her.

What he didn't tell her was that if it was even possible when they finished, he was going to bolt for his own property to check on Manuel and Bismarck. He'd go by himself, unless Pierre felt like taking his life in his hands for another day.

They found the cattle where McMurdy had predicted, a respectable-sized herd that had started milling in a circle. The ones on the outer edge were dead. The warming wind had blown away some snow, revealing heads and horns.

The men cut a path through to the center, where there was still life. They nursemaided the wobbly animals closer to McMurdy's holdings. Preacher and Will bedded down for the night, and Elsie McMurdy tried to convince him to stay. When he wouldn't, McMurdy walked him and Pierre to their blanketed horses, who were eating the generous amounts of hay that their good host provided.

"Be careful, boys," was all McMurdy said and then, "First good day next week, I'm putting Elsie on the train to Cheyenne. She can winter there with her sister. You might pass the word on to Mr. Buxton to think about that for his own woman and kid. Maybe even the others and that mulatto gal."

Jack nodded. *Where would she go?* he thought as he gave McMurdy a little salute and took the blanket off Sunny Boy.

Jack and Pierre rode to the little fenced ranch where Jack's future herd took it easy in the barn. The snow was treacherously deep in the slopes and gullies, but they plodded on, silent to conserve energy. The snow covered the barbed wire fence now, except in spots where the wind had blown it away. They found the fence and followed it to the gate with the crossbars where last summer he had tacked Sinclair Ranch, which Pierre had painted for him, since he knew how to spell *ranch*.

They found Manuel as placid as ever, knitting, and they laughed to see a knitted creation draped over one of the cows. Since Manuel had never specified any particular color of yarn, Jack had bought all colors. The cow sported a green, red, and yellow afghan, tied in place with braided yarn. Manuel had thoughtfully made allowances for the heifer's expanse, as one of Bismarck's offspring grew inside her.

"What do you think, *señor*?" Manuel asked, his eyes bright.

"In Georgia, we'd say 'you're the beatinest.'"

Manuel's face fell. "I do not understand, *señor*."

"It means you're better than anyone else. Beatinest."

They stayed the night with Manuel in the barn, crowding with him for warmth in the little stall he had roofed over. They arrived at the Bar Dot at the same time his hands rode in from the LC, all of them scooting in just before the chinook ended and another blizzard hit. For two days he paced up and down in the cookshack.

Madeleine's X's on the calendar were marching toward December 25 when a worn-out McMurdy stopped at the Bar Dot for the night. He flipped a telegram across the table to Jack. "It's for your boss. I took Elsie and the young'uns to Cheyenne. The postmaster flagged me down before I left town." He accepted the mug of coffee from Madeleine with thanks in his eyes. "The talk in town is that the consortiums are gathering for a meeting," He looked at the telegram between them. "What do you bet?"

Jack nodded. "They usually get together about now to plan how many head they're going to overstock the range with in the coming year." He couldn't help his cynicism, but McMurdy understood. "I wonder if that's it. Fothering's coming to take Luella to the big house for the weekend. He can deliver it."

McMurdy was as good as any man at discerning what was unsaid. "Not feeling the love, eh?" He sipped his coffee. "Sometimes it's good to be the little man out here. I'll probably lose my shirt, come spring, but I'm doing it on a scale a whole lot smaller than the outfit you ride for. Merry Christmas, Jack. Maybe things'll look up in '87."

Sure enough, the long-suffering Fothering brought back a message the next morning for him to come to the house at once. Jack knew Fothering was a reader of moods. "What's in the air? Trouble for me?" he asked.

"Sir Oliver the Great and Mighty is packing," Fothering said, then dropped into Sam Foster–Ohio. "He didn't look like the first dandelion in spring, if that's what you're driving at.

I'll walk you back."

Heads down against the roaring wind, they trudged the few hundred yards to the house. Fothering had called it correctly. Mr. Buxton was doing his own pacing in front of his window.

"If the weather holds tomorrow, you and I are riding to Wisner and I'm catching the train."

Jack felt bold enough. "Why do you need me? You can just leave your horse in the livery stable and get it on your return here."

Mr. Buxton turned red. "You're not going to be here much beyond this spring, if I can help it," he snapped. "I . . . I . . ."

If he wasn't going to be working for the Bar Dot—praise Almighty—beyond spring, Jack reasoned, why not say it? "You don't think you can get to Wisner by yourself, do you? But it doesn't matter to you if I have to return alone."

He waited for the explosion, but it didn't come. Mr. Buxton just narrowed his eyes and continued his pacing. "Tomorrow, hear me?"

❦

The ride to Wisner, only four miles, was longer because of wind, snow, and silence filled with animosity. It might have been fear. Jack couldn't tell what drove Mr. Buxton lately. Fothering's comments about Mrs. Buxton's "fragility" seemed to be a code for "instability" that had nothing to do with the body. Will Buxton used to spend evenings with his relatives in the comfort of their parlor, but lately he had been staying in the cookshack, playing poker with Preacher and a surprisingly adept Nick, with broomstraws as the stakes. According to Lily, Luella was more and more reluctant to leave on weekends. Jack rode in his own self-contained silence, grateful he wasn't Oliver Buxton and happy to put him on a train.

He waited in the depot for Mr. Buxton to buy his ticket. The warmth indoors seemed to unlimber his boss.

"You're not real curious about my trip to Cheyenne," Buxton said.

"You're the boss. You'll tell me what I need to know," Jack replied with a shrug.

"There's been talk of putting the press on you small-time ranchers. The Cheyenne L&C wants its property lines straight. The consortium might want me to make more of an . . . effort to get you to sell. And there's that big bull of yours."

"The land's not for sale and neither is Bismarck," Jack told him.

"We'll see about that. Be here for me on Christmas Day." He turned away.

Jack couldn't leave the depot fast enough, wondering if he had been threatened. He knew his deed for both land and Bismarck were secure, but the Cheyenne L&C, like the other consortiums, had the ear of the territorial governor. They owned Wyoming as sure as if some cosmic force had wrapped a big red bow around the whole territory. *Merry Christmas*, he told himself.

After the Cheyenne Northern pulled away from the depot, he went to the Great Wall for chop suey and saw a morose Mr. Li, who shook his head over slow business.

"Nobody want chop suey," he mourned. "How is a man to make a living?"

"We've had tough winters before, Mr. Li," Jack reminded him. He thought about the hard-working little men from China who ran the restaurants, washed the clothes, and built the railroads. "You'll be here, come spring."

Mr. Li nodded. He handed Jack a sack of almond cookies. "For that pretty lady?" He giggled like a girl. "You maybe marry her some day?"

"She's a lady, Mr. Li," he said, feeling his ears burn and not from frostbite. "It's a nice idea, though."

Mr. Li just giggled and retreated behind the beaded curtain, the subject closed.

He stopped at Watkins' Mercantile, hopeful, even as he looked at bare shelves.

"Food's gone," Watkins said.

"Had something else in mind," Jack said, putting down four bits. "What about a lace collar? Have anything like that?"

Curiosity was stamped all over Watkins's face, but Jack ignored it. The merchant rummaged in one of the deep drawers behind him and pulled out a lace collar. "What do you know, fifty cents. Want a box for it?"

"Sure."

Watkins drummed up a slim white box with cotton padding. He set the collar inside and handed it to Jack, a question in his eyes.

"Merry Christmas," was all Jack said.

He tucked the box into his coat pocket and took the snow-covered road to the Bar Dot, a narrow trail now, with the snow even threatening to close it behind him like a sprung trap. He wished he had enough money to put Lily on the Cheyenne Northern, like McMurdy had done with his Elsie, and keep her safe in some hotel for the winter. He wondered if Lily would leave if he offered to take her to the train.

"Would you, Lily?" he asked the wind. Sunny Boy's ears perked up. Something told Jack she wouldn't. He wasn't really an optimist, but as he rode home, he thought of Lily's comments about reordering her opinions, as she put it. Maybe it was time to reorder his own.

CHAPTER 40

❦

The cold came back, turning the slush to ice. Preacher's horse went down and became another casualty. Lily's brown eyes filled with tears when Jack shot the horse because Preacher couldn't.

"I used to ride, back in England," she said, when he came into the cookshack to explain the rifle shot.

"We'll go riding this spring," Jack told her.

Over his men's protests, he directed them to start moving the huge woodpile even closer to the cookshack and horse barn. When the Sansever children volunteered to help, Lily did too, taking her place in line as they handed firewood from person to person while Will stacked it.

"You don't have to," Jack told her.

"I do too. I live here," she said. She stopped when the wind whistled up her skirt and petticoats and set up a shiver she couldn't control. Jack made the Sansever girls stop too. White patches had appeared on Chantal's face, and she was rubbing the spots.

"They itch," she told Jack, who led her away from the woodpile.

"You too, Amelie and Lily," he said, and it wasn't a suggestion.

In the cookshack, Madeleine scolded her youngest, and then she cried and dabbed white crème on the spots.

"Frostbite," Jack whispered to Lily.

She took a good look at his face, with its own patches of blistered white skin. When Madeleine finished and sent her girls to bed to keep each other warm, Lily dipped her finger in the salve and dotted Jack's blisters.

He smiled his thanks and started for the door. "I'll tell the others to stop now. We'll go at it in the morning again." He touched her sodden and icy skirt and shook his head. "Lily, I hate to ask this, but you'd be a whole lot better off in trousers."

"I couldn't possibly," she said. "The very idea!"

"Lily, don't be a knucklehead," he said. "You can't stop shivering and that's a bad sign. Madeleine?"

The cook came to the kitchen door.

"What can you do for Lily?" he asked.

Madeleine crooked her finger. "Come here. We'll close the kitchen door and you'll take off the skirt and petticoat. I can dry them in front of the stove."

Lily opened her mouth to protest, but they were both looking at her, each equally capable of enforcement. "Very well," she grumbled.

Madeleine closed the door behind them, but not before she heard Jack's laughter.

"I am a source of amusement," Lily said as she stripped off her skirt and both petticoats. She drew the line at removing her two layers of union suits and Madeleine didn't object.

Madeleine gathered up her clothing and draped it over the makeshift clothesline she had strung near the stove. "Amusement? You think that is all you are, *mon cher*?" she asked.

"Well, no, but . . ."

"When was the last time you heard Jack Sinclair laugh?"

Lily couldn't remember a time. She shook her head. "I'm sorry, Madeleine."

The cook patted her cheek and pointed to the lean-to where her daughters crowded together. "Three will fit. Keep warm." She chuckled. "He called you a knucklehead."

By the time her clothes were dry, the men were drinking coffee in the dining hall, and Madeleine was serving stew. She dressed and joined them, grateful for the warmth of her dry clothing, grateful for the small things, which was all anyone had now. Her fingers itched and burned, but scratching didn't help.

Jack took her hand. "Chilblains. I'm going to go through Stretch's trunk and see if he has some wool socks. You can put them on your hands at night." He gestured to Pierre. "We're also going to your father's house and see what clothes of his we can salvage for you. You two are about the same height. I'd loan you mine, but I'm wearing most of them. Now don't you go blush about that! Anything else you want from the house?"

"Paper. Check his desk. I need paper," she said.

She walked with them to Jack's old house. The last wind had knocked the True Greatness sign crooked. She put the least amount of firewood she could manage into the stove, thinking that each stick was precious and that even little Chantal paid a price for it.

They returned an hour later with her father's wool trousers and shirts, plus a shapeless, thick sweater that suddenly looked like heaven to her. After they left, she thought about Miss Tilton's proper school for the last time and put on her father's pants. She found a belt and cinched it tight, then pulled on the blessed old sweater, the one she had been planning to throw out while he was gone to Cheyenne.

Gone to Cheyenne. "Papa, how could you desert me?" she said out loud.

⁓

It was easy enough not to think about Papa as Christmas approached. She had chosen psalms for each of her children to memorize and prepare for a recitation on Christmas Eve. Praise Providence, the paper was dry, thick vellum that Jack had scrounged from Papa's old house.

Her plan to fold several sheets of paper in half and turn them into a journal for each child nearly died aborning, when she found she couldn't even thread the needle to sew the sheets together at the spine because her chilblains made her hands too clumsy. Jack found her in tears two nights before Christmas when he stopped by after Luella was asleep.

Tears streaming down her face, she held out the needle to him. He couldn't thread it either. "What're you making, honeybunch?" he asked.

She knew he couldn't have meant that. It must be a Southern expression, because he had said that to the Sansever girls before. Better just ignore the slip.

"I wanted to sew six folded-over sheets of this heavy paper together to make journals for my children," she said, wishing her chin didn't quiver, because she hated to cry in front of this strong man. She flexed her fingers and winced. "It's much nicer in Barbados."

He laughed at that. "I don't doubt you! Tell you what: let me go get the man who can help." He fingered the folded sheets. "Were you going to make a cover of something?"

Lily shrugged. "I don't have anything."

"Hold that thought. And don't scratch your hands! That makes it worse."

She waited until he left to rub her red and swollen knuckles that itched and burned with no relief. She had spread four separate stacks of six pieces of paper each on the table, folded and ready for the needle she couldn't thread. "I haven't anything else for them," she said to the closed door. "I hope you have a good idea, Mr. Smart Stuff."

He came back with Pierre, who pulled out waxed thread and a needle with a big eye. "I use these to fix my moccasins," he explained. "Thread that one."

She did, delighted to guide the waxed thread through easily. She picked up the first stack of folded sheets, but Pierre stopped her.

"I brought some smoked deerskin. Let me use those scissors."

They watched as Pierre deftly measured the deerskin against the papers. He cut confidently, then sewed through the paper and hide, creating the journal she wanted. He cut three more rectangles of skin and nodded his approval as she sewed the remaining journals. When she finished, she handed back the needle and thread.

"I wish I had gifts for you and the others," she told them.

"Just read to me," Jack said. "Well, uh, all of us."

Pierre just smiled.

⁓⁓

School on Christmas Eve consisted of recitation practice, followed by "Silent Night" and "Joy to the World." The wind had died away to a small breeze, and Lily sensed more than felt a rise in the temperature. They could see their breath in the Temple of Education, same as always, but even traitor Francis, who had abandoned Lily for Madeleine's kitchen, had followed the Sansevers to school, confident enough for an outing. Maybe there would be another welcome chinook.

Lily had borrowed Pierre's needle and waxed thread to string great handfuls of Madeleine's eternal raisins into garlands for the pathetic tree that Will Buxton had located. She had wanted to use the ranch's tin snips to make ornaments from cans Madeleine had saved, but her hands were too clumsy. Raisins would have to suffice.

In the early afternoon, the children, Luella included, walked back to the cookshack, carrying the raisin ropes.

Lily debated whether or not to wear a dress for the festivities and decided against it. Her father's pants were a reasonable fit and she knew the temperature was already dropping as night approached. Better to be warm. Jack had found a nearly new red-and-black flannel shirt among Stretch's few possessions and had presented it to her with a flourish. *Next year will be better*, she thought as she buttoned the shirt that morning. *I will be somewhere else.* Where, she didn't know, but she had the rest of the winter to make plans.

The cookshack was still a sow's ear, but Madeleine had pulled out that white tablecloth again. Someone had painted "Marry Crismuss" on the wall in one foot tall black letters, which made Luella, hands on hips, stare at it a long time.

"Someone can't spell," she said finally with a sorrowful shake of her head.

Supper was everlasting beans, but Madeleine again managed a miracle by seasoning them with the last of the pork from the Thanksgiving pig. There wasn't any flour for bread, but Jack provided a box of Pilot crackers. The little bit of strawberry jelly remaining didn't help much, but it didn't hurt, either.

When they finished, the adults drank coffee while the children strung the raisins around the tree. Lily watched their animation, touched at their pleasure in something so nearly pathetic. Fothering joined them. He nodded to Luella, who whisked out three shiny glass balls. She handed one to Chantal and one to Amelie and they hung them on the tree, which suddenly looked less pitiful.

"I'm glad you could get away," Lily whispered to Fothering.

"Mrs. Buxton's poor, cowed maid is there." He shook his head. "A bad business. I wish Mr. Buxton had taken his wife along to Cheyenne. There must be doctors there . . ." His voice trailed off.

"Maybe in the spring," Lily said quietly, struck by how often she had started sentences just that way. Come to think of it, everyone did.

The chief entertainment was a reading of *A Christmas Carol*, which Fothering had purloined from the big house. With a cup of tea at her elbow, Lily settled herself into a rumpsprung chair from the bunkhouse and started reading. Dickens's timeless tale of redemption worked its own magic in her heart as she read, taking turns with Fothering and his peculiar English accent. If enough time passed, perhaps she might be able to forgive her father for this last betrayal. *Maybe in the spring*, she thought as Fothering took his turn as the Ghost of Christmas Past.

"Silent Night," sung in parts, made Madeleine dab at her eyes. When Amelie sang the last verse by herself as her classmates hummed, the cook gave up all pretense and cried into her already overworked handkerchief. "Joy to the World" brought them all to their feet to applaud, and then sing along as Nick started the song over.

Presents were minimal. Lily reached for her own handkerchief when her children opened their presents from her, presents that began in tears and finished with Pierre's capable assistance. "For your deepest thoughts," she told them, then chuckled. "I only had a little of the lovely paper, so they'll have to be *really* deep thoughts."

To her surprise, her children came forward with a present for her. With clumsy fingers, she opened the newspaper-wrapped package and pulled out a finely polished piece of wood, the edges nicely sanded.

"It's to set your teacup on," Nick said, his eyes lively. "You know how Luella always scolds about rings on the table."

Lily put the little gift under her teacup. She thought of lovely presents through the years, given with no particular thought. "It's a perfect fit, Nick. How kind of you," she said. "I will never need another."

Jack dropped a present in her lap. She looked up, startled, and then watched in amusement as a blush spread up Jack's neck and into his light-colored hair. His crew looked away with smiles of their own.

She opened the narrow little box. Chantal gasped and sighed with pleasure as Lily took out an exquisite lace collar.

"My goodness, Jack," Lily said. She held it up to her neck. "Think how nice this will look against flannel."

"That's all your ensemble lacked," Fothering told her.

"Where in the world . . . ?" she started.

"Tell you later," Jack said. He covered his embarrassment by reaching into a small burlap sack and pulling out four bags made of cheesecloth and tied with colored thread. "All right, you kids. Merry Christmas from all of us."

Chantal opened hers first and exclaimed over Mr. Li's almond cookies and little squares of bittersweet chocolate, probably hacked from Madeleine's larger block in the kitchen, but made special because it was Christmas Eve.

Chantal held the bag and her leather-bound journal for deep thoughts close to her chest. "This is the best Christmas ever," she exclaimed, and everyone reached for overworked handkerchiefs.

They sang "Silent Night" again, then the only thing left to do was pull on sweaters, mufflers, more sweaters, and coats. Lily looked around, laughing inside to see these bundled up monsters, and all for a quick trip to the bunkhouse next door. Jack had already lifted Luella onto Fothering's shoulders for their slightly longer walk to the big house where Luella did not want to live. Still, Luella had whispered to her that her father would be back tomorrow and he had promised a Christmas doll.

Lily tucked her lovely present back in its box and shoved it deep in her coat. There appeared to be an intense conference by the door between Jack and Pierre, the outcome of which meant both of them took one of her arms each and escorted her to the Temple of Education.

"Nice evening, Lily," Jack said. "I have to go get Mr. Buxton from Wisner tomorrow, but Madeleine agreed to hold dinner until I return. She hinted at a raisin pie, but I think all the flour is gone."

"Madeleine has an uncanny knack for holding back things," Lily said as they strolled along, not even needing the rope because the wind had stopped. At her door, she looked up at the stars, remembering a song from her childhood. She glanced at her companions, knowing them not to be too critical about entertainment, and started to sing, "'When in bed awake I lie, watching stars up in the sky, how I wonder, can there be, a Little Child up there like me?'"

"Don't stop there," Jack said.

"'Does he watch the stars go by, in the river of the sky? Is the moon a smiling face, reflected in the sea of space?'"

The words seemed to hang on the magic air of Christmas Eve. "That's all I remember," she said softly.

"Maybe you'll remember the rest in the spring," Jack said, his voice low.

Both men wished her Marry Crismuss, and Lily stood in the doorway watching them return to the bunkhouse, where a few lights shone. When Jack turned back to look at her, she raised her hand and blew him a kiss. It was dark and he couldn't have seen her.

She stood another moment on the doorsill, happy in a way she wouldn't have imagined this time last year. Nothing had gone right, really, except that it had. She patted Jack's little present, figuring he must have paid a visit to Vivian at the Back Forty. He would probably never approve, but maybe in the spring she could meet the faro dealer and thank her for a chair burned up to save their lives, and a present from a shy man who hadn't enjoyed a much happier life than hers.

"Deep thoughts, indeed," she said out loud. "I should have made myself a journal."

Content, she looked at the sky again, and the smile left her face. As she watched, each star winked out one by one, snuffed by clouds moving in fast.

CHAPTER 41

⟨⊶○⊷⟩

The blizzard struck just as Lily was snuggling deep into her blankets, augmented by the blankets from her father's bed, the mound so heavy that she had trouble turning over.

"Drat and blast," she told the ceiling. Didn't the cosmic forces that governed the universe realize that tomorrow was Christmas Day? What would be the harm in two nice days in a row?

She knew self-pity amounted to nothing, so she burrowed deeper into her nest of blankets and closed her eyes with a deliberate snap. The sooner she slept, the sooner spring would come.

Sleep didn't come, mainly because she was getting colder by the minute, despite her blankets. She lifted up her head as much as the weight of the blankets allowed and sniffed the air like Francis. The hairs in her nostrils froze, something she always expected outside, but not in her little house, no matter how poorly insulated it was. This was a deeper cold.

Lily pulled her legs closer to her middle, thinking of Stretch in his frozen ball and the other dead men in the unused tack shed that had become the Bar Dot's morgue. She wrapped her arms around her legs and shivered as the wind roared overhead and snow thundered down with the speed of rain.

Blizzard after blizzard had already acquainted her

with sounds that ranged from a distempered shriek to a low moan. This sound seemed to mimic the Cheyenne Northern, rumbling along and gathering steam. She decided the eerie noise must have some relation to the fact that three days ago the men had taken manure rakes from the horse barn and scraped off the snow from the roof. Time for a new tune, she supposed, at least until the snow piled overhead again. Better to ignore it.

She couldn't, not when the building began to shake as though the wind had decided to lift the house off its foundation. *This can't be happening*, she told herself sternly. No wind was that strong.

Lily had pulled her flannel nightgown over her two union suits and two pairs of wool socks. She lay there, knowing she should snatch up her trousers and baggy sweater from the foot of the bed, except that it would require more effort and let in too much cold.

Maybe she was dreaming. She listened as the wind seemed to be coaxing the very nails out of the eaves, one at a time. She raised her hand to shake her fist at the wind and say what she thought when a screaming vortex lifted the roof entirely from the structure. Snow poured in, followed by deeper cold than she could even imagine.

The roof was gone, leaving nothing but the trusses, and they creaked, as if trying to decide to go or stay. In her terror, she screamed and screamed, coming in a poor second to the wind. She might as well be standing outside her front door, waiting to die.

"No, you don't," she said. She leaped from her bed and slipped and slid into the front room, with its table and bench—her dear school. She knew Pierre had nailed his winter count to the wall this time, but fear gave her strength. She yanked twice and the robe enveloped her into its generous folds. As the wind roared inside now, both windows in the front room exploded outward.

Terrified, she towed the buffalo robe back to her bed

and threw it on top of all her blankets. She pulled on the trousers and sweater and then crawled back into her blanket cocoon, certain now that death was going to be her extra special Christmas gift, but equally determined to fight as long as she could. Someone had to teach the children and read to Jack Sinclair.

She lay there in terror, nearly smothered by the combined weight of blankets and buffalo robe and snow. Pierre had told her how buffalo hunkered down in winter and turned their nose into the wind, rather than away from it. They faced the storm, unlike cows that drifted.

The wind screamed at her and the snow fell heavier and heavier on top of the already great weight. Claustrophobic, she wanted to throw everything off and stagger outside and let death come. It was going to get her anyway. Why prolong it?

In the end, she decided it would take too much effort to move. Her pillow was soft, and the bed saggy in all the right places, because she and its former occupant were nearly the same height. At least her death might be comfortable. Maybe they would dig out the house in a day or two and find her looking as though she slept.

"Oh, bother it," she muttered and closed her eyes, weary of winter and trouble, sorry that she wouldn't know what it was like to fall in love and marry, and have a child or two. There wouldn't be any anniversaries to celebrate, or triumphs to share with anyone, or even just the simple comfort of sitting on a couch, reading out loud to someone who liked her accent.

She did have *that* memory, at least. Lily resigned herself to death and decided that on the whole, perhaps death wasn't going to be all that bad. Death was going to require a massive reordering of her expectations, never high anyway. She could cope.

But that wasn't fair to anyone—not her, not the children, not Jack Sinclair. *I have to stay alive*, she thought, and then she said it out loud to the wind and the storm and the cold. She said it louder until she could hear herself, then drew herself into as small a ball as she could manage. Pierre's winter count had kept five people alive through one blizzard. Maybe its powers would extend to her alone. She closed her eyes and prayed.

⤬

"Lily, I know you're in there."

"Leave me alone. It's cold and snowy."

"I know! I'm not paid seventy-five dollars a month to leave you alone."

Lily opened her eyes to total blackness, the same as before. She felt cold and wretched, with only the distant memory of toes. Surely death would have been more pleasant. Maybe she was alive. It was certainly a prospect to consider.

The blackness grew briefly lighter, and then a whoosh of cold air socked her as though the selfish wind wanted her winter count robe too. She fought for it, which brought her in contact with a flannel shirt that wasn't hers. She patted it, felt arms with ropy muscles, and stopped struggling as relief poured over her, right down to those toes that did still have some blood flowing through them, because they hurt like blazes.

"Jack?"

"The very same. I know this is the height of impropriety, but I don't really care. I'd hold you tight like this even if you were Mr. Wing Li. I'm going to pull you closer. You can slap me later. No, no. Keep your hands in front of you. I want them between us because, boy howdy, they're cold."

He reached down to her toes, sticking his hand inside the sock layers. "This little piggy?" he said.

"Ow!"

"Music to my ears. How about this pig?"

"Stop it."

341

"You've got your parts, Miss Carteret."

What he was telling her penetrated the fog of her mind. At least she wasn't going to die alone, and if the two of them could warm each other, maybe she wouldn't die at all. She wanted to say all this, but maybe he knew.

"Going to sleep," she muttered. "Don't stop me."

"Wouldn't dream of it. You can't die, though, because we haven't finished *Ivanhoe*."

⁓

She woke up to faint snoring right in her ear. The air in their cocoon had been breathed in and out for far too long a time, so she raised one corner of the buffalo robe, letting in the cold, which woke up Jack too. He protested and tried to roll over, but she patted his face until he paid attention.

"What happened?" she asked.

"I've never felt it drop so cold, so fast," he said. "You know that thermometer in the cookshack? It registers to forty below, but the mercury was crowded down in the bulb, last time I checked."

"The others?"

He let out a lengthy sigh. "Bad news, Lily."

"Please, not my children," she said, struggling to sit up and failing.

He pulled her close again. "They're alive, but, oh, Lily . . ."

She prepared herself for the worst, something she had been doing since the first blizzard, so it had no real meaning any more. "Better tell me."

"The Buxtons' roof caved in with all that snow on it." Another sigh, but this one sounded frustrated. "We planned to rake off the snow tomorrow." He fumbled for her hands, sandwiching them inside his own. "Mrs. Buxton and her maid are dead."

"Luella? Fothering?"

"Hey, hey, steady, Lily. Fothering has a broken arm, but Luella is fine." He turned onto his back, pulling her close so her head rested on his chest. "Do you know she's been sleeping *under* her bed? That probably saved her life."

"Good heavens."

"It must have been a scary, grim house. Not even Fothering knew. A joist fell on his arm and broke it, but he managed to get Luella out and make it to the horse barn. Pierre was there, and he carried Luella the rest of the way. We never heard anything above the storm."

Lily digested his words, thinking of Mr. Buxton, probably stuck in Cheyenne now. There wouldn't be any Christmas doll, only sad news for him, one more layer of misery in a winter unlike any other. "Poor, poor man," she said.

She listened to the wind, trying to fool herself into thinking it was subsiding, and failing. "How . . . why did you think to look for me?"

"Dumb luck, my specialty," he said, sounding almost apologetic. He moved restlessly. "When I think—I was helping Fothering to the cookshack when I tripped on the very end of the roof to my humble home. The very end, Lily! One half step in another direction, and I never would have known." He tightened his arms around her.

"How on earth did you know it was your roof?"

"I felt along the roofline and ran into your Temple of Education sign. Yeah, part of the front of the house came off too. So close, Lily."

It didn't bear thinking on, she decided. Too much *what if* already filled their winter. "D'ye think we'll dream about this winter?"

"Probably. I already see cows on bloody stumps when I close my eyes," he told her.

"And I still pat around that woodpile next to the school, trying to find that ax. Jack?"

"Hmm?"

"Merry Christmas."

They spent one day in the house with no roof and three and a half walls. The trusses fell outward, to Jack's relief. All they could do was reach out now and then for handfuls of snow to swish around until it melted and swallow. Calls of nature were problematic, but easier for him, naturally—leap out of the blanket nest and let fly. She cried with humiliation when she couldn't get out in time, but he told her not to be a goose.

He told her about his life in Georgia, chopping cotton, chills and fever, early death for three of his sisters, and then the excitement of war that quickly settled into more chills and fever and early death, this time for comrades. He told her of battles fought and won, and then the losses that mounted higher and higher until all they could do was leave the breastworks before Petersburg and stagger south, starving and depleted. Surrender was a relief.

Her life was infinitely more interesting to him. As the cold deepened, he found himself envying her memories of blue water and warm sand, and that peculiar feeling of walking through seawater as it rushes away from shore and undermines footprints. She hadn't enjoyed England because it was damp and cold, and there weren't any tan people. She had been treated well enough, but without anyone taking a genuine interest in her as her mother had done.

He held her close when she cried about her father and his betrayal. Her tearful, "He said he had a plan, and we were going to San Francisco in the spring!" wrenched his heart around.

When her tears subsided, he asked her to tell him how *Ivanhoe* ended. She refused, and he understood what a fighter she really was. "Not on your life, John James Sinclair," she declared. "That would be bad luck. You'll just have to wait until we're in the cookshack and I am reading it to you."

"Do you even know where the book is?" he asked.

"I'll find it," she assured him, her voice almost fierce. "If I have to dig through your whole house, I'll find it."

Their ordeal ended on the second day, to the welcome sound of Pierre and Will hollering for them. Feeling like a mole too long underground, Jack pulled back the lifesaving winter count robe and peeled away the blankets. The bright sunlight made him wince and turn away, but he hollered back, for one irrational moment afraid that they would walk by and never find them. For another irrational moment, he wanted to stay just with Lily. Funny how wind and cold can work on a man's mind.

Soon, Preacher held him upright while Pierre reached for Lily, who protested the sunlight, but then just rested her head against the Indian's shoulder like a child when he picked her up.

The first thing Jack wanted in the cookshack was a warm drink of water and then another. Lily sat beside him, drinking water too. She didn't protest when Madeleine and Amelie took her arms and gently tugged her into the kitchen. When Jack was certain she was in good hands, he let his men guide him back to the bunkhouse for his own cleanup.

Fothering lay in the bunk that used to be Stretch's, his eyes deep pools of pain. "I couldn't save them."

"You saved Luella," Jack reminded the butler. "I couldn't ask for more."

He looked around the crowded bunkhouse, which smelled like the bottom of a dirty clothes hamper. They were all rank and foul, and praise the Almighty, alive.

They were looking at him, expecting some wisdom. He reminded himself that he was in charge of this train wreck and looked each man in the eye.

"Gentlemen," he said finally, which brought faint smiles. "I've been thinking . . ."

He hadn't, really, but they expected him to be the thinker. They expected him to save them all, so he had better get to it. "I have a plan."

That was all they needed to hear. He watched the relief grow in their eyes and smiled to himself, knowing, as never before, that the Cheyenne Land and Cattle Company didn't pay him enough for such a winter. Come to think of it, could anyone?

CHAPTER 42

⟨≈◇≈⟩

At his quiet order, Jack's comrades in the bunk house gathered their bedding and what clothes left that they weren't wearing and carried them next door. Pierre helped Fothering, who had nothing except the clothes he wore when he staggered from the ruin of the Buxton house, Luella over his shoulder because his arm was broken.

They piled their bedding into one corner of the cook-shack, which began to look even smaller. Jack looked around the room, estimating square footage for the first time. Men in one corner, women and children in the other; they could make this work because they had to. The luxury of heating the cookshack, bunkhouse, and his former house was gone. If they could move the rest of the woodpile closer, they might survive this winter.

Madeleine watched, questioning with her eyes at first, then nodding as she understood before he spoke.

"Madeleine, we're all moving into your cookshack."

"It's about time." She softened her words by blinking her eyes rapidly and sniffing back tears. "We need to stick together."

Lily sat at the table, dressed in her father's trousers and shapeless sweater. How she still managed to look tidy and composed was beyond him. She held Luella on her lap, her arms tight around the child, who had a stare that reminded Jack of soldiers after battle. Every few minutes she shuddered and turned her tearstained face into Lily's breast.

"Madeleine, could you and your lovely daughters get us some coffee? And tea for Miss Carteret, of course." His reward was a smile from Miss Carteret.

While the girls handed around mugs, Nick followed with the coffeepot. Madeleine brought out a bowl of raisins. Everyone took a handful and pushed the bowl around the table.

Now everyone was looking at him, ten serious faces turned his way. Nobody wavered. A man couldn't have a better crew. He had better, by Gadfrey, be equal to them.

"We're up against it," he said. No point in gilding this lily any more. He looked at Luella. "Honeybunch, we mourn your loss, but we are so relieved that you and Fothering are here."

Luella nodded, her face serious. Jack marveled inside how sorry parents could produce stalwart children. He'd put his money on Luella any day of the week.

"We're going to live in here, men on this side—you with us, Nick—and women and children over there, closer to the kitchen." Nods all around. Good. "If we run out of fuel before spring, we'll crowd together with the children between us."

More nods. No one blushed or looked askance, not this crew. "Madeleine, what's the food situation? Don't hold anything back."

He could tell by the look on her face that she must have done an inventory just that morning. "We have beans aplenty and onions." She chuckled, and he saw just how tough she was. "I think the beans will last until next Thanksgiving."

Everyone laughed, and then they laughed harder when Chantal sighed theatrically and said, "Nick is awful with beans. I'm glad he is sleeping on your side."

"We'll survive, Chantal," Jack said.

"That's just it: We will survive," Lily said. She kissed the top of Luella's head and gave Jack such a look that his brains went into a ten-second coma.

"Um, yes. Madeleine?"

"Maybe we have a bushel of potatoes. No sugar. No flour. A gallon of dried apples. Raisins that we will still be eating at the turn of this century. Two quarts of lemon juice. That's it."

"What about coffee?" Preacher had his priorities.

"Lots," Madeleine assured him.

"Tea?" Lily asked.

Madeleine's face fell. "Maybe another month's worth."

Lily slapped her forehead and even Luella giggled.

Fothering struggled into a sitting position, the effort written all over his face. "If we can get to the kitchen pantry, we have some flour and sugar, and cans of oysters and sardines. Salt pork. A case of canned milk."

Madeleine clapped her hands. "Oyster stew!"

"It is the perfect repast for New Year's Eve, Madame Sansever," Fothering replied in his butler voice. He looked at his arm that Pierre had splinted with bed slats. "Enough of that nonsense. My name is Sam Foster and I am from Ohio." He bowed to Madeleine. "You will have to share your kitchen with *moi*."

More laughter.

"I'm still going to call you Fothering because I have standards," Lily joked.

Everyone relaxed visibly, even though the wind seemed to bang on the walls, demanding attention like a three-year-old. "Any questions?" Jack asked.

Fothering seemed to be perking up. "Scurvy?"

"One teaspoon of lemon juice, every other day," Jack said, remembering some bad scenes from the siege before Richmond with men losing their teeth and old wounds reopening.

"I hate to be so practical, but it's going to be tough to keep a path open to the privy," Pierre said.

Madeleine turned a rosy shade, and Lily decided her fingernails were fascinating.

"Good thought," Jack said, wondering if his face was redder than Madeleine's. He looked around. No, Will Buxton had them all beat.

Jack got up from his perch on the table and walked into the kitchen. "Don't you even think it," Madeleine called after him.

"I'm not an idiot," he said patiently. He walked to the lean-to, where Madeleine and her children slept at night, crowded together on two small beds. It would work. He came back into the dining room.

"We'll use the privy as long as we can keep up on a path to it," he said. "If that fails, we're going to use your lean-to, Madeleine. I want you to move the beds in this room, anyway."

Frowns all around. "That's the best I have right now," he told them.

Nick raised his hand, tentative and red-faced, but decisive in his own way. "How about this? We put everyone's chamber pots in the lean-to, then just toss the contents outside when we finish."

"We can dig out a snow cavity near the back door but not too near. The ladies can put the contents in there, and we'll cover it up with more snow," Preacher offered.

"Not just the ladies," Lily said as firm as Nick. "I'm not a great adherent to the idea of just, um, flinging things to the wind."

Oh, she was good with words. Jack decided he could even listen to her talk about privies all day.

"And when spring finally comes?" Trust Luella to look ahead.

"Simple," Jack said, making no effort to hide his amusement. "Luella, you keep a tally. The one who complains the most this winter will get a shovel, a bucket, and a bag of lime."

Everyone laughed, even Fothering, whose arm had to be paining him, and Luella, who had stared down a multiplicity of demons, and Lily, who was raised a lady. Preacher laughed so hard he started to choke, which meant Madeleine had to bang him between his shoulders.

Their laughter had a most healing sound to it. When everyone had subsided to a weak giggle here and there, Jack held up his hand. "You people amaze me. Men, we'll ride when we can, to see if we can find other beeves. This is still the Bar Dot, and we have a job to do. We'll try to check on McMurdy, but we won't take risks."

Luella raised her hand. "What about my father?" She took a deep breath. "He was going to bring me a Christmas doll and candy for all of us."

What about Oliver Buxton? Jack could see the Cheyenne Northern starting out and ending up stranded, but Luella didn't need to hear that, not with her mother dead. "I strongly suspect that the Cheyenne Northern never left Cheyenne. I don't think the train will run again until spring."

Luella sighed. "I'm probably too old for dolls anyway."

"I hope not," Amelie spoke up. "When your father gets here with your doll, we can make doll clothes. Mama has lots of scraps."

Satisfied, Luella settled back against Lily again.

"Everyone will have duties. Lily, you will continue as our teacher."

"Not just theirs?" she asked, indicating the children.

"No, everyone's." If Fothering could admit he was someone else, why lie about his own deficiencies? "I'm no great shakes at reading, and I need to improve. Anyone else have any skills that might help?"

"I'm as good at numbers as Mr. Carteret was," Will said. "Nick, you want a tutor?"

Nick nodded. He cleared his throat. "I have decided to be a cow-roping math teacher when I grow up," he announced, to smiles all around.

"When Lily gets tired of reading, I can tell you Wasichu wonderful stories about the origin of the earth and why muskrats have tails," Pierre said.

"This is going to be the best school anyone ever had," Chantal said, her voice dreamy. Jack doubted she even heard the wind outside. Her hands may have been knobby with chilblains, but her contentment radiated.

"I do have a special job for you girls," Jack said, impressed with how they immediately became serious. "You are in charge of morale." He smiled at Amelie's questioning expression. "You are to write improving things like 'True Greatness' on cardboard—if we have any—and put it on the walls. If we feel down and need songs, you'll teach us. I wouldn't even mind dancing to 'Sur le Pont.' Morale, ladies."

"What about me?" Preacher said. He didn't try to hide his grin. "I know I'm not the best cowhand you ever hired, Jack."

"You can pray for us," Jack said. "We're going to need it."

❧

The storm finally relinquished its iron grip on the Bar Dot after noon. Following bean soup generously sprinkled with onions, Will, Nick, and Preacher went outside to see about a path to the privy and to the woodpile beyond. Pierre headed in the other direction with a shovel to hunt for Lily's trunk and its treasure of books. "I want to see you all back in here in twenty minutes," Jack ordered. "I'll join you in a few minutes, Pierre, but I have to ask Lily something."

He sat beside her. "Luella, I need to borrow your teacher for a few minutes." He looked at Madeleine. "May we go into the kitchen and close the door?"

Mystified, Madeleine nodded. Lily's eyes questioned him, but she followed him into the kitchen and closed the door behind her.

"Did I misbehave?" she teased.

"Nothing of the sort." During the day and night when they had huddled together under the winter count, he had mulled the matter over in his mind. It had made perfect sense then, but as he looked at Lily, he feared he was asking too much. Still, a man could only try, especially an ambitious one. He remembered Lily's calculating look when she got off the Cheyenne Northern last summer, as if she was trying to figure out what she could make of Wyoming Territory. Let's see if he truly understood her expression.

He pulled up Madeleine's rocking chair for Lily and a stool for himself. She sat, curiosity all over her face.

"Two weeks ago when I, uh, escorted Mr. Buxton to Wisner, he made some veiled threats about my land and Bismarck."

"What on earth . . . ?"

"He told me the Cheyenne Land and Cattle Company likes straight boundaries and my piddly little two-thousand-acre jog was messing it up."

"For goodness sakes!" she exclaimed. "How much land does one company need, I ask you."

So far, so good. Her indignation was genuine. "Maybe it's finally penetrating on some level that good breeding stock like my Herferd bull can benefit the range."

"High time, don't you think?" She looked him in the eyes, something her father seldom did. This was a woman with few allusions and nothing to hide. "What does this have to do with me?"

"I have no doubt that if something happens to me this winter . . ." He held up his hand when she tried to speak. "You know it's a possibility."

She nodded and rubbed her arms.

"If something happens to me, I don't want that greedy bunch of weasels to just take my land and livestock. Believe me, they'll try to find a way." He took a deep breath. "There's one way for me to prevent that. I can will my land and cattle to you"—he smiled as she gasped—"but I do not trust their Denver lawyers to let that slow them down much. They'd find a loophole, sure as you're born."

"Your property to *me*?" she asked, her eyes wide. "Jack, that's nutty. I know absolutely nothing about ranching."

"You didn't know anything about teaching when you moved here."

"That's different, that's . . ." She stopped, and he could have fallen at her feet in gratitude to see that calculating look again. "I could learn, couldn't I?"

"That's what's I'm counting on, if this winter kills me."

"I wish you wouldn't say that! But you don't trust Denver lawyers," she reminded him.

"Not even a little. There's one way to double my chances of leaving some kind of a legacy. Lily, will you marry me?"

CHAPTER 43

*L*ily couldn't have heard him right. "Beg pardon?"

"You heard me. If we're married, those Denver lawyers can't touch my property because it will be yours."

She took a deep breath, and then another, unable to speak because the idea was so preposterous, so out of the question . . . She forced herself to think clearly. There wasn't a thing wrong with his idea, drat the man.

"You're a fighter, Lily," he reminded her. "You proved that in the schoolhouse, and you proved it again when the roof blew off."

"Yes, but . . ."

"You'll have a lot to learn, but you won't let anyone steal my land."

"Of course not!" she exclaimed, leaping out of the rocking chair, which rocked harder. She looked at him, from his sandy hair to his frostbitten face with the war scar, to his capable shoulders that had hefted heavy loads all his life.

"Why not Madeleine?"

"I like her a lot, but she's Métis, part French, part Ojibwa. The Denver lawyers would dismiss her claims faster than an envelope would burn in a furnace. Besides, she's not the fighter you are."

She had to ask. "Jack, shouldn't we maybe court each other a little first?"

"We haven't that luxury yet," he said, each word

plainspoken and solid. "Sit down. No, right here." He patted his lap.

She hesitated, then sat on his lap, which put her eye to eye with this man who had just proposed. "It's a crazy notion," she argued, but she couldn't even convince herself.

"Granted. Let's do this: marry me, and if I die before spring, the Sinclair Ranch is yours. If I survive, and you have other plans, we can annul this and move on." He shrugged. "And if you like me a little . . ."

I'd be helping out a friend, she thought. *No, a more-than friend.* She leaned against him, and his arm seemed to naturally curl around her waist. "We can't get to Wisner to find a vicar or a reverend, or whatever you call them in Wyoming. This has to be a legal arrangement." *There. That should end the matter*, she declared to herself, which had the effect of making her suddenly miserable.

He gave her a sunny smile, the triumphant sort of smile she had seen on the face of her father just before he said, "Checkmate," and knocked over her queen, when they played chess. "Preacher is an ordained Methodist minister, someone called a circuit rider. I saw his certificate once. I couldn't read it, but who lies about a thing like that? Well?"

There was one more thing. His casual mention of his illiteracy reminded her. She got off his lap, startled at the look of disappointment in his eyes. "There's another issue. When Pierre finds my trunk, I'll show you."

"You can't say yes or no right now?"

"I cannot."

He nodded. "I'd better help him dig out that trunk." He left the kitchen.

When Lily came out a few minutes later after composing herself, Madeleine and Fothering both gave her questioning looks. Lily shook her head. If she said no, better that they never knew. And if it was yes, she wanted to explain this craziness only once.

Lily helped the Sansevers move their cots—*bed* was too grandiose a word—into the dining area; then she consulted with Luella about their own bed. "We can pile some of my father's blankets underneath, and the rest on top, and be quite cozy, my dear," she told the child. "But you need to help me."

They worked together. Luella started to cry after their pallet was nearly finished, so Lily just cradled her in her arms until she was calm again. When her tears turned into occasional sniffles, Lily handed her another blanket to layer on top. "Get busy, missy," she warned in a gentle voice. "I intend to be warm tonight!"

By the time the men returned from the woodpile, the girls had moved two tables away from the sleeping areas. Amelie had already painted lines on one of the tables to denote their desks in the Temple of Education, which, although battered, was proving to be portable.

And there was the trunk, bashed on top, but still intact. At her direction, Pierre and Jack set it by her pallet. She couldn't open the trunk, but Jack took a crowbar to it and then stepped back, watching, worried, while she rummaged through it.

Thank goodness the books were undamaged. She looked up. "No *Ivanhoe*," she told Jack.

He gave an exasperated sigh. "You mean you won't . . ." He looked around and lowered his voice. ". . . say yes until I can read *Ivanhoe*? Lily!"

"That's not it. Let me look." She searched through the trunk and found the pamphlet, not surprisingly, on the bottom under everything of importance. She had buried the foul thing as deep as she could. She held it up, wondering if he would remember.

"Oh, that's the pamphlet I gave you when you were asking for books," he said, reaching for it. "Seems so long ag—" He stared at the words, which obviously made sense to him now. All the color drained from his face as, lips moving, he slowly read the diatribe against racial mixing that someone had given him years ago, maybe during the war. He read several pages to himself, then ripped the pamphlet in two and stuffed it in the pot-bellied stove. Without looking at her, he turned on his heel and left the cookshack.

No, no, no, Lily thought to herself. She grabbed up the nearest shawl, wholly inadequate to the deep freeze outside and ran after him.

She didn't have to run far. He stood with his back against the cookshack wall, chin down, staring at his boots. She took his arm. "It's too cold to stand out here."

He turned bleak eyes on her. "I'm appalled," he said. "How could I give that to you?"

"You're the goose now, Mr. Sinclair," she said, tugging on his arm until he started to move. "You didn't know what it said, did you?"

He shook his head, mumbled something, grabbed her hand, and pulled her into the cookshack. A few tight-lipped words and the kitchen emptied out. He closed the door.

"Even if this marriage ends in the spring, I have to know if you agree with any of that," Lily asked.

"I never did," he told her, sitting in the rocking chair this time and rocking. "You need to understand: Pa was a poor farmer. He worked alongside slaves. So did I." He stood up and took her by her shoulders. "There wasn't much difference in us, except they stood on auction blocks and we got thrown off our rented land if the crops failed."

"Yes, then," she said simply. "I couldn't even marry you for four months if I thought you agreed with that pamphlet."

"I don't. You *will*?"

"I just said I would." She moved and he let go of her. "And if I decide to stay, you're going to get a lot of rude comments from others about my color." *Stay? What was she saying?*

She hesitated, but it had to be said. "And there's my father, the thief and drunkard. You'll have to live with that too. This might be too hard, Jack."

He took her hand again. "Lily, hard is freezing to death. Hard is finding yourself on the losing side in a war. Hard is eating out of trash cans. Hard is *not* marrying you."

My goodness, she thought. *And he probably doesn't even think he is eloquent.* "I'll help you. I . . . I might move on in the spring, but I can help you now. Yes! That's twice now. Don't press your luck, mister."

He smiled at her phony sternness, which had the unfortunate consequence of making his chapped lips bleed. She reached for Madeleine's white salve—heaven knows what it was—and dabbed some on his lower lip.

"I'll go talk to Preacher," he said. "Let's do this in the morning. While the snow is holding off and it's still light, I want to get the men and move the bodies out of the Buxton house." He looked at her seriously, and his face flooded with color. "Uh, you don't need to . . . this isn't a . . . Oh, you understand."

"I do," she said, her own face warm. "It's no business of Denver lawyers if we're husband and wife in name only."

He nodded and left the kitchen. She watched him go, wondering what on earth she had agreed to. *You're helping a friend, Lily*, she thought.

⁓

Preacher stared at Jack in openmouthed amazement. Once more, Jack patiently explained the whole reasoning behind the marriage, and still he stared.

"Preacher, this isn't hard to understand," he snapped. "I'm protecting my interests."

They had reached the Buxtons' ruined house, shovels in hand, to join the others. Great mounds of snow filled the space where the roof had crashed through the upstairs bedrooms. The men surveyed the destruction of the tidy clapboard house.

"I don't even know where to start," Will Buxton said.

Under Jack's directions, some shoveled snow, and others removed debris from the stairs, hoping to use them. Preacher was the lightest, so he went up first, climbing what stairs remained and crawling under walls where there should have been floors. By the time night fell, the bodies were bundled into blankets and pulled from the ruins.

Pierre had brought the sledge used to haul wood. Gently they placed Mrs. Buxton and her maid on it and tied them down. Jack sent Preacher to try to find Luella's room and some of her clothes, since she still wore only the nightgown she had escaped in. Will volunteered to find whatever food hadn't been destroyed by debris and snow.

Jack and Pierre pulled the sledge to the tack shed where Stretch lay, still frozen into a ball. The blanket slipped off Mrs. Buxton's face and Jack looked at her, noting how relaxed she appeared now. He covered her face. Some women just weren't cut out for Wyoming Territory. He wondered how Lily would fare on her own managing his ranch, and he felt no fear.

He closed the door and stood with Pierre, surveying their world that was getting smaller and smaller. "If we can get a stretch of decent weather, we can dismantle the Buxton's house and the sheds we should have burned years ago. Glory, I'm glad we didn't. We need them now."

"We're going to use it all, aren't we?" Pierre asked. "Down to the toothpicks in Madeleine's kitchen."

"I fear so."

Jack looked at the sky and watched the stars wink out one by one. "Here's comes another one."

When everyone was accounted for and eating skinny beef and one potato each, Jack announced there was going to be a wedding. He looked for surprise on their faces and saw next to none. Maybe Lily had already told them. Pierre looked particularly amused by the matter.

"Miss Carteret needs a dress and flowers," Luella said.

"Amelie and I will sing," Chantal announced.

Madeleine clapped her hands. "Monsieur Will brought me two quarts of flour and some sugar. *Eh bien*, there will be cake!"

"No, no," Lily said. "We need to conserve our victuals."

"'Conserve our victuals,'" Fothering repeated in his peculiar English accent. "You're marrying her because you love to hear her talk, aren't you?"

"You found me out," Jack said, determined not to blush. "Y'all, it's more of a business arrangement, and Lily is a good sport." He glanced at Lily, who was finding the floor interesting. "Yes, cake. Luella, can you make paper flowers? Lily, your best dress, please, and that lace collar. I have one white shirt left."

"What about a honeymoon?" Will asked. "I hear the kitchen with the door closed is lovely this time of year."

Everyone laughed, no one harder than Lily, while the wind blew and snow slammed sideways into their last outpost, and while the roof stayed on and there was food. If they could cram the tables into the corners, there might be dancing to "Sur le Pont." Lily could toss a bouquet of paper flowers and they would fling their own challenge to a winter unlike any other.

Jack couldn't help the feeling of immense satisfaction that washed over him like barely remembered spring rain. He thought of the Lily who got off the train, the Lily who insisted on tea, the Lily who cared about a pack rat, the Lily who kept him warm in a freezing ruin with tales of Barbados, the Lily who would fight and scratch and claw to stay alive and keep his ranch going, the Lily who looked so lovely, even with blotchy spots under her eyes and exhaustion drooping her shoulders, the Lily he wanted to grow really old with. That Lily. How in the world did stuff like this happen?

CHAPTER 44

⁓⊙⁓

*E*yes fierce with concentration, Luella made flowers from newspaper that Madeleine donated, with the promise that they would go in the pot-bellied stove in the dining room when all was done. While she worked, Lily taught her students to sing, "The Flowers that Bloom in the Spring," from *The Mikado.*

"Miss Tilton took us to London to the Savoy to see it," Lily told them.

"You were in London last year?" Chantal asked.

Lily nodded. Was it only a year? She had worn a beautiful dress with a bustle and sat in the grand tier of the mezzanine. And here she was, trying to stay alive in Wyoming, America, the new year upon them with no change in anything. She glanced at Jack, sitting in deep conversation with Pierre. Maybe he was one of those persons susceptible to suggestion, because he turned around and blew her a kiss. Shy, she looked away.

There wasn't much hope for her favorite dress, a green wool sadly wrinkled. Her bustle was buried under mounds of snow in her father's house, not even surviving her removal to Jack's house. Still, the lace collar constituted new, with an old dress. A borrowed and blue garter came from Will, surprisingly, who refused to say where he got it.

Threatening death by butcher knife to anyone foolhardy enough to stroll into the kitchen, Madeleine went to work on the wedding cake. She had requested Fothering's assistance, broken arm and all.

Lily had no plans to sleep that night, not with the wind howling, but Luella cuddled close and warmed her. The room was dark and comforting because she had a roof over her head in no danger of flying off. Pierre and Nick had taken turns that afternoon nailing it down more firmly. The room was far from quiet, with snores and the occasional whimper from Luella, which meant Lily patted her bedmate, hoping to chase away a few demons. In spite of this, Lily felt her eyes closing.

"Lily?"

It was Jack, squatting on his haunches by her pallet.

"I have no plans to change my mind," she whispered. "Go to sleep."

He kissed her cheek. "I just wanted to say thank you." He sighed and lay down on the cold floor beside her. "You're not exactly hitching your wagon to a star, Miss Carteret," he whispered.

"Getting cold feet?" she teased in turn.

"Lily, I wish I had a wedding ring for you."

She turned on her side to see him better. "And I wish I had straight hair and a bank account."

He couldn't help his laughter, which made the other residents of Bar Dot Manor groan and demand silence. Someone threw a pillow.

"Y'all are supposed to be asleep so I can creep around and visit Mrs. Almost-Sinclair," he protested.

"Go to bed, Jack," she whispered. "You're worse than my students."

⁓∞⁓

The wedding was nothing to complain about, all things considered. She dressed in the kitchen, then took the newspaper bouquet Luella handed her.

"I wish they were real flowers," Luella said.

"I don't. They'd freeze in no time. This is perfect." She kissed Luella.

Before Madeleine opened the door, she pressed a dried sprig of sage in the *Cheyenne Tribune* bouquet. "Jean Baptiste gave this to me when we were married," the cook whispered. "He wanted roses, but we live here. Just give it back when you are done."

Madeleine opened the door, and Lily wished she had tucked her handkerchief in her sleeve. Nick cleared his throat and began to hum Mendelssohn's "Wedding March" loud enough to compete with the wind.

Jack stood at the end of the cookshack, wearing his last white shirt and a handsome paisley vest with someone's watch fob stretched across the front. Preacher stood next to him.

To Nick's enthusiastic accompaniment, Lily took her first step toward Jack and his crazy arrangement to keep his ranch. Chantal, Amelie, and Luella stepped in front of her and walked forward, tossing out smaller newsprint flowers with each measured tread. She wasn't certain, because Nick was loud and so was the wind, but Lily could have sworn she heard Luella counting "one, two, three, four."

Another step and Fothering stood beside her. He crooked out his arm. "I'm giving you away," he said out of the corner of his mouth.

Ten more steps saw the journey over. As well-trained as if they were bridesmaids in St. Paul's Cathedral, the girls moved to the side. While Lily stood there with Fothering, the girls sang "The Flowers that Bloom in the Spring," coming in extra loud on each "tra la," almost in defiance of the storm.

Delighted, Lily looked around at each face in the room. The men had frostbite scars. Will Buxton scratched discreetly at his chilblained fingers. Madeleine was already dabbing at her eyes. And there was Jack, a half smile on his face, but calm. She wondered what it would take to make him really angry and hoped she might never find out.

"Dearly beloved!" Preacher shouted to be heard above the storm. Startled, Francis arched his back, and Chantal giggled.

Fothering gave her away to Jack, who stood beside her in front of Preacher, her arm through his now. He trembled noticeably, or maybe she did.

Preacher read a verse from the book of Ruth, which made Lily swallow a few times. He asked them seriously if they would take each other for richer or poorer, better or worse, in sickness and in health until death did them part.

Or spring, Lily thought, unsure of herself. "I will."

Jack's answer was more firm than hers, but she already knew he was not a man to harbor many misgivings about events.

There wasn't a ring, which moved them right along to Preacher's man and wife pronouncement and their first kiss. It wasn't more than a nervous peck, but at least they didn't bump noses.

The wedding dinner was hardly more than the usual fare, but with the menu written in French in Will's lovely handwriting. Each place at the table had a stiff card announcing *Haricot avec des oignons* (beans with onions), *Rôti de boeuf* (roast beef), *Pain san buerre* (bread courtesy of the Buxton's, without butter), and *Raisins sec dans le riz* (raisins and rice, thanks to the recovery of rice from the Buxton pantry).

The wedding cake was a smallish loaf cake, sweetened with Buxton sugar and a little lemon juice from Jack's hoarded anti-scurvy supply. Madeleine had somehow worked the canned milk and a little more sugar into frosting.

Pierre toasted the happy couple with coffee, with tea for Lily and canned milk for the children. He raised his mug. "I'm not sure how this is really done, but Jack says I must." He looked from Lily to Jack and back again. "Be very good to each other," he said simply and drank.

There wasn't anywhere for Mr. and Mrs. Sinclair to go, not with a blizzard outside wanting in like an uninvited guest, but the children threw dried beans because "Mama said to save the rice," then Luella swept them up to wash off and use in the next day's batch of *haricot avec des oignons*. Soon there would be a small sort of dance to "Sur le Pont," and then a livelier one to "Turkey in the Straw," Preacher's favorite. He promised to teach them "Cotton-Eyed Joe," if they weren't too weary with the dissipation of such a wedding.

"What do you think, Mrs. Sinclair?" Jack asked her, after "Turkey in the Straw," accompanied by Preacher on the harmonica, left them close to breathless.

"As weddings go?"

He had given her a wary look, and she nudged him. "I believe it met all my expectations."

"If you had to do it over again, you'd do it differently, wouldn't you?"

His question deserved a thoughtful answer, and she gave it one. Her friends were all here, she had a lovely bouquet, the music was excellent, the flower girls and bridesmaids didn't misbehave, and no one hummed "The Wedding March" with more fervor than Nick Sansever. She smiled and went to nudge him again, but she ended up just leaning against his arm, which went around her in such a natural way.

"I would change one thing. Rice instead of beans. Beans hurt."

❦

In some ways, nothing changed on the Bar Dot. Storms rolled through, dropping a seemingly endless amount of snow. The wind stirred the snow like a petulant child at play, blowing here, then there, until the almost-laughable danger of being lost only a few feet from a building became a harsh possibility.

When the sun struggled into its rightful place in the daytime sky, and the temperatures weren't so low they burned the lungs, the men saddled up and rode, searching for strays. There were more mercy killings than rescues, which made Jack glad that Mr. Buxton was stuck in Cheyenne and not peering over numbers in his precious ledger, now buried under snow.

In other ways, everything was different. For the first time in his life, someone waited at home for him. Jack hadn't known that Lily would do that, but Preacher told him otherwise. Forced to stay in bed because of a racking cough, Preacher told him how Lily opened the door several times and peered outside.

"I asked Lily what she was doing, and she said you were overdue and it bothered her," Preacher said when Lily was in the kitchen helping Madeleine.

"Surely not," Jack said, trying to sound matter-of-fact, even though he was secretly pleased.

Preacher just shrugged. "That's what you get for marrying someone like Lily. She has her eye on you, whether you like it or not."

He did like it. He only half-believed Preacher until one late afternoon he rode in and spent more time currying Sunny Boy in the barn because his horse had broken through ice several times and his shins were scratched and bleeding. When he finally opened the door to the cookshack, he couldn't overlook the sudden raising and lowering of Lily's shoulders, which looked remarkably like relief.

"Don't worry about me," he had told her, which only made her brown eyes well up with tears, something he had no proof against.

"I can't help myself," she had replied. Then she'd busied herself setting the table, preparing for another meal of everlasting beef and beans, made just a little more special because Lily insisted he have her bit of salt pork. "I don't like it," she had whispered to him, but he saw how her eyes followed his hand from spoon to mouth.

They worked their way through January, one day much like the next. In spite of that, even if he and the boys were only outside dismantling unneeded sheds to add to the rapidly shrinking woodpile, Lily always had something to tell him about her day. It might be Francis allowing gentle Amelie to comb all the knots and tangles from his long-neglected fur. Or maybe Nick had mastered long division. Once it was as simple as the first day when Luella didn't cry about her mother and her distant father. Jack came to savor every little detail, because it felt remarkably like his idea of what a home of his own would be.

In early February, all four rode north on a clear day to see how McMurdy had fared. They met the rancher and two of his men hunkered down in a sheltered draw for a palaver.

"It's grim up here," McMurdy admitted. "I have barely any cattle left and no idea if the drifters are safe somewhere."

"Same with us," Jack said.

Not sure why he blushed to give his nearest neighbor the news, but Jack told McMurdy about his wedding. McMurdy just smiled.

"Do you realize that's the first bit of good news I've heard in months?" McMurdy asked. "Not sure what you have that she wanted, but I hope you get down on your knees every night and give thanks." McMurdy slapped Jack on the back. "Boy howdy, can you blush! Do you realize if word gets out, your tough image is ruined forever?"

"I'll trust you to spread it when spring comes," Jack replied. He did have a question for a bona fide husband, and McMurdy was a good sport. "Been wondering, Mac— Lily always has interesting stuff to tell me every night. I can't ever think of anything I do all day that's interesting to anyone."

"Jack, Jack! Just surprise her with some little thing," McMurdy said. He looked around at the white bleakness that surrounded them and joked, "You know, a little bouquet of rabbit brush, maybe a nice haunch of venison, some perfume from Wisner. Good luck, buddy."

Jack thought about that on the cold ride home when Preacher and Will were arguing about the merits of canvas pants versus wool ones, and Pierre was keeping his own council, as he usually did.

Before he went into the cookshack, he had a wild tear and scooped up a handful of snow, shaping it into the best snowball ever fashioned by the mind of man. When he opened the door, Lily looked up from the Temple of Education and smiled at him. He smiled back, then lobbed his weapon at the center of her chest.

Nick whooped and Lily gasped. Suddenly unsure of himself, Jack stepped closer to wipe away the evidence of his sudden madness. Her eyes narrowed and he knew he was in trouble. *Thank you, McMurdy*, he thought as her lips curled sideways, which he knew was not a good sign.

To his amazement, she rushed past him out the door and came back in seconds later with an even better snowball. She hurled it at his head, and he had only a moment to applaud her excellent form before the thing exploded by his ear.

"So that's it?" he said and dashed back outside, returning with another snowy bomb, which landed on her backside.

School was suddenly over for the day as Lily's little angels ganged up on him. He took the fight outside and they followed. Great gobs of monkey meat, was she teaching these hoodlums to *throw*? He started to laugh and ended up with snow in his mouth.

He wasn't prepared for Lily's sneak attack. Someone tapped his shoulder, and he turned around to see a generous handful of yellow snow coming at him. Blamed if he didn't shriek like a girl, screaming something about not playing fair at all.

To no avail. The yellow snow ended up all over his face, and Lily was laughing so hard she started to choke.

"Oh, poor thing," he said and took the moment to push a little snow down the neck of her dress. She gasped and sank to her knees, laughing harder.

"I would never push yellow snow in your face," he said, in an attempt to sound virtuous.

"Just a little food coloring," she said, unrepentant. "Madeleine squirreled it away. I would never . . . you know." Her eyes shone now with an unholy glee that suggested she might keep him on his toes. "Well, I might, so watch out."

The children had trooped inside and his face felt frozen solid. "You have ruined my handsome complexion and noble visage," he teased. "That sounds like *Ivanhoe*."

"Impossible," she retorted and kissed him.

He threw his arms around her, happier than he could ever remember, standing in subzero weather with a wife he didn't quite know what to do with yet. Maybe McMurdy was on to something. He kissed her back.

"Suppose our lips freeze together," she said, letting him hold her close, which wasn't close because he was wearing nearly every item of clothing he owned, and so was she.

"Lily, you're a knucklehead."

It must have been the right thing to say, because she kissed him again. "And you're afraid of a little yellow snow," she whispered right in his ear. "Big baby."

Please don't leave me in the spring, he thought. *Please, Lily.*

CHAPTER 45

✦

*S*pring was a dreadful tease. Another blizzard stopped the icicles from dripping. One horse, already ill, died in the barn. Finding himself stuck in the barn during the blizzard, Francis killed careless mice that he thoughtfully presented to Madeleine at the back door. She shrieked, and Fothering finished them off.

Jack wasn't certain whose idea it was, but he and Lil started to sleep next to each other. He had come to her side of the room late one night, disturbed by her muffled sobs, and held her until morning. After that, there wasn't any reason to stay on his side of the cookshack, not when Lil needed him. No one made any comment except Pierre. "High time," he said, when they were outside hauling in more wood.

They were all noticeably weaker. Chantal didn't dance anymore, and Amelie seemed content just to sit in the tiny patch of sunlight of the mostly iced-over window, moving only when the sun moved. Everyone walked slower. Jack prayed for spring to hurry up.

Then came the morning when Luella simply could not face another bowl of beans. She had been a stalwart child, creative and smart, even after suffering the loss of her mother and her father's lengthy absence. There she sat, staring at her bowl of beans as her tears dropped into it.

God bless Madeleine. She hurried to Luella's side, arms

tight around the child who had borne so much. "Let me see what I can find in my kitchen," she whispered.

She returned after considerable clashing of pans and opening and closing of drawers that everyone knew were already empty. She held out her closed fist to Luella, who had perked up during Madeleine's noisy search. She turned over her hand and revealed a sugar cube.

Luella gasped. "For *me*?"

"Pop it in your mouth, *mon cherie*."

She did and closed her eyes in pleasure. She opened them quickly though and took out the sugar lump, much smaller now, but still a sugar lump. She held it out to Amelie. "I can share."

"No need!" Madeleine exclaimed and opened her other hand. "See? One, two, three for my dear ones too." The cook looked at the others. "I have six more cubes. I don't really care for sugar cubes myself, but who would like one?"

The others assured her that they didn't like sugar, either, too sweet and cloying. Madeleine gave them such a look and then turned to Jack. "You really didn't hire smart people."

"I know, but if no one likes sugar, let the children have it," he said, humbled to the earth by the goodness of the men and women he had shared a winter with in a ten-by-twenty-foot room.

"That's it, Lil," he told her late that night, his arms tight around her. "Will and I are going to Wisner tomorrow, provided it doesn't storm. We have to find more food."

She said nothing, but he felt her fear. "I'm tough, remember?" he whispered in her ear.

The morning dawned clear and cloudless, probably twenty below, but this might be the day it soared to zero. A man could hope.

"You're in charge, Lil," he told her as she walked him to the horse barn.

"Not Pierre?"

"He doesn't like to be in charge, and you do."

She looked at him, hand on hips, and then laughed. "I suppose I do. Very well." She took a small wad of bills from her pocket. "Here's a little of the money I brought from England. I still have a bit more. See how far it will go."

"I can't."

"For richer or poorer," she reminded him, pressing the bills into his hand. "Don't argue with your sweet wife."

He decided to be prudent, considering the warning, and kissed her instead. Will was busy saddling his horse, so the barn was almost private. He kissed her with all the fervor of his heart because he loved his wife. Maybe it was even more than love; maybe what he felt was something nameless, something earned through shared misery, deprivation, and true struggle.

"Lil, you're good at that," he told her after a second kiss just to make sure that first one wasn't a fluke. "Think what we could do if we ever had a room to ourselves," he told her, kissing her cheek more chastely because Will might be watching.

"You're calling me Lil," she said.

"It's your special name," he told her. "No one else can call you Lil, 'cept me."

She lowered her eyes so modestly. He looked around. Will was studying something in the barn, so he put his finger under her chin. "Lil, I love you."

She put her arms around his neck. "Probably not the smartest thing you ever did," she whispered. "I love you."

"Hey, boss, we need to ride," Will said. He chuckled. "She'll keep."

His Lil laughed and gave him a shove. She waved to them both, then hurried inside.

They hadn't ridden far when Will asked, "Why'd you want me along? I know Pierre is your top hand."

"Mostly I wanted you along to tell you how I appreciate what you've done this winter," Jack said.

"I wasn't much of a cowhand when it started, was I?" Will asked, going right to the heart of the matter.

"You weren't. That changed, and for that I thank you."

He glanced at the younger man, warmed to see a job-well-done smile on his face.

"You know something?" Will said after a mile of silence, while they both took in the sight of irregular mounds of snow that must contain cattle. "I was starting to become like Lily's father, a remittance man. Not sure if my cousin Oliver ever told you, but I'd been sent here because no one knew what to do with me."

"Mr. Buxton made me hire you," Jack admitted. "It bothered me at the time, but I'm over it. Not sure what's going to happen this spring, but I hope you'll stay on."

"We'll see."

They rode in what felt like satisfied silence for the mere four miles from the Bar Dot to Wisner. All winter that four miles might as well have been four hundred miles, and even now they struggled through mounds of snow. Jack looked toward his own property, with the high gate leaning but still intact. Snow covered most of the fence line.

"We'll stop on the way back. I have to know what's happened."

"You're a better man than I," Will said frankly. "I'd have stopped first."

It was a long four miles, and slow going. Jack stared into the glare snow that still covered the land, snow whiter than white, and with a brilliance that hurt his eyes. Still, it was better than cold and dark. He rubbed his eyes, wondering why they felt like trail dust had blown into them. He smiled to himself. Maybe Madeleine had a white salve for eyes too.

Wisner looked more put-upon and overwhelmed than any Wyoming town he had ever seen. Great walls of snow clogged all the alleys.

"That's not going to melt for weeks," Will commented.

They went to the train depot, struggling through waist-high drifts to find a place to hitch their mounts. The stationmaster looked up in surprise.

Jack noticed he was reading a *Cheyenne Tribune* dated November 14. "Old news is good news?"

The stationmaster folded his paper. "We've been trading papers all around town." He stuck out his hand. "I'm glad to see the Bar Dot boys are still alive."

"Can you send a telegram? The wire still up?"

"It's been our only link with the world, Jack." He took out a pad. "Shoot."

"I can write it," Jack said and took the pad. "Learned to read and write this winter." He felt his face grow warm. "I also got married."

"My word, you've been busy," the stationmaster said. "That high yaller gal?"

"My wife," Jack said in his foreman's voice. "No more of this high yaller stuff. Got that?"

In twenty stringent words, Jack wrote Mr. Buxton of his wife's death, and their struggle to stay alive. He pushed the note through the clerk's window. "Send that care of the Plainsman Hotel. Mr. Buxton usually stays there when he's in Cheyenne." He handed over some of Lily's money and nodded to Will, who had appropriated the old newspaper.

"Any idea when a train will come through?" he asked.

"Any day now," the stationmaster said, apology in his voice, whether for the train or for his comment about Lily, Jack neither knew nor cared.

They slipped and slid across the street to the mercantile. Mr. Watkins had been watching them cross the street. "You're looking about as independent as a hog on ice," he joked. "The Presbyterian minister broke his leg doing that last week. Glad you're alive, boys. What can I do you for?"

Jack stared at the empty shelves. "We're about starving on the Bar Dot. Got anything at all?"

"I might," Mr. Watkins said. He reached under his counter and brought up, one by one, eight tins of sauerkraut.

Jack had never cared much for sauerkraut, but his mouth started to water. *I could eat all of these right now*, he thought. "How much?"

"Three dollars a can."

Will stepped back in surprise. "That's highway robbery!" he exclaimed.

"Take it or leave it."

Shocked, Jack stared at the money in his hand. Twenty-four dollars for eight tins of number one cans? Lil taught a whole month of school for twenty-five dollars, and the money she had given him represented nearly everything she had brought from England. He leaned across the counter, his eyes boring into Mr. Watkins' face.

"I don't mind a man making a profit, but this winter is fixin' to end. When it does, you'd probably like the good will of the ranchers."

"You threatening me?" the merchant asked, starting to sweep the cans out of sight.

"Just stating a fact, sir. I'll give you a dollar per can. I'm betting that when times are good, you sell them for a nickel each."

Mr. Watkins lost the staring match. "All right. Eight dollars."

"Throw in some peppermint, if you have any."

"For fifty cents," Watkins said, not surrendering easily.

"All right." Jack slapped down eight dollars and counted out fifty cents, which only bought a small bag. There was enough for the children.

On the sidewalk again, Jack looked toward the Great Wall, which sat by itself, a little distance from the main street. "How about it?"

"Need you even ask? Let's see what the Chinaman has."

A much thinner Mr. Li didn't have much except a sorrowful face and a piddly bit of rice with a mysterious brown sauce on top. For a dime, it was heaven on earth. Jack didn't care if anyone was watching. He ran his finger around the rim of the plate.

"Almond cookies?" he asked Mr. Li.

"One, maybe two, old and stale," the Great Wall owner said. "For your pretty missy?"

"The very one." No need to threaten Mr. Li about his manners. He obviously knew a pretty missy, no matter her color.

"I married her this winter," Jack said.

Mr. Li's smile made his eyes nearly disappear. "For you, three cookies!" He put them into a little bag and bowed. "You gonna have pretty children."

"Best plan I've heard all day," Jack said, knowing better than to look at Will, who was probably enjoying this hugely.

"Pretty children, eh?" was all his less-than-top hand said as they rode away from Wisner.

The afternoon sun shone with a ferocity now that made Jack look down at his saddle horn. He blinked his eyes, trying to remove what felt like gravel now. Rubbing made it worse. He opened his eyes wide, and then wider, panicking to see only haze and shadow. When Jack put his hands on the saddle horn and pulled leather, he heard Will's sudden intake of breath.

"Boss, what's wrong? You don't pull leather."

Eyes closed, he handed his reins to Will. "You lead. I can't see."

He heard Will's breath coming faster. This was no time to be anything less than a foreman. "I'll be all right soon," he lied.

"Th . . . th . . . the Bar Dot?"

"My ranch. Bar Dot's too far."

Jack bowed his head over his chest. He wanted to groan with the pain, but knew Will couldn't manage that. He opened his eyes and saw nothing. "Lil," he whispered. "Lil."

CHAPTER 46

~∞~

here's a simple explanation, I am certain."

"They should have been back by now! Don't you tiptoe around me on little cat's paws."

Lily looked down at the floor, wondering if she would leave a deep trough in front of the window. She peered through the darkness, telling herself that if she walked another mile in front of the window, Jack would surely appear. Ashamed of herself, she looked up at Fothering, who was only trying to be nice.

"I shouldn't have snapped at you," Lily said. "It's just . . ."

If Fothering hadn't held his arms out, she wouldn't have thrown herself into them, sobbing. He only winced a bit and assured her that his arm had nearly healed.

She looked over his shoulder and saw her children staring at her with fear in their eyes. With an effort, she forced herself into calmness. "Silly me," she said. "Here I am worrying about two men perfectly capable of taking care of themselves."

"It scares me when you cry," Luella said, her lip trembling.

So endeth the tears, Lily thought later, after the children were asleep. Pierre beckoned her to the classroom table and she sat down. "I'll track them in the morning," he whispered. "We're not in a blizzard, so there is probably a logical explanation. Maybe they stayed in town."

"That's probably what happened," Lily said, mainly

because she knew he wanted to hear that. "I'm going with you."

"No, Lily, that's not—"

"A good idea? At what point in this winter has there been a good idea?" When he said nothing, she tried out Jack's foreman expression and achieved results, because Pierre agreed after one stare.

"We'll leave after chores," Pierre told her, his face stern. As he walked away, she wondered if the sternness had more to do with his own emotions than her intrusion into his man's world. She told herself that if something had happened to her husband, she would be intruding in that man's world more and more.

She lay down to sleep, but closing her eyes only meant reviewing the whole, dreary winter. She already had nightmares about the schoolhouse blizzard. All Jack had to do to banish them was to put his hand over her moving eyelids. She had returned the favor a few times. Where was he now when she needed him?

Exhausted from worry, she tried to find a comfortable spot on the floor. She gave up when she realized that the only thing that had made the floor even remotely accommodating was Jack lying beside her.

"I love you," she whispered, not wasting a minute trying to think back to when it began, mostly because her mind was starting to play strange tricks on her resolve. She was exhausted and hungry and weak and did not need any more winter, not when her life was falling apart.

She woke up to another cold morning, one of too many. She sat up and looked around, hopeful that Jack and Will had come back late last night and crept to bed, to not disturb anyone. Nothing. All winter she had felt crowded and hemmed in. Two men were gone now, somewhere out in the cold. She liked one and adored the other, and the crowded cookshack seemed empty.

She ate breakfast because it was put before her and then

darted for Jack's old house with the roof gone while Pierre saddled up. She pawed in the hardened snow, searching for *Ivanhoe*. Maybe if she could find the book, Jack would appear, because he insisted on the ending.

The lean-to seemed like the last place for *Ivanhoe*, but there it was, crammed underneath a pot, thrown there by some force of wind or snow. Her heart rose at the sight of Sir Walter Scott's dear book, the story of old England that had brought them together. Sakes alive, it was even dry. She tucked *Ivanhoe* in her coat pocket and went to find Pierre.

Clouds scudded across the sun as they rode, and Lily couldn't help staring toward the northwest. A veteran of Wyoming winter, she knew a blizzard cloud now. She relaxed. They were clouds and nothing more.

"We've seen the worst of it," Pierre told her. "We might have another storm or two, but I think the worst is over." He reached over and put his gloved hands on hers. "He Stands with Feet Planted is not going to blow away when spring is here."

"I'm not going to leave in the spring, you know," she said, trying to keep her voice conversational and calm. "Even if he is alive and well and doesn't need me, I'm not leaving."

"I didn't think you would," he said.

They covered the two miles to Jack's ranch with laborious effort, skirting huge snow drifts and avoiding uncovered cattle carcasses. She rode through them, dry-eyed, because she had bigger worries.

"There's the ranch gate," Pierre said, pointing to the crossbar on its tall post that leaned a little from the wind but hadn't toppled. "Wait here."

He continued toward Wisner, then stopped and looked toward her. He stared at the snowy ground and gestured to her. When she reached him, he pointed down. "See here, two horses side by side." He pointed ahead. "Right there. See how they stopped for a while. And then look beyond—one horse following the other."

"What does it mean?"

"Someone ran into a bit of trouble here, and the other one is leading his horse." He made an elaborate gesture that made Lily smile. "Let's go to your ranch, Mrs. Sinclair."

They rode beneath the crossbar. She looked ahead and saw distinct tracks of two horses. The pounding in her heart began to slow down, as real calm took over, not the kind where she put on a false face to keep the children brave, but serenity she hadn't felt in months. Jack was there, and he was going to get all the *Ivanhoe* he wanted.

She barely glanced at the little house with her father's improbable wallpaper, knowing that Manuel had spent the winter in the barn with his charges. There was Bismarck in the corral, raising his massive head to the sun, the picture of contentment.

"What on earth? Pierre, Manuel has knitted Bismarck a blanket!"

Pierre shook his head. "I have now seen it all."

They ducked into the barn, struck by the pungent odor of dung heaped in piles to one side. Manuel sat on a bench facing the sun, knitting and talking to Will Buxton. Lily looked around, determined to remain calm. Pierre dismounted and then helped her down.

"Where is he?" she asked, not caring that her voice was breaking.

"*Hola, señora*," Manuel said. "You want your man?"

"Oh my goodness, I do," she said, not even minding that Will chuckled. "Please, where is he?"

Manuel pointed with a knitting needle. "One, two, three stalls down. We had to keep him in the dark."

She didn't stop to ask why but ran to the third stall, bathed in shadows. She blinked, accustoming her eyes to the dim light, and there he was, lying under blankets with his hands behind his head. Manuel must have smeared soot under his eyes.

"Jack?"

"I thought that was you, Lil. Things'll be all right now."

She sank to her knees beside him and stared at his face. "You can't see me, can you?" she asked, trying to sound like a woman grown and not a squeaky, frightened girl.

"I can see your outline. Lean over a bit. That's better."

He puckered up and she kissed him, not minding when the soot transferred to her face. She lay down with her head on his chest.

His hand rested heavy on her head, and she loved the feeling. "I'll love you even if you're blind," she whispered.

"It's temporary, Lil, that's all," he told her, then stroked her hair. "Snow glare finally got to me. I couldn't see anything yesterday, but I can see you up close."

Lily sat up and took a good look at his dear face. "Soot?"

"Yeah. Manuel's not taking any chances with glare." He outlined her profile with his finger. "Um, you'll still love me, even if I'm *not* blind?"

She kissed him again.

"That's a yes?" he asked, and she thumped him.

"I saw Bismarck in the yard," she said, after another sooty kiss.

"Corral," he corrected. "I'll bring you along slow on ranch duties, but do start with corral. We're going to be a strange enough pair anyway, the British lady of color and the Georgia cracker."

She lay down again, ready to spend the day there, but he sat up. "You probably didn't even notice, but I want you to go take a look at our herd—two heifers. We're off to a good start. Scram! I'll keep."

Lily stopped at the barn's entrance, delighted to see two small versions of Bismarck looking back at her. She knelt down to reach them through the fence. The slightly larger one butted against her hand, and she laughed.

Pierre rested his arms on the top rail, nodding at the little ones. "He did it, Lily. That man of yours is officially the smartest rancher in the territory."

Pierre only stayed a few minutes more, then left with Will Buxton. With a smile to Manuel, who bowed from his chair in most courtly fashion, Lily walked back to Jack's stall and lay down again, sound asleep as soon as she closed her eyes, secure in his arms.

✿

They were two days in the barn, lulled by the lowing of cattle and even Bismarck, who made a sound similar to a soft purr. In the early morning, she woke to her husband staring at her.

"You're still a bit grainy, but I'd recognize you anywhere," he whispered, even though Manuel's snoring thundered through the barn.

"You'd better," she said, cuddling closer. He moved closer too, and one thing led to another. By the time Lily finally sat up, looking for her shirts, she was officially Mrs. Sinclair, as her husband reminded her.

"I doubt this was the wedding morning of your dreams," he teased, "a half-blind lover in a cow barn, with beans and sauerkraut to eat."

"You forgot the peppermints," she added, which earned her another kiss, almost derailing her plans to get up at all. "No, Miss Tilton would never believe this," she said later.

She got up long enough to fetch everlasting beans from Manuel, his expression so kindly, and blessed tortillas, which she had never experienced before. When they finished eating, Lily settled in with a kerosene lantern and starting reading the conclusion to *Ivanhoe*, chapter forty-three to the end.

"You found it," Jack said.

"I had to," she said simply.

By evening, his vision had returned. Lily washed the

soot off his face, planning to reapply it in the morning when he had to contend with the sun's glare on snow as they left. As it was, she had soot all over her face and neck too.

"Anything you want more'n a bath, Lil, my honey-bunch?" her husband asked before he drowsed away into a lover's coma.

"The aforementioned bank account, straight hair, and lettuce," she replied, barely keeping her eyes open. "Leave me alone. I'm tired."

"Ah, it begins," he teased.

⁂

They left in the morning under an overcast sky, which Jack called a relief. He spent a long moment just staring at his little herd, which, in the curious nature of cows, had come to the fence to check him out.

"You're the beginning, girls," he told the cows. "Bismarck, what a lover you are."

"For goodness sake!" Lily exclaimed.

"We're going to have some lean years, but this is the start of something that will cover the range some day," he prophesied. "More land would be nice, but we'll be patient."

He smiled at Manuel, sitting and rocking, so calm and placid, probably the way he had spent the whole, solitary winter. He came closer and put out his hand. When Manuel took his hand, Jack turned it over and kissed it. Lily looked away, tears in her eyes.

"I owe you a debt I can never repay, Manuel," Jack said.

"Señor Sinclair, you gave me a home and a job when no one else would," the Mexican reminded him.

"Someone did that for me once. He told me to return the favor when I could. See you in a week or so, my friend."

As they rode for the Bar Dot, Lily tried to be sly about watching Jack, but he noticed immediately and told her not to worry. "Just a little grainy, that's all," he assured her. "I'll put warm cloths on them when we get home. You'll see; I'll be better in two shakes."

The melt had begun in earnest. Snow-covered trails of two days ago were running with mud now. The wind worked overtime to reveal burial mounds of cattle, which reduced them both in tears.

"I hate this," Jack said as he dabbed at his eyes. "Such a waste, and it never would have happened if folks hadn't been so greedy."

The schoolhouse came into view first. Lily tugged on her horse's reins and stopped. It was easy enough to open the door, now that most of the snow was gone. Feeling shy for no reason, she peaked inside at bare walls and the one remaining desk in splinters and ready to be shoved into the pot-bellied stove. She leaned against the doorjamb, hoping that someday the good times would outshine the terror of their struggle to stay alive.

She walked to the corner where the Little Man of the Prairie, a.k.a. the Wyoming Kid, had probably made his last stand. "Are you in there?" she asked. Curious, she carefully pried up the floorboard and took a look. To her amazement, a whiskered pack rat stared back, lean, yes, but alive and irritated. He scolded her in his churring way but did not run. She sighed with relief and replaced the floorboard. Her children would be delighted.

She stood another moment in the doorway, happy in the knowledge that a temple of education could be found anywhere. She glanced at Jack through the window. So could love.

"All well?" Jack asked. He looked alert enough to Lily's watchful eyes, but she knew he needed to lie down soon because he kept squinting.

Preacher met them at the cookshack door. He took the reins over their protests. "I'll do this," he said. "Boss, we're glad you're alive."

"Same here, friend," Jack said.

He put his hand on the doorknob, but Preacher stopped him.

"Mr. Buxton's here," he said, his voice low. "The train came in."

CHAPTER 47

Oliver Buxton looked the same to Lily, the same high color, the same displeasure at everything marring what must have been a handsome face in earlier years. She saw something else. She recognized the look in his eyes as the same look as anyone on the Bar Dot, that sadness of humans who have been tried to the limit. In her case, she knew that time would determine if that sadness was a badge of honor or a curse. With Mr. Buxton, she could not tell.

He just looked at them, as if mulling what to say. Jack beat him to it.

"Mr. Buxton, we are so sorry for your loss."

Lily took a deep breath, wondering if Mr. Buxton would glare and swear and blame. To her relief, he did not.

"Sit down, Sinclair," he said. "You look worse than most of us."

"Getting better, though. I wish we had a good report for you."

She helped Jack to the nearest bench. He blinked his eyes a few times, then focused them on his employer. Lily glanced to the corner, her school, where the children sat. Luella held what must be her Christmas doll on her lap. The doll's extra dresses were on Chantal's lap, and Amelie was already deep into a book that Mr. Buxton must have brought for Luella too. She sniffed and smelled wonderful things from the kitchen. Did the man bring food? She felt her mouth water and swallowed, eager for something better than canned sauerkraut chased by peppermint drops.

"When will you bury them?" Mr. Buxton asked Jack.

"As soon as we can. Perhaps tomorrow, if the ground will cooperate," Jack replied.

Lily listened for something approaching sorrow in Mr. Buxton's voice and heard nothing but the brusque tones of the businessman he had always been. She noticed that he had barely glanced at her before looking away. Apparently the sins of the father were going to plague the daughter, she decided. That's nothing new, she wanted to tell him.

"Make it happen. I'm taking Luella with me to Cheyenne tomorrow and we're going to Moline, Illinois, where we came from."

At her name, Luella's head came up. "No, Papa. My friends are here."

He barely glanced at her, either. "Tomorrow, Luella, and no argument. There's nothing here for any of us."

"Yes, there is," Luella said with all the dignity of an eight-year-old. "We learned so much this winter in our school, and I have friends here."

You survived here too, Lily thought, suddenly understanding the bond they had formed.

Mr. Buxton ignored Luella and turned back to the others. "As I was saying before your foreman decided to return—"

"That's unnecessary and unkind." Lily gulped. Had she actually said that? At least she hadn't raised her voice. Might as well forge ahead. "As I am certain your cousin told you, they went to Wisner to send the telegram that must have brought you here. Jack has been recovering from snow blindness."

"With your help?" The sarcasm was unmistakable. He gave her a mocking bow. "Congratulations on your wedding. His idea or yours?"

Jack leaped to his feet, swayed a little, and righted

himself, his face pale. "You have no idea what this winter was like. Don't bother to fire me. I quit."

Mr. Buxton threw back his head and laughed. Lily felt her skin crawl at the sound.

"That's precisely why I am here! Sit down. Let's get this over with."

Mr. Buxton directed his attention to the men of the Bar Dot, those stalwarts who had risked their lives all winter trying to round up drifting, confused cattle, the men who had contrived and starved through months of misery, probably while he twiddled his thumbs in the Plainsman Hotel. He glared at them as if daring them to make a move or say one word.

And then he sighed, and it was an almost-human sound from someone tried almost as hard as they had been. "As you can all imagine, the Cheyenne Land and Cattle Company has been receiving disastrous reports from every corner of the range."

"Everyone was hit this bad?" Preacher asked.

"Everyone, without exception. One of our ranches to the south and west tallied ten beeves alive out of three thousand."

"We have two hundred, at last count," Jack said quietly. "Out of five thousand. And that's just the ones we know about."

"Then you are to be congratulated," Mr. Buxton snapped. "Three weeks ago, the Cheyenne Land and Cattle Company dissolved itself."

Lily looked at the others and saw no surprise on anyone's face. She saw tired, hungry men, weak from a winter that would have killed Mr. Buxton.

"That's it then," Jack said.

"As of now, you are all unemployed. What assets remaining to the company are to pay you off. You have a week to vacate."

"Merciful saints defend us!" Madeleine had been

standing in the door between the dining room and kitchen. She burst into tears.

"Stop it!" Mr. Buxton demanded.

Fothering put his arm around her shoulder and led her back into the kitchen.

"I have your wages here." He pulled a ledger from his briefcase and opened it to the Bar Dot page. "You were last paid at the end of August. The amount here is from September through the end of April. Look it over and initial it."

Silent, the men took turns at the ledger, no one bothering to even glance at Mr. Buxton. Jack took the book last and added his initials. He pointed to the blank space under his name and wrote in Lily Sinclair. "You owe Lily two hundred dollars for the school."

Mr. Buxton shook his head. "That was a deal my wife cut, not me. Besides, her scoundrel of a father owes the company two thousand dollars."

"There *is* no company now. Pay her the two hundred dollars," Jack said in his foreman's voice, even though he was foreman of nothing. "She did everything she was asked to do. Ask your own daughter. Don't be so small, Buxton. Just for once."

Silence settled over the room, the kind of silence charged with electrical currents. Lily could hear Mr. Buxton's heavy breathing. To her ears, he didn't sound like a well man. Pierre took out the knife he always wore at the small of his back and gave it a thoughtful appraisal.

"Very well, if I must," Mr. Buxton said finally, the fight gone out of him. "Line up, people, and let's get this over with."

He pulled a canvas sack from the briefcase and doled out back wages that didn't even begin to cover a winter like this one. His face registered no sympathy when Madeleine stood before him, her hand trembling.

"Where are we to go?" she asked.

"That is not my concern," Mr. Buxton said. "Next?"

Fothering followed her. Silent, he took his salary, then stepped back, as if for a better look. "You, sir, are a reprehensible lizard with no feelings," he said in his best butler's voice. He turned on his heel and escorted his weeping co-chef into the kitchen and closed the door.

Lily took her money. He set it on the table and pushed it toward her as if he didn't want to run the risk of actually touching her hand. "Thank you, sir," she said, because she meant it. She had discovered this winter that she was a teacher, a friend, and a surrogate mother to a lonely child. "Please see that Luella gets into a good school in Moline. She is bright and clever and very much a leader." Lily smiled. "She could probably even teach you a thing or two about leadership. For that matter, so could Jack. He's the reason we're still alive here."

The others nodded, and she saw smiles on tired faces.

"Well, hip hip hooray," Mr. Buxton said, sounding remarkably childish. The smiles widened. He closed his briefcase with a snap. "I'm going to Wisner to spend the night." He looked around at the room where they had stayed alive. "This place disgusts me. I'll take the morning train to Cheyenne. Come, Luella."

His daughter shook her head. "I belong here."

"With these haggard, smelly people?" he said. "Come with me!"

"We'll get her to the train in the morning," Jack assured his former employer.

"Wait a moment, Cousin Oliver."

Will Buxton had been silent through the whole dismal, humiliating business. He sat down next to his cousin and gave him an appraisal both long and thorough. This was not the Will Buxton who had begun the winter, Lily knew. This Will Buxton had been tested and proved, his assurance almost equal to Jack's. *Will, you've been studying a master all winter, haven't you?* she thought, pleased.

"I want to buy eight thousand acres of the Bar Dot."

Mr. Buxton laughed, with no mirth even remotely in sight. "You do? Ask Jack how we wore out the land and ruined it with overgrazing. And you want that?"

"The land just needs some kindness, fences, and fewer cattle," Will said. He looked at Jack, his real boss. "Yeah, it'll take a while, but I have the time. What do you say, Jack?"

"I'm in favor. I'll add my land and my herd to yours, and we'll see what happens. How about it, Buxton?"

"That's Mr. Buxton to you," the man said.

"I don't think so. What about it? Are you authorized to even do such a thing for a dissolved company?"

Mr. Buxton sat back, his face thoughtful, now that money was involved. "I can do that. One thousand dollars. The shareholders'll get about fifty dollars each. That should buy'em each ten boxes of Cuban cigars." He had to get his dig in. "Will, this is another example of the stupidity that exiled you here in the first place. Your father will be delighted."

"Not sure I care, cousin."

"I have four hundred here in wages," Will said. "Three hundred from me. Jack?"

Without hesitating, Jack spread out five hundred dollars. "I'll hold some back because I owe Manuel. That's eight hundred. Lil?"

Lily took a deep breath and deliberately counted out all of her money. "That's two hundred and totals a thousand, Mr. Buxton." She smiled at Jack. "Do I get my own brand?"

"Absolutely, Lil. Go in the kitchen, love, and assure Madeleine that she has work here as long as she wants. Nick too. He'll do our books and ride the range, just like he wants."

"Do your books?" Mr. Buxton asked. "Are you crazy?"

"He learned a lot this winter, same's the rest of us."

Lily hurried into the kitchen in time to see Fothering comforting Madeleine in a way that made her a little envious. No matter. She and Jack could swamp out the little house on the Sinclair Ranch and have their own peaceful time soon.

"All right, you two," she teased.

"You found us out, my dear," Fothering said in his pseudo-English accent. "I just proposed and my favorite cook accepted. I think we will open a restaurant in Wisner."

"Wisner needs something besides chop suey," Lily said. She told them what Will and her husband had just done. "We were hoping you would just stay here," she concluded.

Fothering and Madeleine exchanged delighted glances. "We will give it strong consideration," Fothering said.

Mr. Buxton left, after he drew up a contract and extracted three signatures from the new owners of eight thousand acres of worn-out land. "Luella, I will see you tomorrow morning in Wisner. No later than nine, and no argument."

Lily put her arms around the little girl. "We'll have her there." She didn't want to say that at all, but the man glowering before them was Luella's father and she had no choice.

Mr. Buxton left as soon as he could, assuring Jack that he could bury Mrs. Buxton whenever he felt like it. "We'll put up a nice headstone," Jack called as the man rode away from the Bar Dot.

"I don't think he heard you," Lily said, taking his arm. "Good riddance."

They started back to the cookshack. "You don't look too afraid of the daunting prospect before you, Mrs. Sinclair," Jack said.

"What daunting prospect?" she teased. "Oh, you mean who of us gets the chore of cleaning up behind the lean-to now that the snow has melted there?"

"That's the one, I mean," he teased back. He opened the door. "You in there? Wasn't the one who complained the most all winter supposed to 'police the grounds,' as they say over at Fort Laramie?"

Everyone came outside. Amelie, Chantal, and Luella had become better than friends through the winter. They stood with linked arms. Nick walked toward Pierre. How could the boy have grown so tall on beans, onions, stringy beef, and a sugar cube? Preacher was looking over his little flock. Lily wondered how many prayers he had said for them all and said her own silent prayer of gratitude. Madeleine and Fothering already looked like a couple. Maybe all those arguments in the kitchen hadn't been so vehement, after all. Will stood by himself. He would probably always be a solitary sort of man, but he had an air of confidence about him now.

She leaned against her husband's arm, wondering about love and how it happened. When she got off the train in that distant summer gone by, she had only wondered how soon she could leave this Wyoming Territory that was now her home. "God is good to me," she whispered into Jack's sleeve. He had the lion share of the property and Bismarck, this man of hers. No one was going to laugh at him now. Maybe in time the locals would come to understand her.

"Here it is, crew," Jack said. "The one who complained the most this winter gets the lime, a bucket, and shovel."

Everyone stepped forward, which made him look at her, his wife, tears in his eyes. "What do you do with people like this?" he asked.

"Mostly love them," she said. "I'll get the bucket, boss."

CHAPTER 48

༺☙❧༻

The ground was ready to receive the two LC cowboys, Mrs. Buxton, the maid, and Stretch by midafternoon. Everyone took a turn digging the graves. Amelie, Chantal, and Nick spent a quiet moment by their father's grave. Amelie left one of Stretch's *Farmer's Almanacs* on Jean Baptiste Sansever's final resting place.

"He would like to know that we can all read now, and that Nick is a marvel at numbers," she told Lily. "Do you think he does?"

"I am certain of it," Lily said. She held Amelie close, admiring the cemetery beyond the schoolhouse, with its long view of prairie and mountains in the distance. All around them were dead cattle, which made her sigh. She turned precisely toward her new home two miles away. In her mind and heart, the Sinclair Ranch was going to be the spot everyone knew about as the place where ranching changed. Perhaps other ranchers had the same idea. She knew the little spread Jack won from her father in a card game was first, and best.

After the two cowboys were at rest, they buried Stretch, the maid, and then Mrs. Buxton, a woman deeply troubled who was now at peace. By unspoken decision, Preacher handed his Bible to Jack, who turned to the book of Job.

"'For I know that my redeemer liveth, and that he shall stand at the latter day upon the earth.'" He read with real fluency and feeling, which made Preacher smile. "'And though after my skin worms destroy this body, yet in my flesh shall I see God.'"

Jack swallowed and handed the Bible to Lily. "I just can't. This is hard."

"You're good at hard," she whispered, handing it back. "They want you, not me. You're in charge."

He took back the Bible and turned to Psalms. "I like this one," he said, sounding almost as shy an Amelie. "'Yea, though I walk through the valley of the shadow of death, I will fear no evil, for thou are with me.'" He stopped. "We all took that walk this winter." He looked down at the graves and then around at them. "Some of us didn't make it. I intend to make my life count for me and my . . . my own family, and for these dear ones who left us. That's it and amen."

Jack and Lily took the buckboard to town, Preacher and his one suitcase in the backseat. Luella had refused to leave, and no one forced her. "I'll make it right with your father," Jack said. "I'll tell him we'll take good care of you."

They drove in companionable silence to Wisner, Lily's hand on Jack's knee. He kept inching it higher, which made her laugh and pinch him, but she didn't remove it. Preacher, in the backseat, couldn't see anything, but she doubted he would mind. He wasn't that kind of preacher.

"You have to tell me what's so all-fired important in Alabama that you have to go back," Jack said as they reached the depot. "I know it's a Western credo not to ask questions, but I gotta know."

"Easy enough," Preacher said as he took his suitcase out of the buckboard. "There's a young lady in Dothan. I got cold feet and left. If she'll forgive me, I'll make that right too."

Lily clapped her hands in delight. "Preacher, you sly dog!"

"Oh, you Sinclairs. I watched you two all winter, maybe even before you knew you loved each other," he said simply.

"Couldna been that early, Preach," Jack said. "You weren't with us in the Great Wall of China Café."

Lily stared at her husband. He shrugged. "You looked mighty good over chop suey."

Lily laughed, her face flaming hot. She kissed Preacher. "Keep being a good man and come back with *your* wife."

"I just might."

They followed him inside the depot and there was Mr. Buxton, pacing up and down and glaring at his watch, as if it didn't measure up, either. He saw them, then went to the window and looked outside.

"She didn't want to leave," Jack said. "I hadn't the heart to force her. We'll take good care of her."

Mr. Buxton said nothing. He looked at them a long time, as if wondering at what point he had lost charge of his entire life, and then turned on his heel and went out to the platform. He stared at the tracks and came back inside. His shoulders drooped, and Lily had one small moment of pity.

"If she decides to return to you, we'll see that she gets to Moline," she said.

He nodded, took another breath, and was all business again. "Sinclair, I'll take your contract to my attorney in Cheyenne. He'll spruce it up and I'll register it there. Next time you're in Cheyenne, drop by the First National, and you'll have the deed." He held out his hand and Jack shook it. He didn't hold out his hand to Lily, but she hadn't expected him to.

"Well, Lil, let's drop by the bank and see just how pitiful my account is," he told her.

The teller had a smile for them both and turned to Lily. "I'm glad to see you! We've been holding two checks for your father from England. Just the usual. Sign for them and I'll give you the money, so you can take it to him."

"My word," Lily said, stunned. "I forgot he had remittance checks."

"We can understand why no one made it in from the Bar Dot this winter." He ran a finger around his own too-loose collar. "It was a dilly, wasn't it? Sign here, and I'll get the money."

"Grab it and run," Jack whispered out of the corner of his mouth when the teller turned away to complete the transaction.

She did, holding her breath and afraid to look down at the bills until they stood on the sidewalk. "One hundred, two hundred—Jack, five hundred dollars!"

He closed his eyes and turned his face to the warming sun. "I hadn't even thought of those remittance checks. Do you think he'd mind if we used some of it for posts and bob wire?"

"You're the boss," she reminded him, handing over the money.

"So are you," he said as he pocketed it.

They spent the next hour in the bathhouse behind the hotel. The tub was too small to share, which Jack considered a great pity, so they took turns until the water ran clear. "That's a lot of grime," Jack said as he stood there with a towel around his middle and took a careful razor to his battered face. He looked back at her. "You're getting all wrinkled, Lil."

"We're going to have bathhouse on the ranch just as soon as cattle start paying again," she told him.

"Guess we'd better. You're one of the bosses."

Clean and brushed, Lil felt almost self-conscious walking down the sidewalk. She was pretty sure what came next, even though chop suey would never be high on her list. Maybe there had been enough trains coming and going by now to drop off some green tea at Mr. Li's Great Wall.

As they passed the Back Forty, Lily's attention was caught by a group of men standing around one of the still-snowy alleys. As they watched, one of the men ran for the sheriff.

Jack shrugged. "I'm betting they're finding dead cattle everywhere. On to Mr. Li. I insist."

The restaurant looked the same, and the menu had the same fly specks. She handed hers to her lord and master and favorite rancher. "Chop suey, of course."

While they were eating, Mr. Li took a moment from mysterious noises and fragrances from the kitchen to pull up a chair. He gave her a little bow.

"Jack tell me he marry you, pretty missy. May you have many, many children."

"We're working on it, Mr. Li," Jack said cheerfully, which made Lily blush.

Mr. Li nodded and gave Lily his attention again. "Missy, you let me know what day you want me to visit your class. I tell them all about China and bring almond cookies."

"My class?" Lily stared at him. It seemed so long ago that she had given that letter to her father and told him to drop it by the Great Wall. "You . . . you got the letter?"

Mr. Li bobbed his head up and down. "Yes, missy. Mr. Carteret brought it right here and we ate chop suey." His face fell. "It was snowing so hard, and I told him to hurry and run for the train, but he said it would be fine."

Jack leaned forward, his eyes intense. Lily clutched his arm. "Lots of heavy snow?"

"Ah so. I told him after a while maybe he better just stay here and eat chop suey and get the train the next day, but no, he ran out."

Jack took her hand, probably squeezing it harder than he intended to. "Lily."

She didn't know what he was going to say because the door slammed open then and the sheriff stood there, breathing hard. He took off his hat. "Miss Carteret."

"Sinclair," Jack said automatically.

"You'd better come with me. Good thing you're here, Miss . . . Mrs. Sinclair? Jack, don't let go of her."

"Wouldn't dream of it."

Jack kept hold of her hand as they hurried after the sheriff toward the mounded snow in the alley.

"Jack, you don't think . . ." *Think what?* she asked herself frantically, her mind and heart on her father, the man who had delivered her letter to Mr. Li and run out into the storm, the man who had run off and abandoned her.

Jack made her stay at the head of the alley while he threaded his way past snowdrifts and out behind the buildings. "Breathe, Lily, breathe," she whispered.

He came back more slowly, the crowd parting to let him through, his eyes disbelieving. He took her hand and his fingers were so cold. He tucked her close to his side. Two deep breaths. "Lily, your father didn't run away and leave you."

She fell to her knees because her legs refused keep her upright. Jack knelt beside her in the mud and snow of the alley and they clung together. She cried tears of sorrow, anger, relief, and gratitude that Clarence Carteret, that weak man who told her she was the best thing he ever did, had not failed her after all.

When she thought she could stand, she let Jack lead her through the alley and into the open field. She covered her nose with her fingers as they passed dead cattle. The crowd of men parted, and she saw a tall figure wearing a familiar overcoat, face down in the mud, still clutching his valise.

The sheriff put a meaty hand on her shoulder. "I'm afraid it's . . ."

"My father," she finished, calm now. "He got lost in the blizzard, didn't he?"

The sheriff nodded, his eyes solemn and sad. "It happens. One inch and he would've touched a building. Another inch . . ." He shrugged and turned away, leaving her scant privacy with what he thought was simply grief, but which was grief mingled with the greatest relief she had ever known.

"He didn't leave me," she told Jack.

"Not at all."

At her husband's quiet words, the sheriff and others wrapped Clarence Carteret's mortal remains in a blanket, knotting it securely, and carried them to the buckboard that Jack had pulled around. One of the bystanders handed Lily the valise. Tears in her eyes, she traced his initials on the worn bag. "Papa," she whispered.

They rode home in silence, Lily holding the valise tight in her arms, staring straight ahead. *He never made it to Cheyenne*, kept running through her brain. *He never made it to Cheyenne.*

"Stop!" she cried.

Jack spoke to the team. "What, honeybunch?" he asked, his voice so gentle.

With hands that trembled, Lily opened the valise. She pawed through the jumble of clothes, a copy of *King Solomon's Mines*, and her father's ledger. Underneath everything was a canvas bag. She pulled it out, widened the drawstring and gasped.

Jack was looking over her shoulder. She heard his sharp intake of breath.

"I'd forgotten about that," he said finally. He leaned back and started to laugh.

"Jack! How can you . . ." She stared at the money in her hands. "My word. Two thousand dollars that a dissolved company has already written off."

"We'd better hold a meeting of the ranch owners," he said and slapped the reins.

❦

Will looked like he didn't know whether to look serious or let out a whoop. They had taken him aside in the barn. "Who are we supposed to give this to?" he asked, his expression puzzled. "There isn't any company. Mr. Buxton said so. I even have my doubts that he's going to turn that thousand of ours over to anyone. Who should get this? No one owns the Cheyenne Land and Cattle Company, Lily. It doesn't exist."

They were both looking at her as though it was her money. Maybe it was, in a way. Oh, what was she thinking? She was silent, remembering what the old Clarence Carteret would have spent it on. She suddenly knew what the new Clarence Carteret would have done.

"How many of us are there?" she asked, even though she knew. "Counting Preacher."

"Eleven." He laughed. "I believe you're right, honeybunch. Divide it evenly between us all?"

"That's fair."

"Madeleine and Fothering will get the lion's share with the children," he reminded her.

"I know. Good! I have Papa's remittance money, at least until I write to my uncle and tell him what happened, and he shuts off any more."

"That could take a while," Will said. "Even a year or two, if you play it right."

"No, it won't," she said, serene now in a way she had never been before. "I'll write him tonight. There might be a final settlement for me or there might not be. It doesn't matter. We are all honorable people."

Will nodded, even though she could tell his heart wasn't in it. Then he grinned. "Guess I still have some faulty character to work on, huh?"

"Just hang around Lil," Jack said, "but not to close, because she's my special partner in this business." He put his hand on the back of her neck and gave her a gentle shake. "Lil, you're the smart one: how it is that a terrible winter can also be the best winter that ever happened?"

She shrugged. "'Beats me,' as you would say. Let's go tell the others about their good fortune."

They buried Papa at dusk. Lily had saved her newspaper wedding bouquet, and she placed it on his grave, kneeling there after everyone had left except Jack and Pierre, her heart at peace. She looked at the valley beyond, thinking of the days and weeks ahead that would be filled with the bleakness of burning dead cattle and reliving every terrible moment of suffering for man, woman, child, and beast. But Jack's calves would grow and frisk, their little red-and-white faces full of the optimism of young things.

Her husband said he was already making plans with McMurdy to scour the range for the hardy cattle still alive. "I'll buy them, if we know the owners," he had told her as he and Pierre took turns digging a good grave for a man who tried. "The cows will be tough and that's what Bismarck's harem needs." He had leaned on his shovel and looked up at her. "Tough like us, my dear wife."

Mah deah waf. She loved the sound of it, and so she told Pierre as they walked back together, Jack hurrying ahead to make more plans. She'd have him to herself at night, and that suited her right down to the ground.

"I've never properly thanked you for your winter count," she said as they strolled along. "It saved my life twice."

"And I've never thanked you for insisting that I was Pierre and not just Indian."

"What will you draw for this year's winter count?" she asked. "Can't be too hard to imagine."

"Probably you and Jack holding hands. That's what I choose to remember."

She thought about it and agreed. "It's better than snow, cold, and death."

He stopped and took her hand. "Lily, I have a name for you. It's a good one to walk side by side with He Stands with Feet Planted."

"Heavens, I'm almost afraid to hear it," she said, secretly pleased.

He turned away from her as if seeing something beyond her vision. "I watched your face at that first snowfall, the soft snowfall, the one that covers all ugliness and sins and sourness and misdeeds. You're like that, Lily. Probably the closest I can come in English is 'Softly Falling.'"

She rested her forehead against his arm. "Pierre, that's too much."

"No, it's just right, Softly Falling," he said quietly. He gave her a little push. "Go tell your man. He'll agree completely. Go on!"

She did as he said, walking fast, then running, and then waving her hands and calling to her husband. Spring had come, summer was near, and her cup of life was full at last.